M. K. HUME

PROPHECY
BOOK TWO

DEATH OF AN EMPIRE

headline
review

First published in Great Britain in 2012 by HEADLINE REVIEW
An imprint of HEADLINE PUBLISHING GROUP

First published in Great Britain in paperback in 2012
by HEADLINE REVIEW

4

Cataloguing in Publication Data is available from the British Library

ISBN 978 0 7553 7148 8

Typeset in Golden Cockerel by Avon DataSet Ltd,
Bidford-on-Avon, Warwickshire

Printed and bound in Great Britain by
Clays Ltd, St Ives plc

HEADLINE PUBLISHING GROUP
An Hachette UK Company
338 Euston Road
London NW1 3BH

www.headline.co.uk
www.hachette.co.uk

This novel is dedicated to Dr Tom George and Dr Warwick Sapsford, two healers of the modern age to whom I owe a great debt. They have always believed in me even when I doubted myself. Without their unfailing support and faith, I could not have created my Myrddion Merlinus.

M. K. Hume, March 2011

ACKNOWLEDGEMENTS

This book was very difficult to write, for I had to spend many hours researching the tangled and half-remembered history of Europe in the period between AD 450 and AD 456. As a novelist (rather than an historian) who is used to finding and deciphering information quickly, and then building on pre-existing knowledge of ancient cultures, I felt a little over-awed in this new world of the Franks, the Goths and Constantinople without my extensive Arthurian historical data at my fingertips.

However, I rediscovered my passion for discovery as I became aware of the lives and times of fascinating persons who were influential in shaping the world that we now know. I was particularly interested in the latest arguments concerning the effects of lead poisoning and its importance – or lack of it – in Roman life.

My thanks must go to several key people who helped me to understand the details of my research. First, to my editor, Clare Foss, who has taken on the task of mentoring me with so much enthusiasm and who is so supportive. Writing is a solitary pastime and it is all too easy to become dispirited and certain that you are chasing mares' nests as you hunt through computer data, piles of books, photocopies and reams and reams of paper. Clare's encouragement and praise have lifted my spirits during my occasional difficult days via her emails and messages.

Thank you, Clare.

Thanks again to my sounding boards, my friends Pauline, Penny and Robyn who are so very patient with me when I become over-enthusiastic.

Jolene Hill is a treasure. She is a towering support with my writing career and I must thank her with a full heart. Jolene has so much talent and handles all the bits and pieces that I need to be an effective novelist. Jolene, Michael and our IT man Simon are the staunch walls at my back that give me the technical support that keeps me going as I chase the elusive dream of all writers – to be successful at what we love best.

Then there are the many people who are virtually anonymous except in their own communities, especially in England and Wales, whom I met in my travels across Europe, Asia and Britain.

To Gwylym, the elderly gentleman whom I met at the Hole in the Wall, a pub in Caernarfon, my thanks for giving me a name to add to the *dramatis personae* of this novel.

To Inga, Ken, Anan and David in Glastonbury, many thanks for easing my time among strangers, making me laugh and giving this Aussie a bird's-eye view of life in rural Somerset.

To the wonderful people of the Coach House Inn at Chester where I became aware of the existence of the Tempest family: your advice remains with me.

To the many kind people of Carmarthen, thank you too.

I wish I knew the name of every bus driver, newsagent or passer-by who helped me so I could thank them personally, but be sure that I carry your faces and your voices with me as

I sit at my desk, several oceans away, and work through the long night hours.

My thanks also to Dorie Simmonds for making me feel welcome at Christmas when I was far from home, and the people of the Premier Inn chain in London, Nottingham and York. The generosity of people sometimes takes my breath away and I am grateful for every smile and every kind word.

M. K. Hume, March 2011

DRAMATIS PERSONAE

Aetius

Flavius Aetius (c.396–454) was the last of the great Roman generals. Of Scythian descent, he was raised among the Huns and remained friendly with them for life. While in the service of Rome, he was elevated to the rank of *magister militum* by Galla Placidia, empress and regent of the Western Empire and became the protector of Placidia and Emperor Valentinian. In 451, his forces defeated Attila the Hun at the Battle of the Catalaunian Plain near Châlons in France, where he fought Attila's hordes to a standstill. He slowed Attila's advance into Italy and was present at Pope Leo's meeting with Attila at Mantua in 452. In 453, he arranged the betrothal of his son, Gaudentius, to Valentinian's daughter, Placidia. In 454, Aetius was assassinated by Valentinian III, prompting the famous description that the emperor cut off his strong right hand with his left.

Ali el Kabir

A minor Arab king of a small tribe near Damascus, he was the uncle of Yusuf el Razi.

Ambrosius

Ambrosius Aurelianus was a High King of the Britons in the early fifth century. He was the son of Constantine III and the brother of Constans II (who was murdered and succeeded by Vortigern) and Uther Pendragon, all of whom held the throne at various times. Ambrosius went into exile for some years, but eventually returned to Britain and reclaimed the throne in his own right. He succeeded Vortigern and became the last of the Roman kings.

Annwynn   A female healer who resided in Segontium. She was well versed in herb lore and accepted Myrddion as an apprentice when he was still a young boy.

Ardabur Aspar   While on a covert mission to Britain, Flavius Ardabur Aspar (400–471) raped a young Celtic girl, Branwyn, who rescued him after he was shipwrecked near Segontium on the west coast of Britain. At the time, Aspar was in the service of King Vortigern. Branwyn became pregnant and Myrddion Merlinus (later Emrys) was the issue of their coupling.

Ardabarius   Flavius Ardabarius was the father of Flavius Ardabur Aspar.

Avienus   Consul Avienus was part of a delegation, led by Pope Leo I, that met Attila at Mantua and convinced the Hun king to leave Italy.

Ardaric   King Ardaric (died c.460) was a minor ruler of the Gepid peoples who served under the command of Attila the Hun.

Attila the Hun   Attila the Hun (406–453) was the ruler of the Hunnish Empire from 434 till his death and was a fierce enemy of both the Eastern and Western Roman empires. He invaded the Balkans twice. He also invaded Gaul (France) and rampaged as far as Orléans before being defeated at the Battle of the Catalaunian Plain near Châlons in 451. Subsequently, he attacked the forces of the Western Roman Empire in 452 and took northern Italy, thereby threatening Rome. After a conference with Pope Leo and a delegation dispatched by Emperor Valentinian, Attila abandoned his attack and returned to the north.

Bleda — Brother of Attila the Hun. He was murdered by Attila after a dispute between them.

Bran — The Celtic god of regeneration.

Brangaine — A Celtic camp follower who joined Myrddion's healers in the journey from Segontium in Britain to Constantinople as a servant.

Branwyn — Myrddion's mother. She was the daughter of Olwyn and Godric, and the granddaughter of Melvig ap Melwy, king of the Deceangli tribe.

Bridie — A Celtic camp follower who joined Myrddion's healers in the journey from Segontium in Britain to Constantinople as a servant.

Cadoc ap Cadwy — A warrior in Vortigern's service who came from the Forest of Dean. He became

Myrddion's assistant and apprentice and travelled with his master from Segontium to Constantinople.

Captus
A captain in the Salian Frank army who was an escort for Myrddion's party when they were captured by the Franks near Châlons in France. He became friendly with Myrddion.

Catigern
The illegitimate son of King Vortigern and a servant girl. He was the younger half-brother of Vortimer and the elder half-brother of Vengis and Katigern.

Ceridwen
A Celtic enchantress. She possessed the Cauldron of Poetic Inspiration.

Childeric
Prince Childeric (440–481) was the son of Merovech, king of the Salian Franks, and succeeded his father as king.

Cleoxenes
A Byzantine nobleman, Cleoxenes was a diplomat in the service of the emperor of the Eastern Roman Empire. Initially, he was sent to Valentinian's court in Rome as an envoy, and then joined Flavius Aetius at Châlons. He was at the Battle of the Catalaunian Plain as an observer. After the battle, he returned to Rome and was present at the meeting between Pope Leo I and Attila in Mantua.

Clodio
King of the Salian Franks. He was the father of King Merovech.

Constans
High King of the Britons, succeeding his father, Constantine III. He was the older brother of Ambrosius.

Constantine	Emperor Constantine (c.285–337) became emperor of Rome in 311. He divided the Roman Empire in two, with the capital of the Western Roman Empire in Rome and the capital of the Eastern Roman Empire in Constantinople, a city that bore his name.
Constantius	Emperor Constantius (died 421) was the emperor of the Western Roman Empire and the consort of Galla Placidia.
Emilio	An innkeeper in Constantinople.
Erasistratus	A noted Alexandrian physician.
Erikk Horsebreaker	A Gepid warrior who acted as a courier.
Ferreus	A thug, also known as Iron Bar. He was a wrestler and bully in Rome's subura.
Finn ap Finbarr	Also known as Truthteller. A forward scout with Vortigern's army, he became one of Myrddion's assistants and travelled with the healer to Constantinople.
Flavia	The daughter of Flavius Aetius, she married Thraustila, a Hungvari nobleman who served in Emperor Valentinian's guard. She seduced Myrddion and had a brief liaison with him while on a journey from Ravenna to Constantinople.
Fortuna	The Roman goddess of chance or luck.
Freya	The Norse goddess of love and fertility. She was the most beautiful and propitious of the goddesses and was called upon in matters of love.
Galen	A Roman philosopher and physician.

Galla Placidia	The daughter of Theodosius I, Galla Placidia (392–450) was married to various husbands before eventually becoming the empress consort to Constantius III, the emperor of the Western Roman Empire.
Gallica Lydia	Wife of Petronius Maximus.
Gaudentius	The son of Flavius Aetius, he was married to Valentinian's daughter.
Gorlois	The Boar of Cornwall who is the king of the Dumnonii tribe. He is married to Ygerne, and is the father of Morgan and Morgause.
Gwylym	Gwylym ap Gwylydd was a Celtic mercenary who served under Flavius Aetius in Gaul.
Hengist	A Saxon aristocrat who served under King Vortigern as a mercenary for a number of years before leaving to re-join the Saxon invaders. He eventually became the thane of the Kentish Saxons.
Heraclea	The sister of Thraustila Minor, Flavia's husband.
Heraclius	Chamberlain to Emperor Valentinian III.
Herophilus	A famed Greek philosopher and physician.
Hippocrates	A famed Greek philosopher and physician. He is remembered for the Hippocratic Oath.
Honoria	Princess Honoria was the daughter of Emperor Constantius and Galla Placidia, and the sister of Valentinian. During

Attila the Hun's forays through Gaul and Italia, she sent a letter to Attila offering herself as a marriage candidate. The failure of her machinations caused Attila to attack the Western Roman Empire.

Horsa   Brother of Hengist and a mercenary in Vortigern's forces.

Isaac   A famed Jewish healer who practised medicine in Rome and Ravenna.

Leo I   Pope Leo I was a distinguished and competent pope who was appointed to the papacy in 440. Among other successes, he led a delegation to Mantua in company with two delegates of the Western Roman Empire at the behest of Emperor Valentinian in 452. Their task was to meet Attila the Hun and intercede with him on behalf of the citizens of Rome.

Licinia Eudoxia Wife of Emperor Valentinian.

Marcian   The emperor Marcian (392–457) was a protégé of Flavius Aspar. He became the emperor of the Eastern Roman Empire in 450 through the influence of the *magister militum*. He succeeded Theodosius, and was married to Pulcheria.

Magnus Maximus   Legendary Roman ruler of Britain. He was the grandfather of Ambrosius.

Merovech   The king of the Salian Franks was also known as Merovius (415–451) although dates are problematic. He was the father of Prince Childeric, and was reputed to be one of the leaders of the coalition who defeated Attila the Hun at the Battle of the Catalaunian Plain in 451. His mother was believed to have been impregnated by a sea-monster.

Mithras   An obscure deity in Zoroastrianism. He represented the father figure and was adopted as the warrior god of the Roman soldiery.

Morgan   Eldest daughter of Gorlois and Ygerne, sister to Morgause and half-sister to Arthur, who becomes High King of the Britons.

Morgause   Daughter of Gorlois and Ygerne, sister to Morgan and half-sister to King Arthur. Husband of King Lot and mother of Agravaine, Gawaine and Geraint.

Myrddion Emrys   He was named after the sun. His name means Lord of Light.

Olwyn   Daughter of Melvig ap Melwy, mother of Branwyn and grandmother of Myrddion. She was killed by Vortigern at Dinas Emrys.

Optilia   A Hungvari captain in Valentinian's guard. He was involved in the plot that resulted in the emperor's murder.

Petronius Maximus   A senator who later became emperor. His reign was short-lived and lasted for only two months before he was torn apart by the Roman mob after the Vandals commenced their attack on the capital.

Phoebe   Wife of Emilio, innkeeper in Constantinople.

Pincus	Cleoxenes's manservant.
Placidia	The daughter of Emperor Valentinian III and the granddaughter of Galla Placidia. She married Gaudentius.
Praxiteles	A servant in Constantinople who entered Myrddion's employ.
Pulchria	The healers' landlady at their rented premises in Rome's subura.
Pulcheria	The wife of Emperor Marcian of the Eastern Roman Empire, the empress was the sister of Emperor Theodosius who preceded Marcian on the throne.
Ranus	A Frankish horse trader in Gesoriacum (Calais).
Rhedyn	A Celtic camp follower who became a servant for Myrddion's healers on the journey from Segontium to Constantinople.
Rowena	The second wife of King Vortigern. She was of Saxon descent and was the mother of Vengis and Katigern.
Sangiban	King of the Alan nation.
Theodoric	King of the Visigoths, who died at the Battle of the Catalaunian Plain in 451.
Theodosius	Theodosius II (401–450) was the emperor of the Eastern Roman Empire. He was succeeded by Marcian.
Thorismund	The son of Theodoric, Thorismund succeeded his father as king of the Visigoths.
Thraustila	Married to Flavia. A Hun nobleman, he was pro-Roman.

Tofus	Servant of Flavius Ardabur Aspar.
Trigetius	Prefect Trigetius was a member of the delegation led by Pope Leo I that met Attila the Hun at Mantua.
Uther Pendragon	High King of the Britons, younger brother of Ambrosius and father of King Arthur. He succeeded Ambrosius.
Valentinian	Flavius Valentinian III (419–455) was the emperor of the Western Roman Empire from 425 to 455. He was the son of Galla Placidia and Constantius III. His predecessor was Honorius, and he was succeeded by Petronius Maximus. A weak ruler, he is mostly remembered for murdering the last of the great Roman generals, Flavius Aetius.
Vechmar	Personal physician to King Theodoric of the Visigoths.
Vortigern	The High King of the northern Britons of Cymru, some generations before the emergence of King Arthur. He is remembered as the first monarch to welcome the Saxons into his realm to appease his Saxon queen, Rowena.
Vortimer	Prince Vortimer was the son of King Vortigern and the brother of Prince Catigern. They were half-brothers of Vengis and Katigern.
Willa Major	A casualty of Attila's army in Gaul, Willa was the mother of a young babe who survived and was adopted by Myrddion's healers.

Willa Minor	An abandoned orphan who was found during the healers' travels in Gaul.
Ygerne	Ygerne is the wife of Gorlois, the Boar of Cornwall. After his death, she marries Uther Pendragon. She is the natural mother of King Arthur.
Yusuf el Razi	A young man knifed at a brothel in Constantinople whose life was saved when Myrddion treated his wounds.

PROLOGUE

Three years after this, he himself [Constantine,
King of Britain]...was killed by Conan, and
buried close by Uther Pendragon within the
structure of stones, which was set up with
wonderful art not far from Salisbury.

Geoffrey of Monmouth

The Giant's Dance loomed out of the rain and sleet in dark
shades of charcoal. Myrddion dismounted and waded
through the dying grasses, which were flattened by the strong
winds that howled over the great plain. He had never seen
the Giant's Dance, but he had been told about the great stones
that seemed to have been placed in the landscape by a gigantic
child playing with pebbles. Looking at the Heel Stone, he felt
a twinge of disappointment. The Dance was extensive and the
healer had no notion of how the lintel stones had been
winched into position, but he was mildly disappointed by the
smallness of the scale.

Hunching his head and shoulders under the fur-lined
hood of his woollen cloak, Myrddion leaned against a

bluestone column that was slightly shorter than a full-grown man. The slick wetness of the rock was both cold and vibrant under his sensitive fingertips. Listening with that odd other-sense that plagued sections of his family, he could hear a thick humming noise reverberating out of the blue monoliths, and revised his poor opinion of the imposing nature of the Dance. Something very old and menacing dwelled within the strange arcane circles of stones. The origins of the Dance had been lost in the vortex of time, but one local legend suggested that the Lord of Light, Myrddion's namesake, had built it during the ancient days.

'Are you done, master?' Cadoc stood at the very top of the huge, encircling mound, his nose bright red in the chill wind and his hunched figure a picture of cold misery. 'This wind would freeze off a witch's tits.'

'You've no soul, Cadoc,' Myrddion murmured, knowing his servant would be unable to hear him over the howling gale. 'Get out of the wind for the moment,' he shouted. 'I'll come along shortly.'

The apprentice raised one wool-wrapped arm in acknow-ledgement and trudged down into the ditch that encircled the Dance. Every movement of his stolid warrior's body spoke of his dissatisfaction with the weather. Cadoc was loyal and indispensable within the healing tents, but the scarred warrior hated cold weather and dreaded the prospect of sailing to the land of the Franks across the Litus Saxonicum. He would follow where Myrddion travelled, but the healer knew that the ex-warrior with the ugly burn marks on his face and neck would complain irritatingly every step of the way.

Myrddion sighed, but regardless of the invisible yet palpable presence of Cadoc waiting at the wagons he made his way to the very centre of the Dance. One huge, upright stone bore the marks of a blade, and Myrddion followed the shape of the carving with his ungloved hand.

'A knife!' he whispered aloud. 'What in the name of Bran and all the gods caused the symbol of a knife to be carved into these stones? This whole place is a mystery.'

As he peered closely at the slick, icy surface of the stone, Myrddion recognised that the design of the knife was outland. No Celtic swordsmith had wrought this dagger, and only a skilled and observant engraver could have picked out its details on the stone. The healer memorised the shape in case he should ever see such a weapon again.

A pale moon struggled with dense clouds that were pregnant with sleet, and almost unconsciously Myrddion was drawn to the centre of the great horseshoe of stones where a large, rough-cut block of heavy local rock lay like an altar. There, at the very heart of the Dance, he felt a gathering of dark symbols, as if he could pull back a curtain and watch the builders as they laboured through uncounted generations to bring the circle to life. But for what purpose?

Wheeling constellations. A sunrise that sent long bars of light and shadows racing across green grass, while shaggy shapes chanted to the thudding accompaniment of hardened spear-shafts as they struck the ground. He could feel no blood – only the light that flowed in great rivers as it cascaded through his eyeballs and burned his retinas. A star hovered over the central pair of stones with the great cross-piece positioned over it. In a dim, trance-like state, Myrddion realised that he was drifting off to the edges of a fit; that old, much-feared unconsciousness when he said and did things that defied his waking, scientific mind. With a wrench powered by all the anger that hid in the child who was almost grown to manhood, he pulled himself away from the star and the river of light, seeing the figures fade into gusts of rain as he returned to his true self.

His right hand was pressed against the altar stone, which still felt warm from the touch of long dead sunrises. Myrddion snatched his hand away and the connection with the Dance splintered like frostbitten rock under the mason's hammer.

'Never! Never again! I'll not live and fear the past or the future,' he screamed. 'I'll not know.'

But flurries of wind and rain blew his voice away.

'All I want – all that I'll accept – is to find Flavius, who-ever he is. If I have to travel beyond the Middle Sea to the cataracts that support the pillars of the world, then I'll go. But I'll know why my father played dice with my life before I was born. I'll face him and, if need be, I'll kill him if that's what it takes to be free of him. And I'll not use the fits to track him down.'

Brave words! Myrddion's inner self sneered. What we want and what we get are rarely one and the same thing. The healer raised his eyes to the cloud-shrouded moon and laughed at his own foolishness. The gods will not be mocked, he thought sadly. They'll not free us from the curses of our births. But I still want to know!

'I want to know,' he whispered aloud, then turned and ran through the circle, past the bluestones and beyond the Heel Stone, until he came to the mound and saw the wagons huddled together around the makeshift fire that Cadoc was attempting to keep alive.

Again, Myrddion laughed and hurried towards the wagons, his friends and the sense of a purpose that would give him no inner peace until it was achieved. Behind him, the Dance waited as it had done for a thousand years. Not even a Demon Seed could disturb its long dreaming as it slumbered under the whips of the winter winds. It slept and dreamed until it would be needed again.

Myrddion's chart of the route from Segontium to Dubris

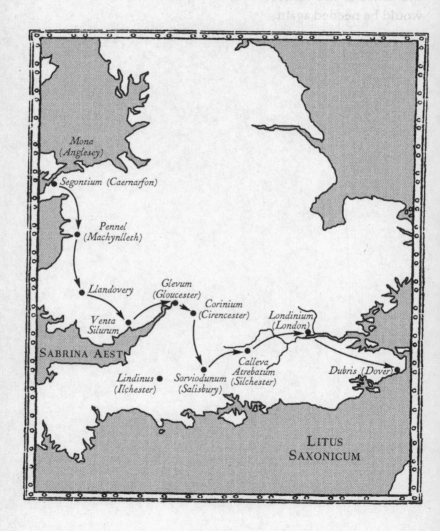

CHAPTER I

AN INAUSPICIOUS MEETING

For how can man die better than facing fearful
    odds
For the ashes of his father and the temples of his
    gods?

Demosthenes, *Olynthiacs*

In far-away Tintagel, where the fortress clung to a barren rock thrust out into a cold, howling sea, Queen Ygerne stood in her forecourt, wrapped in furs and shivering in the gelid afternoon air. To the west, the obscured sun coloured the thin, storm-ravaged clouds with a transparent orange glaze. Light struggled with darkness, like the battle that raged within her spirit. With hands thrust in coarse woollen mittens, she clutched at her flat belly and begged the goddess to be kind. Then, for good measure, she prayed to the Virgin Mary that the immortal mother would intercede with the Christian god and bless her unborn child.

When Ygerne had become certain of her third pregnancy, she had told her husband, King Gorlois, that this time she was sure that her infant would be a boy. Her heart clearly told her the formless child's sex, and she already dreamed of him, soft and milky, nestling in her arms. Gorlois had whooped with joy, for although his girls, Morgan and Morgause, were a permanent celebration of the wonder of their union, his masculine pride was stirred by the thought of a son to inherit the kingdom of Cornwall. Gorlois asked so little of Ygerne, and loved her so generously and purely, that the queen was overjoyed that she could give him his heart's desire. The solstice feasts had been transformed by the fertility and felicity of their shared love.

Then, as the rains of winter set in with a vengeance, the Boar of Cornwall had been called away by Ambrosius, the new High King. With regret, Gorlois had departed, for to leave his wife in the death days of the year was a wrench that made his heart ache. Gorlois knew she would be kept safe through the devotion of his guard and servants, but this new pregnancy gave his absence an additional poignancy that made the Dumnonii king short-tempered and depressed. As he rode across the causeway from Tintagel on his new colt, Fleet Foot, with his personal guard trailing behind him, he dared not look back at the fortress in case he should see the weeping face of Ygerne. He cursed Ambrosius and his demands, then straightened his back and galloped away from everything he loved.

Now, in a grey place of stone, sea and wild things on the wing, Ygerne tried to commune with the developing son who lay in her womb. As yet, the child had no thread of consciousness to speak to her, so she felt very alone on her spur of rock, far from the courts of men. A shadow lay over her mind, as if a blanket had blotted out the warmth of the sun and extinguished all light. She longed for spring and the swelling of her belly, but the skies promised hard weather before the King of Winter perished and the new lord was born in a wave of perfumed flowers and soft rain.

The sudden pain, low in her belly, was so swift and sharp that Ygerne dropped the bag of mending she carried with her during the day. She stared at the spilled clothing on the stones of the forecourt, at one of Gorlois's knitted gloves that had fallen a little way from the woven bag and lay, like a crumpled grey flower, already unravelling at the thumb. To her cringing, shocked gaze, the ruined glove became the centre of her universe as the pain tore through her – and then was gone. Her legs trembled, and she felt a sudden leak of blood trickle down her thighs.

'Are you well, my lady?' A concerned guardsman had approached her, shocked by her sudden pallor. 'For the love of the gods! Alarm! The queen is unwell!' he shouted as Ygerne's knees began to buckle with shock. 'To me! The queen needs assistance!'

As the guardsman swung her delicate frame into his arms, Ygerne knew her son had died and she began to keen, frightening the poor man so that his strong hands shook. Rushed inside the fortress, to her servants and her huge marital bed, Ygerne could only weep with sorrow and lost hope. As her serving women clucked their tongues over her bloodstained legs and hurried to staunch the bleeding, she turned her face into her pillow and asked the gods why Gorlois was being punished.

Light as fingertips on her lips, faint words came to her out of the depths of her mind. 'Not yet, Ygerne, your time is not yet come. Be patient, for you'll have what you desire in time.'

'How will I tell my love that his son has perished?' she asked her serving women, who could only shake their heads and try to comfort her. 'How will I explain to Gorlois when I cannot understand myself?'

Out on the peninsula, the wind howled a message that chilled her spirit. 'Not yet! Not now! You must wait!'

Cadoc leaned against the rough side of the heaving boat and vomited into the sea. Ever since the port of Dubris had been left behind, the warrior had been unable to control his gorge, so that now he hung with his body half out of the vessel, a picture of abject misery. In the inexplicable way of humankind, Myrddion and Finn Truthteller were unaffected by the pitching and rolling of the ancient, salt-encrusted vessel, while Cadoc suffered his seasickness acutely.

'You have to eat something, Cadoc,' Myrddion coaxed, while the man's face spasmed with sudden nausea. 'You could develop a serious illness if you don't eat for days on end.'

He held out a bowl of clear soup, cold, but nourished with herbs, shredded chicken meat and a little poppy juice to settle the stomach, but Cadoc waved it away. The servant's face was grey under his rueful grin, but Myrddion persisted. He depended on Cadoc's superlative organisational ability, and having sold his wagons and livestock rather than risk them on the dangerous crossing of the Litus Saxonicum he would need the purchasing expertise of his servant once the wallowing, wooden vessel made landfall.

'Please, Cadoc,' he urged. 'I'd not give you anything that would increase your discomfort. Sip the soup slowly and the nausea will pass. Trust me, my friend.'

Against his better judgement, Cadoc sipped the thin gruel and discovered that it did have a palatable taste, although he'd have added a little salt if he was able. Led by his master to a nest of blankets prepared on the least frequented portion of the deck, he was persuaded to recline on the scrubbed planks where he huddled in a cocoon of wool so that only his dripping nose was exposed to the cold air. Once his vivid eyes began to cloud over and his head started to nod, Myrddion ushered Finn out of the other man's hearing, hushing him when he opened his mouth to make a joke at Cadoc's expense.

'Be kind to our friend, Truthteller. He's seriously ill from the movement sickness and I need him to be alert and healthy as soon as we are on dry land again. His malady will soon pass once we have docked, but until then he's really suffering. Unfortunately, although the crossing is very short, the pangs of his illness are quite extreme.'

Finn shook his head with the incomprehension of a man who has never been affected by the movement of the waves. 'Of course, master. I'll see him comfortable, although who'd have thought that the irrepressible Cadoc would be laid low by a few pitching waves?'

'We all have weaknesses, friend Finn, even Cadoc.'

Myrddion turned away and returned to the blunt prow of the crude vessel, where he strained his eyes towards the coastline in a wishful hope for the first sign of land. His thoughts ranged back to Londinium, and the dire things he had seen in that mighty Celtic city.

After weeks of weary travel, the wagons eventually reached the broader roads leading into Londinium as a short winter day began to fade into darkness. The open countryside had given way to the unmistakable signs of a large metropolis, in conical Celtic cottages, small plots of tilled land, fences of crude wood and an abundance of inns, shop-fronts and trading stalls along the Roman road. Crudely daubed signs bore the ramshackle air of semi-permanence.

Barca's Food screamed a red sign over one such establishment, a place where bucolics and ragged children stood and played in thick mud and ate greasy stew with shared wooden spoons, or devoured chunks of meat, oozing fat, which they impaled on their knife points. Myrddion observed a crowd of filthy, tangled beards, sly eyes and ragged wools and furs typical of the inhabitants who dwelled on the fringes of any large settlement.

Another sign leered drunkenly above a two-storeyed structure, which indicated its wares with the simple declaration *Best and Cleanest Girls*. Myrddion judged the truth of this boast by a young woman, barely beyond puberty, who lounged at the doorpost and scratched her crotch unselfconsciously. Under flimsy, revealing robes, her goose-pimpled flesh had the grey tinge of old dirt and her long black hair was greasy for lack of washing. Even from a distance of a few feet, Myrddion could see lice crawling through the tangled locks.

Clean? Myrddion thought sardonically. I could become diseased just from talking to her. The girl caught his eyes with her own insolent, ancient invitation to experience the pleasures of the flesh. Under the childish veneer of seduction, he sensed a well of hatred and contempt that she had not yet learned to disguise.

Pointing towards a copse of dispirited, bare trees that survived just off the road, Myrddion ordered his servants to make camp. With the economy of long practice, the servants obeyed, but preparation of the evening meal had barely begun when the first customers appeared in search of the healer. Somehow, with the mysterious genius of those who grasp all opportunities with alacrity, the settlers had already discovered the profession of the itinerant strangers.

Sighing with weariness, Myrddion set to work, lancing boils, drawing a painful tooth from one sufferer and treating the small injuries and diseases common in any semi-rural community where poverty and dirt afflict the citizens.

He was dressing a nasty infection with a pad of cloth smeared with drawing ointment when a huge form entered the tent and inserted itself between the firelight and the healer's view of his patient. Myrddion cursed under his breath, rose to his feet and turned with sharp words of complaint on his lips.

His protest withered.

The figure was a huge warrior, standing well over six feet three inches, more than enough to block out the light. Myrddion was very tall, but this warrior overtopped him by several inches. Although the light from the fire was behind him, the young man seemed even larger and more impressive than he would otherwise appear, for he possessed a wild bush of amber curls that defied the strictures of plaits and the iron helmet designed to contain their vigorous tendrils. The light invested his head with a nimbus like a glowing, golden halo that exactly suggested a great crown.

'Are you proficient with your sewing needles, healer?'

Almost seductive in nature, the melodious, husky voice seemed to promise understanding and support. Myrddion shook his head to clear it of the dulcet offer that the tone implied and peered into the dark face.

'Turn into the light, sir, so I can attend to your needs,' he replied in kind, using his own mellifluous voice to counteract the warrior's silken net of sound. 'Cadoc can complete this dressing.'

Mutely, the warrior turned so that the firelight washed his face with scarlet and held out a bronzed arm to reveal a long, shallow wound that travelled from elbow to wrist.

'I see!' Suddenly all business, Myrddion moved forward and gripped the proffered arm so he could inspect the wound more clearly. 'What caused this injury, sir? The edges are puckered as if something blunt ripped through your skin.'

'Something did.' The warrior grinned engagingly. 'I killed a boar on my spear, but the beast threw itself down the shaft as it attempted to gut me. One tusk managed to catch my wrist-band before it died.' He smiled again. 'It was determined to kill me, so I suppose I'm lucky to have escaped with this scratch.'

Myrddion examined the inflamed edges of the wound and pursed his lips. 'This boar has used his tusks on other, unclean prey, and even now the infection from their blood is attacking your flesh. You are fortunate that you came to me when you did. One more day and we might be mourning your imminent death.'

The warrior watched intently as Myrddion began to wash the wound with hot water, taking care to clean every part of the nasty gash. Although the water must have burned the exposed and tender flesh, the man didn't flinch. Then, while Myrddion heated a long tool until it was cherry red, he asked if the healer proposed to cleanse the wound with fire and seal off the blood vessels. Myrddion realised that the man had a curious and adaptive mind and was able to appreciate the reasons for his actions.

'Aye, lord. It is paramount in wounds of this kind that the evil humours are scarified out of the injury before rot sets in and the limb dies. So easily are we crippled, sir, by things we cannot see.'

'Then my luck holds, healer. I find myself wounded and you arrive on my doorstep, knowledgeable and ready to minister to my needs. What is your name?'

Myrddion looked up into the handsome, tanned face and saw that the warrior was beardless, in the Roman fashion. Mystery piled on mystery with this tall stranger, Celtic in appearance, yet so alien in manner. He didn't flinch as his flesh smoked and burned, except for a perceptible tightening of his lips.

With a little nod of his head, Myrddion answered. 'I am Myrddion Merlinus of Segontium, erstwhile healer to King Vortigern. I am en route to the Middle Sea to study my art under the great minds in Constantinople.'

Except for raising one eyebrow interrogatively, the warrior showed no obvious sign of surprise. Myrddion felt the warmth of the man's wide smile, but observed that no corresponding liking reached the cold blue eyes that watched him so carefully. Somewhere below his ribs, the healer cringed inwardly, as if he recognised someone who would change his life.

'I am Uther Pendragon, brother of Ambrosius the Great, Lord High King of the Britons. You may have heard of me.'

Uther spoke without a trace of prideful self-consciousness. Like an unpredictable force of nature, he simply was. The entire British world had heard of Uther Pendragon. Eloquently, he had expounded his lineage, his royalty and his utter self-belief with just a few simple words. Myrddion shivered, as if a cold wind had crawled over his bare flesh, threatening all kinds of punishment and horror.

'Indeed, Lord Uther, all men who serve the goddess have heard of you and your valiant brother. The Saxons, Hengist and Horsa, were driven out of our lands at your command, while Powys, Dyfed and Gwynedd rest more peacefully because of your actions.'

'You served the tyrant Vortigern?' Uther asked as

Myrddion smeared fresh salve along his wound, taking care to use a small wooden paddle so that his fingers never touched the reddened edges of the wound. Uther's cold voice never wavered, but the blue eyes had hardened.

'Aye. And tyrant is a good description of that unlamented king. He would have killed his own children by Queen Rowena had he not burned to death in his own fortress in the midst of an unseasonal storm.'

Myrddion was choosing his words with a statesman's care, even though Uther's piercing eyes were fixed upon his wound. Uther was a truly dangerous man and Myrddion felt the air drain away around them, as if the High King's brother could suck all the vitality out of the atmosphere with a single intent glance. The healer hardened his heart, composed his face and spoke on with feigned nonchalance.

'Aye, Vortigern paid for his many sins when he ran the length of his own hall, wreathed in flames, as his fortress burned to the ground around him. Believe my words, lord, for I was at Dinas Emrys . . . and I saw the Burning Man.'

Uther looked up then and caught Myrddion's eye as the healer began to bandage the ugly slash. His eyes were frigid, although his mouth smiled with a woman's promise. 'It is said that he was struck by lightning.'

'I saw and heard lightning aplenty that night, lord, but I didn't see what set Vortigern aflame. He was within his bedchamber when the fire engulfed him, so I doubt that the gods sent a bolt from the heavens just to take his life. The actions of men probably ended Lord Vortigern's existence. He certainly had enemies enough.'

Uther smiled. 'So I have been told, healer, so I have been told. How did you come to serve the Regicide?'

Myrddion washed his hands in a large bowl of warm water

and chose his words carefully. 'When I was a boy, I lived in Segontium with my grandmother Olwyn and her second husband, Eddius. Vortigern had me captured because he had been told that blood from the son of a demon should be used to seal the foundations of his tower at Dinas Emrys. I was taken because it was rumoured that I was the Demon Seed.'

Uther raised one eyebrow. 'So I've heard – but I doubted the truth of such a boast. I am agog to hear your ancestry from your own mouth,' the prince added with a white and sardonic grin. 'I've been told the Demon Seed predicted things Vortigern didn't wish to hear.'

'So the rumour says, Prince Uther, but I've no memory of what I said. Vortigern feared to kill me, so he murdered his magicians in my stead. But Fortuna turned her face away from me. My grandmother, who was a Deceangli princess, and the priestess of the Mother, came to save me. Vortigern struck her with his clenched fist, and the blow killed her.'

'So how could you serve the Regicide when your grandmother's blood called to you from the earth? Were you frightened?' Uther's perfect teeth, so unusual in any warrior over thirty, seemed very sharp and lupine. Myrddion wondered if the prince enjoyed the infliction of pain as much as his glistening eyes and moist mouth seemed to suggest.

'I had no choice, for he threatened to kill my mistress, Annwynn of Segontium, who is a famed healer in Cymru. I obeyed, and eventually he told me my father's name. Not that he was much help, for Flavius is a very common Roman gens. However, I'm now free to seek my father out.'

Myrddion checked the prince's bandage carefully and found a small container so that Uther could take a quantity of ointment with him. As he pressed the small horn box into the prince's hand, he felt a shiver of presentiment course through his blood.

'Take care to keep the wound very clean and dry – and use fresh bandages when you dress it, my lord. Evil humours have a way of creeping into the most carefully tended wounds.'

'I am fated to die peacefully in my bed, healer, for so it has been prophesied. But I thank you none the less for your labours.'

Uther searched in a leather pouch and retrieved a golden coin, far too much payment for Myrddion's ministrations, and flicked it towards the healer with a deft and insulting movement of his thumb. Reflexively, Myrddion caught it in his cupped hands and tried to return it.

'That's far too much gold for such a simple task, my lord,' he protested.

'Consider it an indicator of payments for services you will provide in the future. When you return from your journey to Constantinople, I would have one of the finest healers in the land as my personal physician.' Uther laughed as if he had made a good joke, enjoying the flush of embarrassment that stained Myrddion's cheeks. 'I will remember you, Myrddion-no-name, and I will not have forgotten our talk on this day when you return from your travels and enter my service.'

Prudently, Myrddion kept any words of refusal between his teeth and bowed low so that Uther wouldn't recognise the mutiny in his eyes. Then the prince swept away without a backward glance, accompanied by three warriors who had waited near the raised leather entrance of the tent.

Cadoc exhaled noisily with relief once the small party had vanished into the night. 'You can thank all the gods for your skill, master. An arrow was notched and ready for flight throughout your ministrations. Did you not see the archer in the shadows of the wagon?'

Myrddion shook his head as his knees threatened to collapse under him. 'I feel as if I've just escaped from a pit of angry vipers,' he muttered as he sank to his haunches by the fireside. 'Uther Pendragon makes Vortigern seem kindly and generous.'

'That man is a devil, master, a chaos-beast come to tear the land to ribbons for his own benefit. Did you see his eyes? For the first time, I'm glad we're going to Constantinople, wherever that is. He'll not find us there, master, and he would if you remained here. He wants your skills.'

'Perhaps battle will claim him while we are absent from Britain. I've had my fill of arrogant, powerful masters who ride roughshod over the dreams of ordinary men.'

'Not him. He'll survive the worst that fate can throw at him and still flourish. We'd best be gone before first light, for I'd not put it past that devil to steal you away for the sake of his precious honour.'

'Aye.' Myrddion nodded in agreement. 'Wake me at dawn.'

The night was as cold as ever and the dried grasses under the copse of trees made an uncomfortable and itchy bed, but Myrddion was suddenly so exhausted that he couldn't keep his eyes open. He plunged into the river of sleep as if he meant to drown himself, and through the marshes of the darkness night-horses sent horrors after him until his cries disturbed the other sleepers and Finn was forced to wake him with a worried frown.

Londinium was a city that had been infiltrated and defeated by stealth. As the healers rode through its outskirts, heading for the southeastern roadway that would lead to Dubris on the coast, Myrddion couldn't fail to recognise the hordes of Saxon traders clogging the Roman streets and a growing accumulation of filth where the clean outlines of stone drains had become blurred with rubbish. The Roman passion for cleanliness was beginning to fade, while Celt, Saxon and dark-skinned traders from other lands hawked their wares in an argot of many mixed languages. Myrddion spied Roman-ised Celts dressed in togas and robes wearing expressions of permanent confusion, as if puzzled by the changes that had turned Londinium into a slatternly city.

'The barbarians have taken Londinium without a single blow. See the traders? And beyond the villages, there are northern palisades that have no place in these lands.' Cadoc's face whitened a little and he shook his head like a shaggy hound. 'Londinium can't be allowed to fall, lord. What will happen to us if all sorts of wild men gain a foothold here?'

'I don't know, Cadoc,' Myrddion whispered softly. 'Hengist and his sons have set down roots in the north of the country, so many more Saxon ships will soon follow from the east. Before I die, I fear that the days will come when our whole green land will belong to the invaders ... and our customs will be consigned to the middens of the past. Change has come, my friend, whether we want it or not.'

Cadoc was affronted by Myrddion's opinion, so he busied himself by carefully handling the reins of the four horses that were dragging the heavy wagon. 'The Saxons won't be permitted to lord it over our people while we can still fight. I know what those bastards are like. They destroy everything that is good in the name of their savage gods.'

'I hope you're right, Cadoc, but reason tells me that a change has come and only a fool pretends he can stop it. The Saxons aren't wicked, just determined to find a permanent home. Perhaps Uther Pendragon can stop them, if anyone can.'

'Now there's a horrible thought,' Cadoc muttered as he concentrated on controlling his team.

'As you know, the cure is sometimes worse than the illness,' Myrddion whispered, but his words were blown away in the stiffening breeze from the sea.

The inhabitants of the towns of the south were nervous and inclined to be suspicious of strangers, for these people had endured the invasions led by Vortigern's Saxon bodyguards, Hengist and Horsa, and struggled with Vortimer's bloody retribution for their incursions into the Cantii lands, so the local elders now waited for the void created by warfare to be filled by some new, as yet unknown, threat. Strangers were not to be trusted, for lies come easily to the lips of greedy and ambitious men. But healers were in demand, so the wealth in Myrddion's strongbox gradually increased through payments of silver and bronze coin and the odd rough gem, besides the barter of fresh vegetables and eggs in return for their ministrations. Of necessity, such aid as they could offer to the citizens along the road to Dubris slowed their journey as well as enriching them, while bringing new dangers of robbery from unscrupulous and desperate outlaws.

Finn Truthteller had been grimly silent as they passed the hillock of greening earth where so many Saxons had died during Hengist's war, and he shuddered as he spied the standing slab of marble with its carving of the running horse. Knowing that Finn still suffered the lash of memory and a shadow of dishonour, Myrddion joined his servant in the second wagon as they passed an old, fire-scarred Roman villa.

'You need not be concerned to look upon the ruins left by the Night of the Long Knives, friend Finn,' the healer offered when he saw the shaking hands and quivering lips of his friend. 'Hengist's revenge on Vortimer's Celts was no stain on your honour.'

'I am the Truthteller, Lord Myrddion, and Hengist left me alive to testify to the death of Prince Catigern at this place. Many good men perished here, but I was saved to recount the tale. I'll not run from a memory, master. I can't. Better to face my ghosts and save my sanity.'

Myrddion laid one sensitive hand on Finn's arm where he could feel the bunched muscles that were a mute betrayal of Truthteller's internal suffering. 'You're right. I somehow expected the villa to be larger and more oppressive than it is, when you consider its reputation. But, like all bad dreams, its reality is far less impressive than the memories it holds. It has become a worthless pile of fire-scarred bricks and stone rubble. See? The trees are beginning to grow through the open rooms and little will soon remain to remind us of what happened here.'

'Aye,' Finn replied slowly, as Myrddion felt some of the tension leave the man's arm. 'Weeds are covering the cracked flagstones and ivy is breaking up what is left of the foundations.' Then, just as Myrddion thought that Finn had managed to banish his constant companions of shame and guilt, the older man cursed. 'I wonder if Catigern lived for a time under Horsa's body?' Myrddion saw a single tear drop from Finn's frozen face.

'I don't know, Finn. But if he did, Catigern deserved to suffer. He was a brutal man who is better under the sod. He'd have betrayed us all for the chance to win a crown.'

'Aye,' Finn replied once more. He shook his brown curls and used the reins to slap the rump of the carthorse. 'Better to be off on the seas and away from these bad memories.'

*

Dubris still retained its links with the legions in its orderly roadways and official stone buildings, but the healers could see evidence of the growing malaise of carelessness in the pillaging of the old forum for building materials. Marble sculptures of old Roman gods had been carted away to be crushed and turned into lime, leaving empty plinths of the coarser stone so that, uneasily, Myrddion fancied that Dubris was cannibalising its own flesh.

But the docks displayed the bustle and industry of any busy port. Vessels of all types jostled for moorings along the crude wooden wharves, while traders haggled with ships' masters in half a dozen exotic languages. Running, grunting under the weight of huge bundles, or driving wagons drawn by mules, oxen and the occasional spavined horse, servants and slaves moved cargoes to warehouses or loaded ships with trade goods for the markets across the narrow sea that linked Britain and the land of the Franks. Above the din of commerce, Myrddion could barely make himself heard as he gave his instructions to Cadoc.

'Sell our horses for the best prices you can get,' Myrddion ordered as he ran an experienced eye over the rawboned beasts as they strained under their heavy loads. 'Judging by the standard of animals we can see here, you'll get a good price for our horseflesh. The wagons will have to go as well, but remember that we'll have to buy others once we make landfall. Don't let the bastards cheat us!'

'It'll be my pleasure, Master Myrddion. The traders will pay good coin, or I'll make up the difference myself. However, we might need to wait for a few days to win the best prices. They'll fleece us bare if they smell any desperation on our part.'

'We can afford to wait for several days, for the spring sailing has only just begun. Besides, I'm sure we'll have our first customers before the day is out.'

As usual, Myrddion read the tone and desires of Dubris correctly. Even before the travellers had found an inn to provide them with moderately clean shelter, the grapevine of gossip had whispered of a skilled healer in the port and Myrddion, his women and his servants were soon profitably at work.

Nor was it difficult to find a suitable vessel to continue their journey. The ship they chose was captained by a dour northerner who plied his trade between Dubris and the Frankish lands to the east, and was more than willing to bear passengers who wouldn't need to fill his wide-bellied ship with their own goods. Prudently, Myrddion paid a quarter of the agreed price in advance and sealed the deal with a handshake.

A week later, Dubris became a disappearing line of dirty haze in the charcoal skies behind them, and the Frankish port of Gesoriacum became an equally vague suggestion in the heaving seas before them. They were about to enter foreign climes, and Myrddion was still boy enough to feel his heart lighten with excitement. His mother might detest him because of the violence of his conception, and his beloved Olwyn had been buried on the sea cliffs above the straits of Mona isle, but Myrddion was still young and vigorous. Somewhere beyond the haze on the horizon were libraries full of learning, new ideas that would fire his questioning mind and a whole new world of sensation. Somewhere, out in the far-off corners of the world, the object of his quest might lead him to his destiny.

The seabirds followed the wallowing vessel and squabbled

over the food scraps that were tossed overboard. Like all scavengers, they were careless of the needs of their fellows, so they fought for their spoils with the intensity and ferocity of starving beggars. Even their cries were like eerie curses that followed Myrddion, sending his thoughts winging onwards towards the east and to the man he sought out of all the millions who populated lands that bordered the Middle Sea.

And yet his reason called him a fool for allowing himself to pursue such a useless undertaking. An old cliché echoed in his brain, full of warning and threat, so he spoke the words aloud to rob them of their sting. 'Be careful what you wish for . . .'

MYRDDION'S CHART OF THE ROUTE FROM GESORIACUM TO CHÂLONS

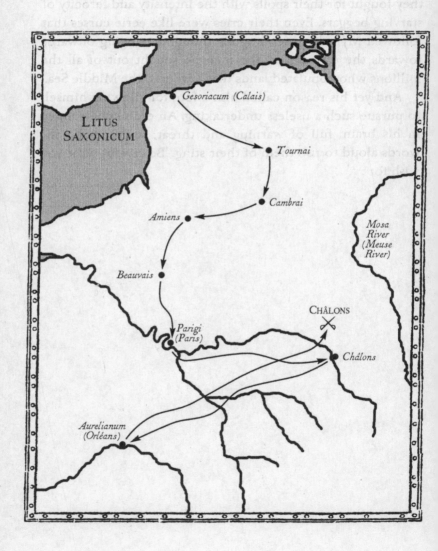

CHAPTER II

ON THE ROAD TO TOURNAI

All journeys end, especially short, wind-driven dashes across the narrows of the Litus Saxonicum. As the sailors responded to the barked orders of the weather-beaten ship's master, expertly using the single patched sail to catch the wind, Myrddion marvelled at the skill that drove the wallowing, wide-bodied vessel to tack ever nearer to the docks of Gesoriacum. The ravenous, noisy gulls, their constant companions on the journey, cursed the ship as it made its untidy arrival at the battered wooden wharves of the old Roman port. With one last chorus of pungent insults, the seabirds departed for mud flats that promised mussels, cockles and the detritus of a very dirty seaport.

Gesoriacum was still ostensibly Roman, although the filthy inns on the seafront were home to men of all races, sizes and degrees of bad temper. While the three women who served the healer protected their master's possessions and made vain attempts to ignore the lewd invitations uttered in half a dozen equally incomprehensible languages, Myrddion and Cadoc sought out a trader who was prepared to sell them two stout and weatherproof wagons and the beasts to power them.

Like all ports, Gesoriacum was grimy, mud-spattered and

vicious, offering every form of vice that brutal men could desire. Dispirited prostitutes of both sexes stood against the salt-stained buildings trying to keep themselves dry in a steady drizzle of rain. Drunkards cluttered up the roadways and reeled argumentatively out of wine shops, eager to take offence if a stranger crossed their path. Ferret-eyed men promised good sport with dogfights, cockfights and even illegal scrimmages between desperate men who would win a few coins if they could beat their opponents into a bloody pulp. The air was stale with the smell of seaweed, drying fish, excrement and desperation, so Myrddion walked carefully with one hand on the pommel of the sword he had inherited from Melvig.

'Shite! Watch where you be putting your clodhoppers, you horse's arse,' a half-drunken sailor cursed before he spotted Myrddion's sword and noted Cadoc's angry eyes. 'Your pardon, master,' he muttered and would have scurried away, suddenly sober, if Cadoc hadn't gripped his torn tunic with a muscular, scarred hand.

'Do you know of any place in this flea-bitten billet where we can purchase wagons and horses?' Cadoc rasped in the Celtic tongue.

Nonplussed, the sailor shook his head, and Cadoc was forced to repeat the question in sketchy Saxon, backed with Myrddion's Latin, which was almost too pure for the man to understand.

Finally, he pointed one grimy paw down a darkening back alley. 'Try that Roman pig Ranus. He deals in horseflesh, if he hasn't sold them all to the army. And if there are any wagons to be had, he'll know where they can be found – at a profit to him.'

Even before Myrddion could thank him, the sailor had

slipped eel-like out of Cadoc's grasp and scampered down a dark lane like a sleek, black rat. Cadoc wiped a greasy hand on his jerkin with an exclamation of disgust. 'Doesn't anyone wash in this hellhole? That bastard's sweat reeks of cheap ale, and my hands will stink for weeks.'

Myrddion ignored Cadoc's complaints and entered the indicated alleyway cautiously. The few cobbles were slick with rainwater, urine and congealed grease that had been dumped out of a nearby kitchen. The smell almost took his breath away with its rancid, sharp tang.

The shadows were oppressive where the two-storeyed shanties leaned together like drunken friends holding each other upright. Where the last of the dusk sent a little light into the shadows, Myrddion swore he could see the gleam of eyes. He loosened his great-grandfather's sword in its scabbard with a dangerous hiss of tempered metal. Avoiding the filthy sludge on the cobbles, the two men picked their way carefully through the looming darkness and the piles of half-visible rubbish. A rat scuttled over Cadoc's foot and he cursed in sudden alarm, but the alleyway was empty of human scavengers and the two healers soon found themselves on a mean, narrow street that was empty and silent.

'Our hasty friend seems to have directed us on a fool's errand,' Myrddion murmured, but almost before he had finished speaking, he heard the whicker of horses at the end of the muddy thoroughfare.

Without bothering to waste more words, he jerked his thumb in the direction of stamping hoofbeats and the stench of horse-dung. Keeping to the very centre of the dark roadway, master and servant picked their way through the ordure-fouled mud until they came to an enclosure in which horses loomed out of the shadows like solid, black standing stones. The presence of the men set the beasts to jerking and snorting in panic, but Myrddion passed them by until he came to a rough building built of split wooden slabs with a roof of crudely shaped, fired-clay shingles. Even in the darkness, the fitful moonlight showed that the tiles were furred with bright green moss and the walls of the stables and outbuildings were so poorly built that lamplight shone through the many cracks and splits in the structure.

'This must be Ranus's establishment,' Myrddion grunted. 'Let's hope that his beasts are sounder than his building skills.'

Cadoc used the pommel of his knife to pound on a flimsy-looking door that proved to be surprisingly sturdy. A string of muffled oaths served as the only response to his knocking, but Cadoc was persistent. Eventually, the door was unbolted and the light from the gatekeeper's oil lamp revealed a prominent, ruddy nose in a face that sloped away into a chinless jaw and an equally narrow, receding forehead.

'What do you want, waking a body in the middle of the night?' The chinless man exposed a set of broken, blackened teeth and large canines that gave his mouth a predatory cast.

'It's barely dusk,' Myrddion retorted in a high-handed fashion, speaking in his purest Latin. The doorkeeper raised one ginger eyebrow at the young man's accent.

'So? What do you want me to do about it? All decent souls are about their supper and preparing for their beds rather than annoying citizens who are minding their own business.'

'We wish to speak to Ranus about the purchase of some horses and wagons.' Myrddion was curt to the point of rudeness, but the doorkeeper seemed incapable of digesting the healer's tone.

'You can tell your master that we have coin to pay, but we

won't waste our time talking with ostlers,' Cadoc added in his Saxon argot.

The doorkeeper grumbled into his thin beard and moustache, ordered them to wait and then promptly latched the door behind him. Master and servant cooled their heels on the doorstep for ten minutes and Cadoc would have put his shoulder to the warped wood had Myrddion not ordered him to be patient.

Just when the healer too was considering intemperate action, the door was thrust open and a plump figure beckoned them into a narrow corridor lit by a single oil lamp. Myrddion's nerves twitched with a presentiment of danger, but he followed the man over a well-worn step which was enlivened by a rather picturesque design of a horse laid out in coloured pebbles and shards of tile.

'Greetings, good sirs! Forgive my servant for his caution, for it's not often that traders come so late to do business. But I say that coin is coin, regardless of when a buyer comes knocking.'

'You are Master Ranus, I presume?' Myrddion began, and then his words withered in his throat when he saw the tawdry magnificence of the room at the end of the corridor.

Ranus was obviously a man of means, if his triclinium was any indication. Although the building seemed ramshackle on the outside, the inner walls were of polished lime render and covered with paintings that aped the old glories of the Empire. Fanciful trees and birds were displayed in a landscape that could never have existed on this earth, while partially clad dryads cavorted lewdly around a drunken Dionysius as he pressed grapes against their naked breasts or caressed their plump thighs. Myrddion shuddered at the thought of dining with such murals as a backdrop.

'They're fine works, aren't they? I spare no expense when I entertain in my house. And I've no doubt that you also believe that quality is worth paying for.' Ranus aimed an oily smile at Myrddion and directed him towards a splendid dining couch with magnificent scarlet upholstery, trimmed with gold fringing that was beginning to tarnish. The healer seated himself with easy grace, trying not to touch a fresh food stain that had left a greasy trail across the head of the couch.

'Of course, my friend. It's only sensible to pay well and pursue the very best, if one is to get lasting value from one's purchases.'

'So how can old Ranus help a young lordling like you, sir? A horse for riding, perhaps? One to impress the ladies? Or are you off to the wars?'

Myrddion explained his needs succinctly and carefully. Now that he and Cadoc could see the horse trader more clearly, they were unimpressed by their host's appearance and manner, even when he clapped his hands imperiously and the doorkeeper shuffled off to find wine and sweetmeats for the guests.

Ranus was a short, thickset man with a colouring and a greasy toga that shouted a mixed Roman heritage. His eyes were very black, like his dusty hair, and were too close together for him to appear trustworthy. A single bushy eyebrow wound above them like a rather nasty caterpillar. His feet in their rough cobbled sandals were none too clean, although his hairy fingers were covered with large rings that had eaten into the puffy flesh. A costly pin of northern workmanship held his toga and tunic in place, while his hair had been forced into a series of curls that trailed across his forehead in an unsuccessful copy of the epicurean style.

Before business began, Ranus insisted that his guests take a draught of Spanish wine in real glass goblets. From Ranus's airy, casual use of the glass, Myrddion saw that the horse trader was inordinately proud of his imported possessions. Cadoc almost choked when he took a deep quaff, and only managed to swallow the vinegary liquid with difficulty. Wisely, Myrddion forced himself to sip his wine and praised Ranus on the quality of his choice. The Roman flushed with pleasure and thrust a salver of sticky honey concoctions upon his guests, who managed to eat without revealing their distaste.

'So you will need four carthorses rather than mounts for yourselves. You're lucky, young sirs, for I don't have a horse suitable for riding, no matter what price you offered me. All the young warriors have purchased any beast that is even remotely battle-ready so that they can join Flavius Aetius in his campaign against those damned barbarians. The gods alone know what'll happen if Aetius fails. I suppose our skulls will be decorating Attila's hall.'

Ranus paused dramatically, hawked, and then spat onto his pebbled mosaic floor. Myrddion tried not to wince, or to betray his ignorance of local politics.

'At any road, I can sell you some carthorses that are too damned slow for battle, but quite capable of towing the heaviest of wagons. They're not young, mind, but they're not likely to die on you either. You have my word on it.' Then Ranus named a sum that left Cadoc gape-mouthed.

The horse trader quickly explained. 'You can search through Gesoriacum all week, my fine sirs, and you'll not do better. A man would be a fool if he didn't take advantage of the times. As my old father used to say, only an idiot ignores supply and demand, so it's up to you. But if you wait too long, these beasts will be sold to a cook from the kitchens who's anxious to make a name for himself.'

'Show us your horses then, Ranus. I'll not buy any animal sight unseen,' Myrddion said. His dark brows were drawn together and Ranus saw a flicker of irritation lurking at the edges of the healer's eyes.

'Certainly, young sir, come along with me. I never cheat anyone, least of all young lordlings such as you. It's bad for business, for a start. Mind the step! Horses are mucky creatures, all told, and their real talent is turning fresh hay into horse shit.'

Ranus led the two Celts through a series of small store-rooms into a tumbledown stable where two young stable hands had made themselves comfortable in the straw and were playing at dice. With highly descriptive and colourful oaths, Ranus drove them out into the yard to bring in the four carthorses. This task took some little time, for the animals had no desire to be penned into narrow stalls after the relative freedom of the muddy yard, with its supply of nettles and long grass that had been left to grow near the fence posts.

Once the horses were in place in their stalls, Myrddion and Cadoc checked them from head to hock and were pleasantly surprised to find them to be in good condition. Ranus hadn't lied, and although the animals were a little grey around their muzzles their eyes were clear, their yellow teeth were sharp and strong and their hairy hocks were sound.

'We'll take them. Now, do you have two wagons that we can purchase, preferably ones that are watertight?'

Ranus rubbed his hands together with oily pleasure and presented two wagons for Cadoc's careful inspection. Like the carthorses, the wagons were old and clumsy, but they came with stout leather covers that would protect Myrddion's tools of trade. A bargain was soon struck and most of Myrddion's store of gold changed hands. As Cadoc harnessed the horses, Myrddion turned back to face the wily old trader.

'Ranus, I'll tell you straight, I've no desire to serve in any conflict outside my own land. Commanders always seem to take advantage of healers, so I've been dragged into a number of disputes in the past. I've found that working for a royal master is never financially rewarding, so I'm sure you understand my reservations, my friend.'

The Roman trader smiled like a shark. In truth, a good war was very profitable for his business, but he took pains to avoid any personal experience of the carnage. 'Aye, young lordling, I can see that a healer would be a valuable addition to any commander's army.'

'How may I avoid the coming war? I wish to travel to the south, eventually to Ravenna, and I don't wish to be side-tracked by the Huns or the Franks along the way. What route would be fastest and safest?'

Ranus rubbed his stubbled chin with a horny forefinger. Myrddion winced at the rasping sound that resulted, while the Roman eyed the younger man with cunning, insolent eyes.

'Well, young sir, if I were to gamble on where Attila will attack next, I'd be thinking of the rich lands to the southwest. He'll pour his warriors into the lands of the Alemanni and strike either at Worms or Strasbourg. He could easily be holding those cities already, but we'll never know until his horsemen come knocking at our own gates. The Huns move fast. Attila will carve through the Frankish countryside like a hot knife through cold butter, using the Reno river as his marker to move his troops from place to place.'

Myrddion frowned. 'So where should I go if I hope to avoid him? This land is foreign to us and I'd rather avoid any pitched battles, if I can – even minor skirmishes. Of course, if I stumbled across wounded men, I'd be morally bound to treat their wounds – but I must reach Ravenna without being delayed by a war.'

'Then I'd take the main Roman road leading into the east. I'd drive my wagons to the river, where Caesar crossed into the north to defeat the barbarians, then head south to Tournai, Cambrai and the Frankish border cities. With luck you'll skirt around the fighting.'

Myrddion grimaced. 'Won't I be heading towards the Huns if I follow your advice? Why not follow the coastal route?'

Ranus shrugged expressively. 'It's true that the best road runs along the coast, but you're likely to run across one of the armed groups from the defending king's forces. The Franks and the Goths are just as dangerous as Attila's warriors, so I'd follow the central route if I were in your position. The roads there are in disrepair and the Romans don't guard them any more. But, I do know that most of the bridges are still standing, so . . . well, it's really up to you.' Obviously sick of profitless chatter, Ranus turned back to his sweetmeats and his execrable wine, trusting his customers to latch the gate as they departed.

The darkness was complete by the time Myrddion and Cadoc had picked up the three widows and loaded their provisions, the tools of their trade, the leather field tents and Myrddion's precious box of scrolls. Distrusting the local inns along the waterfront, Myrddion chose to travel under the rising moon to the outskirts of Gesoriacum where they could make camp in relative safety. Unfed, but safe beneath the wagons among their furs and woollen blankets, the small party were soon fast asleep.

Cadoc woke at daybreak and departed the camp to gather further supplies of food while one of the widows, Rhedyn, scoured the cooking pot with river sand and used dry meat to begin a stew that would sustain them once they were on the move. Another widow, Brangaine, used the last of their wheat to make flat cakes on a griddle. When Cadoc returned, Rhedyn selected several wilting carrots, a turnip past its prime and some soft cabbage to give flavour to the stew. Myrddion awoke to the smell of cooking meat, seasoned with salt bought for a few coppers by Cadoc, and his mouth watered with hunger for the familiar fare that gave him such pleasure on the open road.

Master and servants ate with their fingers, using Brangaine's flat cakes to soak up the gravy as Cadoc recounted the local gossip he had picked up in the marketplace.

'The Huns, whoever they might be, are on the move,' he told them as he demolished his first plate of stew. 'The local people are terrified, although Gesoriacum is unlikely to be attacked.'

'King Vortigern told me that the Huns under Attila threatened Rome . . . although he could easily have been wrong,' Myrddion said doubtfully, knowing that Britain rarely received useful intelligence from the Frankish side of the Litus Saxonicum. None the less, the name Attila caused his tongue to tremble. 'Did the people say why the Huns have come so far to the west – why they are at war with the people of Gaul?'

'A Roman general called Flavius Aetius has pissed them off by returning their gift to its original donor.'

The widows giggled, while Truthteller made an incredulous grimace at the thought that any passably intelligent general would make such a mistake of protocol. Cadoc began to refill his bowl with stew while continuing his explanation of what he had heard from the villagers.

'No, Truthteller. The gift from the Huns was a dwarf called Zerco, and this Aetius seems to take a dim view of treating human beings as inconsequential presents to be exchanged at will. Unfortunately, the Huns chose to view Aetius's mercy as an insult.'

'Does the cause of the conflict really matter?' Finn asked. 'The Huns will invent a reason to be offended if they truly desire a war. Is Flavius Aetius an able warrior?'

'So they say. He is the best that the Empire has left – which isn't saying much. Do you want to become embroiled in this war, master? Perhaps we can recoup our losses from the voyage.'

Myrddion looked doubtfully at his narrow fingers as he cleaned his bowl with a scrap of bread. Was his father this particular Flavius? For the first time, the healer considered the difficulty entailed in finding a man with such a common gens, even though the name had a noble history.

'What else have you heard of this Flavius Aetius?' he asked as artlessly as he could manage. If the general's age indicated that the man could be his father, he might reconsider his decision to avoid the war.

'I only know what the marketplace gossip tells me,' Cadoc responded. 'He is said to be about sixty years old. His mother was Italian, of no real birth, and he is of Scythian descent. He calls himself Roman because he served at the imperial court and was trained at the Tribuni Praetoriani Partis Militaris. He's been the most successful of the Roman commanders for near enough forty years.'

Myrddion nodded with relief, his resolve firming. We

must pass through Gaul as quickly as possible so that we can reach Rome and Ravenna. No more crazed kings, hungry for glory. And no more generals ready to spend the life-blood of their young conscripts like copper coin. He could dismiss this particular Flavius from his consideration on the grounds of his age and the impurity of his blood.

'Then he will have to defeat the Huns without us. I am weary of battles and dying men.'

'But master . . .' Cadoc rubbed his thumb and forefinger together in an age-old gesture.

'Yes, I know we are stripped of our wealth, but we'll not starve. The peasants will keep us fed for the sake of a little clean healing on our part. We will take the road to the east, then turn south for Tournai once we reach the river.'

Knowing their master's moods, Finn and Cadoc did not argue. They were, after all, sensible men. They recognised that it was only because he was still young that Myrddion never stopped to think how high-handedly he made the decisions for the entire party, taking their loyalty and sense of obligation for granted.

Their fast broken, the healers set off on the next leg of their journey and soon put the squalor and vigour of Gesoriacum far behind them. The day was all that early spring should be – soft breezes, puffball clouds and sweet new grass with its clean smell of fresh beginnings. On the Roman road that lay ahead of them, the countryside was flat, greening and welcoming, with occasional small villages clustered in the fecund fields where green shoots had already broken through the brown sod. Exhilarated, Myrddion breathed it in.

In every village, peasants stopped them to request simples that would cure chest colds, or for the more mundane tasks of pulling teeth, alleviating earache, or removing thorns, splinters or chips of metal from inflamed flesh. The villagers expressed their thanks in a language a little like Saxon or in bastardised Latin, and paid for the treatments with vegetables from the winter store, apples put down in the autumn, a brace of coney or quail or, on one memorable occasion, a whole haunch of venison. The weather conspired, along with the gratitude shown by the villagers, to induce a holiday mood for which the healers were extremely grateful. For far too long, they had waded through blood, hideous wounds and the agony of doomed souls to atone for the poisoned desires of petty princelings.

So it was with surprise that Myrddion discovered that he was irritated by the slow, steady pace of their journey. These lands had been tamed and seemed well tended, but there was an alien quality in the lack of heavy forest or hills that raised flinty heads into the sky. So few miles separated them from the lands of the Celts, yet the Roman rulers of this gentle place had felled the ancient forests and killed the old gods in their sacred groves. Something else was beginning to take their place, but Myrddion could not see the shape of the new force that was, even now, bringing death and destruction to these quiet hamlets.

The small party finally reached the river Ranus had mentioned, where the road turned in an arc towards the south.

'Good. Now we must keep our ears sharp,' Myrddion told them. 'The lands around Tournai belong to the Frankish king, so we may stumble across his warriors before too long.'

'That's lovely,' Cadoc muttered sardonically, while Finn Truthteller simply flicked the reins and urged his pair into movement.

After some days of uneventful travel, their horses suddenly became restive and Myrddion felt a frisson of alarm shiver down his backbone. There was no discernible reason for his presentiment of danger, but Myrddion was aware that dumb creatures were often warned of trouble long before the blunted senses of men picked it up. He knew that only a fool would ignore such warnings.

'Go back to the other wagon and tell Finn to keep his sword close at hand,' Myrddion instructed Cadoc. 'Like the horses, I can smell trouble on the wind.'

Cadoc scanned the horizon with his keen, warrior's eyes. 'There's smoke over the forests to the south, master. And the birds are unusually silent. I don't like it.'

'Hmph,' Myrddion muttered, as he retrieved his sword, resplendent in its fine hide scabbard, and slipped it under the seat of the ponderous wagon. 'We go on!'

The first refugees appeared within the hour, on foot, or pushing barrows laden with their meagre possessions. Myrddion's experienced eyes noted that the haggard peasants were all women, old men or children. Several bore nasty burns or sword wounds as they trudged ahead with fixed eyes and the shocked, blank stares of people who had nowhere to go but away from the homes where they had lived their entire lives. Cadoc saw one woman carrying a small child whose arm was burned from shoulder to wrist, and was forced to stand in front of her before she would interrupt her steady, mile-devouring pace.

'Let me take care of the babe for you, mother,' he murmured, making sure that his voice was gentle and without threat. 'My master has a salve to soothe the little one's pain.'

The woman stopped as if her leg muscles had forgotten how to work. Cadoc took the partially wrapped, silent child from her nerveless fingers, while Myrddion wordlessly motioned to Rhedyn to seat the woman out of the sun and see to her comfort. Finn and Cadoc began to set up the wagons and unharness the horses before lighting a fire, heating water and assembling Myrddion's tools of trade.

'Business is coming, master,' Cadoc murmured softly so as not to disturb the almost comatose infant in his arms. 'I can feel it in my water.'

'Aye, fortune has set her face against my hopes for a quiet journey to Constantinople,' Myrddion replied. 'Bare the child's body. The little one is far too quiet, and I fear she isn't long for this world.'

The little girl could hardly have been older than two years. She had sustained an ugly, blistered burn that began across her shoulder and extended down to her wrist, leaving her perfect, delicate fingers untouched. The flesh had swollen under the blackened and blistered skin, but the mother had been unable to treat the gross injury.

'She must have snatched the child out of a burning hut, gathered what she could carry, and fled. Normally, immediate treatment for burns is vital, but in this case the application of goose grease or dirty wrapping would have made our task even harder. For the moment, I must cut the skin where it's not breached to ease the swelling and blistering, so I'll need a little poppy juice.'

The child felt like a rag doll in Cadoc's hands, but he knew his master had the gods' own skill in his sensitive fingers. If Myrddion believed that this child still possessed a frail chance of survival, then Cadoc would also fight for her right to live. The soldier in him remembered the agony of his own burns and his soft Celtic heart ached for the agonies that this little girl would experience – if she survived the treatment. He laid the child down naked on a clean cloth spread by Rhedyn, and fetched knives, salves and the poppy juice.

Once the child had been treated to Myrddion's satisfaction, and laid in a nest of clean wool in the larger wagon, the healer turned his attention to the mother and the growing crowd of refugees who had abandoned their mindless, numbed trek to nowhere. Most of their injuries were minor, including the wounds resulting from the trek itself, such as blistered hands and feet, but Myrddion, Finn and Cadoc took pains to treat each villager, promising them clean water, hot stew and a safe place to rest if they tarried for a while. Several able-bodied women had helped to raise one of the leather tents and those old men and women who had exhausted them-selves to escape the town of Tournai rested under its shelter on the untainted grass.

As for the child's mother, all Rhedyn's skills and gentleness couldn't coax a single word from her bitten lips. The woman seemed impossibly old to have borne such a young daughter, but as none of the other fleeing refugees professed to know her the healers could gain little insight regarding the damage to her mind.

But her body was another matter entirely.

The woman sat hunched over like a crone and rocked in time with the music that she alone heard in her head. When Myrddion and Cadoc attempted to examine her, she tried to beat them off with her fists and her teeth, a resistance that was made more dreadful by its silent violence. With great difficulty, and at the cost of a badly bitten thumb, Myrddion forced poppy juice down her throat until her feverish struggles slowly ceased.

With silent apologies to the woman's modesty, Myrddion checked her body for any sign of injury. Deep in her groin, he found an arrow embedded with a small length of shaft visible above the reddened flesh. His heart sank at the absence of blood loss.

'Is she bleeding inwardly, master?' Cadoc whispered as he wondered at the fixity of will that had kept this nameless woman on her feet over so many agonising miles, while carrying such a painful wound.

'Aye, she must be. This arrow must have pierced her gut hours ago, which is why her skin is so hot and the child hasn't been treated. The evil humours are killing her from within.'

'Should we remove the arrow, master?' Cadoc's voice was sad, for women as brave as this one should die by their own fireside, not maddened with pain on an endless, pointless journey.

Myrddion shook his head and squared his shoulders. Hard experience had taught him that there was no point in struggling with death once the internal organs were breached and poisoned.

'What would be the purpose? It would only cause her more pain. Cool her flesh with soft compresses and ask Rhedyn to stay with her. I'll leave more of the poppy juice with Rhedyn to ease her journey into death. Whoever she was, she is beyond our help.'

Cadoc heard the anger in his master's voice. Although Myrddion had long outgrown his boyhood, his short life had taught him that adult strength meant nothing when he was faced by the ugly truth of his own ignorance. Some wounds were beyond his ability to heal, and he railed silently at the gods who allowed children to grow to the age of love and reason – and then killed them so capriciously.

'We'll go no further today,' he decided. 'We seem to have

fed all who need our services, even if we have been forced to strip our food stores to nothing. They'll need something in their bellies if they are to survive the hardships that lie ahead. Besides, other sufferers will find us soon enough, so perhaps they can replenish our supplies.'

As he spooned food into a wooden bowl for a toothless old crone who blessed him in her strange tongue, Cadoc watched the sun reach its highest point and begin the long slide down the sky towards the horrors of night, although for now it still shone sweetly and the scented air was just as delicate as it had been during their early morning travels. Yet the unmistakable stink of violent death seemed to have wafted to their encampment from the south, where smoke still rose like an impudent finger, or a warning of horrors that were yet to come.

The wounded woman began to convulse at nightfall. Cadoc and Finn held her down, but her whole body was as hot as fire, as if she blazed inwardly from some terrible conflagration of the spirit. As her body arched until only her head and heels touched the earth, Cadoc feared her spine would break, and prayed to the Mother that her death would be swift.

Myrddion laid his cool hands on her feverish forehead and whispered words of comfort in her ear, promising that if her child should live, then he would care for her until her death. Insensible to these words of release, the woman's heels drummed on the hard earth and a long, anguished exhalation of breath escaped through her clenched teeth. Then she slumped as if an invisible hand had cut all the tendons and muscles in her body, leaving a boneless shell of flesh. Her eyelids snapped open, exposing irises that were a strange transparent green, but there was no sense or understanding in them. A single word escaped lips that were bitten and bleeding, and then she was dead.

'Willa,' Myrddion repeated. 'Was that her name, I wonder, or the name of her child? I suppose we'll never know, so we'll let them both be called Willa. It's a pretty name, a version of Willow, I presume, and certainly sorrowful enough for times like these.'

So Willa Major was buried in a hastily dug hole off the Roman road leading to the south. Myrddion was unable to spare any cloth for a shroud and, as she had carried nothing but the child, she was returned to the earth in the clothes she wore, unprotected from the cold and the rain. The moon was down when the first clods of earth struck her white, upturned face, and Finn Truthteller had to turn away as he remembered a crueller interment in his past. Quickly and economically, Myrddion and Cadoc filled in the shallow grave and placed a fieldstone over the spot where her head had lain.

'The Mother will protect her,' Myrddion reminded his friends, 'as She protects all who lay down their lives for their children.'

Brangaine found herself weeping for her own lost hopes of bearing children, which had passed when her man died in Vortigern's army. 'I'll see to the child. Little Willa will not die, I swear!'

'But she'll be scarred, Brangaine, no matter how well you care for her, and I cannot say if her arm will ever work as it should,' Myrddion warned her, knowing that tendons seared by fire often lost all flexibility.

'No matter; the babe will survive,' Brangaine swore and scuttled away to the wagon where the child was lying in her nest of old woollen rugs.

'I swear that woman grows stranger every day,' Cadoc said

to no one in particular as he watched the widow heave her thickened body into the wagon. 'Still, she's a good worker and her flat cakes are marvellous.'

The three men trudged back to the wagons in Brangaine's wake. A light rain began to fall, perfectly matching Myrddion's mood of disappointment and regret. For the healer, every patient who passed beyond the shades hung on his shoulders like a heavy weight.

'Shite!' Cadoc swore. 'Now it's going to piss down with rain. The gods alone know what's in store tomorrow. I can tell you, master, I didn't like the look of that smoke in the distance, and we're heading in that direction. Whatever lies ahead cannot be good.'

'Aye, tomorrow may be difficult, but for now what can healers do but sleep when Fortuna offers us the leisure? To your pallets, both of you, for we must be alert in the morning.'

Yet despite his sensible advice to his friends, sleep eluded Myrddion, no matter how he tried. He had set forth on this quest with the enthusiasm of a boy, without a single thought of what it might cost along the way. He was beginning to understand that the journey to learn his true identity would not be concluded by simply finding his father. Perhaps his quest would only be achieved by learning painful lessons about his self.

MYRDDION'S CHART OF THE ROUTES TAKEN BY ATTILA'S FORCES DURING THE INVASION OF FRANCE

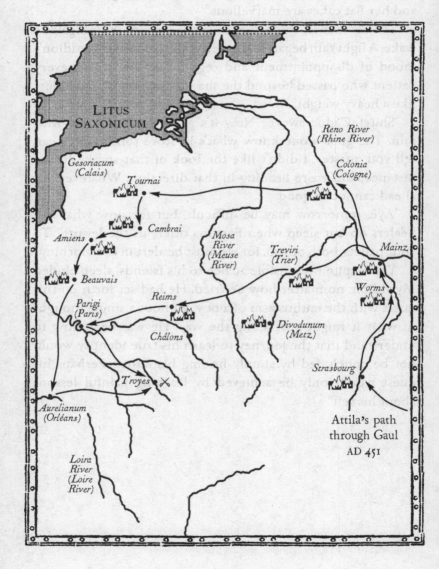

LITUS SAXONICUM

Reno River
(Rhine River)

Gesoriacum
(Calais)

Tournai

Colonia
(Cologne)

Amiens

Cambrai

Mosa
River
(Meuse
River)

Treviri
(Trier)

Mainz

Beauvais

Reims

Worms

Parigi
(Paris)

Châlons

Divodunum
(Metz)

Troyes

Strasbourg

Aurelianum
(Orléans)

Attila's path
through Gaul
AD 451

Loira
River
(Loire
River)

CHAPTER III

A GRISLY TRADE

As dawn broke, the sky was pallid with a light cloud cover, like the face of a corpse whose features were blurred by death. Myrddion awoke with those first frail shafts of light, but on this particularly ominous day his eyes were gritty from too little sleep and soured after the haunting dreams that had pursued him during the night. Throughout the meagre hours of darkness that followed the burial of Willa Major, the young healer had dreamed disjointedly of burning crofts, butchered children and Willa Major's strange green eyes. Wakefulness was a mercy compared with the black beast of his dreams.

Finn Truthteller and Cadoc stirred with equal unwillingness, but what was left of the congealed stew must be heated and fed to a small cluster of elderly, confused peasants who were loath to return to the road that led to the northwest. While Brangaine heated the stew with the child Willa lying close by her, the men set to work dismantling the leather tent and preparing their horses for travel. Once the old ones were fed, they would be eased on their journey away from the town that had bled smoke on the previous day. But Myrddion and his companions must go forward to face whatever horrors lay before them at Tournai.

'Should we take our time, master? Perhaps we'd be wise to bypass whatever is up ahead. I'm not anxious to face whatever these poor people are fleeing. And who are the Huns anyway?'

Cadoc looked so alarmed that Myrddion knew he must explain their situation. Only willing men should go forward into such an uncertain future.

'The Hun is a wild tribe noted for its ferocity,' he replied as calmly as he could in a vain hope of placating the frightened women. 'But we must go on. How far could we safely travel if we went off the road? What would become of us if a wheel broke on the uneven ground? Wouldn't we be more likely to stumble into danger? Besides, we are healers. Like it or not, our oaths bind us to try to relieve suffering.'

He pointed along the roadway leading to the south. 'There is much suffering in that direction. Should we avoid it? Or should we go on?'

Cadoc and Finn shuffled their feet. Myrddion could tell that their first reaction was to counsel caution, but their natural anxiety was at war with their equally powerful sense of service. Cadoc ducked his head and reddened with shame.

'We should go on, master, even if we are frightened of what we might find,' Finn decided slowly, while Cadoc nodded his agreement.

Yet, paradoxically, Myrddion was forced to admit to himself that wiser men would have given the town a wide berth. However, he remained true to his mentor's stricture that the sick must be tended, regardless of his presentiments of imminent disaster. Myrddion was terrified of being constrained and becoming the unwilling vassal of another powerful lord, for he could not forget the bonds that had tied him to Vortigern, broken only when the Celtic king was burned alive in his own hall. He was determined that he would never willingly serve a temporal lord again, but equally determined to remain true to his oath, despite the knowledge that to continue with the journey could bring disaster on himself and on his friends.

Eventually, with their bellies full of food and carrying clean water, the old folk trudged away to an uncertain future, freeing the healers to resume their hazardous trek. Every mile covered weighed on the hearts of the three men, for they had personally experienced the dreadful fact of warfare with its callous disregard for the frailties of innocent flesh. Only Brangaine was happy, for Willa had awakened, had endured the dressing of her burned shoulder and arm with uncomplaining green eyes and was now sucking her thumb and drowsing as she rocked to the soporific sway of the wagon.

The skies seemed wider and bluer than those above the landscapes of Britain for, as Myrddion had already seen, much of the heavy forest growth had been stripped away by the Romans, leaving the sacred groves deserted and bare. The lands of Gaul were filling with strange tribes – the Franks, the Visigoths and the Alemanni. The populace also worshipped alien gods, although Rome still kept a tenuous hold on the reins of power. Flavius Aetius was growing old and tired, and the smoke over Tournai was merely an omen of the troubles that were to come as the wily old general weakened.

The spring sun was pleasantly warm on Myrddion's face and he would have taken pleasure in the new clarity of light in this unfamiliar land had he not seen the piled detritus of fleeing families. A cart with a shattered wooden wheel lay tipped on its side in a ditch beyond the road, while here and there abandoned cooking pots, empty water skins, old blankets and even the bloating corpse of a dog lay where they had fallen. A single, broken sandal was crushed under Myrddion's wheels and he felt a physical wrench as he looked back to see it ground into the soft dust under the hooves of Cadoc's horses. A man had worn that sandal and now must wander barefoot on the cruel stones that clad the roadway.

The day was far advanced when the small cavalcade reached the centre of the thinly forested wood beyond which Tournai awaited them. To their left, a river could be seen and heard through the light veil of woodland that partly concealed its rush-choked banks. The land here was rich and the farmers who lived by the river's margins had fared well off the bounty of silt-rich land and plentiful water. Filled with foreboding and weary to the bone, Myrddion called a halt to their journey, for even the indefatigable Cadoc was beginning to falter. Whatever lay ahead, the healers needed sleep, or they would be of no use to anyone on the morrow.

The night was still and cloudless, and carried no signs of the usual light spring rains. The stars shone clearly like holes picked in black wool hung before an oil lamp. Cadoc swore he could reach out his hand and touch them, while Brangaine sang softly in her deep, slightly off-key voice to soothe Willa as the little girl succumbed to sleep. Finn joined in the mournful folk song, which told of a child stolen away to the Otherworld and of a mother destined to mourn until her life ended, leaving Myrddion to fight the prickle of tears behind his eyes. Unloved by Branwyn, his own mother, the healer knew that an empty space existed in his soul where she should dwell, but she had rejected her first-born son as a consequence of her rape. Indeed, Myrddion still bore a scar on his head where Branwyn had tried to brain him with a rock many years earlier. The sound of Brangaine's simple peasant song made his heart sore, but the past could not be changed, no matter how the young man yearned for Branwyn's love. Eventually he fell asleep to the sound of soft crooning voices and, for once, no dreams pursued him in the still, fragrant night that embraced them under the trees.

Morning brought sadness and a reminder of human brutishness. As the wagons cleared the wood, a wide swath of agricultural land lay before them, divided into small parcels by low walls of fieldstone that had been taken from the cleared paddocks. The walls were unmortared, but careful husbandry had ensured constant repair of these proofs of civilisation and order. Until recently, green shoots had blurred the tilled, brown clods of soil, but now the young grain and vegetables had been trampled flat or cropped by grazing horses and hungry men. Flattened earth, charred cooking fires and burned peasant huts bore mute witness to a large army of cavalry and foot soldiers who had been careless of hygiene and the future uses of the earth. In places, the walls had been breached and the scattered, head-sized rocks had been used to construct temporary hearths. Animal bones and feathers lay scattered randomly around these fireplaces, and rudimentary latrine trenches fouled the air with their stink. None the less, Myrddion reasoned that this force, under its deceptive carelessness, was well organised and travelled fast. Only two days had passed since Tournai had burned, but in that time a large company of warriors had disappeared like smoke into the Frankish landscape.

The town of Tournai lay at the epicentre of a great circle of land that had been scarred by the flotsam of an army. Its walls seemed to be intact, although Myrddion could see the burned inns, huts and primitive shop-fronts that had sheltered around its Roman skirts. Ominously, birds of prey circled its defences and carrion seekers covered a dark mound piled haphazardly against its fire-blackened flanks.

'Dead things,' Cadoc whispered. 'The birds are feeding.'

'And the dogs,' Finn Truthteller added, as dark shapes slunk away from the mound, which seemed to writhe with unclean life.

'Perhaps some people still remain alive in Tournai,' Myrddion muttered, but his voice lacked any real hope. 'At any rate, we must do what we can if there are any survivors.'

Cadoc and Finn shrugged, but each climbed back into his place on the wagons as they resumed their slow journey.

A huge fire had been lit across the road and the travellers paused to examine the scarred roadway. Corpses had been burned here in an ordered cremation, although the remains, once the fire had cooled, had been pounded into splinters. Myrddion realised that the pitiful mementos of once-strong warriors had been carefully gathered for those who waited, far away, for the return of their menfolk.

'At least this army has respect for its own dead,' Myrddion muttered to no one in particular. 'Perhaps they might have spared the children of the town.'

'Not the Hun, if Tournai is their work,' Finn replied in a voice that was pregnant with world-weariness. 'From the descriptions of those peasants who fled from Attila, I doubt we'll find anything but corpses in this accursed place.'

The horses shied away from the smell of death, and Myrddion's gorge rose as he led his pair, afoot, off the road and past the ashes that filled the roadway. Here and there lay isolated fragments of bone from dismembered corpses, such as jaw or knee splinters. Small pieces of metal from oxhide breastplates had been overlooked by the enemy horde who, even though they burned their dead with respect, had clearly contrived to collect every item of armour that could be reused by prudent warriors in battles yet to come.

'This small heap of ash is all that remains of the enemy dead, indicating that very few of them became casualties in comparison with the civilian defenders,' Finn Truthteller muttered as he turned over a tiny fragment of skull with his booted foot. 'Whoever they are, these warriors are skilled in the arts of war.'

'Or the citizens of Tournai put up very little resistance,' Myrddion murmured in agreement.

'Peasants and traders are rarely skilled in the dance of death. Perhaps they threw themselves on the mercy of the attacking army.'

'More fool them, if they did!'

As the road turned towards the walled town, another dark mound revealed itself to be a pile of dead bodies that had been flung haphazardly into one spot to spare the army from any threat of disease. Kites, crows, ravens, domestic cats and even stray dogs rose angrily from their feast and slunk or flew away from the approach of the wagons to wait until they could return to their feeding. By what was left of the dress of the ransacked and partially stripped bodies, the healers could tell that these citizens had been farmers or traders, men who had found that pitchforks and domestic knives were no match against iron swords, spears and arrows.

But of all the casualties, the children affected them the most. The lower arm of one small child lay under a heap of tangled adults, fingers already gnawed away to stumps by scavengers and its palm mutely appealing for mercy, while nearby a large bird hopped away from the belly of a young boy. Finn cursed and threw a rock at the ungainly creature, which turned one baleful, yellow eye towards him before slowly taking to the wing.

'All creatures of the earth must eat,' Brangaine murmured from the wagon, one hand covering the eyes of Willa, who was sucking her thumb in distress. 'Are these dumb beasts any less deserving than us? At least the scavengers clean up the mess that men have left in this place of tears.'

As the wagons moved inexorably forward, the remains of the gates of Tournai slowly hove into view.

Timber trunks had been used to fashion a war machine that could take advantage of the only weakness in the walls of the town. Myrddion could see the large tree trunk that had been used as a battering ram to smash the great latch open, and the remains of fires that had been set to burn the timbers and weaken the planks around the iron-braced supports. The expertise of the attackers was obvious to any eyes that understood the ruthless trade of war. Tournai's defences had been breached by a determined, brutal and well-organised enemy.

Shattered timbers were all that remained of the huge double gates, and the healers soon found more corpses lying in untidy piles where they had perished. As Myrddion and his apprentices walked into the cramped space within the gate, it was plain that these men had tried to defend the town. Their weaponry was clearly Roman in design, but they were obviously incapable of protecting themselves against an army intent on rape and plunder. Most of the bodies were of old men or very young boys on the brink of adulthood, causing Myrddion to wonder about the fate of the able-bodied. A few black-fletched and broken arrows spoke mutely of defences that had been mounted in the stone houses closest to the wall, and Cadoc found the corpse of one boy whose ruined hand still held a slingshot.

Search as they might for any sign of life during the gruesome day that followed, the healers discovered that Tournai was a dead town, stripped of anything of value and then burned. No wounded survivors, no items of value and no hope remained after the passage of an army whose aim was complete destruction.

As the wagons skirted the city walls, Finn caught a flash of light in the trees to their right. For a brief instant, he expected armed horsemen to ride threateningly out of the lengthening shadows under the trees, as if the reflection of light on a sword blade had betrayed the presence of watchers. Then cold reason overrode his moment of panic as he realised that the army was long gone, for their tracks were quite evident in the trampled grasses, heading towards the south where, the healers had been told, the town of Cambrai, a Frankish centre, lay open for plunder.

'I saw something flash on the edge of the forest,' Finn murmured softly to Myrddion. 'Someone is still alive, but they seem keen to remain in hiding.'

Myrddion followed Finn's pointing arm with his quick black eyes. At first the hidden survivor was elusive, but then, just when the healer was about to turn away, weak sunshine struck a reflective surface and pinpointed its position under a coppice of trees.

'We're being watched, master,' Finn said reflectively, as he fumbled for his long knife under the seat of the wagon with one booted foot.

'I see it, Finn! If this observer wants us, then he'll find some way to approach us. I'll not risk the women and our tools of trade to explore the forest. Every tree could hide an enemy warrior.'

The wagons creaked into movement, the groan of the

huge iron-braced wheels almost drowning the sound of the horse's hooves as they slid on the rough stone surface. The steady slap of one open flap of the wagon's leather cover was a comforting counterpoint to the complaint of the wooden axles. With one eye on the far-off forest, Finn Truthteller urged the horses into greater effort with a deft flick of the reins.

No survivors crowded the roads. No terrified peasants clustered around the wagons for an illusion of comfort. The cleared farmlands were fecund with growth, but every wooden dwelling had been looted before being gutted by fire. Even the dead became commonplace as their remains swelled in the sunshine. Sickened, Myrddion gave the order that they should push on to whatever lay ahead, leaving the bodies to be absorbed back into the earth whence they had come. Three men could never hope to bury so many.

The healers travelled for three days, finding game wherever they could in the dark shadows of the forest. Although hunger was beginning to hollow their bellies, Myrddion was not yet sufficiently desperate to hack half-rotted meat from the corpses of beasts that the marauders had placed in streams to foul the water and poison what remained of the local citizenry.

On the fourth day, as they crossed a narrow bridge, the healers saw Cambrai before them. The town had been warned of the approach of the enemy, so the devastation was less obvious outside the solid rock walls that protected the city. Terrified by the smoke from burning Tournai, the peasants had begged for shelter within Cambrai's defences. The walls possessed a cyclopean strength, for the Romans who had built the city had learned to trust nothing and no one in this brutish country. The legions had brought order and prosperity to Cambrai, but ambitious kings now squabbled over the proceeds of peace.

Once again, the travellers saw the evidence of the burning of the enemy dead, as at Tournai, but the patch of scorched earth here was larger in size, the charred remains less scrupulously honoured and the mute possessions of dead warriors less carefully sifted. Myrddion gathered that Cambrai had resisted her rapists, and guessed that the enemy had taken time to ensure that she paid terribly for her impudence. Long before they reached the shattered gates, the stench of swollen corpses, burned meat and hot, cracked stone warned the healers that there would be nothing left alive within.

'Our watcher is still with us,' Finn Truthteller hissed as he caught a glimpse of telltale sunshine reflecting on metal at the edge of the tree line.

'Aye,' Myrddion murmured. 'He's been keeping pace with us for days, but he'll approach when he's good and ready.'

Finn Truthteller stared at his master with the intensity of a mature warrior who is faced with an enigma. Master Myrddion was so young, barely old enough to take a sharp knife to his beardless cheeks, but the lad possessed that rare quality of inscrutability, coupled with the patience of wild things that wait on the edges of dark places for any unwary animal or man who intrudes on their domain. Observing his master's raven hair, and the black eyes that seemed to trap the light so effectively, Finn could understand why King Vortigern had been prepared to sacrifice a younger Myrddion to appease the gods and the spirits of the earth. Sometimes, Myrddion frightened Truthteller with those obsidian eyes that saw everything and revealed nothing.

Impatiently, the warrior flexed his stiff shoulders in rejection of such superstition. His master was clever beyond measure and old beyond his years. If the lad could wait to discover what threat the forest sheltered, then so could he, a grown man and a wounded soul whom only Myrddion had tried his best to heal.

'The town appears to be intact, but the smell is vile. If the Huns are the enemy, they leave nothing alive to betray it.'

'But Cambrai resisted. So let's see the worst. Perhaps someone still lives!' Myrddion pulled his leather satchel onto his shoulder as Finn flicked the reins on the flanks of the horses.

Cambrai could have been Tournai's twin. The gates had been ripped apart by battering rams and fire, and a great slaughter had taken place within the narrow streets that led directly to the gates. On this occasion, the enemy hadn't bothered to pile the citizens into mounds, but had looted them where they fell. Even so, Myrddion could imagine the desperate last battle fought in the alleyways and narrow twisting lanes of the town as old men, boys, and even women had used whatever makeshift weapons were to hand. For the victors, the sacking of Cambrai had been hard won. Every street, no matter how narrow, had been taken with the loss of many men, while the defenders appeared to have perished trying to slow the inexorable advance. As Finn and his master picked their way through the smashed wood, burned stones and heaped bodies, they found the smell of the dead and rotting corpses so nauseating that they were forced to tie cloths across their noses and mouths.

'Who were the people who defended this place?' Myrddion asked Finn Truthteller, struck as he was by the height, the breadth of shoulder and the greying yellow hair of many of the corpses that lay near the inner gates.

Finn shrugged and whistled piercingly to Cadoc to catch

the attention of the scarred Celt. 'You speak the language of a sort, Cadoc. Have you heard anything about these men who fought to the death here?'

'I believe the defenders of this town were Franks, master,' Cadoc replied as he drew his wagon to a halt just inside the gates where the piled corpses forced him to halt. 'See, master! They wear red cloaks, or at least most of them seem to have done so. They have fierce moustaches, but they often leave the rest of their faces bare and their hair is allowed to grow, just like our warriors'. The Franks originally came from the north, and like all good northerners they are totally dedicated to war.'

The Celtic warrior picked his way forward over the uneven stone paving and used his booted foot to turn over the corpse of a grey-haired man who had been hacked by sword blades in a dozen places.

'His hand is bloody to the wrist, so he must have slain many men before he was killed. His gods will honour him in the Otherworld.'

Myrddion observed that the half-naked man was indeed splattered with blood, much of which wasn't his own. An undershirt that was too torn to be worth stealing was soaked in gore almost to the elbow, and his empty fist was still clenched as if it clutched the hilt of his sword.

'This man wasn't a peasant. A finger was severed to remove a ring after his death, and something valuable was torn from his throat.'

'Aye, master. Blood surrounds him – far more than his own body could hold. He made his murderers pay before they cut him down.'

In an action that was very gentle and respectful, Cadoc turned the slain Frank back onto his face so the birds couldn't devour his cold blue eyes. Myrddion nodded his approval, touched that Cadoc should offer this small dignity to a man now deep in the shadows of the Otherworld.

'Aye, Cadoc. Let him go to his gods with his eyes intact. Let him see his enemies perish, as they surely will!'

Cadoc stared up at his master, his own eyes rounded with superstition.

'No, I don't see their destruction, Cadoc. But such wanton carnage will not be permitted to go unpunished by the Romans. Our erstwhile masters are a dour people, even if they are now in decline. We Celts have good reason to remember how they repay blows to the face. Where are our druids? They're dead on the bloody shores of Mona. Where are Boudicca and her daughters? Long executed, regardless of their sex or status in their land. But these invaders go too far, for they leave the good earth barren behind them. When the Romans eventually force them to retreat, where will they find shelter or food for so large an army?'

Cambrai and the atrocities enacted within its flame-scarred walls left Myrddion's heart sick with regret. Girls no older than children had been raped, and then hacked to pieces. Their pitiful flanks, stained with their own blood, were affronts to any decent-thinking man. Even babes had not been spared, although their mothers had fought with nails and teeth when no other weapons had been at hand. Saddened, and feeling unclean, the healers carefully checked the detritus and rubble of Cambrai before leaving to sleep outside the walls where the air almost seemed fresh.

In the weeks that followed, the healers travelled along straight, wide roads into the south: to Amiens, to Beauvais and onward towards Parigi, and in each town the same picture of violence was left as mute testimony to an enemy that showed no pity for the helpless, nor mercy to the innocent. Piles of corpses, burned crops and desecrated temples left a vast, charred track, as if a monster had dragged its hideous body across the earth, killing everything in its path with its poisonous breath.

The Hun had spared Parigi and, once the terrified citizenry had been persuaded to open the gates, Myrddion's party replenished their supplies. While Cadoc sought out what poor fare could be purchased from the skittish traders, Myrddion questioned an old soldier who spoke some Latin.

'The city owes a huge debt to a holy woman called Geneviève who went forward to meet the Hun, barefoot and unarmed,' Myrddion reported to Cadoc and Finn later that evening as they settled into their campsite outside the city gates. 'Attila admired her bravery and permitted the city to live.'

'That's madness!' Cadoc exclaimed. 'How could a commander be so ruthless on the one hand and then spare the wealthiest city in the land because of a religeuse? It makes no sense!'

'This Geneviève is supposed to be a woman of great sanctity, while Attila is a very superstitious man, or so my soldier friend told me. Whatever the truth of the matter, Geneviève is alive and so is Parigi. We must give thanks, for tonight we have full bellies and a small supply of food for our future needs. With luck, we will have sufficient food to reach Aurelianum.'

'It's still crazy!' Cadoc repeated. 'But we must be grateful to the gods that these Huns fear the retribution of prayer. It seems to be the only weakness they have.'

Beyond the ploughed fields surrounding Parigi, their hidden watcher waited among the old trees that rimmed the once fertile patches of soil. Someone continued to follow them, with eyes that missed nothing and cared little if they were seen by the travellers in their wagons.

Myrddion despaired during this journey into atrocity. His skills were useless, for no true battle was being fought. And yet the corpses in the killing fields were always of old men and boys, as if somewhere the able-bodied defenders of the land waited for Fortuna's Wheel to turn in their favour at last. Nor could Myrddion entice the watcher in from the forest. Late at night, convinced that his whole journey to the Middle Sea was a fool's errand fuelled by his own hubris, Myrddion began to wish that he had stayed in Segontium and remained ignorant of the realities of war in this fertile landscape. In this foreign land, only the dead seemed real.

Worse still, he watched his little band of companions with a feeling of acute guilt. Cadoc and Finn worked diligently, driving, cutting firewood and easing their master's way through this perilous land; Rhedyn and Bridie cooked, cleaned and collected herbs as they moved through the landscape and watched the denser forest with frightened eyes; only Brangaine seemed content as she nursed the child, Willa, crooning a lullaby between changes of dressings and giving all her attention to the wounded little girl.

Myrddion felt shame stab through him. He had brought them to this dangerous and lawless land, stripping away their security and their trust in familiar things. Why? To sift through swollen bodies on the faint chance of finding someone alive in this charnel house? As a sop to their master's pride? In search of a man who meant nothing to them? Or did they wander with him because they loved and honoured him?

One night, as the healers followed the road towards distant Aurelianum, their watcher finally decided to approach the wagons. As the fires were dowsed at the healers' campsite and the little group began to settle down to sleep, the moon appeared through the cloud like a huge orange ball that was almost as red as a baleful, bloodshot eye. Willa slept in Brangaine's arms while Myrddion rested on the cooling earth, swathed in blankets against the encroaching chill.

The first sound that warned him of the approach of visitors was the stamp of a horse's hoof and a muffled whicker. He rolled to his feet and reached for the sword that was secreted under the seat of the wagon.

'Don't bother, young sir. My lad Clodinus can split you with an arrow, even in the dark, before your hand touches the sword you're reaching for.'

A dark figure had materialised out of the shadows and even the bloody moon hadn't betrayed his approach. Carefully, Myrddion revealed both his hands, palms outwards, and turned to face his hulking visitor.

'Tell your men and the bitches in the wagons to come to the fire – now! Meanwhile, I think we need a little light, so get those coals burning again. I've never been over-fond of the darkness.'

'You're a Celt,' Myrddion croaked, ashamed that his voice revealed his fear.

'As are you. But that won't save you if I decide you're going to become a problem. I've lived across the Litus Saxonicum for nigh on thirty years, so you're nothing to me.'

The intruder's voice had hardened perceptibly, and Myrddion tried to pierce the gloom so he could see their visitor, but to no avail. Careful to stay in the shadows, the Celt lifted his sword in a gesture that underscored the fact that he was a clear threat to the healer's safety.

'Now, do as I say. Tell those young bucks to drop their

weapons and to come out of the dark with empty hands. I'll not ask again.'

'Cadoc! Finn! Do what he says. Rhedyn, wait with the others beside Cadoc's wagon. Don't be afraid, for our guest has no intention of killing us just yet.'

Myrddion's tone had regained its decisiveness, although the stranger stifled a gurgle of amusement at the tone of authority in the youthful voice.

Cadoc and Finn appeared obediently, although Finn's eyes were silvery and fey in the moonlight. Myrddion snapped out a single, sharp instruction, and Truthteller lowered his head and dropped the knife that he had hidden in his sleeve.

'Light the fire, Cadoc. You've a far better talent for that than I have. Finn, we need not fight this gentleman – and whoever else waits out there where we can't see them. They could have murdered us in ambush days ago.'

The dark shadow snickered again with a suggestion of admiration. 'You're a clever young boy, I'll say that for you!'

'He's no boy, coward!' Cadoc flared, his redhead's temper erupting at the insult to his master. 'Lord Myrddion is the confidant of kings. He was King Vortigern's personal healer, and is renowned for possessing knowledge way beyond his years. You should beware that he doesn't shrivel you with one of his spells.'

'Don't be an idiot, Cadoc!' Myrddion groaned, well aware that Cadoc's threats posed a danger to them all. Then he turned to the invisible face of the intruder. 'I am a healer – that much is true. And, yes, I served King Vortigern in his battles against his sons. But I don't have the power to kill you with spells. If you choose to insult me on account of my age, you may do so without any harm to either of us.'

The intruder chuckled again. 'Those are the words of a

wise man. Light the fire, Cadoc. You three are far too nosy for simple travellers, so I want to keep you in my sight. Other, wiser men would have headed back to the coast after seeing what happened at Tournai. So why are you still here?'

Under Cadoc's expert ministrations, the fire leapt into life and, finally, Myrddion could see their adversary clearly.

At first glance, the short, thickset warrior seemed to pose very little threat. He was almost comically round at the belly and his legs were bandy from years in the saddle, giving him a grandfatherly look that was more suited to the fireside than to the sword. But his florid face spoke eloquently of the dangers of judging by superficial appearances.

The warrior was middle-aged and his long hair was almost white, although a few strands of coal black still threaded through his plaits. He was clean-shaven, like many of the corpses found in the ruined towns, and his moustache was fierce, long and yellowed around the mouth. His sagging jowls and bristling brows couldn't humanise a pair of flat black eyes that showed neither amusement nor friendliness, regardless of what his rather full lips suggested. Two slabs of prominent cheekbones set those eyes into deep hollows, so that his pupils glinted coldly and distantly as if through a veil of snow rather than flesh.

With a deceptively languid gesture, the warrior raised his right arm and five very tall Franks came to stand at the edge of the firelight. We'd never have stood a chance, Myrddion thought. He could have killed us whenever he wanted, so we're still alive for a purpose.

'We travel to the Middle Sea for reasons that are mine,' he replied at last. 'If your men search our wagons, you will find our tools of trade easily enough. I am Myrddion of Segontium, named for the Lord of Light and sometimes called Merlin, and I am a healer. You know the names of my apprentices, who were both warriors like yourself before they were injured and entered my employ. We bear no weapons, except those we use for self-defence and hunting, so you may take what you want from us and leave us to ply our trade as best we can.'

'You are impertinent,' the Celt answered without any discernible emotion. 'However, I'll forgive your foolishness on this occasion because you're blind to the dangers of your predicament.'

He spoke rapidly in a language foreign to Myrddion and a young Frank strode forward into the light. 'This young man is Lord Childeric, heir to the lands of Merovech. He is the son of my master, may he live forever. I am his comite, Gwylym ap Gwylydd, and I serve as his interpreter with the Romans, the Celts and our current enemy, Attila the Hun.'

Childeric and Myrddion examined each other narrowly.

The prince was as fair as the healer was dark. He possessed a quantity of yellow hair that had never been cut, framing a face that was handsome, grim and intelligent. Myrddion could not determine his age, for the young man had an air of gravity that was more suited to one in the prime of life. He would have been an imposing figure even had he not been the son of a Salian Frankish king, although his moustache was still a little downy. He stood just over six feet tall, the same height as Myrddion, although the healer could never hope to match Childeric's width of shoulders or dense chest muscles, visible even through a shirt of leather, which was liberally plated with iron.

Childeric spoke rapidly in a voice that was both deep and measured, while Gwylym began to translate.

'My master's son asks what a youth like you is doing

following Attila's hordes as they rampage through his father's lands?'

'I am a healer, Lord Childeric,' Myrddion answered as he bowed to the young warrior. 'I am obligated by my oath to save whatever lives I may when I see the bitter fruits of war.'

Childeric spoke again and Myrddion listened carefully, trying to grasp the rudiments of this strange, rather guttural language.

'You are far from your home,' Gwylym continued. 'Who gave you leave to enter our lands?'

'No one, Lord Childeric. Healers are free to come and go as they please through all the far places of the Middle Sea – or so I am told. I seek knowledge, for a healer must strive to discover all the skills that will help the sick and succour the injured.'

After the Celt had finished his translation, Childeric nodded briefly and spoke in a staccato growl. 'Know you that my lord and father, Merovech, also called Merovius the Great, has dominion over all strangers who seek to travel through his lands. My father is the son of the mighty king Clodio, who won this kingdom through the power of his sword. But my sire was also born of the *bestea Neptuni Quinotauri similis*, in the tongue of the Romans. This sea beast was a man-bull, sprung from the sea god, so King Merovech is doubly blessed. Every living soul within his realm owes service to the god-king.'

Myrddion would have smiled at the pomposity of Childeric's boasting had he not seen an opportunity to salvage their lives and their tools of trade from this grave young warrior who was so proud of his father's doubtful parentage.

'Then King Merovech and I have much in common, for I was said to be begotten on my mother, a princess of the Ordovice tribe, by a demon from the chaos-lands that hover between day and night. King Vortigern, High King of the Britons before his death, attempted to sacrifice me to the gods of the land in response to an ancient prophecy. As you can see, I still live.'

It was now Childeric's turn to peer at Myrddion's face, as if he sought to see the marks of the godling, or the demon, in the healer's features. At the firelight's rim, Myrddion watched several Franks cross themselves or clutch at concealed amulets in superstitious dread as Gwylym translated Myrddion's description of his parentage.

After almost five minutes of careful thought, while Myrddion, the apprentices and the cluster of women awaited Childeric's decision on their fate, the young prince launched into a rapid spate of words that was far too fast for Myrddion to follow. As he finished, he grudgingly offered the healer a brief bow of his yellow, helmed head.

'You have the very luck of a demon, healer. My master has decided that his father, the gathering of kings and the Roman, Aetius, shall decide your fate. You will come with us to Châlons by the shortest route, although I fear we will see a mountain of dead before we reach the safety of King Merovech's camp.'

'But . . .' Myrddion began, but Gwylym silenced his protest with an icy glance that brooked no disagreement.

'Order your folk to the wagons after the horses have been placed in the traces. Our men will return with our own beasts, for my master's son has decided that we leave at once, under the cover of darkness. The Hun is abroad, and you would have walked into certain death if you had braved the sunshine on the morrow.'

Left with little choice but to comply, Myrddion set Cadoc and Finn to work, after first cautioning them to keep their mouths shut and to make no threatening or aggressive gestures.

'We walk between sword points, Cadoc,' Myrddion whispered. 'So keep that temper of yours in check. Better the Frankish king than the Hun.'

'Aye, master,' Cadoc replied, and then grinned widely. 'Whoever this devil spawn might be, I'll wager he'll be no match for our own particular demon.'

Gwylym gave no sign that he had heard their brief exchange, but Myrddion sensed a great darkness in the Celt that made his flesh creep with presentiment.

Before the ruddy moon had set, the wagons had left Parigi far behind and the party was travelling along a thinly wooded path, far from the Roman road that led to Aurelianum. By Myrddion's reckoning, they were heading towards the east and relative safety, if such a thing could exist in this land of casual, ruthless carnage. As a weak sun rose over the far horizon, Gwylym called a halt to the journey and indicated that they would rest in the shadow of the trees. The horses were soon freed from their traces and hobbled, so the exhausted, hungry and thirsty members of the troop were free to tumble into a brief and dreamless sleep.

CHAPTER IV

THE SEA DEMON

The nearby river was wide, dark and forbidding, and a well-constructed Roman bridge spanned its sullen, lightless depths. Myrddion had been unable to sleep so, cat-footed, he had slid from shadow to shadow until he now stood under a nacreous moon, which was reflected in the sluggish waters. Within the cocoon of night, he felt blessedly alone.

'Courting the Huntress, healer?'

Gwylym had reached Myrddion's refuge in the centre of the bridge without a single telltale sound. For such a large, well-rounded man, his feet were almost unnaturally silent, and in the shadows of his prominent brows only the odd flicker of light betrayed his ambiguous eyes.

Myrddion had been alarmed by the Celt's silent approach, but some deep instinct warned him to mask any concern. Instead, he smiled with a flash of white teeth, endeavouring to show no fear of his companion and captor.

'Aye. We Celts are all a little moon-mad, although my allegiance is to Ceridwen and the Mother, whose name must not be spoken by any man. What of you, Gwylym? What god, or gods, own your soul?'

The older Celt chuckled sardonically. 'None, healer. I

make no apologies for my godless state and prefer to set my star by my lord Merovech, and after him by Childeric, his son. I put my faith in men rather than in gods, and I would have thought that you'd be the same. You seem to be a man of common sense rather than superstition.'

'I give my worship to the gods as my grandmother taught me, but my allegiance to any man is hard won,' Myrddion replied with a spot of colour on each cheekbone. For once, the young man's careful control had deserted him, although in the darkness Gwylym couldn't detect the sudden rush of colour to his cheeks.

'Aaah! I sense a touch of human emotion, healer. I'm flattered! So you are chary of the ties of loyalty.'

'Is it loyalty to serve blindly?'

'Yes!'

This rapid-fire exchange left both men, the young and the old, standing only a few inches apart with fists clenched by their sides. Myrddion was the first to realise the ridiculousness of the discussion and he stepped away from Gwylym's dangerous proximity.

'I serve no one person with blind devotion, Gwylym, but I am pleased to learn of the differences that lie between us. But I'm still confused. Why would a Celt turn his back on his fellow countrymen?'

Gwylym glanced up at Myrddion's dark, largely invisible face and blinked rapidly, like a raptor measuring the space between himself and his prey. Under the enlarged moon, the older Celt's eyes had the sudden sharpened perception of the killer falcon freed from the hawker's glove.

'Harsh words, Myrddion-no-name! I'll give you the answer to that question in my own good time, but for now you must return to your sleep. I know Lord Childeric well, and he'll move us fast and hard through this easy country until we reach the relative safety of Châlons. Attila is upon the land, like a scourge from heaven. The Hun warriors believe that Attila bears the Spirit of Death into every battle in the form of an ancient iron sword that is almost godlike to the superstitious among them. For our part, we are blinded by a lack of good intelligence, so Childeric will lash us onward until we're all half dead from exhaustion. So you will need all the rest you can get to survive the journey – and your interrogation by my king. With luck, Flavius Aetius won't be there to cause you even more discomfort.'

Myrddion stepped away from Gwylym, knowing that he had conceded the argument to the older Celt. The healer laughed quietly and Gwylym frowned in response, as if he was puzzled by Myrddion's reaction.

'Then I'll take your advice, Gwylym. You know the trials we will face, not I. But I fear you'll be disappointed in me, for I'll not willingly serve another master, no matter how royal.'

'You'll not?' Gwylym chuckled from the cool night shadows. 'I warrant you'll serve my master, for he'll find some reason that will tempt you – one way or the other. If he decides he wants you, King Merovech will have you.' With these threatening words, he strode back the way he had come until he merged once more with the shadows.

'That old man moves like a cat – or an assassin,' Myrddion whispered grimly into the soft breeze. 'But he's right. If these local kings want me, then I'll have little option but to obey them.'

Dreams chased the young healer throughout the few hours of his rest. He saw the heavens split and a huge iron sword dive, blade first, out of sullen, livid skies to pierce, point down, into the barren earth below. Thrumming with menace, the archaic weapon reared over an arid plain like a portent of disaster. Then, in the inexplicable fashion of dreams, the blade began to bleed and a tide of sanguine gore seemed to wash over the whole, dry land until Myrddion believed that he would drown in a viscous flood of red.

A booted foot to the ribs roused him from his trance before the sun rose. Rhedyn handed her master a bowl of cold stew and a large wooden spoon. As the healer ate the grey mess reflectively, he saw that his apprentices had already set the horses into their traces and had struck camp.

Myrddion sighed, and poured water over his face from the leather bag that was kept slung over the wagon's side. The cold water shook his blunted wits back into a semblance of order and gave him the illusion of cleanliness. The worst part of any long journey, from Myrddion's point of view, was the lack of opportunities for personal hygiene.

The town of Châlons lay on the bank of a large river flowing through wide plains that were fertile in agriculture and trade. Plentiful water, a gentle climate, rich soil and long rows of poplars and vines had created an ordered, earthly Eden. Only a few low hills set off a countryside that was largely flat, except for the folds carved by the many streamlets and rivers that flowed slowly through the idyllic landscape. In this alien world of green, blue, beige and gold, Myrddion longed for the misty greys and charcoals of his mountain home.

Châlons possessed the obligatory stone walls of any prosperous city, and additional clusters of hamlets had grown up around the outskirts. Green spear-points of growth from fruit and olive trees testified to good husbandry, and vegetables of all kinds grew in neat rows around simple workers' cottages, resembling flower beds in their regimentation and crisp beauty.

The roads and byways leading to Châlons were thick with traffic. Christian Arian priests in dirty white and Catholics in dusty black robes walked side by side with peasants carrying heaped baskets of goods bound for the marketplace. Crisp cabbages as large as a man's head, bags of new turnips, the first legumes of spring and baskets of brown farm eggs nestling in straw competed with new-born lambs, calves and chickens carried in wicker cages as the produce of the rural communities found its way into this major market town. Men in dirty togas, visitors in alien finery and rows of petty princelings bound for the court of Merovech and the Visigoth lords vied for space with peasants on the congested, dusty gravel.

The Frankish horsemen negotiated the bustling traffic with relative ease, forcing a path for the wagons through the throng until Myrddion eventually saw the gates of Châlons looming before them.

'I don't like our chances here if the Huns should attack,' Finn murmured quietly to Myrddion as he urged his horses through the heavy wooden gates. 'I wish we knew where the devils are. We've seen the fate of town dwellers throughout our journey, so I'd prefer to sleep in the open air.'

Myrddion nodded, and then pointed to the wooden ramparts built on the inside of the stone fortifications. 'At least young warriors are manning the walls, which is an improvement on the defences we saw at Tournai and Cambrai.'

Finn peered up at the red-cloaked men who stood at regular intervals along the wall, their disciplined eyes obviously scanning the surrounding countryside for signs of unusual activity. 'Aye! Châlons is definitely not Tournai. This town won't be taken without warning, so I suppose we should be grateful for that small mercy.'

'Yes, we should be grateful,' Myrddion muttered under his

breath as the wagons negotiated roads so narrow that they almost scraped the plastered buildings lining the cobbled roadways. 'Perhaps the gods protect the ignorant.'

An unnatural silence had enveloped the quiet streets and, as they passed, women glanced up at Childeric's face, dropped their heads respectfully, then dragged their squabbling children inside brightly painted doors that were closed firmly behind them. 'Whatever else Châlons might be, its population is loyal to their king and his Roman ally,' Myrddion added, thinking of his earlier conversation with Gwylym on the moon-drenched bridge.

Neither man spoke again until the cavalcade reached a small cul-de-sac of stone and wooden buildings decorated with shuttered window openings. These buildings were narrow-fronted and opened straight onto the cobbled road-way where a guard of red-cloaked warriors directed foot traffic away from the seat of power to other, less important streets of the township.

'You'll be billeted in the guards' quarters until Merovech and the allied kings are ready to give you an audience,' Gwylym explained, as Myrddion climbed down from the wagon's high seat. 'Don't fear for your possessions. As you can see, the king's guards are always alert and no one would dare to filch anything from one of the king's guests.'

Myrddion nodded, but snatched up his satchel and a small pack of personal possessions as he gazed around at the narrow, looming buildings. The upper storeys, where the healers were to sleep, were built of wood, and as Myrddion and his followers negotiated a set of narrow, ladder-like stairs their nostrils were assaulted by the mingled smells of dried fish, cooked cabbage and male sweat. Myrddion's nose wrinkled with distaste.

'If you wish to bathe, a well is situated behind this building,' Gwylym added from the ground floor. 'I'm afraid that no Roman epicures dwell in Châlons.' Then he disappeared into the shadowy interior, his rasping chuckle trailing behind him like a crude insult.

Myrddion examined the bleak room with misgiving. It lay directly under the roof and he could barely stand upright without striking his head on the pegged rafters. Straw had been laid out for pallets, but the mice had found it first, and the dim recesses of the room reeked of urine and the musty smell of long dead vermin. The raw wooden walls were unpainted and the floors could be seen to be slick with grease wherever they were exposed to the light.

Only a few pieces of rickety furniture provided an inadequate promise of comfort. A pair of home-made stools that canted alarmingly off centre, a table with inexpertly formed, uneven legs and a piece of oiled cloth nailed over the single window to keep out the inclement weather completed the depressing list of the room's appointments.

'Rhedyn, find out where food is prepared, will you?' Myrddion asked once the women had trooped doubtfully into their new quarters. 'And we'll need water, Finn! You always know where to winkle out buckets.' He glanced around the stuffy room and absorbed the appalling lack of cleanliness and hygiene. 'Cadoc, see about a broom, or anything that will help us to clean this pigsty. The place stinks of piss and sweat.'

Two of the widows, Brangaine and Bridie, were soon at work, clearing the floor bare of the malodorous hay and then scrubbing the wooden boards, the table and the stools with stiff brushes made of boar's hair. The air soon became golden as motes of hay, dust and the accumulated grime of many years began to float through the room. When Brangaine set off in pursuit of a mouse, her switch broom wielded with murderous intent and Willa giggling at the fuss, Myrddion decided that he would explore the small cul-de-sac until the widows had imposed order on their new quarters.

When they had first arrived, the healer had noted that the bones of the buildings in the small cobbled street were Roman in style, but a local twist invested the narrow stone facades with an exotic, purely Gallic appearance. Wooden shutters gave the windows an odd, blind look that was strangely unsettling. More surprising to Myrddion, who was used to the grey, flinty stone buildings of his home-land, was the use of coloured pigments which had been applied over the plastered stones in faded washes of pastel yellow, brick red and a peculiar hue of charcoal grey. The shutters were lime-washed a brilliant white that added con-trast to these architectural oddities, and large, hand-thrown pots were filled with earth to sustain flourishing young lemon trees that were already heavy with tiny green fruit.

His eyes wide, Myrddion stared around the mellow buildings. A series of rough gates made of lime-washed wood sealed the narrow alleyways between them. Curious, Myrddion pushed open the gate that separated the largest structure from the barracks where they were housed and, to his surprise, the gate gave way with a squeal of rusting iron hinges. Beyond the coarse timber, the darkened alleyway promised cool, indigo shadows after the dazzling sun of the cul-de-sac.

His curiosity piqued, Myrddion passed through the gate-way and entered the narrow, dark tunnel between the stone buildings.

The absence of sunshine had promoted the growth of

lush ferns and moss where water collected in stone hollows against the walls. The sudden coolness was a balm to Myrddion's sun-blinded eyes, but the cobbles under his feet were slippery with black slime. Keeping to the middle of the alleyway for safety, he picked a path towards the rear of the buildings.

As he made his tentative way through the alley, he noticed that there were no windows to threaten the security of the house on either side. Narrow apertures on the upper floors were secured with odd-shaped iron straps that were securely bolted into the stone. Entry into the buildings from the alley was rendered impossible. 'Someone has a penchant for safety,' Myrddion murmured to the empty laneway as he moved towards the brilliant splash of sunlight that signalled the end of the narrow tunnel.

'Ah!' he breathed as he stepped out into the enclosed space that backed onto both the guardhouse and its neighbour. His surprise would have been laughable if anyone had been present to see his slack mouth and round, amazed eyes as he gazed at the scene that lay before him.

The narrow, dark alleyway opened onto a rising series of broad terraces bounded by high fieldstone walls. Within this enclosed area, a large roofed structure protected a fire-pit, complete with spit, several brick ovens and a smaller fireplace constructed for the preparation of lesser meals. Two rock walls sheltered this outdoor kitchen from the elements, while an alcove served as storage space for a neat stack of firewood.

At the rear of the more imposing of the two buildings flanking the alley, a well was centred on the lowest terrace beside which several decorative fruit trees were planted. The petals had already fallen and small citrus fruits were forming on the branches. Myrddion tried to imagine the size, shape and taste of the grown fruit but, as he had never seen an orange, he could only marvel at the pleasant smell of the leaves when he crushed them between his fingers.

A series of stone benches were laid out where idlers could sit in the shade of the building and enjoy the bars of brilliant sunshine, the deep green of several narrow pine trees and a riot of vivid scarlet flowers that created a colourful splash under the impossibly blue sky. Against his better judgement, Myrddion leaned against the wall and drew the lightly scented air deep into his lungs.

'And who might you be, to enjoy the pleasures of my garden without permission?' A deep, resonant voice cut through Myrddion's reverie, shattering the feeling of peace and well-being that had embraced him. He raised his eyes.

The woman who stood on the terrace was slender and very tall, so that she almost reached Myrddion's own height. Her colouring was vivid, with lips that were pomegranate red and glistening over her large, beautiful teeth. Those lips were full, bee-stung and voluptuous, and an incongruous counter-point to her imperious, patronising voice.

'Well, clod, I'm waiting for a very good explanation,' she continued in perfect Latin. 'Or must I set my guards to teach you a lesson in manners?'

Completely confused, Myrddion met a pair of snapping eyes which possessed an unmaidenly directness that made the young man's hackles rise. The fine-boned, aristocratic face was topped by a head of rich auburn hair that shaded from carrot red into gilded bronze. Its owner was obviously wilful and impetuous by nature, her aquiline features suggesting charm and temper in equal measure.

Conscious of his rough clothes and dusty hair, Myrddion bent his head in a deep, courtly bow.

'Forgive me, my lady. I am Myrddion of Segontium in Britain. I have been billeted in the guardhouse next to this building on the orders of Prince Childeric, so that his father might question me. I am a healer and I have come to these lands with my apprentices and servants, seeking knowledge of my craft.'

The lady raised one dark brow sceptically and Myrddion noticed that she had a rare abnormality. Now that he had collected his wits sufficiently to examine her properly, he observed that her right eye was a northern, arctic blue, while her left eye was a clear, dark-rimmed green.

'You are far too young to be a master of men and a scholar. If you lie to King Merovech, he will have you spitted like a pig. He is my godfather, and he is in a vile temper already over the sacking of Cambrai, the city won by his father Clodio, during the great wars. If I were you, I'd consider carefully how I answered your betters in future.'

One narrow foot, shod in gilded sandals, tapped impatiently on the paving. Despite the lady's arrogant rudeness, Myrddion felt his face fall into a rather cloth-witted grin.

'Don't just stand there, idiot! Assist me to be seated! No! Not in the sun! May the gods preserve me from all fools! I want to sit in the shade where my complexion won't be ruined. Now, find my maidservant.'

As Myrddion grappled with the lady's demands, he wondered at a pride so engorged and all-encompassing that she presumed he knew who she was. Tentatively, he cleared his throat to ask. In response, she raised that interrogative eyebrow once more. Both eyes were cold and her expression was patronising.

'Who should I say desires her servant, my lady? I am but newly come to these lands, so I am ignorant of the honour that you do me by deigning to address me.'

The lady sighed with impatience, too lofty to recognise the irony underlying the false servility of his compliments. 'I am Flavia Minor, youngest child of the great general Flavius Aetius, Overlord of the West, who holds these lands by favour of the Emperor Valentinian.'

'Lady Flavia, I shall obey immediately.'

Two tall Franks, both dressed identically in the familiar uniform of the household guard, stood in the shadows near a simple door. Myrddion approached them cautiously, with both hands held palm upwards so that they could see he was unarmed.

'The Lady Flavia requires her maid,' he told them, and watched as the older of the two guards gave a mocking grimace. The rapid-fire instructions that he gave to his fellow warrior in the Frankish language were too fast for Myrddion to even guess at his meaning, but the warrior's tone suggested weary forbearance. Impassively, his companion turned and entered the cool darkness of the building.

'You'd best return to the lady, Master Myrddion, or neither of us will have any peace. Mistress Flavia requires constant diversion.'

Myrddion turned to obey, then stopped abruptly and swung back to face the guard. 'How do you know my name, sir? To the best of my knowledge, we have never met before this day.'

The tall, craggy warrior grinned widely and exposed a broken canine that was grey with rot. 'You and your party are the subject of much speculation and curiosity in Châlons, young sir. You seem to us to be far too young to be a healer, and you have managed to earn the distrust of Gwylym the Celt. At the same time, you have managed to pass unscathed through the armies of the Hun. The men are taking wagers on how long it will be before our master orders your head to be parted from your body.' The guardsman spat on the paving to express his disapproval of unreliable strangers.

Despite a sudden lurch in his stomach, Myrddion grinned at the warrior with reckless defiance. 'Even King Merovech will find I am a very difficult person to kill. Other kings have tried to sacrifice me in the past but, as you can see, I'm still here. What did you wager?'

'Me? I never judge by appearances, young master. While most of the men discount you because of your youth, I take the view that if you're not a boasting child, then you must be a young man of extraordinary talent. I've wagered that you will live, so I'll be very disappointed if you let me down.'

An imperious female voice interrupted the whispered conversation. 'Myrddion of Segontium! Why are you talking to Captus, while I'm left to swelter in this heat? Someone needs to fan me, and in the absence of my lazy maid I must depend on you. Stop talking men's nonsense and act like a gentleman.'

It was now Captus's turn to smile ruefully and step aside so that Myrddion could obey the compelling, impudent and husky command. The healer was reminded of honey poured over shell grit by that oddly attractive voice.

He bowed to Captus and spoke to the warrior so quietly that Lady Flavia couldn't hear his advice. 'That tooth must be causing you pain, sir. It is dying, so you risk ulcers or foul humours inside your mouth if it isn't removed. Come to me tomorrow and I will draw it for you before it weakens your health.

'Now, my lady, where is your fan? Perhaps you would be more comfortable under the pines? It's a pity that the cooling breezes from the river cannot reach us here.'

The lady's skin was alabaster pale, so Myrddion could easily see the blue veins just beneath the surface. Although she had dressed primly in a pale rose peplum of some light fabric, it clung to her full breasts and rounded hips suggestively, and Myrddion felt a hot little knot forming in the pit of his stomach.

Is this lust, he wondered? But years of practice ensured that his face showed nothing of the unfamiliar turmoil he was feeling. Lady Flavia had set his wits tilting crazily in response to her passionate mouth, her deep, throaty voice and the delicious suggestion of a nipple beneath her gauzy pink gown. Myrddion was not entirely without experience of the pleasure to be found in a woman's body, freely and generously given, but he had never before felt the dizzying pull of sexual attraction, nor imagined that his sharply honed brain would respond so irrationally to the desires of his body.

How odd, he thought. So the songs about the madness of love are true. This woman must be avoided if I'm to remain in control of myself.

'I never pine for what I cannot have,' the lady answered, in response to Myrddion's comment about the river breezes. Confused and disoriented, the young man took a moment to remember the gist of the conversation. 'I find that too much effort is wasted on quite fruitless desires. Besides, there's very little I cannot have if I put my mind to it.'

'Then Lady Flavia is a fortunate young woman, and the goddess must favour her on the Great Wheel.' Myrddion's murmured reply was so courtly that Flavia's eyebrows rose once more.

'Luck has nothing to do with it, young man. All anyone really needs to achieve their desires is a little planning, perseverance and the resolution to do what must be done.'

As Myrddion continued to ply her simple fan of painted chicken skin in a gilded wooden frame, the lady straightened her curls and chattered on about the deficiencies of Châlons in the matter of social gatherings. The one-sided conversation led inexorably to Lady Flavia's desire to return to the delights of sophisticated Ravenna, from where she had been removed by her father some three years earlier after the death of her mother. Lady Flavia revealed her egocentricity as she spoke of the status of Flavius Aetius, the dowry that would go with her to the marriage bed and her dissatisfaction with life in Gaul. Barely pausing for breath, the young woman also exposed her ignorance of the world with every word, for Myrddion realised that her veneer of world-weary cynicism was barely skin deep. Although she pretended to be experienced, she was a gently raised Roman maiden who had been kept away from men throughout her youth. No great general like Flavius Aetius would countenance his daughter's attending social events, no matter how liberal her upbringing had been.

She lies! Myrddion thought with amusement, ignoring the appeal of Flavia's husky, intimate voice that almost compensated for the patronising condescension of her words. Almost . . . but not quite.

Still, she had drawn Myrddion's eyes to her dress of rose-petal pink, which complemented her remarkable eyes. She had made his brain feel too big for his skull and sent a wave of heat coursing through his body. Unfamiliar as such emotions were, Myrddion understood enough to know instinctively that Lady Flavia was a danger to his peace of mind now that he teetered on the edge of true adulthood. He was beginning to understand carnality at last.

'Are you listening to me, boy? Or are you daft, standing there like a block of wood with a silly expression on your face?'

Myrddion dropped the fan unnoticed onto the stone bench and stared at his trembling fingers. 'I must go, my lady. I've been absent from my people for too long.'

Like all females, Lady Flavia was wise in the ways of sexual attraction. She laughed, and it was the sound of her throaty good humour that followed him through the unfamiliar rear door of the guardhouse, up the rickety stairs and back into a place of relatively dusty order.

Cadoc looked up from a large bowl of water that he had been using to scrub his hands and face. His eyes swept over Myrddion's dusty hands and sweat-soiled robes. 'We've been summoned, master. The general and his allies have arrived, so we are commanded to attend Aetius and Merovech at the Hall of Justice, whatever that is!'

Without wasting time on words, Myrddion began to rummage through his pack until he found his best black robe, his softest doeskin breeches, his best boots and his bone comb. Taking Cadoc's place at the water basin, he stripped off his soiled robe and exposed a smooth, hairless torso that was both beautiful and androgynous in its sculpted whiteness.

'Master?' Cadoc asked softly. 'Should we be frightened of this Merovech and the Roman general?'

'Aye, we should. By all that I've heard, General Aetius is a clever, ruthless man who will do what must be done to protect the emperor's interests in Gaul. The centuries of Roman power are gone, perhaps, but men such as Aetius remind us why Romans once ruled the world. He'll use us up, then cast us away like empty wineskins if there's some advantage to Ravenna in doing so.'

'Isn't this Merovech just another barbarian king? We survived Vortigern and his sons, and we've managed to avoid crossing swords with Ambrosius and Uther, so why should we fear another minor king?'

'The walls have ears in this place, Cadoc, and these Franks don't think as we do. Merovech believes he is the son of a sea demon, so he'll be very confident of his own powers. Nor is he the greatest of our concerns. The Visigoths, the Alans and a clutch of other tribal lords are also threats to our continued good health. We must walk carefully, my friend, for we know neither the men who await us nor what mantraps have been laid to snare us.'

Finn moved forward into the fading light from the narrow windows. He had dressed in the best garb he had, oiled his long hair and plaited it into the side locks of a warrior before securing the ends with bronze clasps carved with intricate detail. His leathers gleamed in the dusty light.

'I have just been told that this king was raised in Rome to ensure that his father held the peace. General Aetius backed Merovech's claim to King Clodio's throne, and no man dares to breathe in Gaul without the general's permission. Merovech is his protégé.'

'As always, Finn, you keep me supplied with answers before I even know the questions to ask. These two men are dangerous pikes and we are minnows swimming in their pond, so take care and keep your mouths shut, as I intend to do.'

'If they'll let you,' Finn muttered.

Myrddion scrubbed his flesh until it shone before donning his clean clothes. As he chewed a stick of charcoal to clean his teeth and sweeten his breath, Rhedyn dragged his comb through his hair until the raven locks gleamed. As he had no right to assume the plaits of a warrior, the young healer permitted his hair to hang free to his waist. With a last careful rinse of his mouth, his toilette was complete.

'Well, we are as presentable as possible, so let's discover what breed of men these rulers are, and how they will treat us as visitors to their lands.'

Unarmed, and escorted by three hulking Franks, the three healers were led out of the guardhouse and into the narrow stone building next door. Myrddion's first impression was of many dark corridors and small rooms of indeterminate purpose. He noted the lack of ornamentation and luxury in the presentation. Then they entered a bigger, stone-walled apartment at the rear of the building. This chamber was obviously a meeting place for large groups, to judge by the long benches built into all four walls, a dais that caught the light from high, narrow, barred windows, and more banks of benches arranged behind the throne-like stools that stood in the centre of the dais.

Accompanied by their guard of barbarian warriors, the three healers were forced to await the arrival of their noble inquisitors. As they stood before the dais, Gwylym ambled into the audience chamber and whistled softly when he noticed Myrddion's long, glossy hair. The older Celt strolled around the three men, taking in their attempts at finery, before he whispered in Myrddion's ear.

'You're very pretty, healer. Were we in Rome or Ravenna you'd be in no danger from the nobles – for the citizens of the Empire worship young male flesh.'

Myrddion's face spasmed with disgust. 'Faugh!' he gasped. 'Pederasts sicken me.'

Gwylym laughed. 'How very intolerant of you.'

'Perhaps,' Myrddion hissed, and Gwylym walked away, whistling through his teeth.

Flanked by his friends, Myrddion tried to avoid fidgeting as he stood in the centre of the chamber and faced the empty stools. Five minutes went by before a door was ceremoniously opened, admitting five men who radiated the kind of power that only kings could muster.

The eldest man mounted the dais first and seated himself with considerable care, as if his bones were aching. He possessed a shock of thick white hair that was cut militarily short at the sides, although his domed forehead was bald. From his laced army boots to his spotless white toga, the ageing warrior was the epitome of a Roman soldier. Yet there was something foreign about the slightly slanted eyes and the high cheekbones that jutted through the man's skin like knife blades.

The second man appeared to be about forty years of age and was very fair in colouring. His uncut hair was wheat yellow, as was a large, luxuriant moustache. His eyes were pale blue, but the profile that accompanied this typical Frankish colouring was unexpected. His nose was strong, high-arched and aquiline, with flaring nostrils. By comparison, his mouth was thin and almost cruel, with down-turned corners that matched the deep crevices running from each nostril almost to his jaw line. With narrow, dark brows arching over his deep-set eyes, Merovech's appearance suggested that under his conventional Frankish good looks he was a man of stubborn pride and a freakish, inflexible will.

The three accompanying kings sat directly behind Aetius and Merovech, gathering their cloaks about themselves as if they could be contaminated if they touched each other. Each was a man of middle years; each was dressed with gorgeous, barbaric magnificence and each possessed a face scoured by power, ruthlessness and ferocity. Later, Myrddion discovered that they were King Sangiban of the Alans, King Theodoric of the Visigoths and the king of the Burgundians. Elsewhere in the room, lords of the Alan tribe, the Saxons of the north, Amoricans and Sarmatians rested on soft cushions and tried to conceal their growing concern at the prospect of defeat in the coming battles.

One other man was present, standing deferentially to Myrddion's left, and positioned so he could watch the reactions of every man in the room. He was tall, almost cadaverous in appearance, and was dressed with exotic opulence in silks of brilliant blue and green. Myrddion had never seen the like of the man's exquisite, almost feminine jewellery, which included earrings of finely wrought gold basketry set with blood-red precious stones. For the first time, Myrddion gazed at the face of Cleoxenes, the emissary of Theodosius, emperor of Constantinople and the sole ruler of the Eastern Empire.

Aetius coughed briefly, and all eyes in the room swung to focus on him.

'We are here to consider several weighty matters, including the incursions of Attila into the lands of the Salian Franks, the Visigoths and the Burgundians. We shall also discuss his siege of Aurelianum, which you call Orléans. But before we commence our deliberations, we must decide on the fate of these travellers who have entered our lands without our express approval. We find it suspicious that they have followed a wing of Attila's army from Tournai almost to the gates of Aurelianum.' He turned his eyes directly onto Myrddion. 'What are your names, and what is your purpose in entering our lands?'

Aetius's eyes were a greenish-brown, and ice cold. They held no pity or empathy as they scanned every inch of Myrddion and his apprentices in a careful, dispassionate examination that missed no detail of their appearance.

Myrddion stepped forward cautiously. No one thinks to inform us of their names, he thought irrelevantly. They presume that all men here will know who they are. Like father, like daughter.

He coughed apologetically. 'As you have no doubt been told, I am Myrddion of Segontium in Britain and these men are my apprentices, Cadoc ap Cadwy and Finn ap Finbarr, who is also known as the Truthteller. We are healers, come to Gaul on a quest to learn the finer details of our craft.'

Aetius sucked on his teeth in an action that appeared to be habitual whenever he was thinking. Like his daughter's, his voice was husky and imperious, and possessed an edge that abraded the nerves of any listener.

'That does not explain why you were following the Hun army, unless you were in their pay.'

'No sir, we are not in anyone's employ. We took a route that we were advised would keep us away from the fighting. Our destination is Ravenna, and having served Vortigern, the High King of Britain, we have no desire to be in the service of any other king.'

'You are arrogant!' Aetius snapped. 'Who are you to choose your employer? Nor does your explanation satisfy me, so I repeat the question. Why did you follow in the tracks of Attila's army?'

In his eagerness, Myrddion took a short pace forward, and immediately heard the sinister hiss of a sword sliding out of a scabbard in the hands of one of the guards. He stopped immediately.

'We weren't certain of where we were most of the time, my lord. We had been advised to follow the old Roman road, so we did. As we travelled, we met refugees from Tournai and realised we were indeed on the track taken by Attila.'

Aetius turned and faced King Merovech. 'Do you have any questions, Merovech, before we arrive at our decision?'

'Aye! Tell me about your father, Myrddion ap Nobody.'

Merovech's eyes were as hard as chips of ice under a northern sun, so Myrddion knew he would be unwise to lie, for Childeric had obviously told Merovech about the healer's claims of demonic birth. However, to be completely honest about his father could be equally dangerous, so Myrddion decided to speak with the spirit of truth, using the broadest possible definition of honesty.

'Your son has obviously reported my words, great king. Therefore, I am obliged to tell you the truth as I have been told it. My father was a chaos-demon who raped my mother and begot me on her young and innocent flesh. She was a princess of the Deceangli tribe and the daughter of the High Priestess of the Mother – so I was permitted to live. I cannot vouch for the truth of this birth, as I can only repeat what my mother vowed were the circumstances of my conception.'

Merovech frowned. Myrddion understood that the king would be struggling with the knowledge that another man shared the same extraordinary birth as himself.

'A princess! So your family was of royal blood?' Merovech clutched at the one detail that could link them both and underscore their superiority to the ordinary run of men.

'Aye, my Lord. My great-grandfather was Melvig ap Melwy, king of the Deceangli tribe of Cymru. He left me his sword when he died.'

'Bring it to me!' Merovech demanded peremptorily, and

he and the Roman general were soon examining the short, utilitarian blade and the gold-chased pommel with its single, carved stone with the interest of professional fighting men.

'Aye,' Merovech decided. 'This is surely the sword of a king. But how am I to know that you speak the truth? You could have stolen this sword, filched it from one of your masters.'

'But you know in your heart that I didn't steal it, King Merovech. I am demon born, so I have the skills of my sire, although I would prefer that I were free of them. At times I see what will be, as well as what was, just as clearly as if past and future were a scroll that I could unroll and read.'

Two spots of colour mounted on Merovech's cheeks. His jaw clenched and jutted aggressively and Myrddion shuddered inwardly at the king's reaction. Obviously, Merovech did not have the sight, and the healer hoped that he had not overplayed his hand.

'You are a soothsayer?' the king growled menacingly. 'So you knew you would be captured.'

'No, my lord, I did not. When I prophesy, I have no recollection of what I say, although I sometimes catch glimpses of dangers that are present in the air around me. I would surely be free of this cursed birth-sight, if I could.'

Even Aetius, who believed very little that he was told, was forced to admit to himself that Myrddion seemed sincere. The young man's eyes had shown the first flashes of emotion since the questioning had begun. As a good Roman, Aetius paid lip service to many gods, and took part in the rituals invoking the blessing of the soldiers' god, Mithras. But his duty required him to bind the northern pagans to Rome's cause, so pragmatism as well as a natural scepticism ensured he remained detached in the face of all religions.

'But you must have some inkling of the future,' he said with a sardonic grimace. 'Tell us, then, what your demon has whispered into your mind regarding the outcome of this war – if you dare!'

'Lord, do not ask,' Myrddion whispered, but he saw Aetius lower his eyebrows and could tell by the suspicious twist of the general's lips that his gambit had failed. To mention his fits had been risky, but he had gambled that it might save their lives if Merovech and Aetius had been impressed by the account of his demonic powers. Instead, the healers were now in grave peril.

'Do you fear to demonstrate your skills? Or do you lie to us, because you believe us to be credulous barbarians who will believe anything you say? Perhaps you need persuasion?' Merovech gestured with one hand, and a guard stepped forward. 'Choose one of the apprentices and cut his throat. Then, perhaps, this young charlatan will recover his powers.'

'No, my lord! No,' Myrddion cried. 'I'll try. But for the Mother's mercy, hold your hand.'

'Very well, healer. Entertain us! Show me how a demon's son can master the ribbon of time.' Merovech's craggy, handsome face was stiff with scorn. 'Demonstrate why you are no ordinary man. And hurry, because we impatiently await your pleasure.'

With his mind racing and his heart pumping as if he had just completed an exhausting race, Myrddion looked round at each of the barbarian kings. In the many pairs of eyes that were riveted on him, the healer saw no sympathy, but he did recognise an avid curiosity and a hunger for bloody diversion. Cadoc and Finn reached out to him with their hands and hearts, but Myrddion was powerless. His fits did not come at the bidding of a mere king. Nor had his gift ever responded to any attempts on his part to master it.

With a suddenly dry mouth, Myrddion stared fixedly at the narrow strip of light that crawled across the tiled floor, as he tried to dredge up the curse of his birth. The light was fading as the afternoon died; each regal face already had deep shadows about its eyes and mouth as if the skull were trying to burst through the skin.

Myrddion felt the old, hated darkness begin to push through the angled light until the room in Châlons began to shrink, becoming smaller and smaller until it was just a pin-point of light in the blackness of his skull. He had a sensation of falling, and then his consciousness was swept away in a dark tide of great wings.

He knew nothing more.

CHAPTER V

THE SINGER AND THE SONG

Roman, Goth, and Hun,
And Scythian strength of chivalry, that tread
The cold Codanian shore, or what far lands
Inhospitable drink Cimmerian floods,
Franks, Saxons, Suevic, and Sarmatian chiefs,
And who from green Armorica or Spain
Flocked to the work of death.

Herbert, *Attila*, Book 1

When Myrddion opened his gummed eyelids some hours later, he lay in inky darkness. As his eyes gradually adjusted to the gloom of this lightless room, his sensitive fingers fumbled over the surface on which he had been laid out, almost as if he were a corpse. A pallet had been spread on a wooden framework strung with sturdy rope, and someone had flung a woollen blanket over his supine form. He recognised the distinctive smell of horse.

Then the memory of his dilemma came flooding back in an uncomfortable tide. What had he said? Where were Cadoc and Finn? Had he made the situation worse, or had he promised the success that would cement their survival? In his distress, he groaned aloud and shifted on his bed, hearing a complaint of stretched rope.

A shape suddenly loomed out of the dimness. His pupils at their widest, Myrddion made out a silent servant who had been standing beside what he could now see was a barred doorway. A flint was struck and a crude pottery bowl of oil was lit and leapt weakly into life.

'I am instructed to bring you a restorative draught, but you must stay lying down in case you feel nauseous,' the prim, disembodied voice instructed.

Myrddion felt like a child who had soiled his loincloth and was now being lectured, firmly but censoriously, on his behaviour.

The dark shape moved easily to the doorway and a slice of light provided enough visibility for Myrddion to see the far wall of a small, windowless room. Then the door was closed once more and the wall vanished into darkness. Only a brief period elapsed before the servant returned, bearing a horn beaker filled with warm milk to which some powerful liquor had been added. Myrddion coughed as the raw spirit hit the back of his throat, but the initial burning sensation was almost immediately replaced by warmth that radiated outwards from his belly.

The cloth wick of the oil lamp had now caught and details of the room were more easily discerned. Clean, scrubbed and spartan, it offered few comforts and no hint of the personality of its normal occupant. The only clue to its owner was a large wooden chest bound with thin strips of iron for security.

Myrddion sipped his powerful drink carefully and tried to think. The presence of the very superior manservant seemed to suggest a mark of favour, but the room had a distinctly cell-like quality that hinted at imprisonment. The young man was confused.

'So, healer, you've set the hen coop a-flutter, haven't you?'

'Lady Flavia,' Myrddion croaked as Aetius's daughter swept into the room, lifting her trailing skirts fastidiously as if she feared encroaching grime in this sterile little room. A hint of musky perfume caught at his nostrils and made his senses tremble. 'You should not be here if you are unaccompanied.'

'How else would I discover anything in this house of secrets?'

What was it about this brusque, rude woman? What quality in her character forced Myrddion's eyes to follow her every movement and set his heart beating irregularly in his breast?

'Cat got your tongue, Myrddion? I felt sure you would be interested in your situation when you woke from your trance, but here you sit with your mouth hanging open like a dullard. Aren't you a little bit curious about your prophecies? After all, you owe your life to them.'

'I'm terrified of what I might have said during my fit. Believe me, Mistress Flavia, such a talent is a curse and I'd willingly cast it from me.'

'Oh, fie to you, healer! I can see many ways to profit from your *fits*, as you call them. I never inherited anything useful from my father other than an extremely large nose.'

Doubtfully, Myrddion stared at the offending feature. Flavia's nose was aquiline and slender, with delicately moulded nostrils that flared attractively when she became excited. Perhaps it was a little long for true beauty, but, feature by feature, Flavia's physiognomy was decidedly unusual, as well as attractive. When seen in totality, what should have jarred actually charmed and, once again, Myrddion felt that unfamiliar flutter under his ribs.

'So, tell me truthfully, mistress, for I am on tenterhooks to discover my fate.'

'I wasn't present, for such audiences are for men alone,' Flavia teased, her eyes dancing with mischief. 'Such exclusions are dreary and unfair, but I cannot persuade my father to allow me to attend his meetings with the kings.' She sighed with impatience, leaving Myrddion convinced that she had argued with her parent over this restriction on many occasions. 'But Castor here was present, for he was serving my father. Perhaps he can be persuaded to describe your fit and its repercussions.'

Castor moved forward so that Myrddion could see him clearly. 'I believe, Mistress Flavia, that your honourable father would be disappointed by the levity with which you approach such weighty matters. I shall, however, report my recollections of what occurred to the healer, for I believe that such was my master's intention. But I assure you that what I saw and heard was no subject for jesting.'

'You're so . . . so puffed up with your consequence, Castor!' Flavia's eyes flashed with annoyance. 'For Fortuna's sake, say what you mean without all the verbiage.'

'Very well, mistress, I will try.'

Beneath his stiff, formal manner, Castor was a natural storyteller who enjoyed being centre stage, and the word picture he drew was so vivid that Myrddion could soon visualise what had happened as clearly as if he had seen it.

The healer's eyes had rolled back into his head, exciting a sudden chatter of alarmed comment from the seated rulers. His body had become rigid and his fists had clenched tightly at his side.

'Speak, healer, and describe what you see,' Aetius had commanded in a voice that neither quavered nor broke with fear.

Myrddion's eyes had snapped back so that the pupils remained visible, but every man present could see that his senses had fled from his body.

'Woe to the west if the Hungvari succeed in their quest out of Buda. Woe to the west if the Fratricide fulfils the legend of Romulus, for the last vulture has fled.'

Aetius had gasped, despite his stern refusal to admit the possibility of second sight. In his position against the wall, noble Cleoxenes had flinched and made a swift movement of the cross over his breast. Many of the Goth and Frank kings had looked puzzled at Aetius's consternation, but before they could ask questions Myrddion had begun to speak once more.

'Strike while the Huns are sacking Aurelianum! If you hasten, they will be forced to retreat to their great camp on the Catalaunian Plain. The fate of the City of the Seven Hills, and more, rests on your speed. While you are engaged in battle, a great king will die and you cannot save him, no matter how hard you try, for his own horsemen will drive him into the clay. Still, your luck will hold, Roman, though you are closer in blood to the Hungvari than to Rome. Beware of hubris, Aetius. Although your son will sit beneath the feet of Ravenna's golden throne, your own ambitions will betray you, unless you have the will to change your plans. And you must be wary of a high-born servant who will turn against you.'

'If you seek my favour, healer, know that a prophecy such as this is guaranteed to win my enmity rather than my friendship. I will repeat the question, Myrddion-no-name. Will I defeat the Hun?'

'The Dread of the World will take the high ground, but you will have the higher. When you lay the great king to rest, do so where he falls, as a gift to your gods, and, perhaps, the last vulture will tarry a little. I cannot say for sure, as I am only a messenger, and not so beloved of the gods that I am permitted to know all their secrets. Yet I can say freely that you will defeat the Dread of the World.

'You are the last of the great generals of Rome, and, though you lack the strength of arms that is necessary to bring Attila to his knees, you will deny him his ambitions. The Princess Honoria will weep for lost chances.'

Aetius leaned back in his gilded chair with a deep sigh of satisfaction. Although he had little faith in soothsayers, he understood that the details of this prophecy would soon become common gossip and would give heart to his troops and their superstitious allies. Besides, this Celt seemed to know details that were not immediately obvious, even to the Goth kings.

'Blood and death! All I can see is heaped piles of carrion. The streams will run with blood.'

'And what will be my part in this battle?' Merovech demanded, leaning forward on his stool with eagerness.

A short silence followed, before Myrddion continued softly, 'And there you are, Merovech, the front of a line of kings who will forge these lands into a great nation. In future times you will be spoken of with reverence as the foundation stone of a great dynasty and glory will shroud the legends that surround your name.'

'Wonderful!' Merovech breathed, his face shining with awe and hope. 'You offer me eternity.'

'But it must be paid for with blood and suffering.' Myrddion's voice had the measured, sombre beat of a funerary bell. 'You will die before your time with your sword in your hand, but your son will win glorious victories in your name.'

'Then what does an early death matter? I will have eternity . . . and that is sufficient.'

Then the young healer's voice became slower and seemed to be dragged from a dank, dark place deep within his body. The listeners invoked their gods with superstitious dread at the tone and content of his last, dreadful prophecy.

'This land is already soaked in blood and will remain so for two thousand years to come. The dead of Tournai will be as nothing to the millions of men, women and children who will perish on this cursed land in conflicts that are yet to come. Great nations will struggle over it, but they will bleed so freely that they will perish, one by one. What Caesar began in suffering and melancholy will never be finished until the land is satisfied that her rapists have been repaid in full.'

Aetius snorted with anger when the healer accused the great Julian of being the root cause of so much suffering. Myrddion's eyes almost focused in that instant, but then a heavy veil seemed to fall over the healer's face and his eyes darkened once again.

'Be silent, Aetius the Patrician, for the river of time is clear and you are just another Roman caught up in its tides. This day, you will decide to cast the die that will save the land from despoilers, and you will succeed because the gods will strengthen your arm. But you will seek to bolster your family power beyond common sense or personal safety. You will place the knives in your assassins' hands out of hubris. Perhaps you wish to rule in Ravenna; or perhaps you hunger that a son of yours will reign in the fullness of time. Be very sure that such an ambition will not come to pass.

'And with your death, the last blow is dealt to the Roman

Empire. The schism will rip away any pretence that past glories will return and only the Golden Throne of Constantinople will endure – for a time! Your assassins will cut off the strong right arm of Rome, but men are fools and infinitely fragile. They will not count the cost until it is far too late. You might change your fate, Aetius of Ravenna, but you will not choose that safer path. The Scythian Plains are in your blood, so the taint of envy lies deeply coiled in your brain. My words will be forgotten, so your fate is sealed.'

'Enough, healer,' Aetius interrupted. 'I no longer desire to hear the sound of your cursed voice. Do not let me see you again.' The general's face was bloated with rage and his fists were clenched. He would have risen and struck out at Myrddion, but Merovech stopped him by gripping his toga.

'Never fear, my lords. If you think my message is bleak and unjust, I turn the river of time against myself as much as against you. I will be forced to serve you for a time, great general, and your house will make me pay deeply for this day of prophecy over many untold years. I will live alone, struggling to mitigate my faults and to save my own world from disaster. I, too, will know hubris and meddle in the affairs of the gods. I am their tool, as are you, and who can know what they intend for us? I will fail, as thoroughly as you will, for we are all servants of the Mother and the new god who comes from the east. Not one of us can escape the destiny that time has mapped out for us.'

Then Myrddion turned to his left on legs that seemed to be controlled by an invisible giant, as if the healer were a wooden doll in the hands of a monstrous child, until he turned his burning, inward gaze upon Cleoxenes, the emissary of the emperor of Constantinople.

'You, Cleoxenes, have seen the Hungvari, whom you call the Hun. Your master, Theodosius, paid a huge ransom to protect his lands from pillage during their inexorable march to the west. Never fear! Constantinople will stand long after Rome, Ravenna and all their works are pale memories of ruined columns and shattered temples. The walls will stand and a great church will rise beyond the winds of time and war, but the Golden Horn will see you washed away by the scimitar. Remember me, Cleoxenes, when I come to your halls.'

Cleoxenes took an involuntary step forward, but Myrddion had already turned on legs that were incapable of bending. The emissary swore in perfect Latin, its purity rendered shocking by the crudity that spilled uncensored from his lips. Then Cleoxenes crossed himself once more, and his lips moved in either silent prayer or an incantation of a charm against evil.

Within the halls of Merovech, Myrddion's ragged breathing was the only sound that broke the stillness. Then, just as the king stirred, preparing to speak, the healer gave a great cry, his eyes closed and his knees collapsed under him. His head struck the floor with a sharp crack and a trickle of blood snaked over the tiles.

'Then my master ordered me to bind your head wound, and lodge you in one of the guest chambers,' the servant finished. 'As you can see, I carried out his instructions.'

Myrddion was exploring the back of his skull where a small dressing covered a long split in the skin. 'You are an accurate and talented storyteller, Castor. I could almost see the audience chamber as you spoke. Thank you for caring for me. Unfortunately, I have no idea what much of the prophecy means. I suppose my words were the ramblings of delirium.'

Flavia had listened by the far wall where the shadows hid the expressions that passed over her mobile features, but as Castor left the room she moved forward into the light. 'Are any of your prophecies the truth, or simply the ramblings of a brain-sick dolt?' she asked, her face as stiff as a marble effigy.

'How can I say, my lady? I never remember what I have said after these fits take me. Nor do I court such visions. Merovech and Aetius forced me to speak or to face death. I am neither brain-sick nor foolish, and desire nothing more than to travel to Ravenna in peace. Regarding fratricide and vultures, I am as puzzled as you are.'

Flavia laughed softly, but her mirth had no humour in it. 'If Castor has recounted your words accurately, those references were clear for any Roman to understand. Surely you know the tale of Romulus and Remus?'

'They were the twins who founded Rome,' Myrddion answered blankly. 'I'm sorry, mistress, but I still don't understand.'

'Romulus slew his brother and was then granted a vision by the gods. He dreamed of twelve vultures that symbolised the ages that Roman power should endure. Aye, the best part of twelve centuries has passed since Romulus became a fratricide, and the soothsayers look for signs that the end of the Empire is coming.'

Flavia was so serious and so perturbed that Myrddion had to stifle a laugh. 'I see the reference to vultures, but what has Romulus to do with Attila? My words were ravings – they were of little relevance.'

'No! For pious Romans will tremble at the words of your prophecy. I am adept at listening at closed doors when my father entertains, so I can relay the news that Attila has killed his brother, Bleda. Just as Romulus slew Remus to purchase

Rome's twelve centuries of power, Attila has begun to create a myth for his own purposes. Why, I cannot imagine, for I am a mere woman, but my father sits alone on the terrace and broods over your prophecy, because you knew the greatest fear that assails Valentinian, emperor of the Western Empire.' Then she laughed, a sound reminiscent of the tinkling of bells. 'Ah! Perhaps you're no dolt at all, but a man who weaves the skeins of power and chance into a rope that will bind even the greatest men of the west to protect you. Perhaps you're worth my cultivation.'

She would have continued, but Castor returned to the room on silent feet and took the beaker from Myrddion's unresisting fingers.

'Lord Aetius bade me to inform you, healer, that you are now in the employ of King Merovech, who has welcomed your prophecy. When you are fully recovered, you are instructed to make yourself ready for departure to an undisclosed destination. General Aetius would also be obliged if you would refrain from being in his presence from this day onward.'

'My thanks to your master, Castor, but I don't intend to serve the king of the Salian Franks,' Myrddion snapped with a sudden flush of temper on both cheekbones. Avoiding the servant's eyes, he sat up gingerly and swung his feet to the floor.

'My master expected such a response, so a guardsman will ensure that you obey his instructions. Your prophecy is dangerous to both Merovech and Aetius, for Attila would use it to convince the gullible and the superstitious that the Roman Empire is doomed. When you leave this room, you will be escorted back to the guardhouse. I might add that Aetius implied that your apprentices and your servants will be held hostage to ensure your co-operation.'

'Shite!' Myrddion swore pungently in soldier Celt. Flavia laughed throatily, although how she could understand his crudities baffled the young healer. 'That being the case, I will take my leave,' he added stiffly. 'My apologies, mistress, if my prophecies caused you pain.' He sketched a rudimentary bow in Flavia's direction and limped to the door, boots in hand.

The audience was over.

When Myrddion entered the upper room of the guardhouse, accompanied by a very large and humourless Frankish warrior, five pairs of worried eyes looked up with varying degrees of surprise and pleasure.

'You live, master!' Cadoc exclaimed joyously, leaping to his feet and embracing the healer.

'You state the obvious, Cadoc. Have you heard our orders?'

'Aye, master,' Finn Truthteller said, rising slowly to examine his lord's bandaged head. 'Until we received them, we feared we would never see you again.'

'Then you know we must pack and be prepared for an immediate departure?'

'Aye. The preparations are already complete and we were awaiting you, my lord,' Cadoc explained, his eyes shining with relief. 'That Merovech moves fast when he chooses, and all that needs doing is to put the horses in the traces.'

'I'm sorry that we are brought to this pass through my affliction. With luck, Merovech will release us when the Hun is forced to retreat to the lands from whence he came. I hunger already to be free of Aetius and the allied kings.'

'At least you're alive, Master Myrddion,' Finn responded quietly. 'I never saw the like of your trance, and I never wish to see it again. I have never felt such terror as when you defied the general and told him that he was bringing his assassination down on his own head. I was sure we'd all be killed out of hand.'

Myrddion grimaced and anger stirred in his gut, like the sick feeling caused by sour wine. 'Perhaps our new masters are honourable men. Perhaps they're not. Only time will expose the truth. Meanwhile, Merovech, Aetius and the tribal kings intend to go to war, so there'll be red work for us to labour at. I would have wished for a better outcome, but beggars cannot be choosers and the general holds our lives in the palms of his hands.'

Once Truthteller was satisfied that Myrddion had suffered no lasting hurt, the party trooped down the stairs and waited while the ostlers led the unprotesting horses into the traces and secured their harnesses before climbing into the heavy wagons. The Frankish guardsmen were already mounted on large, skittish horses, but the entire group was forced to wait for nearly an hour until Merovech, his son and a contingent of the king's personal guard joined them. The warriors were immaculate, and even Gwylym had polished his plated leather cuirass until the embossed and engraved brass shone like gold.

By comparison with his men, Merovech was a subdued figure. His cuirass was obviously Roman in style, including the plated leather skirts that protected his loins and flanks. The king could have indulged his vanity with gilding, but heavy iron served him well enough without the need for ostentatious finery. A shirt of fine metal links protected his upper arms under the cuirass and greaves of iron were strapped over his leather breeches.

Only his horseflesh indicated his station. His mount was a showy grey whose dappled coat shone with grooming, its fine hocks lacking the fringe of long hair usually associated with horses of such great size and strength. The harness too was workmanlike but heavily decorated with rosettes of brass and bronze.

Merovech glanced across at Myrddion on the high seat of the wagon. His saturnine face creased into a grin of recognition and pleasure.

'Well, healer, you're still with us, although the night has almost fled while we awaited your recovery. The allied army is advancing, exactly as you predicted. Aetius will lead the legions, the Alans and the Burgundians to block Attila should he try to retreat. To the Franks and the Visigoths is allotted the privilege of lifting the siege of Aurelianum. The old Roman name for the city is rarely used now, for most folk call it Orléans. Have you heard of it?'

'Aye, my lord. I have heard of Aurelianum, although I didn't know it was besieged. We would have stumbled into a hornets' nest of Hun cavalry had your noble son, Childeric, not brought us to you.'

Merovech chuckled. 'True, healer! And think what we'd have lost, if Childeric had not been such a clever servant of his father. I'd never have heard you prophesy, Demon Seed, and I'd have been the poorer for that silence. Where we are going, your expertise will be needed, for your prophecy of blood is about to come true. By the way, couriers have arrived to warn us that King Theodoric plans to join us at Aurelianum.'

Myrddion blinked in surprise. 'Why would the emperor of the Eastern Empire at Constantinople come here, my lord? I don't understand.'

Merovech chuckled and slapped his thigh so hard that his grey stallion danced and pulled at the reins, its eyes wide with nervousness. 'Your face! You're confused, young man, for this Theodoric is the king of the Visigoths and rules vast lands to the south and onwards into Hispania. He's not the eastern emperor, although they do have similar names. No doubt King Theodoric's father had great ambitions for his son.'

Myrddion flushed with embarrassment. 'I will pray for the king's safety then,' he answered evenly, although his heart sank. 'I've been informed that part of my prophecy concerns the death of a great ruler, although I have little knowledge of the Visigoth tribe.'

'Theodoric and his warriors are our greatest and most valued allies. Without them, Attila will strip Gaul bare and turn us into more of his vassals.' Merovech looked glum for a moment but his natural ebullience quickly reasserted itself. 'The levies have been ordered into the battle lines, but for the moment Aurelianum is our target, as you suggested. We ride in haste, following Aetius, who has already departed with the legions. May the gods keep you safe, healer, for you are of vital importance to our plans.' Then, with an imperious wave of his hand, Merovech and his guard clattered away into the fraying darkness that was fast retreating before another clear morning.

The countryside west of Châlons was beautiful, and for the first time Myrddion relaxed on the high seat of the wagon and enjoyed the panorama around him. In the distance, a cloud of dust indicated that a large force of cavalry and foot soldiers was on the move. Long rows of poplars grew like golden-green fingers, pointing upwards into the vivid morning sky. The land was rich and civilised but empty, for the peasants had disappeared with the first signs of imminent warfare.

The wagons were, perforce, much slower-moving than the mobile contingents of cavalry and foot soldiers that passed them on the road leading westward to Aurelianum. To protect the small convoy from any groups of marauding Huns, Merovech had ordered a detachment of Frankish cavalry to accompany the healers, and, with pleasure, Myrddion recognised Captus leading the guard. When they paused at dawn to water the horses, Myrddion beckoned the large, rawboned Frank to join him.

'I haven't forgotten that tooth of yours, Captus. I'll see to drawing it when we rest for the night. Does it pain you?'

The warrior shifted uneasily on his saddle, and Myrddion recognised the anxiety in his eyes. No matter how courageous they were, most men feared the extraction of teeth more than the pain from the diseased tooth itself.

'Aye, it does. But I have no wish to miss the siege of Aurelianum because of a toothache.'

'All the more reason why it should be drawn before the infection poisons your blood.' Then Myrddion grinned engagingly, having divined Captus's real source of discomfort. 'Don't be concerned, Captus, for I'm not a sorcerer or a demon who will attempt to ensnare you with spells. I'm a healer, and I know that a man with a bad toothache is not effective in the field. A little pain now will save greater agonies later.'

'I'm not afraid of having a tooth pulled out,' Captus snapped, his manhood insulted by Myrddion's slur on his courage.

'Good! Then I'll see you at dusk, good master Captus.'

Cadoc flicked the reins on the flanks of the sturdy carthorses and the journey recommenced.

At dusk, on the banks of a slow-flowing stream, Captus arrived at the wagons like a prisoner being led to execution. The Frank didn't exactly drag his feet but his bowed shoulders and haunted eyes showed his reluctance to endure the treatment more clearly than mere words. Hiding a smile, Myrddion presented the Frankish warrior with a cup of wine into which he had poured a few drops of poppy juice.

'You need not distrust my potion, Captus, for I have no need for poisons. This draught will simply dull the pain and ensure that you sleep soundly after the extraction. Now Finn and Cadoc will hold you still. Sit yourself down on this stool.'

Captus endured the extraction like a true warrior, although his eyes grew round with apprehension when he saw the size of Myrddion's surgical pliers. Fortunately, the rotten tooth did not splinter and break off in their grip, so Myrddion was not obliged to cut into the gum to remove the root. With a sudden gush of blood, the canine pulled free and the young healer pressed a clean pad of cotton over the empty socket.

'Swill your mouth out with a beaker of water to which you've added a handful of salt. The saline will keep the wound clean until it closes in a few days' time. A glass or two of wine wouldn't hurt either, as long as you rinse your mouth afterwards.'

Captus gazed up at the healer from his stool, his expression one of exquisite relief.

'My thanks, Master Myrddion, for my mouth scarcely hurts at all. Salty water? Well, who'd have thought such a common thing would be a cleanser? Aye, I'll follow your advice.'

For three more days, the healers and their escort travelled the road leading to Aurelianum, while smoke on the horizon suggested that a pitched battle was being fought somewhere ahead of them. On the morning of the fourth day, with Aurelianum almost in view, a huge cloud of dust to the north spoke mutely of the movement of a huge contingent of horsemen.

'Hun or Frank?' Cadoc asked, but Myrddion shrugged. They could only discover what was happening by reaching Aurelianum at speed. For the first time, Myrddion grew impatient at the slow pace of the wagons, for his vanity made him curious about the accuracy of his predictions.

Aurelianum appeared out of a haze of thick black smoke as the noonday sun dazzled the healers' eyes. A fair-sized city, situated at the confluence of rivers on a wide green plain, it had been besieged for over two weeks, but its walls were strong and water was plentiful within their confines. More important, its citizens knew what fate awaited them if they were defeated, whether they fought or surrendered, and the knowledge stiffened their spines. A large contingent of Salian Franks was also trapped within Aurelianum's walls, and the presence of these trained fighting men gave heart to the populace. For the first time, Attila faced a determined, well-trained and entrenched enemy.

Outside the walls, Myrddion saw the remains of a large encampment where many thousands of cavalry had left scarred sod and the dung, detritus and dead cooking fires of a force that had settled in for a protracted siege. His eyes swept across the huge swath of damage caused by the long picket lines of an army that easily outnumbered the forces available to Merovech and Aetius.

As he stared down the roadway, he saw plentiful evidence of a hasty departure. Off to his right, a series of cooking hearths still held iron pots hanging over simple tripods. No warrior would willingly abandon such essential tools of a cavalryman's life. Squinting against the glare, Myrddion could see a wide slash of churned earth where many mounted men had formed up and departed for the northeast. It required very little imagination to picture the hasty collection of food and fodder bags that could be slung quickly over saddles. Yet, for all the speed that was evident in every foot- and hoof-print, the retreat had been disciplined and orderly.

The Huns had finally gained entrance to the city through the use of a battering ram, but the Salian Franks and the Burgundians had counter-attacked while the Hun warriors were trapped within the town's streets and alleyways. This time, fully trained warriors had been committed to the battle, instead of the women, children and old men who had defended the towns that fell to Attila's forces earlier in the campaign. Aurelianum was no Cambrai that would make a token effort to protect itself. Aurelianum knew that defeat would result in an ugly death.

A vicious, hard-fought battle had ensued, although the Franks lacked the numbers to crush the Hun horde totally. After fierce hand-to-hand fighting through the narrow lanes of the city, the greater part of Attila's force managed to escape their entrapment. Then, a highly disciplined and dangerous force once more, they made a strategic retreat to the east to link up with the other half of Attila's army who had taken the towns of Treviri, Divodunum, Reims and Worms. Somewhere north of Châlons, Attila, the Dread of the World, now waited to meet the armies of Aetius.

Instinctively, Merovech knew that Aetius and his allies would be hard pressed to defeat the juggernaut once Attila's forces were reunited. However, for now the allies could celebrate a miraculous victory. Aurelianum had been saved from annihilation and the Hungvari had proved to be human and fallible.

The healers' tents were raised just outside the city gates as quickly as the Frankish guard could assemble them. Then Cadoc lit the fires necessary to boil the surgical tools while Captus organised his men to ferry the injured into the makeshift hospital. But before the first casualties arrived Merovech appeared and greeted Myrddion cheerfully. He was accompanied by a soot-blackened Childeric, whose face was enlivened by a ferocious white smile.

'Aurelianum is ours, although it cost us many good men. Still, Attila has now been warned that we'll not sit on our thumbs while he rapes our land. We've captured part of his baggage train and the gold he filched from our cities, so this battle has hurt him more than it has damaged us. It was a fortunate day when you came to Châlons and gave heart to my warriors.'

Myrddion's face must have expressed his confusion, so Childeric explained that Aetius had assembled the allied troops and revealed that the gods had promised a victory to the Romans and the Franks. This news, coming as it did from such a pragmatic and experienced general, had spread among the warriors like Greek fire, firming their courage and strengthening their arms.

'Don't be surprised if my men treat you like a godling. Any man who correctly predicts the failure of a leader as fearsome as Attila is magical in the eyes of ordinary men.' Merovech clapped the young healer on the back with sufficient force to make Myrddion stumble and strode off, leaving the sound of a cheerful whistle in his wake.

Childeric paused for a moment. 'Stay out of Aetius's way, healer,' he warned softly. 'It's rumoured that the general wishes to broker an advantageous marriage between his son Gaudentius and Valentinian's daughter, Placidia. Even if anything should happen to weaken Aetius's reputation, his ambitions will only be thwarted for a short time, for he is a patient man. And he is very annoyed with you for allowing his secret plans to become common knowledge.'

'I'll take care, my lord, as should your noble father. I wish no harm to come to him, in all truth, for I'm not responsible for what I say when the fits come upon me. I would not earn the enmity of your house at any price.'

Childeric frowned briefly and then nodded at the healer. 'Father prefers a short and glorious life to one spent rusting away into feeble old age. What will come, will come.'

'You're a generous man, my lord,' Myrddion responded with a low, diplomatic bow.

'Just do your job, healer. I will be content if you save as many of my men as possible.'

As Childeric strode away, his face impassive and his body held stiffly erect, Myrddion wondered at the weight the young man carried on those square shoulders. He was sure the prince understood that his youth and freedom would end on the hour that his father died.

This young man isn't like other princelings, Myrddion thought, hungry for power and prestige. He's much stronger and more astute than most tyros with potential. But I pray that we have escaped long before Childeric comes to the throne, for he will never permit us to leave him if he feels indebted to us. That young man knows the value of healers who enter his employ.

Throughout that long day, and those that followed, Myrddion had occasion to be grateful to the long-dead Vortigern for the experience of battle injuries that had been forced upon the young healer and his inexperienced apprentices. The baptism of fire they suffered at Tomen-y-Mur and Glevum served them well at Aurelianum. From the moment the first casualty was carried into the leather tents, three healers and three nurses worked as one, although it was a struggle to treat over two hundred seriously wounded men and an even larger number who carried lesser hurts. The steady flow of patients on makeshift stretchers and the walking, stumbling injured who came to the leather tents would have been too many to save had it not been for the efforts of Captus and the guard. Captus hunted up several women from Aurelianum who were skilled in herbal lore, and begged, borrowed or stole the ingredients needed for salves, poultices and potions. And he set his guardsmen to work: chopping wood, stoking the fires, cutting grass for sleeping pallets, preparing meals and providing the muscle that ensured the efficiency of the makeshift hospital.

Myrddion worked naked to the waist with his chest protected by a large leather apron, but even so he was soon drenched in blood. Scrupulous always, the young man insisted on sluicing himself clean after each surgery, and he refused to reuse his small scalpels and needles for successive patients. Although Captus often became impatient when he saw the long lines of waiting men and women, he had only to gaze into Myrddion's intent, black eyes, which never seemed to doubt that he could find a way to save the lives and limbs of those who awaited his ministrations and to bow to his greater experience. Standing on earth turned to bloody mud, the healer was impressive in his deftness, his stubbornness and his deep, heartfelt empathy.

'You have worked long enough, Master Myrddion!' Captus stated baldly when the daylight had fled and the oil lamps were making surgery a slow, difficult task. 'Your operations can't be successful if you are half-blind with weariness.'

'Could you tell that young man with an arrowhead

embedded in his calf that he must risk gangrene because I need to sleep?' Myrddion asked gruffly, before smiling to show his contrition at the response. 'I thank you for your aid, Captus, because we couldn't have managed without you and your men, but I'll not rest until the most seriously wounded are treated. They require my immediate attention. I can always sleep later.'

'Most of them will die anyway,' Captus muttered, and then he also relented. 'At least let me give you some help. I've butchered enough beasts on my father's lands before I came into Clodio's service. I might be of some use to you.'

Myrddion managed to raise another tired smile, although his shoulders were rounded with exhaustion. 'Are you suggesting that my trade is little more than butchery?' he joked. 'I suppose we both trade in blood.' Then, because willing hands were very valuable, he relented and pointed to the pool of lamplight where his apprentices were binding the wounds of warriors who were not severely injured. 'You can assist Cadoc and Finn, by all means. Both are adept at their task and you can help them to stitch and poultice wounds. An extra pair of hands will always be useful.'

Then, without taking his eyes from a gaping wound that still oozed blood from a young warrior's chest, Myrddion halted Captus with a brief question.

'I haven't seen any wounded Huns. It seems strange to me that Attila would delay his retreat to collect his wounded warriors.'

'He left them behind, which is not his usual practice,' Captus replied drily. 'We killed them. We couldn't allow recuperating Hungvari to remain free within our camp, for they'd cut our throats as soon as they could stand upright. And what of their allies? They're far worse than the Hungvari.

Don't weep for traitorous Burgundians or Goths, for men who raise their swords against their brethren deserve to perish. And we were merciful: we did not torture them for information.'

Myrddion winced, but made no protest. He understood the realities of warfare where prisoners became liabilities to their captors.

His patient's wound bubbled blood as the warrior struggled to breathe, so Myrddion placed a pad over the ugly gash and indicated to Bridie that a poppy draught should be prepared.

'Is it bad, Master Myrddion?' the young man wheezed through bluish lips.

'It's not so very bad as wounds go, lad. I've seen worse by far. I expect you'll be able to rest soon.'

Captus saw that Myrddion's eyes were very sad, and recognised the ambiguities in his reassurances. This patient would surely die. Then, as he gazed down at the youth, who had sighed with satisfaction in response to Myrddion's promise, he understood that healers suffer as much as any warrior.

When Myrddion finally sought his bed well after midnight, Captus was still sluicing down tables and boiling instruments. The groans of the wounded and dying chased the healer into sleep; indeed, so great was his exhaustion that he found even the cries of those in an extremity of pain to be as lulling as Finn's soft singing. Drowning in the mindless languor that comes at the very edge of oblivion, Myrddion dived deeper into the nothingness that engulfed him.

MYRDDION'S EYE-WITNESS RECORD OF THE BATTLE OF THE CATALAUNIAN PLAIN

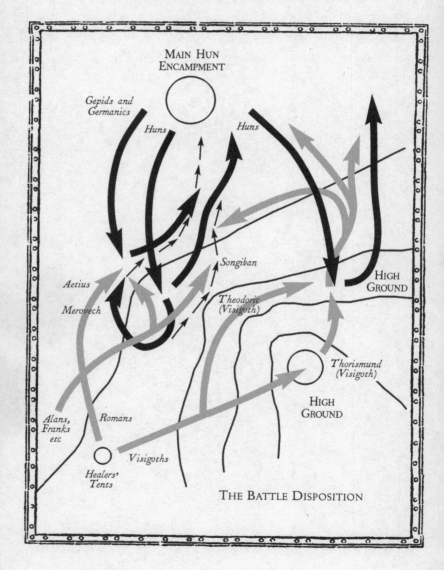

THE BATTLE DISPOSITION

CHAPTER VI

THE CATALAUNIAN PLAIN

> Those whose wounds drove them to slake their
> parching thirst drank water mingled in gore. In
> their wretched plight they were forced to drink
> what they thought was the blood they had poured
> from their own wounds.
>
> Jordanes, *Getica*, 40.208

Cadoc shook Myrddion's shoulder just as a narrow shaft of
sunlight angled through the trees and struck his opening
eyes. The healer swatted at the air as if he could drive the
sudden dazzle away like an annoying insect.

'King Merovech is here to see you with King Theodoric of
the Visigoths, master. They leave today to join Aetius on the
Catalaunian Plain. We have been instructed to finish patching
up the wounded here and make arrangements for the people
of Aurelianum to take care of them. Our orders are clear.
Pack up our tents, and follow behind the king at best speed.
Aetius has need of us.'

The words were a jumble in Myrddion's head and he took
an unusually long time to decipher their meaning. Although

he had slept for four hours, deeply and dreamlessly, his eyes still felt gritty and his brain seemed incapable of retaining any complicated information.

'Give me a moment, Cadoc. Shite, I feel as if I've been dragged through a hedge backwards. Is there any cold water? Perhaps I might come to my senses if I dowse my head.'

'Perhaps if you didn't work yourself half to death for most of the night . . . oh, wait here. I'll fetch some water and try to head King Merovech off for a few minutes.'

Cadoc hurried away and Myrddion staggered to his feet. With an exclamation of disgust, he realised that blood had dried between his toes and now caked his nails in a dark red, muddy paste, exactly like dried mud. He had washed his hands scrupulously before he had tumbled into his pallet, but he had been too exhausted to bathe all over. Now he was aware of smeared bloodstains on his lower body where his leather apron had failed to provide protection.

As soon as Cadoc appeared with the water, Myrddion poured half of it over his head and then thrust both feet into the pliant leather pail. With a scrap of rag, he began to scrub . . . and scrub . . . and scrub. The water was soon stained a rusty brown.

'Master, there are two kings who await your presence. Can't you wash later?'

Without bothering to reply, Myrddion finished scouring his feet and legs and then sluiced them with the last of the water. As quickly as he could, with Cadoc's assistance, he dried himself, threw on his last clean robe and breeches, and pulled a hasty comb through his long hair before securing it with a narrow thong at the base of his neck.

'Will I pass their inspection?'

'Well, at least you're awake.'

Guiltily, Myrddion glanced towards the tent where the seriously ill patients were housed. The widows were already hard at work, feeding their charges and coaxing them to drink a little water.

'How are the patients? Can you deal with them for a time?'

'Aye, master! Why should you trouble to ask?'

With a feeling that he had somehow insulted his apprentice, Myrddion took the time to clasp his friend's shoulders in a sincere gesture of thanks before hurrying away from the wagons to where Merovech was cooling his heels impatiently in company with a tall, ascetic-looking man wearing a finely-knit woollen robe over extremely fine body armour of barbarian workmanship. Before addressing his visitors, the healer dropped to his knees and bowed.

'How may I serve you, my lord?'

'Rise from your knees, Myrddion of Segontium,' Merovech ordered. 'We can't speak to a man if we can't see his face.'

Myrddion obeyed, and surreptitiously examined the expressions on the faces of the two rulers. Merovech seemed almost boyish with enthusiasm, itching to take to his horse to pursue the Hun until they had been driven out of his lands, thus cleansing his honour of the stain caused by the defeats at Tournai, Cambrai and the other ruined towns. His eyes glowed and his skin bloomed with health and youth that belied his forty years.

But King Theodoric of the Visigoths was a different cut of man entirely. Neither old nor young, neither thickset nor unusually slender, Theodoric viewed the world through weary, cynical eyes. His elaborate armour might be gilded and polished to mirror brightness, but, surprisingly, he appeared uncomfortable with a huge sword slung around his waist. Myrddion had been told that Theodoric was a very able warrior and a brilliant strategist with a wild streak of reckless courage, but the man who gazed around Myrddion's camp seemed too introverted and measured for such a reputation. The king's deep-set eyes gleamed with a keen intelligence, so Myrddion peered into the closed face with a healer's curiosity. With disappointment, he noted the early signs of dissipation in Theodoric's skin, which had the open, slightly spotted pores of a heavy drinker. The Visigoth bore Myrddion's calculated scrutiny with the world-weariness of a man who has been weighed down with extreme expectations for all his adult life.

'Lord Theodoric,' Myrddion began, unsure of how to address such an important king. 'May you continue in robust health and rule your subjects well, free from the scourge of Attila and his tribe.'

'Whatever you are, you're the master of a pretty sentence and a well-crafted compliment, healer. Perhaps that explains why one so young is able to rule a field hospital. You may show me through your tents, so I can judge your skills for myself.'

Myrddion groaned inwardly and Merovech stifled a grumble of impatience. No matter how tiresome such tours might be, both men knew that Aetius's major ally would have his way, for he was flanked by a small contingent of the feared Visigoth Guard, soldiers who protected their master zealously. They had killed traitors aplenty over the years, for the king controlled a vast land that stretched from Gaul to Hispania, an expanse that had often seduced pretenders into chancing their luck at assassination. Aetius would support Theodoric of Hispania in almost any endeavour; so important was the Visigoth lord to the alliance. Neither Merovech nor any of the barbarian kings would dare to speak against Theodoric or insult him in any way.

'You have but to ask, my lord, and I will be happy to obey. My apprentices, my servants and my guard will be caring for the bodily needs of our patients as we speak, and I would normally be dressing wounds and assessing the status of each man in our care.'

'We'll not keep you from your duties for long,' Theodoric replied in a soft voice. 'You labour hard if the shadows around your eyes are any indication of your zeal. How late did you work over that table?' He pointed at the bloodstained folding bench that had been constructed to spare Myrddion's spine. The wood had been soaked in gore so often that no amount of careful scrubbing by Bridie or Brangaine could cleanse the wood of its pungent tint, as obvious as an open wound.

'The moon was down when the last patient was put to bed, my lord.'

'He survived your ministrations then. Rare! Very rare! I have seen the work of your ilk more often than I care to remember. Only one healer ever gave me any real confidence, a Jew called Isaac who currently serves Valentinian in Rome. You may use my name should you ever meet him. Isaac saves as many as he kills, although he shuns the acclaim of the world.'

Myrddion felt a tingle in the back of his mind and filed the name away into his capacious memory. 'My thanks for the recommendation, Lord Theodoric. I'm on my way to the Middle Sea in a search for knowledge from healers such as your Isaac.'

'How many servants do you have at your disposal?'

'I have two apprentices who assist with surgery as well as

treating minor wounds. Three widows travel with us to care for our patients once they start to recover. All five are loyal and able, but we are stretched to breaking point, my lord. Should future, larger battles require our services, many warriors will die because we are too few to save the flood of wounded.'

Theodoric's eyes narrowed to gimlet points and even the good-natured Merovech snorted his displeasure. Servants were not encouraged to charge their masters with accusations of callousness, especially towards the plight of casualties on the battlefield. Like the boy who still lurked under the young man he had become, Myrddion found himself gulping at his temerity.

Theodoric scanned the tents and visibly counted the century or so of men who lay or sat around in various stages of recuperation. He stared at his muddy boots for a moment and then offered his hand to the disconcerted healer. 'My hand on it, Myrddion of Segontium! I will send my personal physician, Vechmar, to your tents to assist you, along with his servants and women. Like you, he chooses to use widows and camp followers for basic labour. I trust that King Merovech will also supply what resources lie within his powers.' A quick glance under lowered, crêpey eyelids elicited an immediate agreement from the Salian king. 'Now that your immediate needs are supplied, you may show me how you save as many as you kill.'

For the life of him, Myrddion couldn't tell if the Hispanic king was joking or not. With mixed feelings, he ushered the kings and their suspicious bodyguards deeper into the larger tent. The apprentices had already drawn up the leather sides to allow the free circulation of air and light, so those warriors who were conscious saw the nature and quality of their visitors at a glance. Men bowed or abased themselves, where possible, and the air was suddenly dense with the low, baritone hum of murmuring male voices.

Cadoc came towards them bearing a large basket of dry wrappings; it seemed that Bridie hadn't slept until every used rag in the field hospital had been boiled and hung to dry over any available shrub. Quick to respond, Cadoc discarded his burden and dropped to his knees to pay homage to the regal visitors.

'Rise, good man, and continue with your duties,' Theodoric ordered rather stiffly. Myrddion wondered if he was embarrassed at displays of bowing and grovelling. 'Is this lad one of your apprentices?' the Visigoth asked in a voice that seemed thready now that he was out of the sunlight, as if some vital bodily element leached out of him in the dimness of the tent.

'Aye, lord, Cadoc ap Cadwy has been my loyal assistant for two years. We met at the encampment of King Vortigern, High King of the Britons, after a vicious battle with the king's son. As you can see, burn scars caused the tendons in his shoulder to contract and restricted his arm movements. His injuries put an end to his usefulness as a warrior, but he has become my strong right hand. He makes great progress and will soon become a healer himself.'

'The lands of the Britons seem much like mine – sons rise against fathers and the kinship of blood matters little when a throne is at stake,' Theodoric murmured in a voice so soft that Myrddion had to strain to hear the words. The king's voice was bleak, but his cynical eyes carried a sheen of something that was vulnerable and sad. Is a kingdom worth this pain and loss of trust? Theodoric obviously has faith in no one, the healer thought suddenly, and he drinks to excess to keep his demons at bay in the long watches of the night. Is anything worth such a half-life?

'Do your scars pain you, Cadoc ap Cadwy?' Theodoric asked, switching his attention disconcertingly from master to apprentice. 'They appear painful to me, but I know nothing of healing. May I inspect them?'

Cadoc allowed Theodoric to run a hesitant palm over the raised cicatrices that covered the apprentice's neck and shoulder. Though the king recoiled from the ragged, hairless skin, he asked Cadoc to move his arm so that he could see for himself the full extent of the apprentice's incapacitation. Then, in a very human gesture, he pulled Cadoc's sleeve gently over the old scars.

'Do you regret the loss of your warrior trade, Cadoc ap Cadwy?'

Cadoc's eyes never left King Theodoric's pale face, although a brief flicker of embarrassment slid across his eyes.

'I once took bodies apart for my bread, lord king. But I am now learning how to put them back together. Which trade is the fairest labour for a man, my lord? I am proud to serve a master who is the most skilled healer in all of Britain.'

Theodoric acknowledged Cadoc's pride, but the cynical veil clouded his eyes once more and Myrddion marvelled that a man of such power had decided that feelings of sympathy were signs of weakness.

For an hour, Theodoric talked to those patients who were conscious and asked pertinent and intelligent questions about poultices, painkilling and Myrddion's obsession with cleanliness. The healer gave detailed, considered answers to each query, earning Merovech's gratitude for his courtesy and the care he took to fully explain his trade.

'What are these evil humours that you describe so vaguely, healer? Surely something that cannot be seen lacks the power to harm a healthy man?'

Myrddion treated Theodoric's question seriously and replied as carefully as he could, although he scarcely knew the answer himself.

'I wish I knew, my lord. If I did, I would be the greatest healer in this world, and I would have discovered the means to defeat death itself. But as my craft now stands, we know that something causes plague, lung disease, gangrene and brain sickness, and that these curses are invariably fatal, but we cannot see with the naked eye what causes these ailments. We use the words evil humours, but we are too ignorant to know if that description is accurate. But I do know, in the case of open wounds, that cleanliness increases the patient's chances of survival, even if I don't know why.'

Theodoric nodded reflectively. 'Aye, I understand. Sometimes it's enough to know that a strategy works, even if we're ignorant of the reasons for its success. The ancients built bridges that span great rivers in magical feats of engineering. Today, the builders' skills are forgotten, but we still use their roads and bridges freely. And speaking of roads, healer, your services will soon be needed in other places and the time fast approaches when you must leave. I will ensure that your patients are cared for within Aurelianum, and you may expect my servants to begin moving them within the hour. You will plead that you are needed here, but the battle that is coming will dwarf anything that you have experienced in the past. Yes, some of these men will die because you have left them, but countless others will perish without your skills after we have come to grips with Attila on the Catalaunian Plain. I am sorry to give you no choice in this matter, but kings cannot rule with their hearts – only their heads and their muscle. We leave at noon, so you must pack and prepare to join our baggage train.'

'But I need more supplies, more bandages, more everything, if I am to be effective.'

'Send Cadoc to my guard with your list and they will strip Aurelianum to supply your needs. My physician and his assistants will attend upon you shortly. One other matter comes to mind, and I trust that you will not take offence at my words. I believe you need a nomen to engender trust in those with whom you serve. The lack of a father in your name doesn't shame you in my eyes, but I am not the world. Your birthplace serves to display your heritage, but I would prefer that you select a name that gives you more dignitas. You are the healer for the Western Allies, and your name should reflect your status among our warriors.'

Then Theodoric turned away and re-joined Merovech. Wrong-footed and baffled, Myrddion was left with nothing to say.

The journey back to Châlons was long and tedious, and the wagons groaned under the weight of herbs, bandages, unguents and potions that Aurelianum had donated gladly to the kings. Myrddion preferred to make his own supplies, but time was now a scarce resource, so he knew he must make do with whatever was on hand. Already, fresh bunches of leafy simples hung from the wooden supports of the wagon's leather cover, swinging and drying with every jolt of the huge wooden wheels.

Three other wagons had joined the same cavalcade. Vechmar and his servants had arrived at the camp as Myrddion was preparing to depart, and the Celt met Theodoric's personal physician with open curiosity.

Vechmar was a lean, dark man whose race would have been almost impossible to guess from his saturnine face. The new arrival spoke very little, but even a cursory glance at his fastidiously clean hands allayed Myrddion's concern. But Vechmar was careful to explain that their alliance was only temporary, for he was devoted to Theodoric and intended to serve the king's house for life.

'I understand, Vechmar. While I serve no master willingly, I applaud devotion such as yours. Together we will save many lives.'

Vechmar's lips twisted with open contempt, leaving Myrddion to wonder what he had done or said to offend him.

'I will obey my master, but I tell you honestly that I am embarrassed to labour with a beardless youth. However, I have seen your handiwork, so I hope we can rub together for the coming battle. After that our paths need never cross again. I am speaking bluntly because you deserve to know the measure of my skills and feelings, for I am shamed that my king puts inordinate trust in a foreigner who has no standing in these lands. I will treat those men who come to me in my own way and you are free to do the same.'

Myrddion chewed over this crude appraisal and decided that he was not obliged to like the Spanish healer, merely to work with him. 'That's fair enough. Extra hands are vital and one field hospital will work much better than two.'

As the road unwound before them, Myrddion's thoughts returned to Theodoric's suggestion of a name. Vechmar's opinion of him had stung his sensitivities and he accepted that Theodoric understood the ways of fallible men far more clearly than he did. So, as the wooden wheels of the wagons provided a soporific background to his deliberations, he created and discarded name after name as being either foolish or pretentious. Finally, because he acknowledged that his true life had begun when King Vortigern had tried to sacrifice him at Dinas Emrys under the white brows of Cymru's mountains, he decided on a name that would last for the rest of his life, or until he chose another.

'I've decided, Cadoc, that I will accept the advice of King Theodoric and adopt a more imposing name than I have previously used. I have decided to assume the nomen of Myrddion Emrys of Segontium. At the age of ten years, while King Vortigern's prisoner, I learned what kind of man I would become at that cursed place, so it is probably fitting that it should remain with me always.'

Cadoc shuddered, because he remembered that windswept fortress, dark with rain and dried blood, too well to ever forget it. But if his master chose to call himself a godling or even a fool, Cadoc would accept his decision.

As the weary journey drew towards its completion, the wagons joined the baggage train of an immense army that had been swelled with Aetius's legions, Alan cavalry and the untried Sarmatian warriors. Rumour among the tribes suggested that Aetius had no trust in their king, Sangiban, who had earned a reputation for changing sides whenever there was profit in doing so. In this army, all sensible men were wary around the Sarmatian warriors.

The sight of Roman soldiers fascinated Myrddion whenever he saw them during their forced march to their marshalling point north of Châlons. Too young to have memories of the legions in Britain, he had tried to imagine the appearance of these fearsome and almost invincible warriors, and he found the reality very unsatisfying.

A century of Roman warriors, led by a hard-bitten centurion, marched past the wagons not far from Châlons, giving Myrddion his first close view of their famed discipline. To his surprise, the legionaries were very dark, very short and surprisingly thickset under the daunting packs they carried on their backs. A rectangular shield was used as the basis for each pack, which consisted of a bedroll, a spade, a water skin, a small supply of food and the usual flint, tinderbox and whetstone. Myrddion marvelled anew at Roman organisation that made each man self-sufficient.

Taken individually, the soldiers rarely stood higher than five foot six inches and many men were much shorter. Their serviceable armour and boiled leather protection was weighty, as were the compact thrusting spear, the narrow dagger and the sword that added considerably to the weight each man carried. Myrddion was puzzled by those swords, which lacked the crosspiece of the tribal weapons, but were longer than the Roman blades he had become familiar with in Britain. When he voiced his surprise at the weaponry, Cadoc shrugged with a soldier's cynicism.

'The Romans never waste anything, master, least of all useful weapons. The short sword is probably old-fashioned, given that the Empire has changed, but a weapon is a weapon, and the army won't throw away a serviceable piece of kit. Why would they have sent new swords to Britain? What does it matter, anyway?'

'It doesn't, Cadoc, but I'm curious.'

'It'll be the death of you one day, master,' Cadoc joked.

'I doubt it, friend. Curiosity has kept me alive more times than I care to count.'

'They're runts, master! What good can those men possibly be against the wild Hun cavalry?' Cadoc asked, his lip curling with disdain. 'A strong breeze would knock them over.'

'I'm not so sure, Cadoc. Look at their legs. Solid muscle! Look at the pace they are setting. Judging by the sun, they've been marching for five hours at that pace, but they've hardly broken a sweat. And they march in formation, eating and drinking on the move. If these men are any guide, it explains why Caesar was able to muster his legions faster than his enemies.'

'But they're so short!' Cadoc repeated, his voice almost shrill with disbelief.

'Those swords and spears depend on close contact where height doesn't matter. The size of those shields is interesting too, for they would cover most of their bodies in a defensive position, while the longer swords give them greater reach. I can see now why the Romans ruled their world.'

'Well, I've yet to be convinced,' Cadoc replied in a sulky voice, as if Myrddion's praise for the Romans was somehow a slight on the prowess of the Celts. Myrddion was forced to abandon the conversation with regret.

Summer had come, along with days of sunshine so bright and vivid that Myrddion's eyes were painful from the glare and the dust that rubbed his eyeballs raw. Ripening grain stalks raised their heads towards the sky and sunflowers followed the daily path of the sun through the skies with large yellow faces that were pregnant with seed in their deep, velvet-black centres. The occasional clusters of cottages were empty of both humans and livestock, leaving the land trapped in an eerie silence.

The Catalaunian Plain was wide and almost completely flat, except for a long ridge whose summit, though not high, dominated the agricultural land below it. Streams crossed the ridge, some dry in the hotter months. As night fell and the allied armies set their cooking fires alight, the vast number of men, almost thirty-thousand in total, created a midnight blanket that was dotted with countless small red flowers of flame.

At a vantage point below the left horn of the ridgeline, the allied kings gathered to hear the Roman general elaborate on his plan of action. None of the kings seriously chose to challenge Aetius for the overall control of the battle that was to come. Square, stolid and professional, Flavius Aetius radiated the calm, workmanlike confidence of a man who made his living from the trade of death. Moreover, Aetius bore an almost supernatural luck. In the failing years of the Empire and the new prominence of second-rate minds, Aetius flamed like a comet with his brilliance, his intellect and his capacity for lightning-fast strategies that devastated any enemy so foolish as to chance his arm against the Empire's most successful general.

As he looked up at the ridgeline, Aetius saw, with a lurch in his breast, that the Hun had taken part of the high ground. He pointed to the firefly lights of cooking fires clearly visible on the right horn of the ridge.

'See? Attila has always had the luck of the chaos-lords and, if I'm honest, the skills to capitalise on any landscape that presents itself when battle is imminent. Look to the north!' He pointed towards the spot where the Hun's forces were assembled. 'That's Attila's main encampment over there. He expects us to come roaring onto the plain like tyros and then he'll loose an attack from the heights against our rear. If we were so foolish as to act impetuously, he'd crack us like lice between his thumbnails.' Aetius began to curse like a foot soldier. 'Unfortunately, they beat us to the ridgeline, damn them to the tortures of the gods. But it's not a disaster for us. Given Attila's mistake in concentrating on just a part of the heights, we are still in a position to capitalise on his errors.'

He smiled, and turned to face Theodoric. 'My lord?'

'Aye, general,' the king responded, as he stared into the darkness with a secret smile already wreathing his face. 'What do you require of me?'

'Oblige me by taking the left horn of the ridge, in silence if possible. We will send a contingent to join you, as will Sangiban and Merovech. The bulk of your cavalry and foot soldiers will wait behind the ridge. Let's give Attila something to worry about.' Aetius grinned like a ruffian, exposing worn, yellowed teeth like a sound old horse.

'As I am ordered to take the ridge, it's as good as taken,' King Theodoric agreed softly. 'But why at night? Would the heights be so advantageous to us, General Aetius?' In this setting Theodoric stood easily, finally, as a man who appeared comfortable within his own skin. His son, Thorismund, huge and menacing, stood beside him.

'Yes. A surprise attack, a silent establishment of foot soldiers on the opposing side of the ridge, especially carried out so soon after we arrive on the scene, will be totally unexpected. Attila is not as infallible as his men believe. The Hun will not expect such a tactic, given that neither you nor they like to fight at night. Attila sits in his camp behind the ridge while we stand before it. At dawn, we will engage the Hun on the right horn of the heights, taking them out of the battle's equation.'

He gazed around at his audience who began to nod in agreement as they digested his plans. 'Can you do this for me?'

'Aye!' The voices of the kings were firm, even the higher voice of Sangiban.

'Thank you, my friends, for we were born for this moment. May Mithras protect us all!'

'One moment, Flavius Aetius,' Sangiban interrupted, and Aetius's white eyebrows rose interrogatively. 'Why hasn't Attila taken the apex of the ridge? In his position, I would have no hesitation in doing so, and I like to know the motives of my enemy before I am fully committed.'

Flavius Aetius smiled silkily and every man present realised that the Sarmatian would pay for his interruption. 'I'm sure you do, King Sangiban. I also wonder as to his motivation. What do we know about the Hun? Really know?'

'They like to strike fast and hard on horseback so they can fall back after inflicting maximum damage without risking harm to themselves,' Childeric answered carefully, one finger smoothing his moustache.

'Good, Prince Childeric. Good. The Hun prefers to fight on horseback so, where possible, they leave foot battles to their allies. I believe that a pitched battle on the heights is not part of Attila's battle plan, and would only slow him down. It is a flaw in his strategy and we can use this weakness in his thinking to our advantage. If we take the high ground, Attila's numerical advantage is neutralised.'

'It can't be that simple,' Sangiban snapped, his eyes seeking rapidly for an answer that was more complex and satisfying.

'I can understand Attila's strategy,' Theodoric decided. 'He expects us to come roaring against him after his abortive attack on Aurelianum. He supposes that we will take his retreat there as a victory, and that we will act unwisely in an attempt to finish him off.'

'Mmm ... quite possibly,' Aetius agreed. 'But do his motives matter? If we have the high ground, we take the initiative from him. War is a game, my lords, and advantage, whether real or imagined, tips the balance in our favour.

'Tomorrow we can fight from a position of relative strength with the high ground protecting our rear. The legionaries, together with Merovech and Childeric, will nullify Attila's force on the centre of the plain while Thorismund and King Theodoric control the high ground and engage the Hun forces. We can meet the Hungvari horde with the knowledge that it would be virtually impossible to outflank and surround us. Let these facts be known to your men to give them heart. Tell them also of the healer's prophecy that we shall win this battle in the field. I put no trust in soothsayers, but I will use anything that gives advantage to our cause.' The general gazed around the assembled kings. 'Do you have any further questions?'

The kings were silent for, after all, there was very little left to say.

'Then let's be about our business, and may the gods bless our endeavours till we meet again at battle's end.'

Myrddion watched a contingent of the Salian Franks rise from their cooking fires, mount their horses and fade into the darkness at a walk, leaving their fires to burn throughout the night. His ears strained to hear the sound of a large troop of Visigoth horsemen moving through the darkness, but he could hear nothing except the murmur of other soldiers who remained at their campsites.

'They've taken the time to muffle the hooves of their horses,' Finn explained unnecessarily. 'They're at pains to give no warning of their intentions.'

Later in the evening, as the healers were readying themselves for another night sleeping under the wagons, a messenger arrived to instruct them that they were to assemble the field hospital just beyond the left horn of the ridge. Myrddion protested that late at night was no time to break camp, but the messenger stared at him stolidly and reminded him that General Aetius was in charge and he had made the decision to relocate his healers to a new position.

'Argue it out with him, if you're so stupid,' the man said unemotionally. 'His plans go far beyond such trivial matters.'

'Very well, you may inform General Aetius that we will obey his orders,' Myrddion replied. Vechmar simply grimaced with annoyance. Then, wearily, the two men woke their servants.

Grumbling, unhappy and feeling unappreciated, the healers packed the wagons, harnessed the horses and, using torches made out of heavy branches wrapped with oil-soaked rags, set off for their appointed post. Unexpectedly, Captus and his guard appeared out of the darkness and joined the cavalcade. The tall Frank was unusually silent.

'I expected that you would be taking part in the battle, not babysitting us,' Myrddion murmured.

'So did I, healer. So did I!'

Captus was quietly angry, so he held his nervous horse on a very tight rein. Myrddion could see the silhouette of the captain's profile by the flaring torchlight. His lips were pressed tightly together and what could be seen of his features expressed disappointment and chagrin.

'I'm sorry, Captus. As far as we're concerned, you're released from your duty to protect us.'

Captus responded by reefing up the head of his horse with a cruel twist of his arms. The beast squealed and stopped dead in its tracks, while Captus glared up at Myrddion on the high seat of his wagon.

'You lack the power to order me in any capacity, healer. I am Merovech's man, and he is busy organising a frontal attack while Thorismund takes the ridge that looms so threateningly above us. This peril is but the beginning, for my lord will face the wrath of Attila in the morning. I would serve as the lowliest archer in his army if I were given a choice, but my lord has placed a value on you that is far greater than my honour, or the long loyalty of my troop in his service. Yes, I resent my orders. You have taken more than my tooth, healer, whether it was your intention or not.'

'So leave then, Captus, because we'll not inform on you. Your assistance to us has been too valuable for such telltale, unmanly behaviour. Take my hand and good speed to you, for I know how it feels to be parted from your chosen trade.'

Captus's lips twisted bitterly and he ignored Myrddion's proffered palm, although the younger man could not take offence because he saw, by the set of the warrior's shoulders, that Captus was divided between his oath, his duty and his desire to follow his master into battle. No insult was intended on Captus's part.

'Truly, Master Myrddion, if I were a man of broken honour, I would grab at your offer with both hands. But I am King Merovech's man. Should he die on the morrow, his orders would remain between him and me, but I would always know that I had let him down. I am sworn to obey, and I will, but don't expect me to enjoy my safety.'

'Something warns me, friend Captus, that no one will know any safety tomorrow, so don't torture yourself. But if you decide to stay, then work for me willingly or go on your way. In our bloody trade, a half-hearted man is a liability.'

The healers' wagons moved slowly onwards, but were

passed by dim shapes in the darkness as Sangiban and his warriors began to move into position to make the main offensive into the plain. In the darkness, the Visigoths stole like wraiths towards the ridge, or took up positions immediately below it, ready for a quick offensive. These men would sleep after eating dried meat and drinking plain water, without the comfort of a warming fire during the night.

Puzzled, Myrddion looked down the makeshift road and saw the stolid shapes of Aetius's legions, some climbing, but most massing on the plain, ready to move into the centre of the battle. All combatants avoided clear moonlight until they reached the top of the plateau or the edge of the plain. Only the cavalry, many thousands of them, remained in reserve and these were settling into position along the wings of the ridgeline. Aetius was breaking long-held tactical rules of combat by sending his allies into the field in the dangerous darkness, for warriors were vulnerable on invisible and treacherous ground. Myrddion expected his first casualties before dawn, felled by broken limbs and heads from falls upon the scree-covered slopes. By the light of a fitful moon, he could dimly perceive the central, and highest, point of the ridge that, as yet, had not been taken by either combatant. The healer wondered if it would be the key to the battle that was to come when light began to stain the dark sky.

'We will make our camp on the first piece of flat land on the edge of the ridge, friend Captus. I know such a position puts us in danger and we can be overcome by any determined contingent of cavalry, but my water tells me that there will be a mountain of wounded by the end of tomorrow. We must be prominently placed and clearly visible if we are to be of any use. Please, Captus, ride ahead and find me clean water, the shelter of trees and a position close to the probable battleground. It looks as though none of us will get any sleep, but if we work through the night we might just be prepared for the bloodbath.'

Captus glared at Myrddion's resentful tone, and reached out one mailed fist to grip the young man's shaven chin in order to see the healer's eyes as clearly as the dim light permitted.

'You are no fighter, Myrddion Emrys, and have as little knowledge of the field as a child, so your complaints about working all night are churlish. General Aetius expects that the dawn will bring an attack . . . and he's usually right. So yes, we must work through the night, and you must be prepared to accede to his demands. Your whining does you no credit!'

Myrddion flushed with embarrassment and was glad that the darkness hid the sudden flush of colour on his cheeks. 'You're right, Captus. Consider my rudeness to be that of a boy who has decided his own actions for far too long. My pride prompted my complaints – and I'm sorry.'

Instead of leaving Myrddion to mull over his want of manners, Captus drew his horse back to pace at the speed of the wagons. 'What do you see within your heart, healer? Will we fail on the morrow? I am vowed to protect you so that you may save those who might live, but much depends on our battle plan.'

'We will endure . . . succeed . . . and Attila will feel death coming for him. His supply lines are far too long and his ambitions are disappearing in the night winds. Trust to Aetius and the kings, and the day will be yours.' Myrddion watched Captus pale a little and chuckled. 'No, this is not the product of a dream that tells me what will happen. It's just plain common sense.'

Relieved, Captus also chuckled. 'I'll find you the site you need for the tents. If I must serve in this role, I'll find the best position available to protect the greatest number of men. And, while I'm at it, I'll ensure that we can see the disposition of the battle lines when they are determined. We must have good intelligence if we're to be effective. And I'll make sure that there's a workable space between you and that vain old Spaniard.'

'Since honesty appears to be the coin of conversation on this night, Captus, please explain to me why such puissant kings as Merovech and Theodoric would abdicate their power to an ageing Roman general who has little under-standing, or care, for their people. I don't understand it. Theodoric rules a land far larger than all of Italia and Merovech's lands are nearly as rich and as wide, yet they defer to a short, autocratic tyrant as if they were mere boys.'

Captus flushed, and Myrddion saw the big Frank's fist clench. For a moment, the healer prepared to duck the warrior's swinging arm, but Captus's good sense reasserted itself as he realised that Myrddion meant no offence. Carefully, the Frank tried to explain the strange politics of the lands of ancient Gaul.

'Flavius Aetius deserves respect, not because we revere the Romans, but because the general really is a *magister militum*. We are aware that the empire is all but dead, but Aetius is a master of battle, a lord of carnage who holds a long view and an instinct for the field of conflict that is lacking in the tribal kings. They accept that they are his inferiors in this regard. And because no tribe, nor the Romans themselves, have the strength to repel the Huns alone, we must unite to repulse a common enemy. No army can have five or six heads or, like the hydra, it will thrash around aimlessly until each head is cut off, one by one. So an army of many component parts must have one head. Who better than Flavius Aetius?'

Myrddion bit his thumb reflectively. What Captus said made sense, but the healer was still puzzled by the deference that such redoubtable kings offered so freely to the Roman.

'But why him? Surely the empire has less venal, more amenable generals?'

Captus snorted with repressed humour. 'You don't like our noble Roman, do you? No, he's the best that's left. He's the wiliest, the most ambitious and the man most determined to succeed. The empire is full of greedy, second-rate minds who would seize power with hands stained with blood shed in ambush, but Aetius is a man who'll face you from the front. The mind that doesn't fear the darkness before the battle begins contains an intellect that can defeat Attila and the Hungvari hordes.'

'I hope he comes at me from the front, if he decides to sweep me from his path.'

Captus began to laugh, but softly, for the night was still and dangerous men could well be listening. 'He warned you, didn't he? He'll not bother with you, unless he starts to wonder how you read his mind. You must learn to keep your head down, healer. My master may admire you, but if it comes to a trial of strength he will follow Aetius until such time as the Roman has outlived his usefulness.' Then Captus shrugged. 'Don't look so perplexed and worried, Myrddion. Your fears may never come into being.'

'By the gods, Captus, I thank you. I think I'm finally beginning to understand my place in the puzzle of this strange land. It seems we're all in the hands of the gods, whoever they are. I'll trust in my skills, my two hands and my ability to stay out of the general's way. Fortunately, I inherited my father's devilish luck.' Myrddion grinned, and the torch attached to the wagon's side lit his eyes with a lambent sheen of red and gold, as if the young man saw the world through a veil of blood or fire. 'I give you my promise that you will win glory, Captus, even though you believe you've been given a minor role in the coming chaos. These words are not prophecy, but reason. I can swear that you will be more important than even you believe you could be, for those who serve with a pure heart never labour in vain.'

'Excuse my doubts. Now I must be about my master's orders.' Flushed with embarrassment, Captus kneed his horse into a canter. Then, with a muffled sound of hooves and sliding gravel, he was gone.

'Even with skins to cover our allies' hooves, I can't believe the Hun is ignorant of the movement of so many men. General Aetius is taking a huge gamble,' Cadoc muttered as he slapped the reins on the rumps of his pair and set them into a trot.

Myrddion did not reply. He was reviewing Castor's description of the prophecies, with their promises of the death of a great man, and hoping that, in this instance, he was wrong.

And so they travelled under a dying moon until they reached a small, elevated plateau to the left of the ridgeline, a position that permitted some visual understanding of the plain below.

When Captus found the rise and deemed it suitable for their requirements, he set up a guard to secure the make-shift camp that would soon be erected. Then, as soon as Myrddion's party arrived, the remaining guardsmen and Myrddion's workers set to work to cut grass for sleeping pallets and raise the huge leather tents. Vechmar's apprentices settled into their tasks like parts of a well-oiled machine and Theodoric's gift of widows and camp followers soon found ready work in the collection of water, which was stored in large, sealed leather containers that folded easily when they were empty. Bridie, Brangaine and Rhedyn enjoyed ordering the new women to complete the most onerous tasks such as chopping herbs and roots and preparing them for use. Although they were urged to be silent, the women still gossiped together in whispers as the newcomers were told what tasks would fall to them in the morning. With relief, Brangaine was able to allocate the cooking to a plain, raw-boned woman who claimed to prefer the sight of food to the sight of blood, which 'no decent person should have to see'. Brangaine herself set to work pounding herbs in a mortar so that their medicines would be ready for the casualties that would come. Willa hung in a cloth round her neck, sleeping and crying thinly by turns as she struggled for her foster-mother's attention. Stolidly and patiently, the servant woman worked on, infusing feverwort into boiling water and creating a rather smelly mix of radish paste in pottery jars.

Cadoc performed marvels by unwinding large bolts of new cloth provided by the grateful population of Aurelianum and cutting lengths into usable bandages. Later, he boiled them over fires that were shielded by tree branches to minimise any chance of discovery from the ridgeline above. As the light of day broke through the darkness to the east, the camp was fast settling into the old patterns of the healer's craft.

Now the time of waiting began in earnest.

Accompanied by Captus, Myrddion moved away from the

wagons and stared up towards the crest where, initially, the fates of the peoples of the west would be decided.

The ridge was long and curved into a sickle shape. While not high, it would cause any determined attacker to think twice before charging up its treacherous slopes, which were bisected with narrow, dry watercourses. Scree, the lack of heavy cover and the constant threat of an enemy above created a hazardous field of combat. Any young boy with a slingshot, or the strength to move medium-sized boulders, could hold a dozen men at bay for a time, inflicting damage with the destructive earth slides that could be engineered so easily. Above them, although not visible to the healers below, Thorismund and his father held the horn of the ridge. The Romans and the Franks had moved into position on the plain during the hours of darkness, and now banners were unfurled to the sky; Attila's black standards ranged against the eagles of Aetius. Above the warring camps, the highest land lay bare, stark and vulnerable. It was a prize to be won, its peak tantalisingly close with its promise of advantage in a battle that threatened to be long, hard and vicious.

Myrddion spotted a narrow smudge of smoke in the distance. 'What's that? Who else is abroad on the plain?'

'That's the camp of the great Attila,' Captus replied. 'You can see it clearly now. You can see his cohorts, waiting in the wings to the north. There's movement, Master Myrddion! See? Theodoric is circling towards Attila's position on the high ground, and Thorismund's Visigoths are attacking downhill. Attila's troops are hurrying to cut them off.'

'The sun is barely up and it has begun already,' Myrddion shouted. 'Ready yourselves, for the battle is about to begin.'

'Look down at the plain!' Captus cried. 'Aetius has sent Sangiban forward in the centre. Damn me, but the Roman general is clever. Only a blind and deaf fool would trust that bastard, so Aetius puts him where he'll absorb the full shock of Attila's cavalry. That's one way to fix a problem, especially when Merovech commands the other flank.'

'Why is Aetius taking such a risk, Captus? What virtue is there in trusting a potential traitor to attack Attila's centre?'

Captus grinned like a fox. 'He has deployed his weakest link at a point where he cannot run, at the place of greatest danger.'

As if on cue, Attila unleashed his cavalry.

From the slight rise in the ground, Myrddion could see the mass of horsemen, their arms bare for greater mobility as they charged towards the positions held by Sangiban and Merovech. Long, black banners underlined the ruddy light of dawn. Meanwhile, savage hand-to-hand fighting between Theodoric's troops and another contingent of Hun warriors was just visible through the churned dust. Inexorably, the taller Visigoths were pushing forward until Myrddion saw a taller, mounted figure upon the highest point of the ridge. This warrior swung his sword in a great parabola of light and the Visigoth warriors surged forward.

'Ayeee!' Captus screamed, pointing to another part of the battlefield. 'Look! The devils are breaking their backs on the Roman square.'

Myrddion followed Captus's pointing arm.

A skeleton troop of Visigoths still held the left flank on the ridge. Meanwhile, the Salian Franks and the Romans had moved onto the centre of the plain, swinging wide towards the left to prevent the Gepid and Germanic tribes from flanking Sangiban's men, who were now engaged in vicious hand-to-hand fighting. Theodoric was on the move as well, fighting through a wall of Huns to reach his son, Thorismund, who had attacked Attila's Hungvari troops on the heights.

The battle had fallen into two huge engagements.

On the flat, watercourse-seamed plain, Aetius's infantry met the Gepid force directly in front of their encampment. To their right, Merovech and Sangiban felt the full might of the main Hungvari force with a clash that Myrddion could almost feel through his bones. The whole engagement hung on a thread as men fought breast-to-breast, and died in great swaths on the blood-soaked earth.

In the second engagement, the Visigoth forces, who had split into the two wings led by Theodoric and Thorismund, smashed the Huns as they met and then pursued them from the heights. Then Myrddion saw the Visigoths turn and plunge behind the Hun who were engaged on the plain, encircling them and enclosing the main force in a ring of steel.

Like waves on the sea, the black-clad Gepid and Hungvari warriors, many of them half naked, drove their horses desperately at the Roman squares. Like the shock of the ocean pounding against a rocky shore, Myrddion felt the crash of that meeting down to his toes. Horses screamed as Roman spears impaled their bellies, shafts slid out of legionaries' hands as beasts fell backward, their hooves scrabbling for purchase at the empty air. And the line, five deep behind their interlocked shields, wavered ... and held. The dead began to pile up like cordwood as the Hungvari came at the Romans again and again, but still the squares held in place.

'Dear heavens,' Myrddion breathed, as he tried to visualise the breadth of the slaughter. In the centre, Sangiban had been beaten to a standstill by the Hun cavalry as they threatened to break through to the allied defensive line.

'Merovech has seen them! He rides! He rides!' Captus was screaming, his eyes feral and wild with blood lust.

The Franks struck at the flank of one wing of the Hungvari cavalry as they were poised to attack an isolated outpost of Germanic allies. Red cloaks flying, and with their long swords and spears flashing as they commenced the reaping of a harvest of souls, the Franks struck the Hun on the flank, and in the crazed melee that followed Myrddion saw both black and red cloaks fall like sheaves of wheat.

Like many-headed monsters, the armies snapped at each other in a chaotic series of individual battles where friend and foe alike were both confused and confusing. German fought German and Visigoth fought Ostrogoth. Myrddion became dizzy with the vast scale of the battle and was unable to see any pattern behind the tangle of foot soldiers and cavalry.

Captus was wiser in the ways of warfare. Patiently, he explained how Attila's numerical advantage was dissipated through the tactical and strategic superiority displayed by Aetius and Merovech on the battlefield. Under the expert tutelage of the captain of his guard, Myrddion saw the ebb and flow of the heroic contest through more educated eyes. He was particularly impressed with the intimidatory dourness and discipline of the Roman troops, who did not give an inch, regardless of how many warriors were thrown against them.

The day was long and hot, and Myrddion couldn't imagine how men could fight effectively under the weight of their armour. Even from a distance, the healer could tell that the Hun momentum had gone. The Visigoths had fought them to a standstill, and as the first long rays of the afternoon began to slant over the battlefield the Hun army wheeled and retreated, heading for the safety of Attila's encampment. As they headed northeast along the slopes of the ridge, they left drifts of dead and dying men and horses in their wake. The carrion birds came as they always did, called by the strange telepathy of their kind, to feast on the detritus of war. As he saw the ungainly bodies of vultures and the sleek, black shapes of ravens settle onto the mounds of dead, Myrddion stirred himself at last.

'Send out the men, Captus. We must start to move the living out of this charnel house and into my hospital tents. Gods . . . there are so many of them that I don't know where to start.'

The carthorses, as well as the guard's destriers, were soon pressed into service to bear those who still lived to Myrddion's tents, while Vechmar, Myrddion and Cadoc began their preparations to perform surgery as soon as the patients arrived.

But very few men were alive. Those who had fallen during the morning had mostly bled to death by the time Myrddion's searchers reached them. Enemy and allied warriors were all the same to the young Celt, and some Hun warriors were transported back to the hospital tents. Captus was kept grimly occupied killing wounded horses and he was soon awash with blood. Every step the searchers took was through puddles of viscous gore until they despaired of finding warriors who could be made whole.

Then, as the last bloody rays of sunlight lit the huge plain, Childeric rode through the havoc of the battlefield with scant concern for the bodies that were trodden beneath his destrier's hooves until he found Myrddion, spattered with the paint of his craft.

'Come, Myrddion! As you foretold, King Merovech is sorely wounded and is like to die, even with your skills. But I will not sleep well unless we try to save him. Besides, he is calling for you.'

'Very well,' Myrddion said sadly. 'But it will take me some little time to reach him.'

'You can ride behind me. Merovech has no time.'

Pausing only to sluice his body with clean water and to snatch up his familiar satchel, Myrddion left the tent. He was half naked, wet and glistening like a pale, sleek seal. Childeric extended his armed hand and Myrddion took it, and with an agile twist of the prince's shoulders the healer found himself elevated onto the rump of Childeric's destrier. He barely had time to grasp the prince's sword belt before Childeric thrust his heels into his horse's flanks and the huge beast leapt away in the direction from which it had come.

From horseback, the battlefield was even more ugly and bloody than Myrddion had imagined. The stench made his gorge rise and he was a man who was familiar with the reek of blood, entrails and body waste. Blood had soaked into the earth, forming a gross, red mud that had fouled the combatants, tangled their feet and weakened their straining leg muscles.

When Childeric pulled his horse to an abrupt halt and the two men dismounted, they found the king of the Salian Franks lying on the bare earth, propped up on a saddle, with several red cloaks padded behind his head to assist his breathing. Merovech looked unchanged, especially facially, for his eyes were still reckless and somehow happy, while his mouth was turned up in a smile, even though a trickle of blood ran down his chin. Myrddion knelt beside the Frankish king and pulled aside his mailed shirt, which must have risen up above his waist as he delivered an overhead blow to an enemy, for the wound was beneath the narrow steel rings.

'You've been severely injured, my lord,' Myrddion murmured soothingly as he examined the small puncture wound in Merovech's right side. The weapon had stabbed through the king's shirt and heavy leather jerkin, leaving a bluish hole with puckered edges that oozed a deceptively small amount of blood. 'How long ago did this happen?' Myrddion's hands eased away the heavy leather trousers that protected the king's lower body, and he noted that Merovech winced, and then sighed, as the belt was released. The healer's gentle fingers explored the king's pelvis, and felt a thick swelling in the abdomen several inches below the wound.

Merovech was bleeding inwardly, and Myrddion had no idea how to stem that inexorable, invisible flow. He knew that he lacked the skills to repair internal organs that had been breached by a bladed weapon, so Merovech would soon weaken and die.

Pulling his satchel from his shoulder, Myrddion found a small horn container of powder that contained poppy seed and other painkilling ingredients. As a last resort, all that the healer had to offer was this – an anodyne against pain. Merovech understood when Myrddion asked for a little wine, and placed one bloodstained hand over the healer's narrow fingers.

'Can't you offer me anything better, Myrddion-no-name? No lancing? No surgery? Never mind! In truth, my wound pains me, but I'd as lief not sleep away my last hours. I have too much to explain to my son.'

'If you wish, I can mix a draught that will kill your pain but still leave you conscious.'

'I do wish. I'll not have death steal up on me when I'm not looking. Better to face him. Aye, it's better to fight for my last breath. Still, I would be grateful if you could relieve the pain, friend healer. It was a good day when Childeric brought you to me.'

Myrddion shook a little powder into the red wine and swirled it until the surface was undisturbed. He handed the mug to Childeric, who began to sniff it suspiciously, but Merovech gripped his son's wrist with the last of his strength.

'No, lad. Trust the young healer, for he'll not kill me.' Merovech laughed painfully, and then began to cough, a sound as hacking and raw as gravel underfoot. 'I'm already a dead man – a Hun bastard saw to that. Let me drink his potion, and have done.'

Myrddion had no time to wait and watch Merovech die. Living men were suffering in the healers' tents and he was looked for at the place where his skills had some value. Still, he was unable to turn away from the dying man whose spirit was almost incandescent in the torchlight.

'Fare thee well, King Merovech. May the Mother enfold you in her warm arms and may you sleep on the bosom of your gods for as long as men remember your name.'

'You've already promised me that I will live forever.' Merovech laughed, although his mirth rang hollow.

Childeric bowed his head and wept soundlessly.

As Myrddion retraced his course through the battlefield, he saw Frank warriors slaying the last of the wounded Hungvari. He turned his face away from the bloody butchery, unable to watch the ugly realities of defeat. Still, as he picked his way through the gruesome detritus of the slaughter ground, he realised that he had not heard a single Hun beg for his life, or weep, before blade or axe ended his agony. Perhaps these warriors are wiser than I am, for I only look for the best and the worst in men, Myrddion thought, as he came to the healers' tent and began the bloody trade of saving lives.

The work continued through the night as the dead were dragged away to deep ditches or cleansing fires, leaving fewer survivors to be treated at the field hospital. As dawn approached, Vechmar, Myrddion, Cadoc and the servants laboured on as if that dreadful night would have no ending.

CHAPTER VII

SACRED EARTH

The horse screamed shrilly like a betrayed child, just once, as its legs collapsed and a great jet of arterial blood marred its glossy black coat. Its beautiful, dead flesh collapsed into the hole that had been dug for it, so that it lay like a useless mass of unresponsive muscle and plaited, gold-adorned mane and tail, a toy cast away by giants. The harness of a valuable destrier was laid beside it, ceremonial and heavy with gold wire and heavy embossing. Then Flavius Aetius stepped forward from the press of notables who viewed the execution with inscrutable, flat-planed faces.

'Bane of thy master, lie here until his hand seeks your rein and his legs hunger to feel your body under him, ready and eager for battle. Though you left him, wounded and afoot in the press of battle, no blame attaches itself to you, his fleet-footed and beloved servant. Go with your lord into the abode of heroes.'

Women wailed in a chorus designed both to honour the dead and to chill the nerves of the listeners. In the Roman way, Flavius Aetius had hired peasant women and camp followers to rend their clothing and score their cheeks with their nails, so that they appeared to weep blood instead of tears. The shrill ululations of their purchased grief gave the ceremony the drama of a Greek tragedy.

Myrddion raised his eyes skywards and allowed the gentle morning breeze to cool his feverish, gritty eyes. A river lay just beyond the field with a village huddled on its bank, but few farmers and bucolics had come to gawk at the proceedings. The air was too charged with grief, distrust and despair for ordinary men to choose to become involved. The long grasses soughed and whispered in the light wind, twining with the sounds of the mourners to emphasise that the earth, and all things that lived upon it, felt the loss of this great king.

To the right of the felled horse, another huge grave pit had been carved out of the sod. Four times the size of a normal grave, this pit had been dug with much labour and even greater respect, for it was no ordinary man who would lie under the heavy summer sun of the Catalaunian Plain.

As the wailing of the mourners increased in tempo and volume, six warriors carried to the graveside a litter draped with heavy woven wool that had been hastily dyed a rusty black. Thorismund paced before the bier, his pace measured and solemn, his face harsh and suddenly older, as if his youth had been squeezed out of him by an invisible clenched fist. His armour gleamed with polish and ornamentation, his helm was so bright that it dazzled in the noonday light and his hair was plaited, greased and noble with clasps of silver and electrum. Round his neck was the torc marking his status as a prince of the Visigoths and across his brows was the new band of his kingship. Yet, vital and strong as he was, Thorismund presented a pale imitation of regal power. The corpse of his father, Theodoric of Hispania, still radiated the inscrutable, magnetic aura of a god. Under his cleaned and fabulous armour, never used in the realities of combat,

Myrddion knew that the king's body was smashed and broken by the hooves of his own cavalry, but none of this damage was visible on the still face. Chance, or some last instinct for survival, had caused Theodoric to curl onto his front as the war horses swept over him, smashing his skull and driving his face into the mud of the battlefield. Now, washed and perfumed, his features were almost unmarked, so that Theodoric could be sleeping on the heavy black litter on which he lay. As in life, his face spoke of secrets and careful control, so that Myrddion sought in vain for a trace of the personality that fired those angular features.

With a respect so deep and palpable that no man doubted its truth, the six Visigoth lords lowered the bier into the pit before abasing themselves on their knees so that their foreheads touched the earth. Then, careless of the dirt that marked their knees, their faces and their hands, they stood up and stepped away from their master to take up positions at the edge of the grave pit, still on guard, although their king had departed for a place where they could neither follow nor protect him.

Aetius approached the edge of the pit and ceremoniously tore the neck of his tunic with a strong, gnarled hand. This simple gesture, so common to mourners from one side of the Middle Sea to the other, was imbued with more than the respect due to a dead ally. With his accustomed deliberation, Aetius honoured Theodoric as a Roman warrior, the highest praise the general could give.

'Look your last on Theodoric of the Visigoths, king and man, gone to his gods so that Attila would fail in his ambitions. The priests tell us that Fortuna demands a price for any great victory, and Theodoric was the cost of our success, struck down by cruel chance after he saw that the conflict was all but won. Our strong right arm is gone! Our kingly, noble adviser has gone! Our greatest ally has been sacrificed to spare us from the Hungvari. Ave, Theodoric, man and king! Ave!'

The oratory was stirring and the Visigoth lords responded with a resounding cry of triumph and grief, but Myrddion turned away to avoid any eye contact with Aetius across the yawning grave pit that lay between them. The general could not have seen the healer in the ranks of mourners, even if he had cared sufficiently for Myrddion's reaction to seek him out. But the young man feared that his traitorous face would attract the general's eyes. And he couldn't fool Aetius.

Myrddion knew that Aetius's fine words were only for show. Yes, without Theodoric and the Visigoths, all of Gaul would have fallen to Attila. Sheer numbers had turned the tide on the Hungvari. Yes, Theodoric had been a clever strategist and a brilliant fighter, and he had defeated the horde again and again as Attila tried to find a means of escaping from Aetius's trap. But, like Theodoric, Myrddion understood that Aetius cared nothing for the Visigoth king, except that his death caused a problem. Thorismund lacked his father's cool intelligence and reasoned patience, but the young man had proved himself to be a hero.

Now, the newly anointed king took Aetius's place overlooking his father's grave. In the crook of each arm, he bore a naked sword.

The first weapon was a plain thing, a steel blade that seemed to ripple in the noon sun. The pommel was undecorated, except for a binding of sharkskin designed to prevent a warrior's hands from slipping on blood. Theodoric had carried this superb weapon into battle, but many men who were seduced by surface values would have rejected its utilitarian beauty.

'My father needs no pretty words to praise either his courage or his loyalty,' Thorismund began with a soldier's economy. 'He understood that Attila and his barbarians posed the single greatest threat to his throne, so he served the Roman Empire because he understood the need for combined action by good and reliable allies.'

A rumble of agreement followed this brief beginning of a speech that Myrddion sensed would carry more of a threat to Aetius than a simple paean of praise to his father's might.

Thorismund raised the second sword, gripping it by the centre of the blade, careless of the risk of cut fingers. This sword was ceremonial and beautiful with cut gems, freshwater pearls and chasing in orange gold. The blade was workmanlike but heavily decorated with a pattern of hunting beasts. Myrddion doubted that it was good for anything much but display.

'This blade is the sign of my father's kingship, inherited from his father and his grandfather as tangible proof of his right to rule. Let it go into my father's grave so that the gods will recognise it when he joins them at the feastings of heaven.'

Respectfully, one of the guards took the ceremonial sword, jumped into the grave pit, and laid the weapon along Theodoric's left side.

'I will win a sword of my own so that my father will know that I honour his shade, and will find my own renown.'

Aetius watched Thorismund under lowered, shaggy brows as the Visigoth warriors roared their approval.

'But this blade was my father's pride, regardless of its lack of gems or its ordinary appearance,' Thorismund cried, raising the first weapon so that it flamed briefly in the noonday light. 'Sky Weaver is its name, and its blade will cleave even the invisible air. With this weapon, my father won and held an empire to rival the size and strength of Rome itself.'

Now the Visigoths howled their approval and Myrddion sensed a deep, ancient enmity towards all things Roman that still survived beneath the treaties and the polite compliments of the allies.

'This blade reminds us of Theodoric's commitment to the Goths, to his ancestors and to the ascendancy of our people. His battle sword represents what our king stood for, a strong homeland free from the demands of strangers as overlords, while still honouring the treaties that give us security and power. This weapon must go into the ground with him, but I will make another so that the might of no other peoples will ever enslave us or demand allegiance from us, without honour or deference. Hail, Theodoric of the Visigoths.'

This time, as the weapon was placed in Theodoric's sword hand, the gathered Visigoths did not cry out their approval. Something deeper and more primal stiffened their mouths and squared their shoulders. Aetius frowned, and Myrddion saw one of the general's hands clench briefly.

Thorismund steps on dangerous ground, but so does Aetius, Myrddion thought. But is Thorismund another Theodoric, to avoid the mantraps that the Roman general will lay for him?

As golden ornaments and wooden chests of precious objects joined Theodoric in his last sleep, the crowd stirred like the fields of grass by the riverbank. Imperceptibly, the mood had changed, and Aetius must have felt the chill memory of old, broken treaties on both sides. Then, as the first clods of earth began to fill both grave pits, the general gathered his toga around his body and bowed to Thorismund before leaving the field.

Myrddion watched the Roman contingent depart and was surprised to see several heavily cloaked women being carried back to the Roman camp on litters. A flash of red curls was visible under one closed hood, and when the woman turned her head back towards the graves, a pair of brilliant eyes sought him out.

The glance, so swift and intense, touched Myrddion viscerally so that, for a moment, the sun ceased to shine and the breeze to blow, although he could still feel their touch on his face. That fleeting, shared intimacy of eyes stirred the young healer's romanticism more than a sexual touch or a lewd thought. The meaning of her silent communication was hidden from him, but Myrddion had recognised Flavia by her mismatched eyes and by his body's immediate response to her presence. 'Is this love?' he muttered to himself, then was grateful that no one had heard his foolishness.

Back at the field hospital, there was work to be done, although four days had elapsed since the Battle of the Catalaunian Plain. Many patients had died, for the conflict was bloodier than anything Myrddion had ever experienced or imagined. Even the dying had hacked at each other, using teeth and nails when they had no other weapons, and the sheer scale of the hatred exposed by the battlefield had left wounds that laid bare the human body in ways that Myrddion had never seen before. Grimly, he acknowledged that he had learned more of the secrets of the flesh on that red day, and in the days that followed, than he had discovered in all his years of apprenticeship. He had much to think about.

Merovech had died within half a day of his wounding.

Myrddion had been told that the end was quiet and painless, as the king of the Salian Franks slowly sank into a deep sleep from which he didn't awaken. Childeric had covered his reddened eyes as he reported his father's death to Aetius, and Myrddion had experienced the familiar bitterness of the tradesman who cannot master his tools.

'What will King Childeric decide now that Merovech has gone to his ancestors?' Myrddion asked Captus in a bleak voice. 'And what will Aetius do now that one of his most loyal and enthusiastic allies is dead? King Childeric is a man with a cold, measured mind. He'll not bow the knee as Merovech did. Don't look at me like that, Captus! Merovech was no one's pet hound, and never Aetius's. But he was raised in Rome as a hostage to ensure Clodio's compliance. Your master had a bond with Rome, but he took care to ensure that his son had none.'

Captus's affronted face slowly relaxed. 'How you've come to know and understand the tangled treaties of the great ones is a mystery to me, healer, but you are right. Merovech made sure that Childeric owed no one. Nor in death will my master be a vassal of Rome. I'll wager my new king will take Merovech home, regardless of what Aetius thinks, just as soon as Attila is cleansed from our lands. No Roman praise will send Merovech to his gods.'

'Such hatred, Captus! Yet you explained clearly why Aetius was the sole leader of this campaign. The twisted, complicated dealings between you Franks and your masters are near as convoluted as are ours in Cymru.' Myrddion's face puckered swiftly into a smile, but he felt no humour. This battle had been too huge and too costly to spark even a trace of amusement or triumph, for man-gods had perished. As always, only the clever and the cold in spirit had lived to kill again.

'Rome is done and our time is coming. You made a promise to Merovech, and I heard your prophecy with my own ears. My king died convinced that even the ultimate sacrifice was as nothing to the ascendancy of the Franks. When Aetius is dust, Childeric will rule this blood-soaked land and this battle will become the stuff of legend. I have lived to see a great change, healer, so what do we need of Roman pomp and ceremony? Childeric will bury his father, and my lord, in our way and on our soil.'

On the day after the battle, Aetius had summoned the allied kings together, and Myrddion had chosen to attend, hovering on the fringes of the crowd. Bowed with grief but cold at heart, Childeric and Thorismund had arrived to take the places of their fathers at the head of their armies. With the irony of warfare, Sangiban had survived almost without a scratch. After a day of licking their respective wounds, the two armies sat poised, ready to recommence hostilities.

'I have received word from a Gepid warrior concerning a crisis in Attila's camp. Because any further battle weakens us all, you must contribute to my decision. But first, bring in the traitor.' These last words were spat out, underlining Aetius's disgust for turncoats from whatever side they came.

The Gepid warrior was dragged to the fireside in chains, although he showed a remarkable lack of humility, considering he had deserted his master's liege lord.

'Why are you here, traitor, when your king still serves his master loyally?'

'Not for much longer, Flavius Aetius, *dux et patricius, magister militum* of Gaul. I am here on the express orders of my lord, Ardaric. My king begs for safe passage through your lands so that we may return to our home. My task is to offer you intelligence that you may use as you choose.'

'Why doesn't King Ardaric come to me like a man, if he is so desirous of changing sides?' Aetius's voice was contemptuous, but the Gepid warrior stood up straight and unyielding. His blue eyes became two chips of glacial ice as he scornfully swept his eyes over the short stature of the Roman general.

'I expected better of the *magister militum*, who should have some understanding of the strategic realities under which we live. My lord Ardaric rules a land that has been under the control of the Hun army for years. We struggle to retain Gepidae honour on every day of our captivity. My king has acted in accordance with his duty to his subjects when he sends me to you as his envoy. He does not choose to ally himself with you, for to do so would be to break his oaths to Attila. But he does not wish to have his warriors slain in a fruitless struggle against an enemy who is our brother in race and history. You speak with contempt, Roman, but the other kings here understand the realities of Gepidae life.'

Thorismund nodded, a trifle too quickly to have really considered the Gepid's argument, but Childeric, Sangiban and several lordlings inclined their heads slowly in agreement, for it is beholden on a king to keep his people alive as best he can.

'Tell the people of Tournai, Cambrai, Worms, Mainz and Amiens that Attila will understand if a king chooses to disobey him. I can hear them laughing beyond the shadows.' The Gepid warrior raised his manacled hands high. 'I am Erikk Horsebreaker, lord of many acres, not some slave to be treated like a starving dog stealing food from your fireside. Hear my words and decide what they are worth. But you harm your honour, Flavius Aetius, when you treat me like a cur.'

'Release him,' Aetius snapped, his face drawn into a tight

mask. Sensitive to the mood of his allies, he could not ignore the sympathy for the Gepid warrior that existed at the allied fireplace, but he hated to be countermanded even if he was forced to give the orders himself. If the Gepidae tribes came within his sphere of influence, and he could harm them without personal damage to himself, then Ardaric would be reminded why the Romans had ruled the world.

'We feared defeat before the battle even commenced. Attila had ordered his diviners to sacrifice a sheep so that its entrails could be read. When this task was undertaken, Attila tried to hide the results, but the rumours soon leaked out that the portents were bad – and you know how rumours spread.' Erikk shrugged in a wholly foreign manner, while Aetius and the other kings waited impatiently for the diviner's prophecy to be revealed.

'The Huns were promised a disaster and Attila was urged to change the site of the engagement, or pull out completely and attack Châlons instead. No one wanted to fight a pitched battle on that cursed ridge. Only one detail of the prophecy gave hope to the Hungvari, a prediction that one of the great leaders of the allies would die in the conflict to come. Attila sent his men to fight in the full knowledge that they were doomed, hoping that *you*, Flavius Aetius, would be the one to perish on the Catalaunian Plain.'

As Aetius raised his eyebrows, Thorismund uttered an exclamation that was partly a cry of pain and partly a snarl of fury at the capriciousness of the gods of war. Erikk Horsebreaker turned to address him.

'Yes, we were aware that King Theodoric of the Visigoths was dead, for my king and I both saw him perish. He fought to his last breath but was accidentally slain by his own friends.'

'Tell me!' Thorismund roared.

'After King Merovech defeated Ardaric during the night before the main battle, we were already a spent force. King Merovech and his valiant son, Childeric, were responsible for the loss of at least five thousand of our warriors. Yes, lord kings, five thousand Gepid warriors perished at the bidding of the Hun bastard. We who remained were used to stiffen the Germanic king Walimir's troops, but we were already in retreat when Theodoric fell. I had a clear view from a tumulus of stone behind Attila's front line. King Thorismund, your noble father was at the head of the charge against King Walimir, who was attempting to remove his forces from the field. A spent javelin struck King Theodoric and both horse and rider fell. I saw Theodoric rise to his feet just as his own Visigoths rode him down, for they were unable to halt the charge. Your father raised his sword and swung it at the sun, as if to call his cavalry onward, even if it meant his own end. Then he fell! Aye, your father had a good death and I would wish for the same.'

'It may be useful to know how our noble ally died,' Aetius interrupted, 'but I can't see that it has any bearing on Attila's plans.'

Aha! Myrddion thought. The general's diplomacy is slipping badly. Perhaps the old fox is afraid.

Erikk Horsebreaker bowed ironically and far too deeply for courtesy, causing Aetius's telltale brows to twist and writhe with a life of their own.

'When night came, we were attacked by a small contingent of Visigoth cavalry. I believe you were at their head, King Thorismund. You were forced to fight yourself free from the encounter with great loss of life, but Attila was incensed that his base camp should be so easily breached. The Dread of the World, as he calls himself, expected a further night attack and further retribution, so his warriors were forced to remain awake throughout the long hours until morning. Attila is a little mad!

'In the early hours of this morning, he ordered that the saddles of the dead should be raised into a tower, like a funeral pyre, in case the camp fell. Attila seated himself at the very summit of the pile. Before us all, and under the relentless volleys of your arrows, he swore that no enemy would ever capture him alive, which terrified his allies, who expected to die with him. No other king has the strength of purpose to supplant Attila. We fear him as much as you do.'

'So what are his plans now?' Aetius demanded urgently. 'Tell me, Gepid, for the lives of many men hang on your answer.'

'For the first time, we saw fear in the eyes of Attila. Ardaric looked at him as he sat, high on his pyre of saddles, and could clearly see that the end of a long tyranny was upon us. And so he determined to send me to you as his emissary. The latest sheep intestines speak of further disasters and Attila will be forced to retreat.'

Aetius paced around the fire while the allied kings and Erikk Horsebreaker waited in silence. The flaring light from the burning logs outlined the Roman's high cheekbones and turned his sunken eyes into black pits. He sucked on his teeth, spat, and made his decision.

'We have lost thousands of men, and the accounting will take many weeks to finalise. King Merovech is dead and King Childeric wishes to return his body to the north for burial, while King Thorismund would inter our noble ally Theodoric at the place where he fell while charging his enemy. We will let Attila decide our course of action!'

The allied kings looked puzzled and the Gepid warrior

would have remonstrated with the general had Aetius not silenced them all with a glance.

'Hear me! If Attila turns towards Buda and his lands, then he may pass in peace. I am afraid that we lack the strength to defeat him so easily on a second occasion. If he is so unwise as to turn towards the south, we must ride against him. We will have no choice. Childeric, ensure that arrows pepper the Hun camp right through the nights to come. Aiming scarcely matters, for it's the impact on Attila's nerves that we seek. He has never experienced defeat, so we'll let him feel it in his gullet until he chokes on it.'

Then Aetius turned his attention to Erikk Horsebreaker.

'And you, Gepid, may tell your master that he is free to return to his homelands with no hindrance from us. But hear me, Erikk whatever-you-call-yourself. Do not cross my path again, for I dislike your manners, your face and your presumption. You will stay beyond the Reno river and we'll agree to leave each other be. Thorismund!' The Visigoth responded with a look of sheer contempt. 'There are matters we need to discuss.'

Erikk Horsebreaker chuckled in Myrddion's general direction as the fireside slowly emptied. 'Well, well, well!' he whispered softly. 'Thorismund will need to hide his feelings more carefully in the future. Methinks there's no love lost between those two!'

'You spoke to me?' Myrddion asked, imperious in his rusty black, and alien in this far, violent place.

'Aye,' Erikk replied. 'Apart from the hulking Visigoths who brought me here, you're the only person in earshot. Your Roman friend rides far too high and he'll fall from his saddle faster than Attila at this rate.'

Myrddion paused to lift the edges of his robe away from a

burning log that had rolled out of the fire. 'Be careful what you say, Erikk, for Aetius might yet refuse to return you to your king unscathed. Perhaps these warriors might escort you to the edge of the camp and give you a horse – just to make certain that Aetius's orders are obeyed to the letter. And if I were you, I'd watch my back for stray arrows until such time as I was well on my way back to my master.'

The captain of the Visigoth guards grinned like a shaggy northern wolf. These men understood the nature of their Roman masters. And they did not approve of broken promises, even to erstwhile enemies. 'I will organise a small escort, healer, to ensure that the Gepid avoids the general's belated clutches. After all, we are only obeying his orders. King Theodoric would have enjoyed the irony of all this subterfuge.' The Visigoth kicked the log back into the fire with a brief shower of sparks.

'I'd be grateful for such an escort,' Erikk responded, and bowed to his captors with genuine respect.

Once the fireside was deserted, Myrddion sat and thought carefully. He knew that the situation at the field hospital was in hand and he could absent himself for an hour or two.

Aetius was old-school Roman, Myrddion decided, but he lacked the moral core that those ancients were rumoured to have possessed. After all, he's half Scythian, Myrddion reminded himself, and the Scythians are closer to Attila in thinking than to the old Roman senators. The general would kill Erikk out of hand, without a second thought, for the sake of a perceived insult.

Myrddion was still deep in thought when Thorismund came charging through the darkness from the direction of Aetius's tent. He was muttering savagely under his breath. 'Oh, it's you, healer! Where's the Gepid?'

'I sent him off with your guard for protection. I hope you aren't angry at my decision, but I feared he'd not reach the outskirts of our position alive without an escort.'

Thorismund laughed drily. 'A good guess, healer! I can see why my father set such store by you, although I must warn you that Vechmar doesn't like you – as if his opinion matters! What do you think Aetius should do?'

'Smash Attila while he can,' Myrddion replied economically.

'I agree, but he won't do it. He informed me that he wanted to counsel me on my tenuous position as heir to the throne. Yes, healer, in the middle of a war, Aetius wanted to advise me on the security of my succession. What does that tell you?'

'That you shouldn't be talking to me,' the young healer responded. 'Or anyone who can't be totally trusted. You must watch your back at all times from now on.'

'Frankly, Myrddion Emrys, you don't matter sufficiently to the success or otherwise of the alliance to be any threat. If I ask advice of anyone, you are one of the best choices, because no one will listen if you inform on me.'

Myrddion nodded at Thorismund's convoluted, but accurate, assessment of his worth.

'I was lost when I rode into Attila's camp.' Thorismund laughed sardonically. 'I was looking for Father – and I had no idea where I was. Now Aetius thinks I'm a fire-eater and a threat! He'd rather strip the alliance bare than have the Visigoths snarling at his back. Believe it or not, he fears me because I got lost in the darkness. The man is so used to treasonous thinking that he expects such behaviour from everyone.'

'Did you explain your mistake to him?'

'Do I look crazed, healer? Of course not! When you lie down with wolves such as Aetius, you'd better make sure your teeth are very sharp, as my father always said. I'll let the Roman think I'm more audacious and courageous than I really am.' Myrddion nodded in agreement. 'As for the situation at home, Aetius is half right. My brothers might be tempted to chance their arms against me. Perhaps! Do I stay with Aetius and wait for a knife in the ribs in the dead of night? Or do I return to Tolosa and secure my throne?'

Myrddion placed his finger directly on the seat of the problem. 'Can Attila hurt the Visigoths now?'

'No. He can't hold this part of Gaul, even if he wins tomorrow's battle. He must be nearly out of supplies for that vast horde. He can't hurt the Visigoths any more than he has already done.'

'Can the Romans hurt the Visigoths?'

'Ah, now you have it in a nutshell. If I die, my brothers will scrabble for power like dogs and my son will have little chance against them. I need time!'

Myrddion smiled at the older man and laid one hand on the bowed shoulders. 'You know the answer then, my lord. The blood that is shed in the name of ambition is much the same the world over. Your position must be bolstered in foundations of stone. But first your father must be buried, as must your many dead, so leave your decision for a while. Aetius will go down his own road, no matter what I or my prophecies might promise him.'

Thorismund raised his head and grinned fiercely. 'Aye. You were right with every detail of your cursed predictions. I should hate you, Myrddion Emrys, but how can a man hate the wind that carries the promise of a storm? Better I should be your friend than your enemy. Should you pass through my lands, call on me or mine if you need assistance. I will remember the kindness you showed to my father when you did not tell him that he would surely die. My father was no Merovech who assiduously courted death, so your silence was generous.'

'Your father was a closed and secretive man whom duty sorely harried. How could I add to his woes? Lord, acquit me of a kingly generosity, for I was silent because your father carried too many woes already. Besides, I think he already knew his fate.'

Thorismund sighed, and his love was plainly written on his face. 'Yes, my father was the centre of power for too many years to ever sleep soundly in his bed. He loved beautiful things, you know, and he was concerned for every man who gave him loyalty, so their deaths affected him deeply. His life had been hard, and he feared death. He might have known his fate in his secret heart, but suspecting and being told are very different things. No, you were generous.'

Silently, Myrddion nodded and left the campsite, leaving the new king to ponder over brutalities and broken alliances.

As the red morning dawned on the second day after the battle, Attila sat in his camp and brooded, while Aetius paced his tent and worked out strategies that would save Gaul for the Empire. The Catalaunian Plain was wreathed in smoke, for the armies were burning their dead. Myrddion feared disease more than he feared Attila, and he welcomed the acrid smoke and the stink of roasting flesh.

If Attila was destroyed, then the Visigoths would be the uncontested rulers of this whole wide land, and Aetius understood that he lacked the power to stop them from consolidating their control. If it served his purposes, he would murder Thorismund and send the Visigoths scurrying back to their rat-hole at Tolosa. That he might spare the Dread of the World, a man responsible for hundreds of thousands of deaths, was of little importance to Flavius Aetius, *magister militum* and king-maker. The balance of power must remain tipped in Rome's favour.

'Needs must!' Aetius told the silence of his campaign tent. 'Needs must!'

Myrddion understood the edges of the Roman general's thoughts, for he retained a memory of his trance, a strange after-shadow that warned him that Aetius was a truly danger-ous and ruthless man who lacked even the justification of patriotism. Aetius sought to elevate his family to the throne of the Western Empire, and if allowing the Hun to live would ease that path, then he would not care if a million further men died on the altar of his hubris.

Myrddion realised that King Vortigern had not been so very bad after all. He had sought to achieve and retain power over his vassals, but he had ruled well for many years. Vortimer, Ambrosius and even Uther were Celts or Romano-Celts who were devoted to their land and their subjects in their own different fashions. But Aetius was obsessed with the acquisition of personal power and the elevation of his family, even if the Empire was destroyed in the process. Myrddion searched his heart and his memory to find those motives in the great men he had known, and failed.

'I am learning, Cadoc, what true wickedness is. And it's not always to be found in cruelty or in violent murder. Sometimes, wickedness can wear a fair and reasonable face and swear that it fights for the lives and welfare of all. True wickedness cannot tell the difference between a lie and the truth.'

'Whatever you say, master,' his apprentice replied blankly. Sometimes, Myrddion spoke in riddles, and Cadoc, being a plain man who dealt with what he understood when it crossed his path, always took the line of least resistance.

In his secret heart, Myrddion felt his slow anger building. When powerful men exerted their influence to harm those who were weaker than themselves, or less intelligent or more sensitive, then the healer felt his temper ignite somewhere under his ribs. He had seen too much violence and random cruelty to be unmoved by the death of even one man.

The following day, the funeral of Theodoric was celebrated and then, regretfully, Thorismund put his nation first and led his army out of bivouac, away to the south and Tolosa. Vechmar went with them, along with his wagons and the Visigoth wounded.

That evening, four days after the Battle of the Catalaunian Plain, Prince Childeric summoned the healer to the campsite of the Salian Franks. Myrddion dressed carefully for the occasion, for he planned to say his farewells to Merovech. The dead king was his avowed lord, unwanted, but his liege none the less.

Before speaking to the healer, Prince Childeric led Myrddion to a small tent on a low rise some distance from the campsite. Four warriors guarded the outside of the tent, one for each corner of the world, and each wore a muffler of wool across his mouth and nose.

Myrddion could smell the green, acid stink of corruption long before he reached the rise, as the prevailing wind brought the smell directly to them. Childeric watched the healer closely for a reaction, and Myrddion knew that he was being judged. But his trade was to deal with death on a daily basis, and Myrddion had learned to breathe through his mouth so that he was no longer sickened by decay. Far worse than the smell of the dead was the same deadly reek within the flesh of those who remained alive.

Merovech was laid out in a wooden sarcophagus that

Childeric's smiths had sheathed with lead to minimise the outward signs of corruption. The lid lay to one side, ready to be nailed into place when the new king gave the order.

Washed, dressed and with his hair freshly oiled and combed, Merovech looked surprisingly young under the grey marbling of his flesh. The body was swelling under the rich armour and the nails of the fingers that held his sword's pommel were purpled and seemed to be loosening in their beds. Childeric and Myrddion looked down with shared regrets at the reckless, masculine face that possessed a special, marred beauty.

'I didn't know him well, but your father was an honest man and he was a wise and able ruler,' Myrddion said as he looked down on the ruined flesh. 'He asked very little of me and treated me with respect.'

'Aye, healer. He has passed on his duties to me, but he would have appreciated any words or prayers that you could give him to speed him on his way. He believed that, under the skin, you were his brother.'

Myrddion searched his memory for one of his grandmother's prayers to the Mother, and intoned an invocation to the midnight Lady of Winter who rules when the old king perishes and is replaced by the King of Springtime. 'May the Mother who loves us all guide this good man's journey to the abode of the gods. May she take his hand in the darkness and lead him along the dim paths from this life into the next, so that his feet neither falter nor stumble, and he comes at last to the Father and the great halls of the Otherworld. May he bless his son from beyond death and help him to rule wisely and well, so that the Franks live in peace and prosperity in this land that Merovech helped to save. As the Mother wishes, so shall it be.'

If Childeric was insulted by this women's magic, he gave no sign of it. He called the guard into the tent and instructed them to seal the lid on Merovech's sarcophagus and place it in the great wagon that awaited it. Then, once the carpenters had come to nail the coffin shut and caulk every crevice with pitch, Childeric led his guest back to his tent, where wine, fruit and nuts waited them.

'You will wonder why I have called for you, Myrddion, now called Emrys. First, I release you from your service to my house. My father never liked to constrain you, but he needed your skills, even if he felt guilty at forcing you to obey. Believe me in this, for we spoke of it in the hours before he died.'

'Thank you, my lord. I am grateful for my freedom, as you can imagine, although I doubt that Aetius will let me go so easily.' Myrddion smiled, and Childeric laughed ruefully in agreement. 'How did your noble father die, my lord? I know that I foresaw his death, but the scrolls of time are imprecise and I confess to curiosity.'

'The Alans and the Germanics were under attack and my king commandeered a troop of cavalry to relieve the pressure on them. He slew many men with his sword, but was taken by an underhand blow even as he killed the man who slew him. My father was content to die, believing your prophecy that he had founded a dynasty of kings. Did you speak the truth?'

The air Myrddion breathed felt odd and he remembered those rare times when he had spoken consciously of feelings he didn't truly understand. Now he struggled to describe accurately the half-formed images that chased themselves through his brain.

'I spoke the truth, Childeric. You will die an old man and you will be known as the leader of a great people. You will fight many battles and I see you serving the Western Empire for a time, although I also see a scroll that is torn in half as if a treaty is broken. You will then serve the Eastern Emperor in Constantinople, with greater willingness.'

'But what of the Frankish people? Will they endure?'

'This whole land will bear the name of your tribe, Childeric, for over two thousand years. Do not despair in the hard times to come. Your son will eclipse both you and your father, and will wrest a great throne out of chaos. You may have faith in your gods. I do not lie, although I cannot know if I speak the whole truth.'

'Thank you. Now drink, and I will be an ordinary man for one more night. I'll leave for the north tomorrow. True or not, your vision gives me heart, for truly the governance of men is a hard road and one I would not willingly choose without some trust in the future to which it leads.'

When Myrddion finally left the tents of the Salian Franks, he stumbled a little from weariness and the good Frankish wine he had consumed. Although he was bone tired and sickened by his part in this most pointless of battles, he picked up a clod of damp earth and squeezed it between his long fingers.

'The Battle of the Catalaunian Plain should have been a great victory, but with the Salian Franks and the Visigoths gone Aetius must let Attila escape. So much carnage for no clear result. This earth has become red with the blood of countless warriors and what has come of it?'

Myrddion had spoken aloud, for such heart-sickness demanded that he give it voice. But then he fell silent, smelled the scent of sun-warmed grass and watched the stars wheel above him in strange patterns that he couldn't read. Only time will show if all this sacrifice has any purpose, he decided, and then started as an owl began to scream from a small coppice of trees.

'The hunt,' he muttered to himself. 'Always the hunt!'

Then, drunk and sick of thinking, he staggered off to a warm bed on the sweet, green grass.

CHAPTER VIII

THE ROMAN WAY

Gorlois rode through the fields of summer, heavy with grain and pregnant with ripening fruit. Even the hedgerows bore a bounty of berries ripening under a clean sky that seemed a world away from the chills of winter. Yet although the sun warmed his leather jerkin and beaded his bare arms with sweat, Gorlois felt a chill in the region of his breast bone.

Since his queen had miscarried, she had failed to thrive. Tortured by thoughts of a lost son, Ygerne had sunk into a deep gloom through which her night terrors had returned. For years, the harmony of Gorlois's house had been free of Ygerne's frightened, haunted fancies, but now her imagination conjured up images of bloody babes and dead bodies piled in ugly drifts like cordwood. Increasingly, she searched for meaning in a universe that seemed crazed and disordered, and only an itinerant priest had brought her a fleeting period of peace.

So pagan Gorlois, still faithful to his household gods, had ridden to Glastonbury, the holy place that had been revered for a thousand years and even in the forgotten years before those times, when goddesses had wandered through its long grasses and sung by its sweet waters, to beg one of the holy men of the Christian god to journey to Tintagel to succour his wife.

Never alone, for this land was still wild and dangerous and far from the rules of law, Gorlois led his detachment of six men towards the wooden buildings that clustered a little way from the flanks of the tor. Springs rushed out of the side of the hill, and he could hear the subterranean murmur of a hidden river and noted that water lay in deep trenches beside the verdant fields, so the land appeared to be stitched together with skeins of silver thread. Long before the group of armed men reached the timber outbuildings, several cowled figures in homespun robes walked serenely out onto the roadway in welcome.

'Who disturbs the peace of Glastonbury?' a compact man murmured, his hands buried in the sleeves of his robe.

'I am Gorlois, king of the Dumnonii tribe. We are your neighbours. I seek a priest to advise my queen, who has been saddened by the loss of a child.'

Quietly, the man lowered his cowl and Gorlois saw a Roman head, austere in its carved beauty, atop a heavily muscled body that seemed out of place in its homespun robe. The hand that ushered the king towards the rough, barn-like building where visitors and penitents were housed was strong, calloused and blunt-nailed, and would have been at home wielding a short sword. Gorlois summed up the priest at a glance. An ex-soldier, he thought. And a man dedicated to the strategies and arts of war.

The priest's eyes were dark and dignified, but Gorlois saw knowledge behind those brown irises, and a deep well of sadness that matched the greying, close-cropped hair which seemed to beg for a helmet.

'If I may be so bold, Father, what is your name? Did you

serve in the legions?' Gorlois knew the questions were impertinent, but kings can always cover any social gaffes with the cloak of their position. He grinned with unconscious charm, and the priest immediately forgave him for his curiosity.

'I am Lucius, a humble servant of the one God. I was a soldier once, long ago, and in another life. In those long-gone days, I washed my hands in blood until my brain sickened, but I now labour in the fields in expiation for my many sins.'

Every war eventually ends, as do the darkest thoughts. Childeric had already left the encampment, heading towards the road leading to the north. In a pall of heavy dust, his troops rode protectively around the wagon that carried Merovech's body, offering their last respects to a noble king. Then, when the camp was stripped of its strongest allies, news came of Attila and the Hungvari horde.

That dawning, Myrddion had felt a physical wrench when Captus came to him as the first stains of another day coloured the sky.

'Wake up, Myrddion. Come on, man! Do you need a dowsing in cold water?'

Myrddion opened one bleary eye and realised that the pounding in his head was a result of four mugs of red wine in honour of the dead Frankish king. Swearing off the excessive consumption of alcohol forever, Myrddion raised his head from his pallet and saw that the sun was rising. Around him the field hospital was abustle, as wounded Franks were loaded into wagons with as much care as possible.

'Damn your eyes, Captus! I was with Prince Childeric until after midnight. I drank more wine than I'm accustomed to, and now I'm paying the price. Speak . . . quietly . . . please.'

Captus had hunkered down beside the simple pallet, but

now he rose to his feet with a wince of protesting knee joints.

'Getting old, friend Captus?' Myrddion quipped acidly, as he used the back of one hand to block the steadily rising sun. 'Serves you right for waking me.'

'If you're planning to be unpleasant, I'll leave without saying goodbye,' Captus snapped, only half joking.

'I'm sorry, Captus, you're leaving? Of course you are! How foolish of me. You'll accompany your new king as he bears Merovech home for burial.' Myrddion sat up on his pallet, swung his legs sideways and rose to his feet with the fluid, athletic flexibility of youth. Captus experienced a momentary stab of envy for the recuperative powers of younger men.

'Damn! I didn't undress last night, so I feel dirty and gritty all over.' Myrddion shook himself like a dog or a small boy, and the waves of his black hair flew around his face disarmingly. 'I will miss you, friend. You've made the task of healing infinitely easier in many ways. You have also taken the time to explain the battlefield to me. I'll not forget your lessons, Captus, you can be very sure of that.'

The Frank captain thrust out his sword arm in the ancient gesture of friendship between warriors. Each man gripped the wrist of the other and Captus expressed surprise at the strength in Myrddion's deceptively slender fingers.

'You've watched me at work, Captus, so you know the strength it takes to set a broken limb or to remove an arrow-head that is deeply embedded in muscle. Healers must be strong, not in the way of warriors where heavy muscle is needed, but with whipcord and wire.' He paused and smiled across at his friend. 'But I'm lecturing you again, which is fast becoming one of my worst sins.'

'I'll miss your jibber-jabber, Master Myrddion. I've learned things that I never thought possible and I'll try to keep your patients alive until we reach the north. Cadoc has given me clean bandages and I promise to boil them after each use. He's even given me some of his precious salve to promote healing, and I know what to do with radishes. I won't be eating them again, which is unfortunate as I used to really enjoy them.'

'Take care of yourself and your new master, Captus. He'll need loyal servants with good heads on their shoulders.'

Embarrassed, Captus drew a small wrapped bundle out of a leather pouch at his waist. 'This gift isn't much, I fear, but fighting men don't have the leisure to acquire many belongings. I'm told it came from Constantinople, and as you plan to visit the heart of the Eastern Empire it seems appropriate that you should take it back to its homeland. Use it, and remember Captus, who served you well, even though he whined continually.'

'That's not quite true, Captus. In fact you hardly ever complained.' As he spoke, Myrddion unwrapped the small scrap of wool and found a delicate eating knife of intricate design lying within.

The haft of the knife was decorated with hard paste glass that had been fired in a kiln at a high temperature. An artist had depicted a hunting bird on each side, one with its wings spread and its claws extended towards an invisible prey, the other at rest, but with its talons buried in a dead coney. A clever folding action enabled the blade to be thumbed into the haft when the knife was not in use. When the blade was open, it locked into position and became a wicked, double-edged toy for peeling fruit or eating meat. Yet it was quite sufficient to bury itself in a man's eye and kill.

'This is a beautiful thing, Captus. And it's far too valuable to be given away. Please take it back, for I really can't accept such a princely gift. I've never seen its like.'

'Can you imagine me holding such a toy in these great, clumsy paws of mine? No, Master Myrddion. Take it with my best wishes, and remember Captus whenever you use it.'

Myrddion realised that he would insult the Frank if he remonstrated any further. Besides, his hands itched to examine the clever mechanism that made the knife a miracle of design, small enough to fit in a waist pouch and free of the need for a scabbard.

'Very well, I'll take it to Constantinople, gladly and gratefully. I thank you, my friend.'

Myrddion walked with the captain to his horse and helped him to mount.

'One more thing remains to be said, my friend,' Captus added as he climbed into the saddle. 'Keep your eyes peeled for that bastard Gwylym. I know he's a Celt, but he's a Breton and hails from Brittany, which the Romans called Armorica. They're a strange, prickly people. Childeric has never liked him overmuch, but Gwylym could have continued in his service for life had he wished, because he served Merovech well. But the bastard has been bought by General Aetius for some unknown purpose. One thing is certain: your countryman's not overly fond of you.'

Myrddion shrugged. 'Gwylym told me that he came from Britain thirty years ago.'

'Then either he lied, or he had to leave Brittany in a hurry, because I know where he was born,' Captus said dourly.

'He has no reason to cause me any harm,' Myrddion murmured. 'I doubt that our paths will cross again.'

'Just keep it that way, lad. I've always believed that you can't trust a man whose loyalty can be bought with coin.'

Captus looked around him and saw that the last of the patients had been helped into the wagons, so he gave a shrill whistle and the cavalcade pulled away from the field hospital. Regretfully, Myrddion stood and watched until the dust of their passing had dissipated on the morning breeze.

On the heels of the Frank departure, the news came that Attila was on the move. Dust marked the passage of many horses and a token effort to burn the campsite sent plumes of smoke up into the sky that were torn to shreds on the morning breezes. Aetius had given orders that the Hun were free to depart without hindrance, although the minor tribal kings who remained argued over the merits of such rank stupidity. Even Finn Truthteller voiced an opinion on Aetius's decision and Finn rarely bothered to speak his mind, preferring to keep his thoughts to himself.

'This general is supposed to be the most able strategic thinker in the Western Empire. So why does he allow the greatest threat to the west to just walk away? The man's daft!'

Myrddion could only shrug, for Truthteller was right. 'I can't believe Aetius doesn't understand exactly what he's doing. He's too astute, and too good at battle strategy not to understand the implications of letting Attila go free. Wild boars don't turn into domestic pigs: they will always be savage. Aetius knows that the Hun will return with a fresh army.'

Finn pursed his lips. 'All true, master. In short, he could have killed Attila but he hasn't. He's either a traitor or there's some advantage to the general in letting the Hun go.'

'Yes. Either greed or admiration fires Aetius. I wonder which?'

Before the day was half over, Myrddion was to discover part of the motivation behind Aetius's inaction. A Roman centurion arrived at the field hospital within half an hour.

Attila's dust had barely settled and black smoke still hovered over the Hun campsite.

'I seek Myrddion of Segontium, sometimes called Emrys,' the hard-bitten veteran demanded. He was taller than the usual Roman warrior and his face, under hair cropped close to accommodate his helmet, was more Goth than Italic in shape and bone structure. Many, if not all, of the Roman soldiers were auxiliaries called librones, mixed-blood warriors who had once been regular troops, but were now called on in times of great need when manpower was short.

'I am the healer, Myrddion Emrys, whom you seek. What can I do for you, centurion?'

The Roman was forced to look up into Myrddion's face, an experience that the man obviously found intolerable, for he visibly bit his lip and stood at attention with both fists clenched.

'I am instructed to accompany you to the Hun camp in case there are living casualties left behind. Be quick! I have a horse ready for you, if you know how to ride.'

'One moment,' Myrddion murmured, although Finn's face was stiff with insult. 'I'll need my tools.'

'Master, are you sure you wish to accompany this ... person ... sight unseen?' Finn whispered. 'Why would Aetius want to save the lives of wounded Hungvari? After the battle, the Romans killed all the Hungvari prisoners.'

Myrddion smiled at the centurion. 'The *magister militum* has no plans to hurt me, does he, centurion? He's a clever, able general who would never publicly harm a non-combatant, even if he had some issue with me. And he doesn't, does he?'

'Of course not,' the centurion replied dourly.

'See, Finn? Of course not! I shall be back very shortly.

General Flavius Aetius is simply concerned about any wounded men who might inadvertently have been left behind.'

Carrying his satchel, Myrddion trotted behind the centurion until they reached two horses tethered to a small shrub. Out of bravado, Myrddion loosened the tied reins and vaulted into the saddle, checking the beast's instinctive dance without the slightest sign of difficulty. 'As you can see, centurion, some Celts do know how to ride.' Then, without a backward glance, as if he was free of care, Myrddion kneed his horse into a gallop and headed towards the Hungvari encampment. He suspected that Aetius was exercising his power over the field hospital simply to waste Myrddion's time and demonstrate Roman superiority.

If that's his plan, then he's out of luck, Myrddion thought, for I've been longing to see how the Hungvari set up their bivouacs.

The stench of unburned bodies was sickening – a vile, greenish smell that seeped into the pores of the skin and lingered in the folds of garments. Attila had sought to delay pursuit by leaving a wall of dead surrounding the huge encampment. Even now, allied warriors were using wild-eyed horses to drag away rotting bodies piled high on wagons, sleds and other makeshift vehicles and dumping them in a dry watercourse some distance away, preparatory to burning. Only fire would kill the threat of disease.

'I doubt I'll find anything living in this charnel house,' Myrddion grumbled at the centurion, but curiosity still made him eager to see the disposition of the enemy camp. 'From the look of this place, you will be burning Hun corpses for weeks.'

Attila had fled leaving everything behind, having come to the conclusion that the lives of his warriors were of greater worth than the gold and plundered wealth taken from the cities he had sacked in his earlier campaigns. This great accumulation of wealth, piled onto huge wagons, would only have slowed the retreat.

With a jolt of active dislike, Myrddion watched a crew of Roman librones who had obviously been trained in clerical skills as they unpacked, counted and then repacked chasubles, crosses, reliquaries, caskets and precious paintings that had been looted from the Christian churches in the East. In other strongboxes, belted with beaten iron but opened for counting, the healer could see Roman coins, jewels and golden ornaments spilled in a tangle of unimaginable wealth. Still more slaves were collecting camphor-wood chests from the Orient containing fine fabrics, silks, pure wool and dyed linens that were almost as fine as spun spiders' webs. The treasure of Attila had been captured and Aetius had avoided sharing it with the Visigoths and the Salian Franks, his major allies, who had been encouraged to leave the plain.

'Will such wealth buy a throne, I wonder?' Myrddion asked the empty air guilelessly. The centurion stared dourly at him, but held his tongue.

The healer rode through the huge campsite, seeking any wounded warriors as he had been ordered, but Attila had left nothing alive behind him, not even stray dogs. The cooking fires were stone cold, so food had been perilously short by the time the decision to retreat had been made. Myrddion was quietly glad that he didn't live in the path of the vast horde of hungry Huns and their allies, who were far from their homes and short on supplies.

One memento of Attila's presence had been abandoned

intact, like an impudent finger, to dominate a landscape that had been laid waste by men. Attila had left his tower of saddles in place, a mad, teetering affront to the Catalaunian Plain and the thousands who had perished there.

'That ... thing ... should be torn down and burned,' Myrddion snapped, pointing at the offending tower. 'Attila meant it as an insult.' What am I doing here, if Aetius doesn't plan to kill me? he thought. Is this excursion really just a sham to humiliate me?

The sound of raised voices suddenly shattered the oppressive noonday heat. Myrddion's eyes sharpened.

'Have you finished then, healer?' the centurion demanded. 'There are no wounded left for you to treat, which makes you superfluous to our needs.'

'Just a moment!'

'We leave right now, healer. The day won't wait for you to be deciding what should be done by your betters.'

But Myrddion held his horse on a tight rein on the softly rising slope.

In what was left of Attila's burned tent, an argument in purest Latin was in full spate. The raised voices carried to them easily, although the centurion seemed oblivious of the shouting. The young Celt knew at once that the *magister militum* owned one of the heated voices, although he couldn't recognise the other, and was riveted to the spot as he listened to the dispute. The centurion, for all his status as a Roman officer, appeared unable to understand what Aetius and his companion were saying, and Myrddion was reminded that most men in Gaul spoke a bastardized patois, a combination of Goth, Frank and Latin words cobbled together for convenience. The bulk of the population also spoke Gaulish, a language very similar to Celt. Myrddion considered how useful it was that Aetius was ignorant of his proficiency in Latin.

Within the half-burned tent, the two men were very angry.

'Do you plan to rob the two empires of their share of Attila's treasure? You already appear to have more than enough, having removed the Visigoths and the Salian Franks from your encampment.'

'It's none of your business what I choose to do with the spoils of this war, envoy. Valentinian charged me with saving Gaul from Attila's hordes – which I have done – so I'd be obliged if you minded your own affairs.'

'As *magister militum*, and the greatest general of this age, I expected better of you, Flavius Aetius. You allowed Attila to go free after he had murdered thousands of innocent peasants and civilians. How many more innocents will feel the lash of the Hungvari so that your clerks can count his treasure? In Constantinople, we know the Hun well. The sacred icons out there came from our churches, and our priests were butchered at their altars. Attila will expect to regain his booty in the spring – probably at the expense of our hides.'

Aetius's voice was particularly cutting. 'Attila would not have stopped until he reached the ocean if I hadn't defeated him here. It was I who halted his advance – not Emperor Theodosius, your master in Constantinople. I stopped him to further the cause of the only true emperor, Valentinian of Rome and Ravenna. To the victor go the spoils, although you may keep the sacred pictures as my gift to your emperor. My master, Valentinian, will be given the greater share.'

'Your words are very comforting, Aetius. But I heard the prophecy given by the Celt in Châlons, and I found it . . . illuminating. He's clever, that young healer, even if he's a charlatan. Theodoric of the Visigoths thought highly of him after a very short acquaintance, as did Merovech, your protégé. They fought at the very front of the engagement, whereas you were on the flank. The barbarians bore the brunt of the assault and earned a share of the spoils. Don't stiffen up on me, Aetius, for it's been an age since I last saw that cold face of yours register any human emotion. I welcome any sign that you're still human. I'll take the golden icons gladly, small recompense as they are, but I can assure you that we're watching you in the east. You should be careful that you don't bite off more than you can chew.'

Myrddion suddenly realised that listening in to a private conversation between the great ones of the world could be prejudicial to his health. He turned his horse with a sudden downward tug of the right rein, ignoring the beast's complaint and dancing hooves.

'Thanks for the tour, centurion, but as I'm unnecessary now, I'll return to the field hospital where I can be of some use. I'll dispatch the horse to your encampment with a servant.' Before the centurion had a chance to complain, he dug his heels into the flanks of his mount and galloped away.

Cleoxenes came out of the ruined tent, his narrowed eyes picking out Myrddion's retreating form as he passed through the entrance flap. Through the cloud of dust churned up by the hooves of the departing horse, the envoy could still see the black banner of the young healer's uncut hair, and his mouth twisted with wry humour.

He heard us, the envoy decided inwardly, but does he understand Latin? That young man warrants closer study, especially as he's not Aetius's creature. Would he be useful, I wonder? And those eyes! Should I say aloud what I think?

Unaware that his fate was prominent in the minds of two

great men – for Aetius still harboured a great dislike for the Celt – Myrddion occupied himself for the next two days in the mundane tasks of boiling, washing, herb collection, poultice making and root drying that had to be done if the healers were to continue their trade in peace.

Each day, he waited impatiently for word that he could leave the ridge of the Catalaunian Plain, and each day he was disappointed as, one by one, the Roman allies took what booty Aetius allocated to them and rode away to their homelands. Summer was hammer-beat cruel and Myrddion's patience eventually ran out. Fearing that he would alienate Aetius even further if he approached him in person, he sent a carefully worded letter to the Roman general by the hand of the most disarmingly harmless of his widows, the wide-eyed, pretty Bridie.

In the letter, couched in Latin for a number of reasons, not the least being that the Gallic patois was never written, Myrddion begged Aetius to free him from further obligation so that he could continue his search for knowledge. The healer assured the general, in a self-effacing fashion, that he would ensure that all the remaining patients would be taken to Châlons for recovery.

Although well aware of Flavius Aetius's active dislike, the Celt didn't really expect the reaction that followed. Air that was sweet with corruption fuelled disease, and Myrddion assumed that Aetius would be happy to see the last of the healers and their patients.

When Bridie limped back to the healers' tents several hours later, weeping as quietly as she could, it was some minutes before Myrddion realised she had returned. Then he became aware of hushed voices and snatched up a pottery bowl of oil, complete with a burning cotton wick, before easing his way into the smaller tent where the widows cared for the wounded and slept at night.

'What in Hades has happened?' he hissed when he saw the other two women engaged in the task of dressing a cruel gash across the back of Bridie's knee. Brangaine was tenderly washing the nasty slash with warm water, while Rhedyn used clean rags to staunch the steady flow of blood that oozed down Bridie's leg and stained her robe an ugly sanguine.

'Bridie didn't want you troubled, master,' Brangaine whispered, as Willa, sensing the tension that charged the air, began to cry.

'Show me, you silly girl. It was I who sent you to the general, so any mishap you've suffered is my fault. Were you waylaid on the way back to the camp? I should have sent one of the men with you.'

Myrddion's full attention was on Bridie's wounded knee. With a sinking feeling under his ribs, he realised that a tendon had been severed, turning her foot unnaturally inwards. So daunted was he by the impossible task of re-attaching the tendon, which had retreated up into the thigh, that he scarcely heard her reply.

'What did you say, Bridie?' he asked, as his bloody fingers sought for the slippery, elusive cord. 'Who ordered this injury?'

Bridie hiccupped with distress. 'You'll be angry, master.'

'So you know who did this thing? Tell me immediately so I can demand some form of reparation for you.'

Bridie was now weeping in earnest, great gusts of misery and pain that caused her whole body to tremble as if she had the ague. She pressed her face into her pallet and shook her head.

'She doesn't want to say, master,' Brangaine explained in a

voice that was sharp with distress and suppressed fury. 'There's nothing you can do, because Bridie believes that they plan to kill you if you complain.'

'What do you mean?'

'General Flavius Aetius became angry when he read your letter. He sent Bridie back with this wound to remind you that you are crippled without him.'

Myrddion felt a sudden, visceral surge of rage so primal that he couldn't speak. He could understand Aetius's argument with him, for he had goaded the Roman with a prophecy that seemed to lay bare his most secret ambitions, and had been neither an obedient nor a willing servant. But to cripple a harmless woman, sent in broad daylight to deliver a letter, besmirched Myrddion's honour with such devastating thoroughness that the young Celt felt he couldn't live with the shame.

'Were you hurt in . . . other ways?' Myrddion demanded. 'Don't shake your head at me, Bridie, or I'll draw my own conclusions, I swear.'

Bridie wailed, causing Rhedyn to shoot a warning glance at Myrddion that was both reproachful and feminine in its world-weariness. 'They said it didn't matter what they did to her as she was only a jumped-up camp follower. She was even less important because Celts have no standing now that the island of Britain has been lost to the empire.'

'Who said this?' Myrddion hissed between his teeth.

'The guard. The librones,' Bridie whispered, lifting her face so that Myrddion saw an ugly bruise forming across one side of her face. 'It doesn't matter, master, truly it doesn't. I suppose I became a camp follower after losing my Llywarch when he was fighting for King Vortigern. We'd been hand-fasted for a year so I thought of myself as his wife, but . . .'

Then Bridie began to sob in earnest, and the soft-hearted Rhedyn took her into her arms and rocked her as if she were a child.

'This tale gets worse and worse!' Myrddion exclaimed with loathing. 'Someone should pay for your pain. And someone will! Cadoc!' he roared, and the apprentice came running in response to a voice that seemed too raw and violent to belong to his master. 'Stitch Bridie's wound together for me. I have tried to grip the tendon where it has slid back into the sheath of muscle, but I have failed. Do what you can with forceps, because I am required elsewhere.'

'Master, please take Finn with you wherever you're going. Please?'

Cadoc's words were drowned out by the tide of fury that robbed Myrddion of any rational thought. Without pausing for reflection, or considering the distance he had to travel, the healer stalked through the encroaching dark. The days were shortening, for autumn would soon wrap the plain in russet, gold and saffron. But Myrddion was careless of the smell of ripening fruit or the warm perfume of sweet grasses that were carried on the evening wind. He was fuelled by rage, and pity for Bridie, who would never walk properly again.

The physical marks of her rape would fade but, unlike most men, Myrddion understood the crippling of the heart and mind that women suffer after such an ordeal. The fact that unattached women were fair prey in the minds of many warriors had never struck the healer before, because his servants had always been treated with respect. His eyes had now been opened, and he felt a heavy contempt for his sex.

Flavius Aetius's tent was a mellow golden glow in the midst of the smaller flares of light that indicated the Roman fire-pits. Myrddion stalked past wagons already piled high with strongboxes filled with plunder, and the attention lavished on these inanimate objects made him feel even more heartsick and angry. Aetius's passion for gold and treasure was greater than his care for the dead Theodoric, his loyal Merovech or any unimportant little woman who acted as a messenger and brought him unsolicited, unwelcome news.

Without breaking stride, Myrddion used the flat of his right hand to burst through the partially closed flap, and entered the tent.

Two of the general's guards reached out to stop him, but Myrddion was faster. The taller of the two men, the centurion who had accompanied him to Attila's camp, received the heel of Myrddion's still out-thrust right hand on the side of the jaw. Surprised by the force behind the blow, the warrior fell, his eyes momentarily blank and dazed. The other auxiliary began to draw his sword, but Myrddion turned his back on him and focused his furious black eyes on the startled face of his quarry, General Aetius.

The general had almost reached his feet when the Celt stretched out for him across the low eating table with long iron fingers that were curled into claws and aimed unerringly for the throat of the *magister militum*.

Whether Myrddion would have succumbed to his killing rage or come to his senses would never be known. Two strong, silk-clad arms gripped him round the chest from behind and pinioned his arms so that he couldn't move, regardless of how desperately he struggled.

'Take him out and cut his throat,' Aetius ordered, and the two guards would have obeyed if a cultured voice had not brought them to a confused halt.

'Stand down. Now. Wait outside until I call for you. Obey

me, damn your eyes! I am Cleoxenes, envoy of Emperor Theodosius, overlord of the east, and also his personal strategist. As a Roman nobleman whose ancestors sailed up the Tiber with Aeneas, I demand that you step aside and stand down.'

'I gave you an order,' Aetius cried angrily, and upended the small table. The remains of a meal and some crude pottery plates tumbled onto the hard-packed earth, where the terra cotta smashed with a sound like the crunching of old bones under heavy boots.

'You will obey me.' The urbane voice of Myrddion's captor had not risen in volume. 'I too have the ear of Emperor Valentinian, who will not choose to alienate his brother emperor and kinsman in Constantinople, no matter how valuable you are to him. After all, as you have pointed out to me, you have already routed the Hun. That task is now complete.'

Reluctantly, the two guards backed out of the tent, leaving a small, dangerous tableau of three men standing in the ruins of a simple meal.

'Sit down, general, please. Do you want those ruffians to hear you shouting and raving over an unarmed and ineffectual healer? Even your reputation is not safe from vicious gossip, my friend. Besides, ranting and threats of violence are crass, vulgar and needless. I've never thought of you as one of those buffoons who think they can silence any opposition by imprudent, ill-considered violence.'

Even through his rage, Myrddion was surprised when Aetius righted his toppled campaign chair and sat down.

'And now for you, young idiot,' Cleoxenes said calmly. 'Surely an attempt to assault your master is not a part of your craft. I have read the writings of Hippocrates and I'm tolerably certain that he wrote quite forcibly against all forms of violence.'

'First, do no harm!' Myrddion hissed, as he tried to fill his cramped lungs with air.

'Precisely,' his captor murmured, as if the young Celt was a particularly bright schoolboy reciting his lessons. 'So, young healer. If I release you, will you promise to refrain from trying to rip out the general's throat? Do you carry a weapon of any kind? You can be assured that I'm quite prepared to strip you and search you, if I have any doubts about your truthfulness.'

'Yes, I promise. And no, I'm not armed,' Myrddion snarled, too angry to feel any gratitude for the envoy's intervention. 'I won't touch him, but I want to know why a man of his pedigree would cripple a servant woman who posed no threat to him. Was it just a whim, or is he some parody of a man? And then to give her to his men for a plaything is . . . not the behaviour of an honourable Roman.'

'A reasonable question, and, if true, it's all very unpleasant. But I have no idea what you're talking about.' There was still no trace of anger, disgust or anxiety in Cleoxenes's voice.

'I sent a letter to General Aetius begging permission to depart the Catalaunian Plain and recommence my journey to find a new master. I am no longer needed here, and plague or disease caused by the ill humours in this place could kill those few patients who remain if we don't repatriate them to Châlons.'

'So?'

'My servant, Bridie, a widow woman, delivered my message. I chose her because she does not understand Latin and because she is biddable and gentle. She is certainly incapable of rudeness or impropriety. I know how much the general dislikes me, although I swear I am no threat to him, and am not responsible for my ravings when I'm in a trance. I sent my request in good faith, using a messenger because the general told me to stay out of his presence. Had I known what would happen here ...'

'Tell me,' Cleoxenes ordered brusquely. 'And without the soul-searching and high drama. It's irritating.'

Myrddion flushed hotly, but his response was free of hyperbole. 'Bridie returned to the camp hospital with the tendon behind her knee severed by some form of weapon. She will never walk easily again, for all my skill at treating wounds.' Cleoxenes clicked his tongue behind his teeth. 'The message sent to me by the general stated that I should remember that I am crippled without the support of the *magister militum*, who presents himself as a noble Roman. If this is the way of the Roman aristocracy, then perhaps the rule of Attila would be less painful and more honourable.'

Cleoxenes freed Myrddion from his harsh and painful embrace. 'Fighting words, young man. Are you saying that General Aetius crippled your servant himself?'

'No, I imagine the general ordered his guard to cripple Bridie. I don't know if pack rape was part of his instructions, but she suffered that indignity as well.'

The expression on the envoy's face did not change. Myrddion could have been discussing the beauty of a sunset for all the emotion it showed. The healer's heart sank and he prepared himself for imminent death.

'Kill the Celt and have done, Cleoxenes!' Aetius snarled. 'Or are you too squeamish for red work?'

'You know that I'm not the least bit squeamish, my friend, but I hate waste. This young man is an asset to us. It's true that he's a difficult asset, but he could be a useful tool for your hand, or to provide some service for Emperor Valentinian.

I'm reluctant to waste such a man because he failed to control his temper. A lesser man would have simply poisoned your drinking water.'

Despite his rigid control, Aetius paled a little. Healers had a wide knowledge of poisons, as everyone knew, and Myrddion could have taken his revenge in any number of gruesome ways.

'As for you, Myrddion Emrys, I never took you for a fool, but I'm prepared to change my mind. I cannot speak for the general, but the guardsmen consider unprotected females to be tasty morsels to be taken at will. Generals cannot be held accountable for the crude behaviour of their men when they're chasing an available woman. However, you have now informed the general that your servant has been raped so he will, as an honourable commander, take action against the perpetrators. Flavius Aetius is an honourable man.'

Myrddion snorted and, surreptitiously, Cleoxenes ground his heel into the Celt's sandalled instep. The healer barely suppressed a yelp of pain. Aetius sat in his campaign chair like a stone effigy. Only his eyes seemed alive, while his face was ugly with malice.

'Because we understand your very natural anger at the treatment meted out to your servant,' Cleoxenes went on, 'we will allow you to go free – and unpunished – if you give your solemn vow never to raise your hand against the general again, and swear to give him loyal service for as long as breath remains in your body or the general releases you from this vow. Do you hear me?'

Through a throat that was raw with anger, Myrddion agreed to make the vow demanded by the envoy. He was a little frightened by how close death had come to him and the servants whom he valued so highly. For the first time, the red tide of bloodlust ebbed from behind his eyes and he began to think clearly.

The envoy was so willowy and delicate in build that Myrddion had seemed the more vigorous man, but Cleoxenes had restrained him as if he were little more than an infant. Already, Myrddion was mulling over the acquisition of the physical skills of defence with one part of his brain, while another train of thought was dominated by admiration for the strategic and manipulative gymnastics demonstrated by the diplomat.

'There now, Aetius, my friend. The healer is tied to you for your lifetime. He cannot, and will not, harm you or move against you in any way from this day onward. You'd be foolish to smash shell and kernel with your fist when, with a little reflection, you can enjoy the nut itself.'

Aetius wasn't convinced, but he could see that a moment's anger had the potential to destroy his plans of an advantageous marriage for his son, if the matter should come to the ears of Valentinian. Rumour of unnecessary brutality, even against a camp follower, could make Aetius look incapable of controlling his own troops. Better that the healer should meet with an accident, totally divorced from his dealings with the general.

But Myrddion wasn't yet ready to permit the matter to rest. 'Roman honour means nothing if a helpless peasant woman can be hamstrung or brutalised on the orders of a general. She is not a slave, but these are punishments meted out to slaves. She is not a thief, but her treatment would be a thief's just deserts. She is only a woman who wiped away the shit, piss and blood of Roman soldiers. She helped them to drink water when they thirsted and she cleaned the pus from their wounds. She is only a Celtic woman – but she is free and honest and gives comfort to the dying. Because of Roman anger and pride, she will now be unable to walk unaided for the rest of her life. She deserves reparation.'

Aetius had calmed, and was now steely in his disdain, but Cleoxenes was a different man entirely. For the first time, he demonstrated that he followed the Christos by making the sign of the cross on his breast.

'I am of Roman stock – almost pure, although my name speaks of my Greek lineage. I will pay red gold so that this widow shall not suffer hardship because of her incapacity, for my lord Jesus would expect me to succour those who are heavy laden or bowed down with suffering. Should General Aetius wish to contribute, his gold will be added to mine.'

Cleoxenes pushed Myrddion forward, for the younger man was confused by the whole charged conversation between the two Romans. He was out of his depth and he knew it. 'You will now beg General Aetius's pardon, healer, for you had no right to raise your hand in anger against your master, regardless of your feelings of compassion towards your servant woman. Do it!' the envoy ordered, when Myrddion was slow to respond, and, hesitantly, the healer found the words to offer a grudging apology.

'I will see this young fool on his way,' Cleoxenes murmured to Aetius. 'Wait for me, general, for my business with him will not take long.'

Outside the tent, away from the two guards, Cleoxenes shook Myrddion as a fox shakes a rabbit.

'The general will ensure that you have an accident unless you leave immediately. Do not fret for your patients, for I will see that they are returned to Châlons. You must go south as quickly as your wagons can travel. Aetius won't try to stop you – not openly. Are you listening?'

'Aye,' Myrddion answered. 'But where do I go? And why should you bother to help me?'

'After Châlons, continue south until you reach the mountainous headwaters of the Sequana river. Cross the river and travel further south until you reach Alesia. From there, you will see a narrow valley between low mountains that will lead you to the Rhodamis river. Lugdunum is the first great city you will reach. Follow the Rhodamis in a southerly direction till you reach Arelate and then follow the coast to the port of Massilia. Once you reach the sea, do not take ship. Hear me, Myrddion? Do not take ship! Flavius Aetius will expect you to go to Rome by the speediest possible route and his spies will soon find you and arrange your assassination. Instead, follow the coastal strip until you reach Italy, and then head south once more. All roads lead to Rome, but you would do well to avoid Ravenna at the moment.'

'Why should I run like a frightened dog?' Myrddion's voice was sulky, and achingly young.

'Aetius is aggrieved and will seek revenge on you and your party. Of course he gave the order that your woman should be hamstrung, although I acquit him of complicity in her rape. As far as Aetius is concerned, Bridie isn't real. She's just a small piece of ivory in a board game. Believe it or not, he did it to annoy and frighten you. I doubt he expected your reaction, but if I hadn't been dining with him he'd have had you killed immediately to remove that nasty itch at the back of his brain. That's all you are – an itch! And Bridie matters even less. When his plans reach fruition, as they probably will, he'll forget you if you're not under his feet.'

Myrddion said nothing. In the face of the envoy's lucid assessment of his situation, there was nothing he could say.

'You must trust me to enact some justice on your behalf. I'll make it plain to Aetius that, for the sake of appearances and the maintenance of discipline, the guilty guardsmen must be publicly flogged. Will that satisfy you?'

'I suppose I must accept.'

'You must. As for reparation, I will handle those details. I will catch up with you on the road and see to the future of your widow. Do not fail me in this matter, Myrddion Emrys, for I have plans for your future.'

'Why are you helping me?' Myrddion repeated. 'What have you to gain by saving our lives?'

Cleoxenes laughed quietly. 'I'm damned if I know. Something tells me that if I keep you alive, then I am doing the work of both my master and my God. Consider the possibility that my God speaks to me the way yours does to you. But, for the sake of your dependants, you must learn diplomacy, young man. Sadly, many Romans are worse, much worse, than Flavius Aetius. In his way, he is noble, and almost impossibly brave. The empires depend on him.'

Myrddion looked at the sky, where the stars seemed more distant than ever. His hare-brained scheme to find his father while dragging his faithful servants to this alien land had brought them nothing but trouble. And now Bridie had paid for his reluctance to face up to Aetius man to man.

'I should have presented that letter to the general in person,' he whispered softly. 'Bridie is crippled because of my cowardice.'

Cleoxenes heard a world of regret in that simple sentence, and he responded by slapping Myrddion's face. But the blow was gentle, almost like the caress of a lover.

'You would be dead if you had delivered that letter in person, so you should learn from Bridie's pain. The Lord Jesus has some reason to test you, but don't look to me for answers. I'm too old to be certain of anything.'

'But I have no allegiance to your Jesus. I am sworn to the Mother and Lady Ceridwen, my ancestor.'

'Sometimes the Lord has need of us whether we are pagan or Christian,' Cleoxenes said. 'I would be a saint if I fully understood the ways of my God, but, as you know, I'm not a saint. Time will reveal the purpose that heaven has laid out for us all. But walk carefully, boy, for not all great men possess Merovech's joy in living or Theodoric's love for his people. Kings are only men, as fallible as you or I.'

Myrddion walked away, his shoulders slumped in despair, and Cleoxenes sighed with irritation. He would need to speak to Flavius Aetius and warn him that he would suffer great loss if he raised his hand against the healer and his party. Threats might not work, so the envoy was already seeking out the honeyed words of warning that a sophisticated strategist such as Flavius Aetius would recognise. If all else failed, Cleoxenes was prepared to be blunt and give Aetius an unvarnished assessment of the situation. The chicken and peppers he had consumed with such gusto only an hour earlier were churning in his gut with the promise of a hot, salty attack of vomiting. All his life, Cleoxenes had managed to straddle spear-points with a certain natural elan, but his stomach pained him often and fierce stress headaches sometimes confined him to his bed.

The envoy sighed again as the smell of burning bodies wafted to him on a wind change, and caused his nose to twitch with a sharp, gut-wrenching smell of pork. 'Oh, to be among civilised company in a place as far away from here as I can travel,' he whispered in Greek, trusting that no one would understand his words if eavesdroppers were spying on him.

Aetius was capable of almost any treason, even the accidental death of an envoy, no matter how nobly born.

'And now to frighten the old fox,' he muttered. 'If all else fails, I'll remind the old devil that I remember how he lived with the Hun for years, ostensibly as a hostage, but ultimately as a friend. Yes, Aetius, I remember the days when you held up the Hun as a people to be admired. Are you playing both sides against the middle, as usual? Or are you simply making a last grab for power before it's too late? Be damned to you, you turncoat. Even in Greek, your actions sound despicable.'

Then Cleoxenes swept into Aetius's disordered tent with the assumed confidence of a king.

MYRDDION'S CHART OF THE JOURNEY FROM CHÂLONS TO MASSILIA

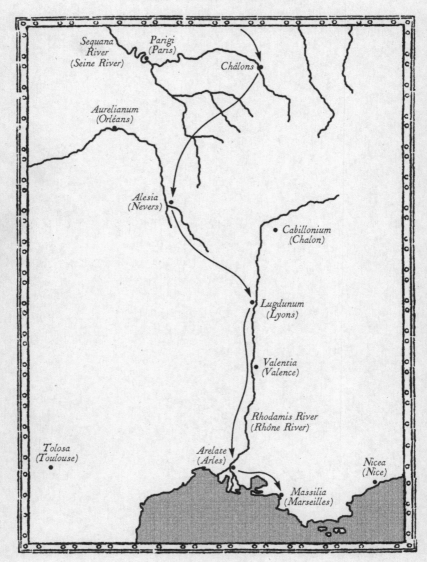

CHAPTER IX

THE ENDLESS ROAD

Urgency spurred Myrddion into action.

True to his agreement with Cleoxenes, he ordered Finn Truthteller, Rhedyn and Brangaine to begin packing up the larger of the tents and prepare for an immediate night departure. As Cadoc had finished stitching Bridie's leg and covered the wound with radish paste and salve to prevent infection, he enlisted his long-suffering apprentice's help in moving the last of the patients out of the smaller tent.

Although the night was well advanced, humidity rendered the air thick and muggy, and Myrddion and his companions sweated in the sullen heat. Somewhere far away, a distant rumble of thunder spoke of approaching storms. The healer watched moths flutter towards the oil lamp, drawn by the flame, until their wings caught alight and they perished in sudden little flashes of golden light.

'We must be gone before dawn or we will all be dead. I wish we'd never left Britain.'

Cadoc, returning from some errand of his own in time to hear the heartfelt murmur, longed to reply with the trite response of 'I told you so', but a hint of unshed tears in Myrddion's voice stilled his tongue. The boy was exhausted and carried loads far heavier than someone his age should be forced to bear.

'Well, we did leave, master, so let's shake the dust of this cursed place off our clothes and our feet as quickly as possible.' He picked up a basket of bandages and clean rags. 'Where are we going?'

Myrddion was busy putting bunches of drying herbs into a rush container. In his haste and upset, he jammed the woven lid into place with more force than was necessary, and Cadoc heard several of the dried rush stems snap.

'To Rome. We'll travel by way of Gaul and much of Italia.'

'But that'll take months. Or even a year, if the weather's bad,' Cadoc protested. 'Why not head back north where life is safer?'

'Gaul virtually belongs to Aetius and no part of it, especially the north, is free of the weight of his hand. The general would catch us and have us killed long before we reached Parigi. No, Lord Cleoxenes is right. We must head south, and away from Aetius's influence, at best speed. No doubt he will want to reach Ravenna without delay, but with luck his treasure will slow him down and give us time to escape.'

A glow of light flashed along the ridgeline, and Myrddion registered that a storm was coming closer, although there was still a short interval between the lightning and the roll of thunder. The smothering heat seemed to increase, as the eerie silence that heralds a storm enfolded the plain in a thick, dry blanket.

'Please, master, promise me we won't be using a ship to take us to this Italia. I couldn't stand another long sea voyage.'

'You're in luck, Cadoc. Lord Cleoxenes has insisted we

travel the whole way by wagon. Perhaps we can purloin some extra horses. Heaven knows there are many abandoned beasts running wild at the moment.'

Cadoc grinned in the darkness. 'I'll steal as many horses as we need, as long as we can stay away from the sea. Another team would speed our journey, especially if we men find mounts to ride. Less weight to pull.'

'Then hop to it, Cadoc. But don't get caught . . . please? I doubt the Romans will even realise that half a dozen beasts are missing. If you want saddles, steal some from Attila's infernal tower.'

Cadoc almost cackled with glee. The possibility of stealing from the Romans was a bonus, especially in conjunction with his relief at leaving the plain and removing from the stink and the danger of the field hospital. The gods would forgive any theft in these circumstances. With no hope of any payment for their services and with the general's pointed enmity, escape from the plain and its environs couldn't come soon enough for him.

'I'll fetch Finn so we can get started on our little expedition at once,' he said, a smile animating his face. 'Can you finish here once the tent is packed? I've procured some smaller tents used by the soldiers for our patients, few as they are, and there are about a dozen women who have agreed to care for them until Cleoxenes repatriates them to Châlons.'

'I know we must take to our heels and run, but it seems wrong to leave sick men behind,' Myrddion said.

'Please, master? Cleoxenes has organised it all. Where do you think I obtained the tents?'

Myrddion shot his apprentice a look of friendly scorn, then sighed with relief as Cadoc set about dismantling the leather tent into a series of folded sections that he unlaced as he went.

In a trice, the tent posts were taken to pieces and packed into the supply wagon, quickly followed by the sections of the larger tent, rolled into manageable packs and lashed together with straps constructed for the purpose. Then, with a spring in his step and a wide grin on his scarred face, Cadoc waylaid Finn as he was packing a box of ointments and whispered to the other apprentice with much gesticulation before both men slipped away into the darkness.

Myrddion, Rhedyn and Brangaine settled the few remaining patients into their new quarters with a smooth economy of movement, assuring them that they would be looked after until they were well again. When their task was almost completed, Myrddion asked the two widows to make Bridie comfortable in the second wagon with little Willa nestled beside her.

Myrddion had been raised to be scrupulously honest and would normally have rejected the idea of stealing food from his master as an unmanly and dishonest act. But the oaths he had given to King Merovech had been severed by death, and Bridie's humiliation had changed everything. He owed Flavius Aetius nothing, neither loyalty nor honesty, and would take payment for his medical expertise in food and supplies rather than gold. Not that he expected Aetius to even consider paying for the services the healers had rendered. The Roman might have been a skilled general, but in Myrddion's opinion he lacked the dignitas and the scruples essential to his class.

Midnight had come and gone, and no moonlight betrayed Myrddion's stealthy return to the Roman quarter of the depleted bivouac. Thick cloud obscured the stars and the rising humidity was thick enough to cut with a knife. The thunder peals were closer now, and the air had the charged heaviness of a storm. Myrddion felt the fine, fair hairs on his arms rise and stir. Good, he thought. The rain and the wind will destroy our tracks. All I need do is to find as many supplies as I can carry.

When he reached the supply tent he realised how over-confident Aetius had become, for it was unguarded. Now that the Hun had retreated, who was there to fear? Tiny, two-man tents encircled the stores but the night was quiet and unnaturally still. Even the fires had died, so that Myrddion left no shadow as he moved swiftly from one deep pool of blackness to another.

On the highest point of the ridge, Aetius's tent was in darkness. Guards patrolled the perimeter, but their main purpose was to protect the many wagons that were heavily laden with plunder. Myrddion smiled. Let Aetius have his precious treasure trove. The healer preferred grain and dried meat.

Soundlessly, he crossed the bare ground between himself and the heavy canvas tent. Rather than risk a frontal entry, he wormed his way under the bottom of the rear wall where a small hole flawed the heavy, oiled cloth. Then he spent the five minutes necessary to rip a large breach at its base where the canvas was already weakened. With luck, if he moved some barrels in front of the tear, the commissar would never notice his stores had been plundered, because Myrddion needed time to put as many miles as possible between himself and the Catalaunian Plain before his absence was discovered.

In his first foray, he hefted a bag of wheat, wrapped several strings of spiced sausage round his neck, and slung a large section of dried goat meat over his other shoulder. Then, as quietly as he had come, he slid back into the shadows once more. In the lee of a small coppice of scrawny shrubs, he dumped his haul and made two more trips, reasoning that he could move the lot more easily once he had completed his theft.

By the time he had finished, Myrddion had purloined dried fish, a string of onions, a bag of withered apples and some dried jerky, as well as three bags of grain, from the supply tent. Dried figs, a jar of honey and an amphora of pressed olive oil completed the provisions necessary to help his party to survive the journey to Italia. Pausing only to rearrange the huge pile of supplies that remained in the tent so that his theft was disguised, Myrddion left the Roman camp as silently and as deftly as he had come. Thankful that the ground was dry and rock hard, the healer left no tracks as he began the physically taxing transport of his ill-gotten gains back to the site of the field hospital. Once the supplies were loaded in the first wagon, Myrddion felt confident that his party could survive for weeks without the need to forage for food.

Brangaine's eyes widened with pleasure as Myrddion stored his booty in the larger wagon. She exclaimed over the barley and apples, although she was puzzled by his selection of figs. But she entered into the spirit of the theft, and carefully stowed the breakable jars so that nothing could be jarred loose as the wagons jolted along the rough road.

Then the two of them moved the horses into the traces of the larger wagon with as little noise as possible, despite the fact that there were no guards to see or hear their preparations. The horses were restive as if they could sense the advance of the storm, and Myrddion had to use all his strength to manhandle the beasts into position. Then master and widows used the remainder of the time for one final check on the patients while awaiting the return of Cadoc and Finn Truthteller.

For Myrddion, the hour that they spent sitting beside the wagons was the hardest and most nerve-stretching part of the whole enterprise. The healer imagined any number of disasters, ranging from the capture of Cadoc and Finn during the theft to accidents through misadventure in the wild darkness. As the fat raindrops began to splatter into the dust, Myrddion began to think that he had sent his two faithful servants to their deaths.

Then, as the rain began to fall in earnest with a fierce drumming sound on the dry earth and the thunder began to peal in almost continuous dull rumbles, a darker series of shapes began to detach itself from the edge of the ridgeline, having taken a wide route around the Roman bivouac to avoid detection. As Myrddion stared, the figures resolved themselves into a string of ten horses, three of which were fully saddled. The others were strung together on long leads and all ten wore skins tied over their hooves to muffle the betraying sounds of their movement.

Myrddion ran to the two servants and gripped Cadoc's hand in thanks before leaping into the saddle of one of the riding horses. 'Harness a team to the smaller wagon and tie the other three to the rear,' he shouted over the drumming of the downpour. He turned to the widows. 'Brangaine, take the reins of the lead wagon; Rhedyn can manage the second. Bridie will nurse Willa for you, Brangaine, and that will keep her occupied during the journey. Let's make a hasty departure while the rains last, and with luck our tracks will be washed away.'

And so, for the first time in his life, Myrddion stole another man's property.

*

With two teams of horses, the healers were able to travel fast and hard for the first two days until Châlons was far behind them and Myrddion allowed the group to stop for a true rest. During the thirty-six hours that had elapsed, they had stopped only long enough to feed and water the horses and attend to personal bodily needs, so the women were exhausted by the time Myrddion ordered the wagons to halt beside a slow-moving river late on the second afternoon. At last, they could sleep, cook hot food and treat the small injuries that the group had collected while on the road.

As he eased the bandages from Bridie's wound, Myrddion could see that it hadn't healed properly. Perhaps the jolting of the wagon or the stress of being unable to rest properly had caused the gaping, suppurating hole that had begun to form at one end of the stitched gash. Myrddion sniffed the wound carefully, but as yet the distinctive, sweetish smell of putrefaction wasn't present. With a sigh of relief, he began the necessary preparation to reopen the wound and treat the damage.

Cadoc sterilised the instruments while Finn prepared the herbs and the poppy needed for the operation. Both apprentices were well trained, for Finn had now absorbed all the herbal knowledge that Annwynn had passed on to Myrddion so long ago, while Cadoc had developed a deft hand with a knife and a needle. Now, as a well-trained team, they prepared an area for Myrddion's ministrations, avoiding the worried eyes of the widows. Surgery in the open air was never an ideal option, but the day was clear and fine without a hint of rain, although the afternoon light was shrinking with the approach of dusk. If Myrddion was going to treat Bridie's infection in a safe environment, now was as good a time as any other.

Finn administered a measured dose of poppy tincture to the patient and Bridie soon fell asleep, ensuring that Myrddion could work with little chance of her waking. However, Myrddion was a superior healer because of his reluctance to take chances. With her face turned to ensure that her breathing was unimpeded, Bridie was gently placed on her stomach and tied down on the surgery table. Once the limb was immobilised, Myrddion took a deep breath and cut the stitches with a swift movement of his sharpest knife. Only three days had elapsed since the original operation, but most of the wound seemed to be holding together.

Without pausing, Myrddion's scalpel reopened half of the long gash. A vile oozing of yellow pus began to well at one end of the wound, so Cadoc leaned forward to mop up the mess with clean rags.

'Burn them and wash your hands thoroughly with hot water and sand before you touch her again,' Myrddion ordered briskly, and used his flask of fruit brandy, now much depleted, to wash out the cavity that he had exposed. Then, as Cadoc and Finn watched closely, he began to remove some of the flesh around the abscess until fresh, clean blood oozed from the pink tissue.

'I'm going to pack the wound with rags soaked in the special salve. You know the one I mean, Finn? Do we have enough of the radish paste? Good. Don't use your hands, Finn. I know you wouldn't do anything to deliberately harm Bridie, but I'm worried. I'm not going to close the abscess – just cover it, so it can release any further poisons that might build up again. I don't know if my surgery will work, so I think we should immobilise the leg with a splint. If Bridie can't move, perhaps she'll heal faster.'

The apprentices moved smoothly to obey their master and Myrddion felt a moment of pride in their efficiency, before anxiety for Bridie chased all other thoughts out of his head.

'Brangaine! Rhedyn! Set up a soft bed in the wagon with the medical supplies. We won't want to disturb Bridie, so make sure that any items we might need for the treatment of villagers aren't under her pallet. I want her to remain in a reclining position for at least a week to give that wound time to heal. No movement at all, do you hear? She must lie on her side or her stomach, so we'll need some kind of cushion to put between her good leg and her wounded knee. Do you understand?'

'Aye, master,' they said, but Brangaine put into words what both women were thinking. 'But what if she needs to go to the privy?' She coughed in some confusion. 'The privy . . . you know, master?'

Myrddion smiled at their embarrassment. 'Find an old receptacle of some kind, ladies. I'm afraid that Bridie must remain in the wagon, regardless of her sensibilities. I know it won't be pleasant for her, or for you, but you've done these tasks before when you've cared for wounded warriors. I trust you to care for her needs, to wash her and to make her comfortable. Finn will be in charge of preparing dressings for her at least twice a day. I know such frequency seems excessive – and certainly more than usual – but I don't want to take any chances. As for Willa – she'll need to travel with you, Brangaine. You can use your sling, although she's almost well enough to sit beside you. But Bridie must have no distractions that might harm her leg, even the care of a small child.'

Little Willa had healed slowly and Myrddion had laboured hard to mitigate the extent of her scarring. But the wounds of the mind are deeper and more lasting than physical pain, and the child was silent and needy. She would welcome travelling on Brangaine's lap because she craved close contact with her rescuer, although it would make the task of driving the cart more difficult.

'I'm sorry that I've made your days more trying, Brangaine, but Bridie could lose her leg, or even her life, unless we're very careful.' Myrddion's voice was regretful and he ruffled Willa's black hair distractedly. Brangaine scowled at him.

'How could I complain when you've saved my girl from death? Of course poor Bridie must be our first concern, and Willa will enjoy watching the horses, won't you, petal? See, she's nodding. My girl won't be a moment's trouble, will you, darling?'

The child nodded again, gazing at Brangaine with huge green eyes that were shiny with adoration. One problem solved, Myrddion thought, as his mind ranged out to the next problem that would require a solution.

He turned his attention back to Cadoc. 'Can you find more herbs and raw radishes? Oh, and some brandy or like spirit? Our supplies are low, and I need to check the wound regularly until it begins to heal naturally.'

'Will it knit properly if it's not stitched, master?' Cadoc asked reasonably.

Myrddion shrugged. 'I don't know, but I'll seal in the poison if I stitch this gash. I'm certain that Bridie would rather have a nasty scar and keep her leg.'

They lingered by the side of the road for a day, although they could ill afford the time. Bridie needed a chance to recover, and although she was teary about delaying their departure and placing the party in danger, Myrddion insisted that they could catch up the lost hours after the horses had rested.

Cadoc took a horse and sought out an isolated community where a wise woman provided the raw materials that he sought for their medications. As he told his master, the woman was none too clean and her blackening teeth and dirty nails inspired little confidence, but herbs and radishes could be washed, and the spirit, made from some kind of root vegetable, made Cadoc's eyes water when he tasted it, speaking eloquently of its potency.

After a short rest and some light toil completing the many tedious but necessary chores involved in maintaining the wagons, the small party continued its journey. Finn was assiduous in his treatment of Bridie's leg. When Myrddion checked the wound every evening, he was pleased to see the shiny, pink growth of healthy new flesh. Finn contrived to spend all his spare time in the medical wagon. Myrddion would hear him telling Bridie stories or singing to her late at night when she couldn't sleep, and was happy when he saw the glow return to Bridie's small, ordinary face whenever she saw Finn moving his horse close to the wagon.

As for Finn, the secretive, damaged Celt seemed as happy as his melancholy nature permitted. He would always carry the memories of Hengist's revenge on the Night of the Long Knives, following the defilement of his brother Horsa. He had earned the title of Truthteller for bearing the dire news of his son's death to Vortigern, and since there was no escaping it, Myrddion had advised him to embrace the name and to employ his remaining days living up to the demanding description. So far, Finn had remained true to the great responsibility of his title in every aspect of his life, and not just in Hengist's cruel requirement that he should describe the Saxon revenge as payment for his life.

Day followed day in a seamless ribbon of dawn, noon, sunset, evening and night. The weather became cooler but the southward journey took them into gentler climes where autumn blessed the land with mild weather, ripened fruit and heavy fields of grain. Berries ripened prolifically in the hedgerows, and Willa's mouth was frequently stained the red and purple of juicy, bursting fruit that had been plucked whenever they paused to feed the horses or rest for the night. Small, misshapen apples and plump nuts were there for the harvesting and the healers augmented their dried rations with the bounty of this fecund land. The country was not heavily populated, and the road was little more than a rutted track that led them from one settlement to another, all of them small and wary of newcomers.

The good earth was beautiful in ways that Britain was not. Here, the colour of gold seemed to cover every surface, unlike the dove grey and charcoal tones of Cymru. Poplars grew profusely like golden fingers; long grasses were edged with gilt and the very air seemed to have been kissed with gold dust by a benevolent god. The Celts could understand why such a land had known so many invaders, for its rich soil and sweet waters spoke of agriculture that could not fail. But years of turmoil and the movement of those seeking new pastures created populations that were nervous, distrustful and divided by different tribal loyalties. Like farmers and herdsmen the world over, they were pragmatic and insular, choosing to avoid strangers as outlanders who had no place in their quiet existence.

But healers provided a service more precious than gold to those who lived in a dangerous world where a broken limb spelled possible death and a simple childhood illness could maim or kill. Most communities possessed a wise woman who was well versed in herbal lore to one degree or another, but these women served within their communities' isolation, without the wider experience of illness and injury that Myrddion and his apprentices had gained in abundance, first on battlefields and then in their long travels. While the inhabitants of these far-flung settlements might have few major accidents, Myrddion was surprised by the number of sufferers of chronic diseases who were brought to his wagons.

In the months of their weary journey, the healer experienced the emotional failures of his craft over and over again. At the end of every dispiriting day when he failed to help those who sought his aid, he regretted anew his ignorance of the many diseases that mocked his learning and left him with an increasing sense of powerlessness. What could he say to the parents of a child whose mind had been damaged at birth? Had fate been kinder, the tiny misshapen child who was unable to walk, speak or even feed itself would have died in infancy. Myrddion knew that some parents killed such damaged infants, but his heart went out to the mothers who wouldn't submit to Fortuna's curse and struggled to keep their children alive in the teeth of constant illness and infirmity. When such parents brought in a drooling child whose eyes rolled uselessly in its head, he was forced to explain that he could do nothing, and watch the hope die again in their faces. He prayed to the Mother to lift the spirits of these children and their loving, long-suffering parents, but his own spirits were hard to support.

Leprosy was crueller still, although it was a rare affliction and Myrddion had only seen three cases before coming to

Gaul. Now, he saw two cases in as many months, each at a different stage of the disease. One was a boy who seemed untouched, except for swollen knuckles and loss of feeling in hands, feet, nose and lips. Myrddion's heart quailed when he was forced to tell the widower who had brought him that his eldest son had been stricken with the curse. Merely ten years old, the happy boy would soon be ostracised, lest the disease should begin to spread among other members of their community. By the defeated slump of the father's shoulders and the haunted look in the man's brown eyes after his diagnosis, Myrddion knew that he had struck the poor man a deathly blow. Later, Myrddion confided to Cadoc that the father would probably kill his son to put the child out of his misery.

The other leper was an elderly woman who lived on the fringes of a wood in abject poverty, maintained only by food left near her hut by a priest and a small group of pious Christians. Myrddion visited her in her shack, which was held together by slabs of rotten wood nailed into position. The mean dwelling was as clean as she could keep it with her numbed, damaged hands, and her pitiful possessions filled Myrddion's heart with sorrow. When he noticed a cracked piece of pottery that had been crudely repaired with pitch and then filled with gay field flowers, her brave attempt to beautify her room caused a tear to well in the healer's eye. The poor woman walked with the aid of simple crutches, although every step on her ruined, suppurating feet must have been agonising. Her hands retained their thumbs and at least one other digit, so she had some dexterity remaining to her. Although he realised he was being cowardly, the healer was shamingly relieved that she had covered her face.

With simple pride, she showed Myrddion her newly

weeded vegetable patch. Beside the hut, an old apple tree still bore fruit on one branch, although she was forced to wait until it fell to the ground because she lacked the strength or the dexterity to pluck it. Everywhere he looked, Myrddion saw evidence that the heart of a warrior was hidden within her shapeless woman's body.

'I was beautiful once,' she told him in a voice so cracked and rasping from the disease and disuse that she could barely be understood. 'I don't expect you to touch me, for I know I'm unclean. All I ask for is some salve to ease the pain in my joints, and something to slow down the rotting of my feet.'

As she moved her ungainly body to ease the pressure on those feet, the heavy bell strung round her neck clanged raucously. Myrddion would have dressed the lesions himself, but she recoiled at his kindness.

'No, master. I would not pass this dreadful scourge on to you. I can see to my own sores if I have the ointments and bandages. Any advice you can give me would also help. I have been forced to remove my own fingers and toes, although it doesn't really hurt. Still, I'd prefer to keep what limbs I still have.'

The woman was obviously intelligent and responsible, so Myrddion returned to the wagons and made his selection from the prepared unguents and his store of cloth obtained from Aurelianum. He also explained the usefulness of radishes and other plants, while advising the old woman to grow these greens herself and harvest them for her own use.

Before he left, Myrddion gave her a small quantity of poppy seed in a screw of rag. 'Should your mobility be seriously impaired, these seeds will bring a speedy death,' he explained regretfully. 'I promise they won't give you pain if you grind them carefully. The poppy seeds are very bitter and can make you vomit, so mix them with food that will help you to keep them down. I'm sorry I lack the skills to help you in any other way, but I will pray to the Mother to take pity on one as brave and as noble as you have proved to be.'

'I am a Christian, master, and the priest counsels me that it's wrong to take my own life.' She sighed wistfully. 'However, I will take your gift – for I know what fate lies in store for me as my illness progresses. May God hold you in His hands, my lord, and protect you always.'

And so Myrddion learned that there were many diseases that he could not heal, and vowed to remember to be humble whenever he drove death away from a cottage door.

Their patients rarely paid in coin, but fresh vegetables, eggs, fruit and even the odd chicken found their way into the cooking pots. Soon, Bridie's face began to shine with health, and although her leg would barely hold her weight and she needed a stick in order to walk, her injury began to heal cleanly under the dual blessings of good care and healthy food. Little Willa also glowed and developed a plump layer beneath her soft skin, although she remained silent. Occasionally, on the edge of sleep, the child would whisper to Brangaine in the Gaulish tongue, although her new mother reported to Myrddion that the little girl was picking up Celt so quickly that she seemed to understand almost everything that was said to her.

As winter came, with frosts and biting wind, the healers reached the Middle Sea and turned towards the great port of Massilia. They had spent months travelling across Gaul and had seen no sign of pursuit during all that time, but Myrddion with Cleoxenes's warning in mind knew better than to lower his guard. The enmity of great men doesn't dissipate quickly, for such men become powerful because of their willingness to crush those who stand in their way. Myrddion ordered his small family to approach their business in Massilia with caution, so they made their camp on the outskirts of the city close to a well at a place where a stand of poplars raised their naked branches towards the grey sky.

This ancient port, doorway to Gaul and the west, was bigger than any city the Celts had ever seen. They had always considered Londinium to be large, but it was a mere village by comparison with Massilia. The port was full of Roman galleys, Greek biremes, slender boats from Egypt, and square-rigged ships from Phoenicia. As they walked through the crowded wharves, leading their horses, it seemed to the Celtic men that people of every race, colour and creed jostled, shouted, carried loads and cleaned the decks of moored vessels. The whole world came and went from Massilia, adding to its vividness and exotic beauty.

Myrddion marvelled at men from Africa, Nubians, with their silky black skin and close-cropped curly hair. Their glazed bead necklaces and strings of seeds and shells jangled and rang like so many tiny bells. Other men possessed sallow skins and slanted eyes that spoke, Myrddion learned later, of Asiatic or middle-eastern backgrounds. Their dress was brilliantly dyed, almost hurting the Celts' eyes with the strength and contrast of the colours. Egyptians scratched their stiff horsehair wigs as they worked, or exposed their shaven heads, glossy with perfumed oils, as they bartered. Their dress was of super-fine cotton, almost transparent in its delicacy, and the pleated magnificence of their loincloths, robes and skirts was only matched by their wide necklaces and breastplates of cornelian, lapis lazuli, amethyst, malachite, rock crystal and enamels set in gold and electrum.

But it was the noise that was most noticeable, a cacophony of different languages, the calls of street entertainers, shouted encouragements from stall merchants, and the jangle, peal, thud and clash caused by the movement of mountains of trade goods. To this impossible jumble of sounds was added the lowing of oxen, the cries of exotic birds in cages and even the snarl of a black-maned lion, securely caged and destined for the arena. Cadoc's eyes were so round with amazement that Myrddion found himself laughing with excitement at the carnival atmosphere.

'I hate the sea and it hates me, but I take back all my complaints about this journey. We've had our troubles and seen some terrible things, but it was worth it all to see Massilia. No one will believe me back in Cymru when I tell them of the marvels I have seen. Who would think that men can be as black as old wood, with yellow eyes and full lips the colour of mulberry stains? It's wonderful!' Cadoc spread out his arms expansively to encompass the harbour that sparkled in the winter sunshine and the passing, haggling throng around them.

'Yes, Cadoc, Massilia is surely a wonder,' Myrddion murmured. 'What then will we find when we reach Rome and Constantinople? Massilia is but a small part of a much larger world than we Celts or the Saxons could ever imagine.'

'I never thought I'd see men with the white skin and red freckles of my friend Cadoc,' Finn whispered to Myrddion with a rare grin. 'How remarkable are these people from far-off places.' He pointed out a woman who was draped in diaphanous robes that left her breasts and belly naked, over which was coiled a brilliantly patterned snake. Her long hair was the colour of fresh blood and tiny brass bells rang from a chain around her waist. As she danced to entertain a crowd that had begun to gather, many ribald comments about what she should do with the snake were shouted from man to man, while a greasy Phoenician handed out small tablets that advertised a house of entertainment. 'Look at her hair, Cadoc. I thought yours was red, but it's a pale imitation of hers,' Finn joked, although his eyes caressed her pert breasts and the hollow in her belly.

'Perhaps her hair isn't real,' Myrddion joked, trying not to dwell on her ripe flesh.

'There's only one way to check,' Cadoc said crudely, and stared at the woman appreciatively. She winked at him and his cheeks flushed with a bright tinge of pink.

While his companions watched the woman's swinging hips, Myrddion examined the dress of the Phoenician trader. His curiosity aroused by a dagger in a decorated scabbard that hung at the Phoenician's waist, he approached the man, who smilingly allowed him to take a closer look. The leaf-shaped weapon was exactly like the carving that had been picked into the great trilithon at the Giant's Dance. Myrddion's ever-curious mind filed away the information that Phoenicians had come to Britain sometime in the past, and he wondered at the vast distances that were covered in the name of trade.

Of the whole throng who passed before them, a group of northerners who disembarked from a primitive pegged wooden boat were the most exotic. White of skin and pale of hair, with eyes so blue that many men of a superstitious bent stepped aside from their paths, they strode through the throng as if the crowd were invisible.

'Who are those hulking brutes?' Cadoc asked, with nervous respect for the height of the northerners. 'They must stand inches taller than you, master. And look at the size of their hands and feet.'

Myrddion relayed the question to a stallholder who was selling roasted chestnuts. Although the short, dark man frowned a little at Myrddion's Latin, he replied with much gesticulation and animation.

'They are Jutes from a country called Jutland,' Myrddion explained to Cadoc. 'They rarely reach the Middle Sea, but they are great sailors and fishermen. I can add that they pose a threat to the north of Britain where they have taken to raiding in the spring. Heaven help us if they make treaties with the Saxons and invade in earnest.'

'Shite! And I thought the Saxons were large,' Cadoc muttered, and a pall was cast temporarily over the brilliance and excitement of the day.

Massilia had a large marble forum and a plethora of Roman buildings of all kinds, including a hospital for the Roman auxiliaries who kept the peace. Warehouses, inns, shop-fronts of every kind, tanneries, slaughterhouses and the slums of the poor made Massilia a port of both beauty and ugliness, with over it all a great vividness that reminded Myrddion of a huge human body that was bursting with life.

After purchasing some essentials at the open-air markets, the three men returned to the outskirts of the city where they had erected their large tent and settled in to earn coin by offering their skills to the public. The widows were impressed by the men's tales of the waterfront, the fresh vegetables they had purchased and a gift from Myrddion of roasted chestnuts and strange sweetmeats made of pastry, honey and almonds. With sticky fingers and beatific smiles, the women set about preparing their evening meal.

After three days in Massilia, Myrddion's cash box was fully replenished. On several occasions he was asked to present himself at the mansions of the wealthy where his cleanliness, his pure Latin and his male beauty quickly earned him approval. When he lanced the infected wound of a young man who had been treated by a charlatan attempting to fleece the family of a wealthy trader, Myrddion suddenly found his skills in great demand. Master and apprentices discovered that there were not enough hours in the day to respond to the queues of poorer patients and the new, wealthy clients who clamoured for attention.

Myrddion was already feeling restive because he knew he was drawing attention to himself and creating a trail that Aetius could follow, when fate conspired to change his plans once again. The healers were about to eat a frugal evening meal of rich stew, hot griddle bread and fresh fruit when several men entered the encampment.

'Who goes there?' Cadoc called, as Finn drew his sword from behind his seat.

'Come into the light where we can see you,' Myrddion shouted.

Two servants bearing torches came first, followed by two brawny bodyguards armed with long wooden staves. Last of all, Cleoxenes strolled into the cone of light surrounding the fireplace and gazed around the encampment with interest.

The demeanour of the envoy had scarcely changed, although his clothing was more dishevelled than usual and his boots were filthy from the dust of a long journey. His narrow, clever face was as indolent as ever, but a new urgency underlay the courtly exterior.

'Well met, friend Myrddion. I see you are continuing to practise your craft – and are doing quite well at it, or so I've been told. I've come with the coin I promised for Bridie and to advise you of the changes that have beset the world since last we met.'

Myrddion leapt to his feet, his face falling into a smile of welcome. He gripped the envoy's hand with affection. 'I am pleased to see you, Lord Cleoxenes, and grateful you remembered your promise. And yes, we have found Massilia to be a very profitable city in which to ply our trade. However, I have begun to believe that we are attracting too much attention and should prepare to depart on our journey to Italia. Another day and we would have missed you.'

Cleoxenes grinned as he gripped Myrddion's shoulder, and the healer noticed the whiteness of the envoy's teeth. As their visitor was introduced to the women, Cleoxenes kissed the hand of each in turn, a gesture that sent them into embarrassed fits of giggles. Bridie, in particular, was treated with touching gallantry when Cleoxenes pressed a leather drawstring bag into her unresponsive hands. When she pulled open the thong and upended the purse, a cascade of golden coins fell into her lap, making her gasp with surprise and delight.

'Thank you, Lord Cleoxenes,' Myrddion said. 'With this coin, Bridie will never have to fear for her future.'

'I only paid what was due. I'm offended by wanton cruelty, so offer me no thanks for doing what was a duty. Fortuna favours us both, although I prefer to think that my lord, the Christos, has helped me to find you at a time when we have an urgent need to speak together. The political situation is grave, and we must change our original plans and take the first available ship to Rome.'

Myrddion frowned. 'Why? What has happened to make such a change imperative? We would leave a clear path for pursuit once we set sail for Rome.'

'Flavius Aetius has more to occupy his mind than the fate of a Celtic healer, no matter how irritating he might find you. Everything we feared has come to pass, for Attila did not return to Buda. He has set the whole of the north of Italia aflame and now he threatens the heart of the empire. Yes, Myrddion. We are part of a new and deadly war.'

Myrddion's chart of the voyage from Massilia to Ostia

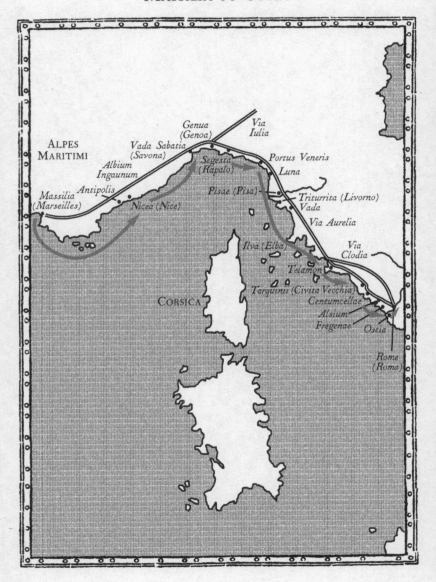

CHAPTER X

INTO THE WESTERN EMPIRE

'Why did you become a priest, Father Lucius? You are obviously a man of culture and learning, and you sometimes make me feel like an ignorant savage. How did you find your way to Britain?'

Queen Ygerne smiled with a delicate curve of her well-shaped lips. She knew she was being overly intrusive, but in the months that Father Lucius had lived in Tintagel, through autumn and into winter, she had poured out her heart and exposed her deepest, most private fears to him. Her natural curiosity fired her, now that her mind was slowly beginning to mend.

Lucius smiled in turn, and considered his loosely folded hands as if some mystery lay within his intertwined fingers. Should he answer, or should he retain his secrets? The priest was a man of intense, contained emotions and was unused to the pain of memory. Twenty years ago, he had fled from his past as if from a plague.

'To remember the man I once was causes me to regret one third of my life, my lady,' he began awkwardly, without his usual measured calm. But as Queen Ygerne's eyes moistened with sympathy he crushed his pride for the folly it was, and lurched back into speech.

'I have listened to your secrets, Queen Ygerne, so I should repay your honesty with frankness of my own. I grew up where the Seven Hills pierce the blue skies of Italia. My family was immeasurably old and full of arrogance, for their scions enriched Rome and themselves during the Republic and the Empire. I'll not tell you my gens, for I still owe something to my family and I'd not drag their name through the mud of my own folly, but I can assure you that consuls and senators fill their death masks and our history can be traced back to the early days of the Republic.'

'I understand, Father Lucius, or at least as much as any woman can who claims nine generations of Britons in her heritage. Family name is a great burden, isn't it?'

Lucius grimaced with weary self-knowledge. 'I agree, although I enjoyed a childhood of privilege and power as an eldest son. I would be a liar if I denied the casual arrogance that my birthright entailed. I drank and whored as do all young men, I practised swordplay on the Field of Mars and thought little of the future, understanding the duties that my position demanded. I was mad to win honour on the field of battle, so my father sent me to the east where I served under various commanders from Constantinople. I never understood what it really meant to be a noble Roman until I killed my first man.'

Ygerne saw the dark shadows of unwelcome memory cluster behind Lucius's eyes and regretted her curiosity and the pain it brought to the priest. He had helped her to understand her place in the world, and to appreciate the love that enlivened her life. Her darker gifts were overborne by the devotion of her husband and daughters, so that Ygerne had put aside the mourning that had terrified her family. Prayer had brought serenity and opened her eyes to a life beyond the frail grass of flesh. Under Father Lucius's gentle gaze, she had explored the promise of heaven and the gentle nature of the Christos.

'I was wrong to awaken painful memories, Father Lucius. In truth, I also know the privileges and disadvantages of high birth. I was immeasurably lucky that my father, Pridenow, hand-fasted me to a man who loved me, so my life has been blessed.'

'You were fortunate. Many women, including my sisters, were betrothed to old men whom they would never love.' Once again, a haunted look appeared in Lucius's eyes. 'Anyway, I followed the tides of war across the Empire and I learned what it meant to be a leader of men. The deaths of my soldiers haunted me in ways I could never have imagined. But in Gaul, I learned what war truly was as we fought the Vandals in blood up to our armpits. Bloody slaughter turned us into scarecrows bathed in gore and brain matter, and no soldier who survived those battles was the same man ever again. I still try to wash the memory of that guilt off my arms and face when I rise at dawn. And at night I still fight my faceless enemies through the dark hours until my mind reels in confusion.'

Ygerne sat quietly and listened, as if their roles were reversed and she was the priest hearing a halting confession.

'I was wounded in the head outside Tolosa twenty years ago and my wits were addled. The surgeons could do nothing for me and I ran wild like a lunatic, sickened by the carnage I had seen and taken part in. I cannot explain this period of madness, or even remember it very well. But I fled from my duties and my life like a coward, and I disgraced myself and my family forever.'

'But you were ill – your actions weren't those of a coward,' Ygerne protested, aghast.

'I was a deserter, even if I wasn't in my right mind. Had I not been taken in by a group of penitents heading for Britain, I would have been executed, to the everlasting shame of my family. As it was, I was brought to Glastonbury and nursed back to health within the holy precincts of the church. Somewhere in those lost years, God found me and gave me a new purpose. I forsook the barren gods of my childhood to follow in the gentle steps of my lord, and in doing so I relinquished the sword to labour in the fields like the slaves my family had once owned. I found myself again through the nobility of sweat and toil. I was redeemed in the contemplation of green and growing things and my days are now full and happy. But enough of sad memories. You are well again, my lady, and my heart rejoices in your happiness. It is time for me to return to the monastery at Glastonbury, but you must call for me again if ever you are in need of consolation. I'll not fail to come if I'm freed by my bishop. I believe that my lord has touched you and His purpose works through you in some mysterious and inscrutable fashion. I cannot say whether your daughters, a child of your body yet unborn, or yourself in your role as queen of a brave people are His tools. But I can feel His touch upon you and your destiny. May He protect you from all harm and bring you His own ineffable peace.'

Embarrassed, Ygerne dropped her eyes and prayed.

On a stone bench on a flagged stone terrace, the priest and the queen sat quietly, wrapped in their own thoughts as the day lengthened towards another cold evening.

Above, the birds of Tintagel wheeled, cried and hunted, in the ways of all wild things.

*

The galley hugged the sandy shore, keeping beyond the teeth of stone that stretched out into the azure sea in long, fanged jaws. Always within sight of land, the ship caught every breath of breeze in its big-bellied sail, rarely having recourse to the oars that could power the heavy vessel at an astonishing speed.

Once again, and practised from their experiences at Dubris well over a year earlier, Cadoc had sold their string of horses and their wagons in Massilia for a significant profit. Cleoxenes had arranged their passage with the easy elan of a man used to wielding power and charming what he wanted from the world. Almost effortlessly, they had embarked upon the long sea voyage.

Myrddion chafed under the length of the journey. Rough maps of the land between Massilia and Rome showed that a straight line away from the coastline was the fastest route, but few captains dared risk the perils of open waters. 'But why?' he asked Cleoxenes with puzzled curiosity. 'When we follow the coastline, we lengthen our voyage enormously and delay our arrival in Rome. At this rate, Attila will have taken the City of the Seven Hills before we arrive.'

'Sensible captains fear to lose sight of land. The Middle Sea is capricious and one storm can muddle the thoughts of the most experienced navigator, leaving him unsure as to which direction to take. We could be lost forever. In the Odyssey, the great Greek writer, Homer, describes how Ulysses was lost for years while sailing through the Greek islands. Sailors steer by the stars when they travel at night, but such directions are hardly accurate. Do you want to die of thirst?'

Myrddion had never heard of Homer's Odyssey, although he had read the Iliad in Latin, so he stored this piece of information away as a valuable source of knowledge.

However, the notion that ships had no means of navigating their way around the Middle Sea was a revelation to him. Maps seemed to be rarely used except by the better-educated sailors, and even then such aids were rudimentary.

'So how do northerners cross the wild, cold seas when they come to Britain? Because they do, you know.'

Cleoxenes shrugged expressively. 'I haven't the faintest idea what methods the barbarians use. I can only explain why no captain will cross the seas between here and the islands of Corsica and Sardinia.'

The names meant little to Myrddion, but once again he filed them away as places of interest should they be discovered on any charts that he might find. He felt obliged, however, to accept Cleoxenes's explanation and to assuage his curiosity by making his own chart of the coastal route from Massilia to Italia.

Cadoc suffered from seasickness for several days until, almost miraculously, he became accustomed to the motion of the ship and his nausea passed. The sun-bronzed sailors laughed at him and teased him about finally acquiring his sea legs, but the Celt retained his sense of humour, spending all day above deck and becoming quite sunburned, especially around the glossy, damaged areas of his scars. Other than a whole new scatter of freckles across his nose and unscarred cheek, he took no other hurt from the warm spring sun.

Ports and towns slid by daily, linked by the coastal Roman road that was still maintained as a route into the west. Antipolis, Albium Ingaunum, Vada Sabatia, Genua and Segesta passed by as the ship made its ponderous way to the east. Above the towns and the road, the mountains of the Alpes Maritimi raised their craggy crowns towards the heavens. Myrddion was fascinated by the height and imposing beauty of the mountains, which reminded him of his home. The sailors told him that these peaks were part of an even higher range that formed a near impenetrable barrier for travellers who wished to access the headwaters of the Padus river that crossed Italia and spilled its waters into the Mare Adriaticum.

When they called at Portus Veneris for fresh drinking water, Cleoxenes strolled into the town to learn what he could of the troubles in the north. He returned biting his lip and frowning so that his dark brows met in deep furrows on his usually untroubled forehead.

'The news of Attila is bad – very bad – far worse than I expected. I have also received unsettling tidings from Constantinople that may or may not be true. I pray they are false.'

'Tell us the worst then, Lord Cleoxenes. We may not understand everything you say, but ignorance is even more dangerous than a little knowledge,' Myrddion urged, alarmed by the sadness in the envoy's voice.

'Rumours have reached Portus that my master, Emperor Theodosius, is dead and has been succeeded by the Emperor Marcian. I have been absent from fair Constantinople for far too long.'

'Will a change of emperor mean trouble for you, lord?' Myrddion asked, his sympathy quickened by the audible upset in the envoy's voice.

'No. Definitely not. But Theodosius was a good man, and brave of heart. He was the first to attempt to halt the ambitions of the Flagellum Dei, or Attila, as you from the western countries call him. I regret his death, if the rumours are true.'

Myrddion kept his face under control so that his features only registered polite interest. Cleoxenes wouldn't welcome overt solicitude.

'As for Attila, he has counter-attacked and now holds all the lands of Italia down to the Padus river. The north is his and Aetius is forced to mount defensive raids against the Hun outriders. The general can only slow the Hungvari advance, not halt it, for he lacks the troops needed to meet Attila in open warfare. He must surely regret his churlish treatment of the Visigoths and the Franks. If she is to survive another burning, Rome will need all her allies.'

'Such a response was inevitable,' Myrddion murmured. 'Given that tower of saddles I saw on the Catalaunian Plain, Attila was certain to seek revenge.'

'Attila has such pride that he dared Flavius Aetius to attack him when he was sitting high on that leather tower. As the world knows, he is unused to defeat. He must have been raging as he rode northeast and skirted the mountains until he came to the Roman road that cuts through the Alpes Carnicae. Turning south instead of north would have seemed the only way to avenge his losses at the Catalaunian Plain and regain his power and position. We brought the Hun down on our heads when we submitted to the general's greed.'

'Don't berate yourself, my lord. I suppose that we'll learn more when we make our next landfall, for I'll wager that the towns of Italia will be speaking of nothing else.'

Sea journeys never seem to end when travellers are eager for news that will reshape their lives. To starboard, the healers could see the blue waters of the Middle Sea, unvarying, stretching to the horizon without blemish or change. Cadoc swore that staring at the ocean gave him the drearies, even though he had mastered his illness.

'There's not enough to amuse us when birds have become the chief topic of interest,' he complained.

'You can amuse yourself by helping Finn to chop the herbs we purchased in Massilia,' Myrddion retorted. 'When we disembark, we'll need to be ready to earn a living.'

Privately, however, the young healer agreed with Cadoc. He preferred to stay to landward, where the shield of mountains was gradually giving way to wide green plains. The Roman town of Luna passed by, and small fishing boats surrounded the galley like a flock of impudent sparrows teasing a raven. They milled and swooped around the larger ship, chasing shoals of silver fish while brown-skinned, half-naked little men cast their nets and grinned up at the sailors and delivered rapid-fire, ribald jokes.

Pisae passed by on the port side, and the occasional river mouth opened into the waters of the Middle Sea, staining the waters brown with silt and the detritus of human habitation. The mountains had retreated, and the galley had turned southward to follow the coastline. Triturrita and Vada passed and Myrddion's young eyes could just make out the wide Via Aurelia as it wound along the coast like a serpent before disappearing inland.

The view on both sides of the galley now showed smudges of land as the great island of Corsica rose out of the ocean with a spine of mountain peaks. The galley slid between the island of Ilva and the coast and Cleoxenes informed the healers that the captain planned to take on more fresh water at Telamon, little more than a flyspeck on the land mass of Italia, lacking even the virtue of a decent harbour.

'Why do we pause, then?' Myrddion asked logically, having adjusted to the rhythms of life on a sea voyage. 'Why not head towards a more hospitable spot to collect our water?'

'Actually, we aren't really stopping. The captain has received a message from a fishing boat that an important personage needs transportation to Roma, and will come to us on a smaller boat that will also deliver our water barrels.'

'Who in their right mind would sail south, when Roman roads would take them directly to the capital much faster than sail or oars? In their place, whoever they are, I'd have ridden.'

'So would I,' Cleoxenes answered with his secretive smile. 'But I suppose they believe the sea is safer than the land. Perhaps our journey will be enlivened by a convivial companion or two.'

When the galley hove to, the passengers could see that the village was a collection of white and pink buildings clustered above the shoreline. No sooner had the galley dropped anchor than a fishing boat left the rudimentary wharf and began to scud out beyond the breakers with the land breeze filling its sails. The crew of the galley clustered on the deck, staring towards the land, and treating this unexpected pause in the voyage as a brief holiday from the unvarying sameness of their duties.

The healers stood with them, eager to be diverted by any change in the predictable rhythms of life on the ship. Even Bridie left the widows' cabin to join them, leaning on an elaborate stick that Finn had fashioned for her on the voyage. He was inordinately proud of his gift, which was rich with carvings of fish and sea serpents and adorned with glowing pink and white slivers of shell.

A rope ladder was cast over the bulbous side of the galley and Myrddion decided that he was glad he didn't have to make the awkward climb on the heavy, twisting rungs of woven sisal. A man clambered up first, a soldier wearing Roman armour that was much decorated with rich embossing and gilding under a heavy red woollen cloak.

'It seems our visitors are persons of some importance,' Cleoxenes informed the healers as the Roman officer heaved his body over the rail. 'The tedium of our journey might be broken.'

Myrddion looked at the climbing ladder and saw only the covered heads of two women who struggled with their robes and peplums as they clung to the ropes with beringed fingers. One of the fishermen assisted them from below while a limber seaman climbed down to offer them a strong brown arm on the way up. Such was the obvious wealth of the new passengers that the sailors, clustering on the rigging and rails, resisted their usual urge to make ribald comments, even when a gust of wind revealed a shapely calf and thigh to their interested stares. The women had barely reached the deck before brown fishermen, as dexterous as monkeys, began unloading chests of possessions and pitch-sealed barrels of water.

Cleoxenes and Myrddion examined the newcomers with frank curiosity, and even the apprentices and the widows gawked covertly from under lowered lids at the two women, who wore hooded cloaks to hide their faces from the open stares of plebeians. The captain appeared, bowing obsequiously even before he reached his wealthy clients, and the Roman officer proceeded to demand his best cabins for the accommodation of the ladies. As Cleoxenes had the biggest one and Myrddion shared the other good-sized compartment with Cadoc and Finn, the only available space was either the widows' inadequate quarters or the captain's odorous, fish-tainted cabin. Myrddion sighed. 'Unless we want the widows to be turned out to sleep on the open deck, I imagine we'll be giving up our cabin.'

The captain of the galley had already come to the same

conclusion. The noble Roman officer was induced to share with Cleoxenes, an arrangement that neither man welcomed, and the healers packed their few possessions and took up a position at the stern of the vessel where they would be protected from the weather. The captain offered them space in the crew's quarters far below the deck, where Cleoxenes's bodyguards and manservant had stolen the best hammocks by virtue of their size and nasty dispositions, but the healers had already experienced the foul smells and stygian darkness of the lower decks and Myrddion announced that a little rain would be far better for their health than hammocks strung in tiers under low ceilings and overfull slop buckets fouling what little air there was and the grimy planks alike.

If the healers expected any thanks for their generosity, they were out of luck. The two women never so much as looked in their direction before they hastened to their new quarters.

'They won't like their new accommodation overmuch,' Cadoc predicted drily.

'They'll like the bunks even less,' Finn added. 'I swear they have lice.' He scratched reflectively at his forearm, and Myrddion and Cadoc immediately began to itch.

'Perhaps they'll have some news to share with us,' Myrddion suggested, his curiosity piqued by the arrival of the Roman party. 'I wonder where Attila is now? We all know how fast the Hun army can move, so they could have taken Rome already.'

'Judging by their friendliness so far, they'll not be talking to us,' Cadoc replied sardonically. 'I doubt even Cleoxenes will learn much from that gilded bag of wind he's stuck with. Cleoxenes may be noble, but he's become very brown in his travels and he's not as fussy about his dress as he was at the start of the journey.'

Myrddion was inclined to agree. Considering the difference in their stations, he had found Cleoxenes to be a charming, erudite companion to whom he owed much, not least his life. But weeks at sea had relaxed the older man's personal dress code and made him less starchy in his manner than in previous meetings. It was indeed possible that Cleoxenes would also be judged as being beneath Roman consideration, unless he dressed as if he were at the imperial court at Constantinople.

'Perhaps we're judging our fellow travellers too harshly,' the healer murmured without much conviction.

'I doubt it, but you could be right,' Cadoc replied. The servant's face suggested that he wasn't the least convinced.

The healers had much to occupy their time, now that Ostia, the port of Rome, was only a few days away. Myrddion's clothing was becoming decidedly shabby, so the widows had purchased several lengths of wool and linen in Massilia with the intention of making garments for their master during the sea voyage. There had been much giggling over their needle-work, while the cloth had always been hidden whenever Myrddion came within their ambit. He had no idea what they would create for him from the black, grey and white fabrics, but until their agile fingers had finished wielding their needles he must make do with the ragged, over-washed and faded garb that had travelled with him from Cymru. He was still young enough to feel shame at his dishevelled appearance, and hoped he would cut a more imposing figure once he reached Rome than he did now.

He had decided to seek out the Jewish healer, Isaac, whom the dead Theodoric had praised in their fateful discussion outside Aurelianum. So far, in his quest to find his father, he had gained neither knowledge nor gold to validate such an upheaval in his life. Perhaps Isaac would take them all on as apprentices and share his knowledge with them. Excitement briefly surged through him, but was soon replaced by self-doubt. Wiser to the Roman world than he had been in Britain, Myrddion doubted that three shabby Celts would be acceptable servants for a man of such fame as Isaac, even if he was a Jew and derided by the nobility of Rome – unless they needed his services urgently. Respectability in Rome, it seemed, increased considerably with usefulness.

'I'm becoming as cynical as you are, Cadoc,' Myrddion confided to his apprentice that afternoon after relating his immediate plans. He was staring idly over the side and watching the cobalt blue depths pass beneath him as a slew of gulls followed the galley, screaming for the slops that the cook cast overboard at this time of day, after the preparations for yet another fish stew had been completed.

'Never, master,' Cadoc answered absentmindedly. He was learning to make fishing nets out of very fine twine with a narrow wooden hook, so he was forced to concentrate hard so that he didn't drop stitches and spoil the mesh.

Before Myrddion could respond, he saw Cleoxenes moving easily along the deck in company with the Roman officer, who had discarded his heavy cloak but was still wearing his magnificent armour. His face was red and puffy, and sweat stained his tunic.

'Myrddion!' Cleoxenes called peremptorily, although his voice wasn't unkind.

Myrddion felt his shoulders stiffen, as their relationship had never previously been one of master and servant. 'Yes, my lord. How may I serve you?'

The healer's voice was exaggeratedly servile, and Cleoxenes's eyebrows rose in surprise. I'm being stupid, Myrddion thought. He realised, with a pang of guilt, that Cleoxenes had probably been unaware of the autocratic tone in his voice. Unfortunately, Roman manners were catching.

'Ignore my mood, my lord,' he added. 'I'm a little on edge, now that our journey is nearing its end. Forgive any lapse of courtesy on my part.'

Cleoxenes still looked puzzled, but as Myrddion was now smiling easily in his customary manner, the envoy from Constantinople put his concerns aside.

'This gentleman is Flavius Petronius Maximus, senator of Rome, patrician and adviser to the Emperor Valentinian. He is accompanying Lady Flavia, daughter of General Flavius Aetius. Lady Flavia is chaperoned by her noble kinswoman, Heraclea, who is the daughter of Thraustila Major, a cousin of Aetius's third wife.' The envoy's tone was neutral, and he explained later that Thraustila came from a noble Hun family, one whose members were loyal to the interests of Rome. He turned to the senator.

'May I introduce to you Myrddion Emrys of Segontium, a healer of extraordinary note. This young man is travelling to Rome to extend his knowledge under the greatest Roman practitioners of our age. Myrddion served General Flavius Aetius with distinction at the Battle of the Catalaunian Plain, where he ministered to many Roman warriors and saved the lives of countless wounded.'

Myrddion bowed gracefully, careful not to shame his friend. For his part, Flavius Petronius Maximus gave a haughty nod, so Myrddion decided that he would irritate the great man by introducing his apprentices to him next.

Another Flavius! Myrddion thought irritably. And this one

is the right age, give or take a few years. He's a reasonable figure of a man but no one, no one, could ever say that he possessed a hyacinth beauty.

Fortunately, the Roman was unable to read Myrddion's mind.

'Noble Cleoxenes tells me that you are a soothsayer as well as a healer,' Petronius said.

'That's not exactly true, my lord. Sometimes, unbidden, I am afflicted with strange trances during which I utter prophecies, but this state is beyond my control. Nor can I vouch for the veracity of my words for, frankly, I don't remember them.'

'Myrddion is overly modest, Petronius. This young man predicted our successes on the Catalaunian Plain in minute detail. Even more amazingly, he foretold the death of King Theodoric of the Visigoth tribes. Myrddion is also literate and speaks and writes fluent Latin.'

Petronius raised one eyebrow sceptically and made excuses to continue his private conversation with Cleoxenes. As the Roman and the eastern aristocrat moved away, Myrddion was free to examine Petronius at his leisure.

Flavius Petronius Maximus was a middle-aged man, and Myrddion guessed that he had lived for at least fifty years. Fortune had smiled on him at his birth and he was sturdy, athletic and handsome in a rough, florid fashion, although good living had thickened his waist and padded his shoulders with a layer of fat. His jaw was a little jowly and the suspicion of an incipient double chin marred a broad, clean-shaven face with regular, well-shaped features. Under a tonsure of fair hair, which Petronius constantly patted down across a central bald spot, the Roman's appearance was pleasing in spite of a snub nose. Myrddion was particularly impressed by the way the light caught his pale hazel eyes, lending them deceptive depth.

He's like Narcissus, in love with his own reflection, Myrddion thought as Petronius Maximus obviously referred to something personal once more, and his beringed hand patted his breastplate. But the senator's hands had authority and Myrddion saw the calluses that were only built up from years of practice with the sword.

Fascinating as Petronius was, Myrddion had been surprised at his own lack of response when he learned that Flavia was a passenger on the galley. His heart didn't leap in his breast, and neither did his hands tremble. The young healer smiled slightly, for he had been a little afraid that the daughter of the Roman general still held him in her thrall. With luck, he would not be obliged to see her during their final days aboard the galley.

After the Roman senator had sauntered off to order a decent meal for his ladies, Myrddion rejoined Cleoxenes, who was frowning darkly.

'Damn that Aetius! I knew his weakness would cause us to lose thousands of lives . . . and so it has proved. The Hungvari have burned the north. Cities have been sacked and churches reduced to smoking ruins. But the worst news of all is that Aquileia has been utterly destroyed. Petronius told me that Attila ordered a wooden fortress to be built nearby from which he could watch the city as it burned with the last of its citizens trapped inside.

Myrddion shuddered. The cold-bloodedness of Attila's revenge could not fail to repulse any right-thinking man.

'Attila now holds the entire north of Italia, while nothing stands between his army and Rome itself. Valentinian has fled from Ravenna, whose swamps and waterways will not protect her this time. So grave is the situation that Aetius has sent his daughter south, and if Rome is threatened she will be packed off to Sicily.'

'If the Hun are as close as Petronius Maximus suggests, it would make sense to send her to Sicily immediately,' Myrddion grumbled. 'A battlefield is no place for a woman.'

'Master!' Cadoc had joined them. 'Where would we be without our widows? Badly fed and half dead of exhaustion, I'd reckon.'

'I meant gently born females,' Myrddion said quickly.

'Worse and worse, master. Are you suggesting that the battlefield is appropriate for the poor, the indigent and the ignorant? Or do you say that the daughters of patricians are unfit to face the bloodbath of war? The philosophers could call you to task for these assumptions, master.'

'He still has all the niceties of youth.' Cleoxenes grinned at Cadoc. 'Myrddion still believes that women are gentle creatures, whereas we know that they are ruthless to the bone, at least where love is concerned.'

With the laughter of his apprentice and Cleoxenes echoing good-naturedly in his ears, Myrddion escaped to the hard deck and his ragged woollen cloak. Eventually, under a blanket of stars, he fell into a deep sleep.

Now that they were approaching Rome, the population grew denser and the shore became a rich scroll of villages and towns that clustered along the coastal road. Tarquinii passed, and Cleoxenes entertained Myrddion with stories of the warriors who first built the city and ruled this ancient land long before the Romans ventured out of their mud huts. Centumcellae, Alsium, Fregenae ... historic names that sang with magic, but the galley soon left the towns behind until, in a huge belch of brown and filthy water, the Tiber river emptied itself into the sea and Ostia hove into view.

With synchronised oars, the galley was manoeuvred towards a berth at the port, and with superb discipline the crew rowed towards the stone pylons to which the ship would be tied. Suddenly, they reversed their oars and the ship shuddered and began to back into position. The oars were raised, the galley slid smoothly into place and a strong length of rope was attached to the waiting mooring ring.

Flavia and Heraclea, dressed in their finery, hurried onto the deck, and Myrddion bowed low in the expectation that the Roman party would disembark quickly. However, some feminine capriciousness drove Flavia to draw back the hood of her cloak to reveal her marvellous, curling hair as she approached the healer with a sweet, seductive sway of her hips. Myrddion noticed that her elegant hands were rouged on the palms with henna, her eyelashes and brows were darkened with stibium and her already pale complexion was further whitened to hide her charming freckles. He had difficulty equating this beautiful creature, so poised and autocratic, with the Flavia he had first met in Châlons. That girl had been equally composed of fire, honey and sour wine, but she was now eclipsed. Only Flavia's extraordinary, mismatched eyes were the same, crackling as they were with life and fierce with a desire to experience everything that Rome had to offer.

'Well met, Myrddion of Segontium. I have often wondered if we were destined to meet again.'

'I'm pleased to see that you are well and that you have kept yourself safe from the dangers in the north,' Myrddion murmured with formal courtesy.

'Still a master of pretty words, I notice. Offer me your

felicitations, healer, for I am betrothed and will be wed at the end of the spring when my father sends Attila back to Buda.'

'May you experience much joy in your coming nuptials,' Myrddion responded with a smile. 'May I enquire who the lucky man might be who has won the hand of the daughter of Flavius Aetius?'

Flavia smiled coquettishly, while her cousin, Heraclea, frowned with disapproval. Now that Flavia was forbidden to him, Myrddion experienced the familiar lurch of his stomach as if he had fallen from a high cliff. He lowered his lids with their long lashes, curlier than those of any woman, in an effort to conceal his telltale eyes.

'I'm fortunate,' Flavia murmured. 'I am to be wed to Thraustila Minor, the brother of Lady Heraclea and master of many broad acres north of the Padus river. He is the lord of Durostorum in Moesia Inferior. His family has been linked to ours for several generations, and Thraustila and his kin are good Roman citizens, besides being fabulously wealthy.'

She couldn't help herself. Her voice became boastful in the old way, while her chin lifted imperiously and her eyes embraced Myrddion's handsome face with the measuring glance he remembered so well. Unsettled, and feeling off balance and awkward, he bowed low to both ladies as Flavia covered her rich hair and submitted to Heraclea's attempt to hustle her away. At the galley rail, she turned back and fixed Myrddion with her unnatural eyes.

'I hope we will see each other when I am mistress of my own house in Ravenna.' She smiled one last time. 'Be careful of your life, Myrddion of Segontium. Your death would be a very great waste.'

Then, flanked by Flavius Petronius Maximus and her chaperon, Flavia reached the gangplank and departed from the galley, leaving behind the heavy, erotic scent of her musky perfume.

'Whew!' Finn whistled. 'What a woman, master, and no better than she ought to be, if her manners are any indication of her intentions towards you. She did everything but drag you into her bed. The invitation almost curled my toes . . . and it wasn't even aimed at me.'

Finn looked so disapproving that Myrddion felt the urge to laugh, but in truth Flavia's implied invitation was not amusing. How could he extricate himself if Flavia threw herself at him? With gratified regret, Myrddion determined to steer a course as far from Aetius's daughter as possible.

Many hours passed in the practised discipline of unloading the tents, the medical supplies, and the precious collections of herbs, potions and concoctions, as well as the three widows and their meagre possessions. Willa clung to Brangaine's hand, wide-eyed and silent as ever as she took in the strange new surroundings. In the meantime, Cadoc had worked his usual magic and purchased two commodious wagons, two teams of horses and three mounts for the men. But some little time would elapse before Myrddion had the luxury to gaze around at the city of Ostia in all its tawdry magnificence, its wealth and its squalor.

Ostia had been a port of huge importance since, according to legend, Aeneas of Troy first saw the Tiber and sailed up the broad river until he beheld the seven hills that would become the city of Rome. Its geographical position was ideal, with the port itself situated at the point on the north bank of the wide river where it flowed into the sea. Myrddion felt a frisson of distaste at the huge tangles of rubbish that had been swept downstream, which included raw sewage as well as flotsam consisting of old cloth, light timber, and even several bloated, unrecognisable corpses both human and animal tangled in nets and webs of dislodged water hyacinth. Myrddion was no novice. He knew that human beings often used rivers for rubbish removal, in every sense of the phrase.

Ostia dwarfed Massilia, for Cleoxenes whispered that some fifty thousand men, women and children called it home. Most of the grain and trade goods that eventually found their way into Rome passed first through Ostia's vast warehouses. Nothing in Britain had prepared the party for the size, complexity and capacity of the wharves. Although much depleted, the naval base for the Western Roman Empire was located in Ostia. Cleoxenes explained the differences between the neat rows of galleys of every shape, size, armament and complexity of oar-banks used to propel these strange vessels. The figureheads on their bows incorporated huge battering rams at the waterline, sheathed in iron and decorated with embossed brass sculptures.

'Over there are the saltpans that made Ostia so important in the early days of the Republic. At one time, Ostia was the largest port in the Empire, but . . .' Cleoxenes shrugged his shoulders regretfully. 'Now that the city drowns in its own waste, grain ships come less frequently, and malaria brings illness and death with every summer.'

'I'm not surprised, if the famed Tiber is any indication. No one would dare to drink its waters.'

'No one does drink from it,' Cleoxenes muttered, and laughed. 'Wine is drunk throughout the Empire, making its deluded citizens believe that Rome is still as vast and as powerful as it once was.'

As Myrddion helped the widows heft their possessions onto the stone and timbered wharf, Cadoc and Finn reloaded their goods into the wagons with the smooth efficiency of a well-trained team. The healer took note of the wharf's rusted iron fittings and crumbling stone, and saw that the warehouses cried out for repairs, paint and cleaning. Yes, Ostia was visibly in decline.

Thanking the gods that they had arrived in late spring and not during the virulence of the summer months, Myrddion mounted his new horse, a showy grey gelding that seemed weak in the hocks, and sought out Cleoxenes, who was preparing to depart in company with his bodyguard.

'I'd like to thank you, my lord Cleoxenes, for all your efforts on my behalf. I've nothing to give you of any value, but if a Christian is not offended by the prayers of a pagan, I will beg the Mother to keep you safe until you reach the sanctuary of your home.'

For all his urbanity, Cleoxenes was embarrassed by the gesture of friendship. But he accepted Myrddion's compliments in the spirit in which they were offered and promised to seek the healer out in Rome before he left to join his new master in Constantinople. Then the envoy fished a cloth-wrapped package out of his saddlebag.

'This gift is for you, healer. I saw your eyes light up when I first mentioned Homer's Odyssey. Unwrap it. Yes – it's yours, and without any qualification. Enjoy the writings of the master, although Homer reads a little better in the original Greek.'

Myrddion gazed down at the scroll cylinder in his hands. The extensive carving on the container indicated its worth and a quick glance at the Latin script showed it to be a beautiful example of the scribe's art.

'I read Greek, my lord,' Myrddion answered automatically, and because his eyes were riveted on the scroll in his hands he missed Cleoxenes's dumbfounded stare at his admission.

'This gift is far too valuable. You have been my friend and my mentor, and those gifts are so great that I will never be able to return them. But this . . . ? The Odyssey? I cannot accept such largesse from you.'

'Oh, for the sake of all the saints, Myrddion! Just say a simple, polite thank you, and I shall have been repaid many times over. No! I won't listen to another word.'

Then Cleoxenes dug his heels into the flanks of his horse and the beast leapt sideways in a nervous prance.

Once the envoy had ridden away, accompanied by his brawny guard, Myrddion felt a profound sense of loss. Cleoxenes had smoothed Myrddion's path in a hundred different ways, but his careless friendship too had been much cherished, for never before had Myrddion had a true companion of his own class. It was not that Myrddion cared about birth, but that Cleoxenes had filled a void in the young man's mind, and they had shared the easy camaraderie of intelligent, educated and curious men.

Noble forums, huge marble baths, a circus that made Myrddion's head spin in its complexity and the multi-storeyed buildings of the subura were evidence of a culture so superior to anything the healer had known that he felt a pang to see derelict buildings falling into ruins. The city was angry with gangs of hollow-eyed, half-starved unemployed who frequented the wine shops and roved the streets in search of vulnerable prey. Fear of the swords and daggers carried by Cadoc and Finn was all that protected the healers from robbery, murder and rape.

'Ostia is a cesspit that is still beautiful on the surface, but rotten at the core,' Myrddion told his apprentices. 'I long for clean air and the green of the countryside. Let's blow the foul stench of this place out of our lungs.'

And so Ostia began to recede into the distance.

Although the afternoon was advanced, the small party shunned the nearer inns, preferring to push forward along the well-constructed road until the city was only a memory. As darkness fell, and the buildings of Ostia started to thin out into isolated pockets that were linked by plots of rubbish or desultory, half-hearted agriculture, Myrddion breathed freely at last. He discovered that he preferred the blood-soaked battlefield to this world that seemed to be rotting from gangrene of the spirit, even as it lived.

'If Ostia is a corpse not yet buried, what then will we find in Rome? What can I learn in an Empire that is falling to pieces as I watch?'

Cadoc turned his head in the darkness, and Myrddion realised he had voiced his despair. Wisely, both Cadoc and Finn maintained their silence.

Myrddion's chart of Rome
and its environs

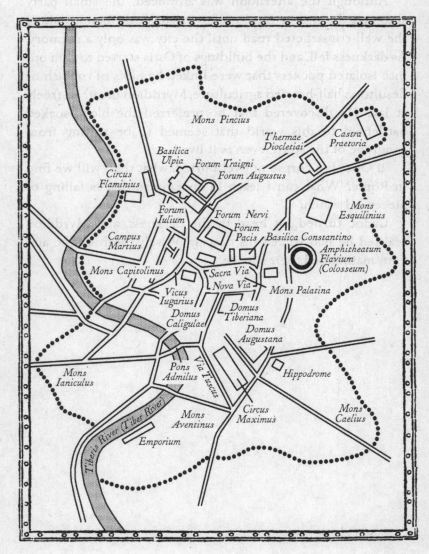

Mons Pincius

Thermae
Diocletiai

Castra
Praetoria

Basilica
Ulpia

Forum Traigni
Forum Augustus

Circus
Flaminius

Forum Nervi

Mons
Esquilinius

Forum
Iulium

Forum
Pacis

Basilica Constantino

Campus
Martius

Amphitheatum
Flavium
(Colosseum)

Mons Capitolinus

Sacra Via

Nova Via

Mons Palatina

Vicus
Iugarius

Domus
Tiberiana

Domus
Caligulae

Domus
Augustana

Mons
Ianiculus

Pons
Admilus

Via Tuscus

Hippodrome

Mons
Aventinus

Circus
Maximus

Mons
Caelius

Tiberis River (Tiber River)

Emporium

CHAPTER XI

THE CITY AND THE SUBURA

The healers spent the night sheltering in a stand of olive trees. Myrddion scented danger on the night wind, as pungent as corpse smoke and as sour as bad wine. Out of patience with his instincts, he told himself that months of travel had left him jumpy and filled with the anxiety that men feel when they venture into strange places. Dawn found the companions awake and the air was ripe with reheated fish stew, the sharp scent of crushed olive leaves and a cinnamon sweetness that Myrddion didn't recognise. Even at this early time of day, the air had a stultifying heaviness, as if fine dust hung constantly in a hot haze.

Daylight revealed bare, exposed countryside that seemed too spent to bear life. Even the old olive trees seemed tired and malnourished. An early gust of wind blew little dust devils into being in a field of dispirited green shoots that were struggling to survive.

'What's wrong with this land?' Myrddion asked Finn, whose family had been farmers for generations. The Celt went down on his haunches and took a handful of pale soil in his fist. He squeezed it, but the earth refused to knit and began to sift through his fingers like sand.

'It's played out, master. All the goodness in it has been sucked away over years and years of constant cultivation. The soil must be replenished if it is to bear. Every few years, my father would grow a crop simply to plough it back into the ground to provide nourishment for our fields. Then he would permit the earth to rest for a season. If a farmer becomes too greedy, or too needy, he will kill the soil by making it bear beyond its strength.'

Myrddion sighed. 'Veterans from the Roman legions have been given small plots of land all over Italia for hundreds of years as a reward for their service to the Empire. It's sad to see this once-fertile land destroyed by ignorance. Men trained for fighting usually know nothing of farming.'

'Aye, master. It's little wonder that Rome now depends on grain from its Empire – what's left of it.'

'It's time for us to leave, Finn. At speed! We still have some rations remaining that will be valuable, if the quality of this crop is anything to judge by. Rome is close, so we shall soon see what the Empire has become.'

In the tiring journey that followed, though he marvelled at the imaginative engineering that created the roads, complete with channels to drain water away from the surface, Myrddion also saw how damaged the landscape had become. While olive trees still survived on the slopes of the low hills, deep ravines of erosion scoured the flatlands and exposed the sour subsoil. Goats devoured any tender shoots that managed to burst through the weary soil, and their hooves trampled the dry ground into dust for the wind to blow away.

Any farmers whom the healers met on the journey were tired, bowed at the shoulders and defeated by years of struggle. One by one, the smaller farms had been devoured by affluent landholders, so that the original owners toiled for coppers in order to enrich absentee noblemen. Resentment shone out of the eyes of the peasantry, as their landlords demanded more and more income from depleted land they never saw. The hands that had once carried swords for the honour and glory of Rome clenched and unclenched in anger at the sight of the healers, for although the travellers were ragged they rode horses, and were therefore wealthy. No one sought treatment. No one spoke.

For the first time since they had left the Catalaunian Plain, the small party was forced to guard the horses and their wagons as they slept that night by the side of the road. The men rested in shifts so that the campsite could be protected in the event of an attack, and were fearful of lighting a fire lest they be discovered by footpads. Myrddion now understood why Cleoxenes travelled to Rome with well-armed bodyguards.

'Italia is far more dangerous than Cymru, and the population is hostile and angry,' he told Finn on the last morning of their journey, although his companion was obviously aware of their peril. Myrddion had been struggling to understand the bitterness in the farmers' eyes as they travelled through this dangerous, depleted land. 'The countryside seethes with resentment, and we can only hope that Rome must be better than this.'

Late on the second day they reached the outskirts of Rome itself, and made camp so they could enter the city during the relative safety of daylight.

That night, the stars were harder to find in the dark night sky. The city generated its own light through cooking fires, oil lamps beyond counting and flares lit in the streets to guide the throngs that prowled the thoroughfares throughout the night hours. For as far as the companions' eyes could see, little flares of light outlined unshuttered windows or revealed half-seen shadows of walls, columns and what appeared to be multi-storeyed buildings.

Sound carried to them on the night wind, too, as if the city was growling deep in its throat. Myrddion knew the ugly hum was composed of hundreds of thousands of voices, crying, groaning, talking, lovemaking or dying, as well as the barking of dogs, the noise of cattle being prepared for the slaughter yards and the cries of exotic animals in the pens below the arenas.

After an hour of listening to the heartbeat of the great city Myrddion fell asleep, to dream of dead earth that offered up the bones of countless victims who had been sacrificed in the name of Rome for over a thousand years. In his dream, the bones poisoned whatever they touched, until the river itself became an acidic wasteland of bloated corpses. Skulls smiled at him with shattered teeth and lifted bony fingers that begged for healing.

When the night horrors finally released him, Myrddion awoke with the taste of ashes in his mouth and salty tears on his lips.

In the early morning light, Rome was stranger and more exotic than Myrddion could ever have imagined. For much of the previous day, the Roman road had hugged the Tiber, with all its attendant smells, and now the healers approached the city from the south with mingled feelings of excitement and trepidation.

The going was slow, for the road was crowded with vehicles of every kind, farmers afoot carrying baskets of goods for the markets, horsemen and peasants riding on spavined donkeys. Myrddion's wagons could only crawl along as the loud, discordant throng shouted, cursed and forced their way into the city.

Ahead of them, the travellers could see a small cavalcade approaching. A noble personage reclining in a huge, gilded divan, complete with gauzy curtains for privacy, was borne on the shoulders of eight coal-black Nubian slaves. Guards accompanied the little procession, and Myrddion judged by their fine clothing and luxurious accoutrements that the traveller was a person of considerable prestige. The Celts had never seen such opulence and stood gape-mouthed at the ostentatious display until one of the guards slashed at the lead horse of their first wagon and ordered them out of the way in curt, crude Latin. As the Nubians trotted past carrying their heavy load with scarcely any sign of sweat or effort, the companions were struck anew by the lack of common courtesy and the automatic assumption of preference shown by such men as the one who lounged within the drawn curtains.

'No wonder the farmers are angry, if great wealth is thrust under their noses by the aristocracy for whom they labour so hard for so little profit,' Myrddion murmured, affronted despite his acceptance that the healers had no status in this city.

'I, for one, would like to tip that bag of wind onto the roadway on his fat arse,' Cadoc replied with unusual venom. The warrior rarely became upset at the foibles of the aristocracy, but in this instance he was thoroughly disgusted by the indifference displayed by master and slaves alike to the needs of anyone but themselves.

'How can you tell that he, she or it has a fat arse? The traveller is completely invisible in case the peasantry might contaminate him by looking at him. But I know how you feel, my friend. Such arrogance! Lady Flavia is a rank amateur in matters of pretension.'

What this trivial incident confirmed for Myrddion was the great gulf that existed between the rich and the poor. The Celts, the Saxons, the Franks and even the Hungvari had their wealthy citizens who arrogantly flaunted their status over the peasantry, but within those lands the farmers and the poor had some recourse to justice through their lords. In Rome, the poor had nothing, while the nobles owned everything, even the souls of their slaves. Above all, rich or poor, to be Roman was everything. As outlanders and non-Romans, the healers were less than nothing.

The visitors' first impression of the city was its sheer size, a vastness that battered the healers' concepts of the needs of such a huge populace. Rome was huge, enclosing and covering the seven hills of universal fame, shining in the noonday light with marble of every colour and size. The Circus Maximus was large enough to contain a chariot racecourse and more. The Palatine rose above it, brilliant with the Hippodrome, the Domus Augustana, the smaller Domus Tiberiana and the infamous Domus Caligulae. Temples glittered with forecourts of shimmering white marble columns, while palaces and mansions raised their careless, ordered heads towards a brazen sky.

But for those who had eyes to see below the glory, the architecture and the marvels of engineering, the same signs of neglect that had afflicted Ostia were exposed to the world. Fifty years earlier, Alaric's Visigoths had sacked Rome and burned it, and even now some buildings still showed the scars of that fire. The population of the city had declined since the sacking, and many of the multi-storeyed tenements that covered the lower ground were empty and crumbling, especially close to the river and its noxious smells. Only here and there did brave displays of trees, dry fountains and even wild drifts of naturally sown flowers indicate that a tenement was at least partially occupied.

Eventually, Myrddion stopped at one of the cleaner tenements, which had a whitewashed stair beside an empty shop-front. Evidence of past grandeur was displayed by the width of the roadway, which permitted the wagons to pass along it without blocking traffic. Other buildings rose three, four and five storeys high, in various states of disrepair, but terra cotta pots of bright red geraniums rested on the sills of the upper windows of this particular one. The shutters were in good working order, and although the pigment was cracking and fading, traces of red, blue and ochre paint could still be seen against the grey of weathered plaster and stone.

'Cadoc! Let's see what we will need to pay to rent some rooms.'

'Perhaps you'd allow me, master? This district is quite run-down in places and rentals shouldn't be too high for respectable tenants. I'm sure I can handle it.'

The two men walked up the shallow steps, which led to an iron grille that acted as a door yet still permitted the free access of any breeze that was available. A brass bell, obviously regularly polished, was attached to the grille to enable visitors to summon the landlord of the building. So it was a surprise to be confronted by a buxom woman, approximately five feet three inches in height and almost as wide in girth.

'Why do you ring my bell, young sirs?'

The woman's voice was melodious and beautiful, turning her simple words into a song. Something in the cast of her features was exotic, especially the slant of her dark eyes and the narrow brows that slanted upwards in the outer corners.

Myrddion could imagine the attraction of those sloe eyes when she was younger, for even now the young man found his lips twitching as she looked up into his face like a plump, perky wren. Her dark hair was liberally streaked with white, and long creases marred her golden skin from her nostrils to the corners of a mouth that smiled widely in welcome.

Cadoc grinned artlessly and Myrddion watched her eyes cloud momentarily as she noticed the scars that twisted one side of his face and disappeared into his coarse tunic.

'Madam, I am Cadoc ap Cadwy of Cymru in the isles of Britain. As you can imagine, we have travelled many weary miles to the centre of the world. This gentleman is Myrddion Emrys, a healer of uncommon skill, who is my master and my teacher. We need a place to treat the sick as well as rooms for living purposes. Your building appears to be superior to many of your neighbours so here we are, eager to discover your rates.'

The little woman eyed both men closely, taking in their shabby clothes, and doubt was written clearly in her dark eyes.

'I have no prejudice against foreigners,' she said, then folded her arms under her ample breasts. 'But you don't look much like healers, I must say. Are you sure you can afford a shop and an apartment?'

'Depending on your rates, perhaps two apartments. My master has two apprentices and three widows who act as nurses. Our clothes are ragged from months of travel, salt from the sea and the vicissitudes of a great war. Don't judge us by first appearances, fair lady, for we are exactly what we claim to be.'

Cadoc could charm the birds out of the trees when he chose, but Myrddion suspected that he might have met his match in this property owner. Her eyes were too bright and far too knowing to suggest that their owner could be easily taken in by flattery.

Myrddion bowed his head and gave her a smile. When he spoke, he was careful to use his purest Latin rather than the patois that Cadoc had mastered.

'You have my assurance that you'll have no cause for regret if you decide to trust us, mistress, despite our dirt and our threadbare clothing. I will bring many patients to your shop and cachet to your house. I bear references from wealthy patrons in Massilia and I can acquire a recommendation from Cleoxenes, the envoy of the emperor of the Eastern Empire. We'll not cheat you or bring trouble to your house.'

'Fair words,' she murmured, surprised at his accent and his obvious education. Then her smile burst forth again, brilliant, whole-hearted and delightfully full of sexual promise for a woman long past her youth.

'Very well, call me a fool, but I'll take a chance. The gods know that there are few takers for empty rooms.' Then she quoted a figure that Myrddion considered remarkably low, but Cadoc laughed as if she had told him an amusing joke. With obvious relish, he was ready to commence haggling.

'For quality tenants – who'll not be drunken, noisy or slow to pay? I've seen the style of most of your clients. Perhaps we should look elsewhere.'

He turned to leave, Myrddion following helplessly in his wake, and the landlady had a sudden change of heart.

'You'll not find better than my rooms,' she called after them. 'But perhaps I could lower my charges a little if you plan to take all three apartments.'

After some further haggling, Mistress Pulchria demanded a month's rent in advance, and Myrddion found his purse lighter by much less than he had dared hope. The healers were now in possession of a shop and two apartments. All that remained was to unpack the wagons and discover a stable prepared to house and feed their horses, a task that Finn promised to organise before nightfall.

The widows descended on the building with the sworn declaration that the premises would be far better after a good scrubbing. Fortunately, Pulchria had no idea what they were saying, or that good lady would have been mortally insulted. Staring a little wildly at the Celtic women and the small child, she retreated up the central hallway and led her new tenants up another small flight of stairs to a higher level around a central atrium that was open to the sky. The adjoining apartments were far from large, but both contained basic furnishings, a tiled space suitable for cooking and long windows that allowed light to enter from the courtyard. The doors and shutters could be securely bolted and locked, and the public privies outside the building were clean enough, although rather pungent.

'If you wish to bathe, as I would recommend to all of you, there's a public bath two streets over that only costs a copper coin. The one great sin in our community is to be dirty in one's personal habits.'

'Thank you for the advice, Mistress Pulchria,' Myrddion murmured, suppressing a smile. 'I will explore the baths immediately.' It struck him as ironic that Romans should place such a high value on personal cleanliness when the streets of the city were filled with refuse, except where some house-proud Romans like Pulchria sent out servants or slaves to clear around their buildings. Great aqueducts brought clean water to the city, so wells and fountains could be found at most major crossroads. No one considered drinking from the Tiber. In fact, if Pulchria was to be believed, very few Romans drank water at all.

Pulchria had two more items of good advice, although Myrddion laughed off her warnings. 'Don't take your purse with you and mind how you speak to others when you go to the baths, young man. You're altogether too pretty to travel unarmed.' She dissolved into giggles as she waddled away down the stairs.

Myrddion informed his apprentices of his intentions, and took the precaution of sliding one of his narrow surgeon's knives into his boot. Then, with a clean change of clothing in his empty satchel, he ventured out into the streets, which were still crowded in spite of the approach of night.

The young healer found the public baths without difficulty and paid one coin for entry and another for a clean towel. Unfamiliar with the use of oil and strigil, he watched a range of men of all ages and occupations as they stripped naked without embarrassment and stowed their clothes on little wooden shelves, supposedly watched by a sharp-eyed slave. For the first time, Myrddion was grateful that his clothes were so ragged. Surreptitiously, he slipped several coins into his mouth, retaining one for the hire of a very battered strigil and a bottle of rancid oil. In the changing room, where the floor was warm and the air steamy, he oiled his body and scraped it vigorously with the small tool while keeping one eye on his fellow bathers. Then, before he lost his nerve in his vulnerable nakedness, he plunged into the hot pool.

Initially, his body seemed on fire, but then his flesh became acclimatised to the heat and his muscles began to relax as his pores opened. He immersed his head and then wrung his long hair free of streaming water.

'Look, friends, we've got a woman,' a coarse voice joked in

the crude Latin patois of the streets. 'But this one's got no tits.'

Myrddion turned and came face to face with a thickset man much shorter than himself whose body was knotted with muscle and seamed with old scars.

'You spoke to me, friend?' Myrddion asked with one eyebrow raised.

'La-de-da! It talks! Perhaps it's a castrato, although the voice sounds deep enough to be a man. Then he's a fancy bum boy, come slumming and looking for customers. Will I do, sweetheart?' The man blew Myrddion a juicy, exaggerated kiss, and Myrddion turned his back. 'I'm talking to you, pretty boy. Aren't I good enough for you?'

Myrddion felt his slow temper begin to ignite. 'Enough, sir. I've no desire to quarrel with you, so leave me be.'

With a smooth, elegant dive beneath the hot waters, he made his way underwater to the steps leading out of the pool. Slick as a seal, he climbed the heated tiles with water streaming from his waist-length hair and beading his rosy skin with glistening droplets. His height, his smooth skin and his beautiful proportions made more than one man stare with hot, lascivious eyes. Several slave girls were also open in their approval, but Myrddion walked between them with his head held high. At the frigidarium, he plunged into the cold water to close the pores of his skin, careless of splashing several giggling youths and earning a hard flash of dislike from several pairs of older men. Then, without a backward glance, he walked back to his clothing as if he was fully dressed. His pleasure in cleanliness now ruined, Myrddion barely paused to dry himself before dressing and striding out of the public baths.

Unfortunately, the muscular dwarf hadn't yet done with him. Myrddion had walked for only two minutes when a broad hand with fingers like iron claws reached up to his shoulder. 'Who said you could walk out on me, boy? I'm inclined to feel insulted.'

Wrong-footed, Myrddion was swung round and saw, with a sigh of fatalism, that he faced four men, as hard and as vile as any creatures of his night dreams. His chief tormentor smiled like a toad with lewd, thin lips, and his red tongue flicked the corners of his odious mouth in feigned sexual gratification.

'Don't you know who I am, boy? I'm Ferreus, sometimes called Iron Bar when I boxed for the pleasure of the high, mucky court. I've eaten boys like you, no matter how tall you are. I think I'll change that pretty face so your clients aren't quite so keen on you.'

He prefers to talk rather than act, Myrddion thought, as his anger began to grow into a hot, scarfing thing that was quickly developing a life of its own. Realising that to beg or reason with his aggressor would only give the brute pleasure, he drew his lips together into an uncompromising line and stared at the thug as if he were a cockroach under his heel.

Ferreus flushed until his facial scars stood out like thick white ridges. He feinted with one hand and lashed out at the younger man with the other, causing Myrddion to rock from a blow to the ribs. As he felt one rib crack, he knew that Ferreus would kill him while the gathering crowd laughed and enjoyed the spectacle.

Another blow fell, almost in the same spot, and Myrddion realised the fighter was trying to finish him off by driving his broken ribs into his lungs. He found himself on his knees, his chest burning, and something rose in his head like sour vomit, obscuring his vision. His fingers found the knife in his boot and he surged to his feet, careless of the pain in his ribs.

The blade shone in the early evening half-light and Ferreus reared back from a narrow slice across his chest. 'You shite! You cowardly shite!'

The contempt in Ferreus's voice triggered Myrddion's fury and the scent of blood made his head spin.

'You may intend to kill me, Ferreus, but I assure you that you'll die earlier than I will. Beware whom you try to harm, for I can see the strangler who comes for you in the cells. If you are fortunate, he will kill you at once. Whatever he decides, your dead body will be thrown from the rock, and will flavour the Tiber so that men will never know that you have ever lived and died in shame.'

Ferreus stepped back, alarmed by a real, red glow in the eyes of this stranger whose unnatural height had so angered him only moments before.

'I have marked you now so that men will know you by the signs I make on your body. When you come closer, as you will, I can finish what I started with ease. I, Myrddion Emrys of Segontium, promise that the fish will devour your eyes before another week has passed.'

Ferreus's friends melted into the crowd like smoke in rain, but Ferreus had been the victor of countless contests in fine mansions where he had fought for fat purses of gold. His courage was limitless whenever he competed against easy targets, for Ferreus couldn't imagine losing any contest where his strength gave him a decided edge. He stepped forward. 'I'm not afraid of your piddling little blade, nor of any sodding threats that you care to make, bum boy. I'll just drive your pretty nose back into your brain.'

He rushed at Myrddion, who absorbed a punishing blow on his shoulder. But even as the young man twisted and turned to minimise the effect of the punch, he managed to run his blade back over the narrow wound above Ferreus's ribs and left a large, shallow cross in its wake.

'It's mostly done now, Ferreus,' Myrddion whispered. 'My patience is at an end, as is your fate. I've done with you.'

'But I've not done with you!' Ferreus screamed, and Myrddion would have been pummelled into bloody strips had not a burly soldier grasped the boxer round his arms, effectively pinioning him. As more members of the guard came thudding up the street, Myrddion turned on his heels and fled.

He reached the subura without pursuit and, clutching his side with one hand, rang the brass bell with the other.

'What has happened, young sir? Your face is as white as winter snow. Come in! Come in! Did you lose your key?' Pulchria fussed around him like a speckled hen, but she let him in swiftly, checked the street behind him and then locked the door in his wake.

Myrddion apologised. 'I still have it, mistress, but I forgot to use it.'

His rapid breathing, and the hand planted over his ribs as though to protect them, caused Pulchria to pull the inner door wide and place a supportive, plump hand round his shoulders, allowing the healer to stagger into the long corridor and lean against the wall.

'Could you call for my apprentices, mistress? I've been caught up in a public brawl, so I hope the watch doesn't come to your door to disturb the peace of the house. I'm sorry.'

Pulchria swallowed a lump in her throat. She had borne children, but she had been a slave in her youth, working in a house of ill repute and saving desperately to buy her freedom. Her sons had been sold, as was the way of the world. And now this boy-man was looking at her with a child's wounded eyes and she melted – although she told herself that she ought to know better. 'Wait here, young master. I'll fetch your boys straight away.' She paddled off on her tiny feet, scrambling up the stairs with as much speed as her bulk permitted.

Cadoc and Finn appeared at Myrddion's side within moments. With relief, the healer leaned his head against Cadoc's shoulder as his apprentices picked him up bodily and bore him up to their apartment and his newly made bed.

'Where are you hurt, master?' Cadoc whispered, for Myrddion's fingers were red with blood.

'It's not mine, Cadoc. Ceridwen forgive me, for I've marked an unarmed man with my scalpel. But I think he's broken some of my ribs and a bone in my shoulder.'

Finn gently cut Myrddion's ragged shirt and sleeve away and bared the healer's chest. Unnoticed, Pulchria had followed the men, and now she gasped aloud to see the ugly, purpling marks of Ferreus's fists on Myrddion's left side and shoulder.

'Gods be!' she exclaimed. 'Someone who knows what he's about has tried to hurt him. I've seen injuries like these before, when I was a young girl. The nobility like sex and blood with their wine. Oh, yes, masters. Men fight to the death with their bare knuckles while fine ladies and gentlemen eat fruit and chatter, or lay wagers. If you'd seen what I've seen . . .'

'What this man has done to our master is more than enough, thank you, mistress,' Finn protested. 'But why would anyone want to hurt him? I'd have thought that the people of Rome would respect healers, not harm them.'

Myrddion flushed with shame and Pulchria knew at once the reason for his injuries. Her hand lingered gently in his damp hair as she smoothed it back from his forehead. 'Your

master is too handsome, lads. He excites envy and lust just by
being alive. I think someone with fighting skills has tried to
seriously hurt him.'

Cadoc's blunt, soldier's fingers had found small green-
stick cracks in two of Myrddion's ribs and the bone across his
shoulder. He shook his head, unable to fathom how a man's
male beauty could bring such punishment down on his head.

'In your own words, master, I'll have to hurt you just a
little.'

'But no poppy, Finn. I want to watch what you two are
about when you're working on my body,' Myrddion hissed
through gritted teeth.

Quickly and efficiently, his ribs were bound tightly, no
other treatment being possible for such injuries. The shoulder
bone was manipulated back into line, and his upper arm was
strapped against his body and then eased into a sling.
Myrddion only groaned when Cadoc hurt him, but Pulchria
felt his pain more acutely than he did and wept silent tears of
sympathy. She had become very fond of this beautiful young
man after only a few hours in his company.

'I managed to cut Ferreus with my scalpel – twice. I made
a very obvious cross with the blade so I would recognise
him if ever I saw him again. I lost my temper, Cadoc, and
said such dreadful things to him. I told him that he'd be
thrown from a rock and the fish of the Tiber would be eating
his eyes within a week. How could I place such a prediction
on anyone?'

'He deserved it,' Finn answered economically. 'Now you'll
drink this water with a little poppy in it so that you can sleep.
No, master, I'll accept no excuses. I'm your herb apprentice,
so you will obey me.'

Myrddion was puzzled as well, a concept that added to his

emotional turmoil. The curse had come so easily to his tongue that he had to consider that it came from the same place in his soul as his prophecies, except that in this case he remembered every word he had spoken. His head spun in confusion.

Myrddion drank the draught, but as he drifted off into a drugged sleep it did not prevent him from despairing of setting up his healing reputation with his left arm out of action for at least six weeks. Fortunately, he did not dream.

When Myrddion awoke, not only were the widows fussing over him, but Pulchria was adding her mite as well. Because of her injured leg, Bridie confined herself to combing and braiding Myrddion's long hair and binding it with woollen bands, ostensibly to prevent it from knotting at the base of his neck. Rhedyn cleaned the men's apartment with thorough ferocity that impressed Pulchria mightily, while Brangaine, with Willa in tow, produced a stew and flat bread she had miraculously prepared on her simple iron hearth.

As for Pulchria, she was in charge of gossip. The local streets were buzzing with news of the incident, although such a minor fight would normally have been soon forgotten had it not been for the tragic sequel. Ferreus had struggled with the guard and those fists, so used to dealing out damage to human flesh, had struck a patrician centurion just under the jaw, breaking the young man's neck. The unnamed officer had died instantly, and Ferreus had been dragged away.

'I'm sorry that Ferreus killed someone, but I'm not surprised. When he hit me, it felt as if I was being struck with an iron bar. By the gods, he only dealt me three blows and he broke a bone each time. Where is he now?'

'That's the whole point, master. You said he'd be thrown from a rock and fish would eat his eyeballs. It is now common knowledge that he's set for execution at the Tarpeian Rock in the old way.'

Myrddion shuddered. He had never heard of the Tullianum Prison, or the Tarpeian Rock that hung over the Forum, but to die in this way seemed a terrible thing. Pulchria gazed at her tenant with an expression composed equally of affection and awe.

'The whole district is talking of nothing else, young sir. It seems we've a soothsayer and a healer all rolled up in one. They'll flock to our door just to see what you look like.'

Myrddion closed his eyes with distaste. Without his volition, rage had unlocked something in his head. Well, no matter, he thought. It's too late now to regret it.

'Cadoc, get the shop in order with Brangaine. She's a genius at putting things to rights. Our first customers will be here shortly, so we need to put on a brave face. I'll dress and join you. Can you help me dress, Rhedyn? Finn can assist at the door. Bridie, find me something clean to wear. The people of Rome want to see a show, so let's give them one.'

Bridie hobbled away and returned with a black cloak which sported a narrow collar of fur, a black tunic and a grey robe. Proudly, she presented her handiwork to her master, and Myrddion thanked her with a child's awe and gratitude.

'Where did you get the fur, Bridie? It's beautiful.'

'You can thank Finn and Cadoc for it, master. When the apprentices were stealing . . . er, finding our horses on the night we left the Catalaunian Plain, they stumbled over the body of a Hun officer wedged into a narrow fissure in the ground. He must have been wounded and crawled away to die. What was one more theft . . . liberation, I mean, after so many others? They stripped the body of its wealth and this fur was around his cloak.'

The fur was thick, soft and the colour of very dark mahogany in the light. Myrddion stroked it and struggled into his new clothes, after Bridie had pottered away with her odd, hopping step to fetch his boots, which had been freshly cleaned. With a pang of affection, Myrddion realised that every tiny hand-stitch in his new clothes had been an act of love. He was humbled.

Once he was dressed, Bridie returned with the boots and a belt of heavy leather, bound with small brass plates that had been polished until they shone like gold. A scabbard decorated with some form of hunting cat was attached, with a knife of particular sharpness and beauty sheathed within it.

'You'll not have to use your surgical knives in future, Master Myrddion.'

'But Bridie, this belt and weapon should belong to Cadoc and Finn. They found them, so the spoils are theirs.'

'Don't worry your head about them. They have his purse and jewels. I know they didn't tell you about the valuables at the time, Master Myrddion, you being a little touchy about robbing the dead, but otherwise that dreadful Aetius would have added these mites to his treasure ... and he's got more than enough. Please don't be angry with them, master.'

Bridie stared up at him with such anxiety that Myrddion felt like a brute. 'I'm sorry, Bridie. Whatever Cadoc and Finn found on the Catalaunian Plain is theirs, by all the rules of war, since time beyond counting. I'm grateful for the fur collar, and Ceridwen knows how much I need to go armed, so I'm not angry at all. In fact, I'm touched that you all care about me.'

'But we love you, master. Didn't you know? You cared for us when no one else saw any value in our existence. You've given us a trade ... so we rely on you. Now, no more of your jibber-jabber. There is only one last detail we have to complete and you'll begin to set all the tongues in Rome a-wagging. Hold still – for just a moment.'

'Ow!' Myrddion bellowed in surprise as well as pain. Bridie had driven a thick needle through the lobe of his ear. 'What was that for?'

'Very still, master, and the bleeding will stop presently. There . . . very still. Done. Finn was right. It looks wonderful.'

Myrddion's ear was hurting, and when he explored it carefully with his right hand he discovered that Bridie had driven an odd-shaped spike through his earlobe. Instead of the usual ring or stud that men sometimes wore, Myrddion's jewel was a small arrowhead of gold, electrum and ruby chips, with a shaft that went through the lobe and then hooked back to attach to the top of the shaft for stability. When Myrddion examined his reflection in a bowl of water, he felt a frisson of pleasure. With his dark hair and eyes, the bejewelled spike made him appear exotic and dangerous.

Myrddion smiled and Bridie's face lit up as if a lamp glowed behind her pale skin. 'Do you like it, master?'

'I do, Bridie, although it hurts. I hope you boiled the earring and your needle?'

Bridie was so happy that she actually punched her master lightly on his good arm with her small fist. Then, realising what she had done, she flushed with embarrassment. 'Of course, master. How could I serve you without learning your ways?'

With an urge to preen that was quite new to him, and his left arm loosely resting in a white sling, Myrddion descended the stairs to the shop, which was now laid out as a makeshift surgery and apothecary's shop. The folding battlefield table was in position and built-in shelves housed Myrddion's jars of salves, drawing poultices and painkillers. The many bunches of herbs and small pails of chopped roots that had been dried during their journey were either hung from the ceiling or piled in rush containers on a rickety table. The baskets of rolled bandages were neatly stacked along one wall, as were the many boxes of boiled rags that had been prepared for service over the preceding months.

The room also boasted two stools of doubtful origin and strength, another low table that Cadoc had used to lay out Myrddion's surgical tools, and his precious chest of scrolls. The crudely tiled floor had been scrubbed clean and swept until no dust dared to make an appearance and even the rather dingy walls had been washed. Dimly lit, because the large exterior doors were still closed, the healer's surgery was as professional and as clean as the three dedicated women could make it.

Myrddion surveyed his small kingdom with elation. His fingers caressed the large pottery water jars and he wondered where Cadoc had found them. The apprentice had also discovered a small terra cotta and iron stove that would be used to heat water or cleanse wounds with fire. Even though the shelves were sparsely stocked, Myrddion's fertile imagination filled them with row upon row of the many herbs and simples that his trade demanded. Filled with hope, he was eager to begin purchasing more of the raw materials that were so essential to his craft.

'Open the doors, Brangaine, and let's satisfy the curiosity of any patients who need our services. I feel like a king today in this strange and dangerous place, and I'm happier than I have ever been in my whole life. I am deeply in your debt, my friends, and I don't know how to repay you.' Then he grinned irrepressibly. 'But I'm sure you'll think of something.'

Red-faced, shuffling and pleased, his five companions accepted their master's gratitude with protestations of devotion and duty. Then Brangaine swung the two doors wide open, letting in the brilliant morning sunshine.

'And so it begins,' Myrddion shouted with a joy nearly as incandescent as Bridie's face and the wide, white smiles of his apprentices.

CHAPTER XII

THE GARDEN OF PAIN

From the moment the wooden doors of Myrddion's first clinic were thrown open, a crowd gathered, several persons deep, to peer into the premises in order to catch a glimpse of the barbarian who had predicted the death of Ferreus. In the subura, word spread like wildfire from tenement to tenement, and the new occupants of Pulchria's building were far more interesting than the unvarying routines of poverty. They came – men, women and children – to stare blatantly through the doors in the hope of gossip, entertainment or, in some cases, an understanding of the reasons for their many bodily ills.

All day, a steady stream of patients, gawkers or personages of importance passed through Myrddion's doors. As the long hours advanced, the healer worked to the point of exhaustion, his cracked ribs protesting every time he bent to examine rotted teeth or asked a crying child to show him the cuts, abrasions or wasted limbs that had brought its parents to his clinic. Cadoc and Finn did all the hard physical work, washing instruments and drawing teeth, and even, under Myrddion's direction, setting simple broken bones. In a multi-coloured, multi-racial stream, the denizens of the subura flocked to the small shop-front with every ailment that Myrddion knew and a frightening number of symptoms that he didn't.

Several family members presented in a very emaciated condition, although there was no lack of food available. The distraught parents swore that their children had lost their appetites and could only be tempted by sweet treats that they frequently vomited up as soon as they had eaten them. The children were listless, very small for their age and slow in their responses to his questions.

Myrddion prescribed a purgative herb and forbade the parents to permit the children to eat the sweetmeats they craved, asking them instead to provide them with fresh fruit, vegetables, eggs and meat. Privately, the healer knew that the parents were unlikely to be able to do so, for unfortunately the poor had little money to purchase the bare essentials of life.

More worrying were four adults who complained of blinding headaches that prevented them from carrying out the most basic of tasks. These chronic patients had visited many other healers but had received no lasting relief from their symptoms. After observing the patients closely, Myrddion noticed a common affliction with all four patients – that they were having difficulty walking. The gait of each was unsteady and all four had a peculiar walk in which the front of the foot took most of the weight. They were also having similar difficulties with their hands, so Myrddion deduced that something was causing problems with their tendons. He offered pain relief for their headaches, but the underlying cause remained a total mystery to him. His brows knit with perplexity, for although he consulted the scrolls until his eyes ached with strain, he was unable to offer even an elementary diagnosis for such a large group of patients.

Failure settled over his shoulders like a cloak of frustration.

Even so, the healers accepted payment for their services, initially a uniform amount, but soon adapting the fees to fit differing financial needs of their patients. Myrddion refused to deny treatment to ragged slum-dwellers with nothing to give. Still, he understood the emasculating nature of charity and agreed to accept whatever payment his patients could afford at a time when they were in a position to pay for his services.

At the end of the first day, the healers had amassed a small store of silver and bronze coins, several eggs, a brass ring, a basket of ripe olives, a tiny stone carving of a household god and a small bird in a wicker cage. As the tiny creature would never survive if it was set free, and was far too small for eating, Willa was given the yellow bird to feed and to love.

Willa was now at least three years old, with burn scars much like the injuries Cadoc bore, but she lacked his natural ebullience and was a self-contained, mute little girl. Months ago, Myrddion had established that there was no physical damage that prevented the child from speaking; her silence was more likely to be caused by the trauma of her injuries and the death of her mother. Willa took one look at the dejected bird and then, like the sun finally emerging from rain clouds, her face broke into a wide smile and she went in search of water for the tiny creature.

After the second day of solid work, their store of coins had increased and Myrddion's perplexity regarding his undiagnosed patients was deeper. Among the stranger forms of payment for their services, they had received a small bunch of radishes and peppers and, inexplicably, an orange tree in a pot. It was a tiny, malnourished thing, but Myrddion accepted it with grateful thanks before giving it to Pulchria. She was delighted, and promised to plant it in the central atrium where it would grow and thrive.

Day followed day in the same unvarying pattern of illness and pain.

Myrddion discovered that he could ease the suffering of many of his patients, but life for the poor underclass of Rome was far more dangerous than in any city he had ever known. As the heat of summer beat down on the stone of the city, causing the roughly cobbled streets to become painful underfoot, illness flourished in the subura, breeding in piles of rotting refuse and excrement and spread by the flies that swarmed over the detritus of Rome. Children came to Myrddion with suppurating eyes and sores turned septic from poor hygiene. To his utter dismay, one hysterical mother brought in a babe with nasty bites all over its body. The healer recognised those tooth marks immediately. Rats had tried to devour the infant as it slept.

At night, by the light of his precious oil lamp, Myrddion kept notes of the strange ailments that he saw daily. But observation and recording weren't enough. Somewhere in this teeming mass of humanity was the man he sought, Isaac the Jew, although none of the people of the subura had ever heard his name. Myrddion waited impatiently, hoping that Isaac might hear of him and, out of curiosity, seek out a fellow healer. However, after the first month in Pulchria's tenement without hearing anything of his elusive quarry, Myrddion began to despair.

Nor had Myrddion forgotten his father, the mysterious Flavius who had given him life so carelessly and so brutally. But the Flavian gens was huge, and many scions of the family were spread throughout the Roman world. As surreptitiously as possible, Myrddion sought news of a man called Flavius who would be in his forties or fifties, but without further information to support his search his enquiries came to nothing.

Perhaps Myrddion would have wearied of the ugly life of the subura and become restive for the excitement of life on the road and the battlefield. But destiny came knocking at Myrddion's door once more when two vaguely familiar men presented themselves at his shop-front at the end of a long procession of patients.

Myrddion was treating a carbuncle on a sandalmaker's neck when the two burly men walked deferentially through the double doors. The sandalmaker flinched at the sight of the strangers and their long staves, so Myrddion finished with the nasty swelling as quickly as possible and called Finn to apply a drawing poultice. Then, after washing his hands in hot water, he turned to face his visitors.

'How may I be of service?' he asked, wincing as he eased his left shoulder back into the sling that offered relief when he wasn't working.

'We are servants of Lord Cleoxenes, master healer. He has an ailment which requires your urgent attention, and has asked that you attend him.'

The servant who spoke sparked a dim memory of two men armed with similar iron-tipped staves who had acted as Cleoxenes's bodyguards in Massilia. Myrddion nodded and fetched his satchel, which he always kept ready for emergencies.

'So your master hasn't yet departed from Rome? I had expected that he would have set sail for Constantinople by now.'

The guard merely shrugged, for the minds of the great men they served were of no interest to those who worked in the dangerous but simple trade of guarding their bodies.

In silence, the three men entered the street and began to walk, but Myrddion soon lost all sense of direction in the confusing alleyways and long intersecting streets that were both ordered and haphazard in their planning. As he hurried in the wake of the bodyguards, Myrddion realised that the streets were becoming cleaner and better lit, and guessed that they were approaching the Palatine. Larger single houses lined the streets and foot traffic was much reduced. Only those men and women who belonged in this district, and their anonymous servants, dared to venture into the sacred heart of Rome. Before an imposing villa lit with torches on its portico, the bodyguards relinquished the care of the healer into the hands of a superior servant dressed in a tunic of bleached light wool who was clean, well fed and autocratic.

'I am Myrddion Emrys, summoned by Lord Cleoxenes to treat him,' Myrddion began, but the servant simply gestured imperiously and entered the mansion on silent feet. Myrddion had no choice but to follow.

The villa was palatial, two-storeyed and profusely decorated with frescoes and mosaics of great naturalness and beauty. Myrddion tried hard not to gape like a bucolic at walls painted to resemble olive and orange groves, at living trees growing tall within the atrium and a fountain that pumped a delicate mist of water over a profusion of herbs and flowering shrubs in the very centre of the structure. The scent of fine oils, nard and cleanliness wafted through the echoing rooms.

The servant led Myrddion to a sleeping chamber of some opulence. It boasted a small balcony that overlooked the atrium and was linked to the corridor by long shuttered doors. More shuttered windows permitted the entry of the evening breeze. A low wooden bed, uncarved but polished with oil that emitted a strong citrus smell, dominated a room that was sparsely but elegantly furnished with several clothes chests and carved wooden stools softened with cushions. Myrddion noticed that the whole house was bare of the household gods that usually occupied niches in the walls. Cleoxenes sat on a wool-stuffed pallet, cradling his arm, which was bandaged from elbow to wrist.

'Greetings, my lord. I had not hoped to see you again so soon, for I understood you were leaving for Constantinople. How may I serve you?'

'Be seated, Myrddion. Pincus will fetch wine for us.'

As the servant turned to leave, Myrddion stopped him with a glance. 'I don't wish to insult your hospitality, Lord Cleoxenes, but I would prefer water. The wines of Rome are far too sweet and heavy for my taste.'

Cleoxenes grinned, and then winced as he moved his arm after momentarily forgetting his injury. 'Most assuredly. I will also have water, Pincus. No doubt it will be better for me.'

As soon as the servant had removed himself, closing the inner shutters in his wake, Myrddion approached the bed and laid his satchel on the timber floor beside the coverlet.

'Now, my lord, what have you done to yourself? I'm surprised that you called for me when Rome is reputed to have some of the finest healers in the world.'

'Perhaps. One such healer, at exorbitant cost, suggested I should wash my arm in the waters of holy Mother Tiber. I'd as soon drink the water as immerse myself in it. The cut began as a trifling injury sustained a week ago and was treated immediately, but it won't heal and now I'm beginning to feel feverish and unwell.'

Myrddion sighed. Summer in Rome was a particularly dangerous season for open cuts, whether the sufferer was patrician or plebeian. Myrddion carefully unwrapped the linen bandages but the cloth had adhered to the weeping wound, and his gentle attempt to peel the last layers away caused Cleoxenes to bite his lip until a spot of blood appeared at the corner of his mouth.

'Relax, Cleoxenes, I'll not hurt you further.'

Pincus returned bearing a tray on which two fine goblets and a jug rested. The metal jug was beaded with condensation, and as the servant poured water into the goblets Myrddion heard the distinctive clink of ice. His eyebrows rose involuntarily.

'The ice comes from the Alpes Maritimi in wagons filled with straw and is then stored in underground icehouses so we can enjoy pure, cold water,' Cleoxenes explained, although his lips and face were pale with strain.

'Pincus!' Myrddion ordered, and Cleoxenes smiled at the autocratic tone in the healer's voice. 'I require two bowls of water, one at room temperature and one that has boiled and is still hot to the touch. Do you understand me?' Affronted, the servant nodded. 'And I need an open flame – an oil lamp will do – and a quantity of clean cloth torn into strips. Don't bring me anything that has been used, because I won't accept it. The cloth must be clean, boiled in hot water and then dried in sunlight. Can this house supply my requirements?'

'Of course!' Pincus's voice was almost sharp, but years of service had taught him to keep his feelings to himself.

'Please bring them at speed then, for your master is suffering.'

Pincus vanished soundlessly, and Myrddion assisted Cleoxenes to drink the chilled water. 'Don't use your arm, my friend,' he warned him. 'I'm going to soak the bandage away from the wound so I can see exactly what is wrong.

There's no need to fret, Cleoxenes, for I'll not do anything to you without explaining it first. You can trust my judgement.'

'I do, Myrddion. That's exactly why I sent for you when I became ill.'

The healer took a sip of cold water and marvelled privately that a city of such sophistication could still be so terrible and unfair in its contrasts.

'Let's talk of other matters while we wait for Pincus,' Cleoxenes whispered, trying to smile. 'Have the people in the subura heard the latest news of the war?'

Myrddion realised that the envoy was very frightened. Cleoxenes's elegant feet tapped the floor with a nervous tic, while his good hand flexed and unflexed unconsciously.

'The people of the subura hardly mention Attila. Their enemies are starvation and disease, which can be just as fatal as a Hun arrow. No, I don't know anything about the progress of the war. For the five weeks I've been in Rome, I could be as far from the battlefront as Segontium for all I've been told.'

'Then they'll not be alarmed to know that Attila is massing his troops for a single fast cavalry strike across the Padus river to the very doorstep of Rome. He's demanded the hand of Honoria in marriage in the misguided belief that Valentinian's silly sister will hand him Rome on a plate. It seems that Honoria is less than pleased with her brother's choice of an elderly Roman senator for a husband.'

Myrddion was shocked. Had untold thousands died because the emperor's sister disliked her future husband? His amazement must have shown on his face because Cleoxenes laughed naturally, his arm momentarily forgotten again.

'Yes, this whole mess stems from a fractious female and Attila's hurt feelings over the gift of a dwarf. Ridiculous!'

Pincus chose this moment to usher in three servants carrying Myrddion's medical requirements. Drawing the stool up to the bed and discarding its cushion, Myrddion ordered the cooler basin to be placed on its flat top so that Cleoxenes could soak his forearm in the water.

Pale again, Cleoxenes continued to speak as Myrddion laved the soothing water over the hidden wound, bandages and all.

'Pope Leo has decided that only God can save the city. He is determined to lead a delegation of prominent citizens to the north, in order to persuade Attila that his ambitions concerning Honoria are pointless. As I represent the Eastern Empire, I have been summoned to attend on Attila along with Consul Avienus, Prefect Trigetius and several wealthy patricians. We are meant to leave in two days for Mantua on the Padus river – so I cannot afford to be ill, Myrddion. There is simply too much at stake.'

'Don't fret, Cleoxenes.' Myrddion's voice was calm and confident. 'Incidentally, I enjoyed the Odyssey. Homer writes with such vividness and spirit, even if most of the story is sheer nonsense. Still, the constancy of Penelope affected me deeply and I regretted the death of the faithful dog.'

'The animal was old and it had lived to see the fulfilment of its greatest desire – the return of its master. They say that Homer was blind, you know.'

Myrddion's hands were busy easing the wet bandages away from the angry red flesh, but his voice never wavered in its soothing, competent tones. 'Then he wasn't born so, I'd lay a substantial wager. He writes with such compelling imagery that I can see the one-eyed Cyclops and hear the voice of Circe as she enticed the travellers to their doom.'

'Isn't it amazing, Myrddion? Even a thousand years and

more after his death, Homer still lives on through the magic of his words.'

The wound was now completely uncovered, and conversation ceased as both men looked down at a livid, suppurating gash that ran from just above the wrist almost to the elbow.

'Ah!' Cleoxenes sighed. 'I thought that Roman healer was a charlatan. I just didn't expect to discover how poor his skills were in this fashion.'

A red line of infection ran up the arm almost to the shoulder. Myrddion clicked his tongue and lifted Cleoxenes's arm out of the water, supporting it carefully from underneath.

'Pincus,' he said quietly. 'Remove the bowl and the bandages. Throw the cloth away and try not to touch it in case you become infected. Immerse the basin in boiling water and then clean it and return it to me, filled with warm water.'

The wound was swollen, but not gaping. Myrddion's heart sank. Normally, he would consider amputation as a last resort, and he would do so for his friend, but only when every other avenue had failed.

'I'll not lie to you, Cleoxenes. This wound is septic and it's poisoning your body. Perhaps it's too late already to save the limb, but we'll not give up just yet. I must send for Cadoc and Finn. To ease any difficulty, please instruct Pincus to obey me as he would you – and trust me, my friend, for I'll do everything I can to save you, I swear.'

'I cannot lose my arm until after the deputation meets Attila. My duty to my emperor is more important than my life, and I would be shamed forever if I put my personal safety before my orders.'

Myrddion shook his head with irritation. 'Your life is worth more than being a part of this delegation, but as it is so important to you I'll do my part.'

Pincus returned to the sleeping chamber and set the basin on the stool. Myrddion had already placed his tools in the basin of boiled water to sterilise them, and now he asked Pincus to lower his master's arm into the new bowl. Somewhat gingerly, the servant obeyed.

'Pincus, as the healer might have to drug me, I want you to obey any instructions he gives you as if I had given the order myself. You will obey me?'

'Of course, master.' The servant's face revealed very little, leaving Myrddion to marvel at the reserve and dignity of slaves when, so often, their masters were crass and ignorant. Pincus was thin and ascetic in appearance, and his face was almost featureless in its smooth blankness. Only his hazel eyes expressed any emotion, and then only fleetingly, before he mastered his dislike of Myrddion. In fact, Pincus showed more nobility than most Romans Myrddion had encountered. The young healer smiled with as much charm as he could muster, which was considerable, gave Pincus his instructions and then thanked the servant unreservedly. At the doors, he lowered his voice so that Cleoxenes couldn't hear him, to whisper conspiratorially to this reserved, self-contained man.

'Pincus, your master is gravely ill, so we must both be very careful. I have no doubt that he is a kind master. I have known him well for some time now and acknowledge he is ever considerate to all men, regardless of their station. If he seems sharp in his manner at the moment, it is because he is fearful that he will fail in his service to the Emperor Valentinian and Pope Leo, so we must do everything in our power to ease his mind. I depend on you, Pincus, to continue to run the household with the efficiency I see around me.'

Pincus unbent sufficiently to smile rather sourly, and Myrddion hoped that he hadn't overdone the flattery. This servant was nobody's fool.

'I'll send those idle bodyguards back to your lodgings to bring your assistants here, along with any supplies you might need. Those hulking bags of wind have nothing better to do than dicing and drinking, so they might as well be put to some use. Lord Cleoxenes only rents this establishment, but I'll own that he is a generous master and never punishes his slaves. Yes, I can assure you that I'll do whatever I can to make him comfortable.'

Well pleased with the result of his stratagem, Myrddion returned to his patient and explained that he was using the heat in the water to draw out the poisons. Cleoxenes was in no particular pain, but his forehead was hot and he eagerly gulped several goblets of the ice water as if he was parched with thirst.

When Cadoc and Finn arrived, the practised calm of a team effort swung into action, relaxing Cleoxenes with its deftness and expertise. Not by a flicker of an eyelash did the apprentices reveal their concern at the condition of the wound. Without being instructed, Finn mixed a sleeping draught so that Myrddion could open the wound and ascertain how far the infection had spread. As soon as Cleoxenes began to drowse, his legs were swung onto the bed and the battlefield table was set up beside it so that Cadoc could cover the wooden surface with a clean cloth and lay the infected arm along its length.

'It looks very bad, master.' Cadoc spoke quietly and with

regret. 'Lord Cleoxenes has permitted the infection to go too far.' Like Myrddion, he had seen many such infections before and knew that they were difficult to check. Amputation or death was the most common outcome. 'We might save his life if we removed his arm.'

Myrddion shook his head briskly. 'He'll not permit me, for he plans to ride north in two days.'

'Then he'll join his ancestors soon after.' Finn added his opinion. 'No jaunt is worth dying for!'

'Cleoxenes is adamant that he must accompany this delegation, so we'll try to save both his life and his arm, even if I have to go north as well, with him travelling on a litter. So let's be at it.' Myrddion expected no answer, for Cadoc had already cleansed the scalpels over the flame of the oil lamp and had a number of clean cloths ready to staunch any bleeding. 'I'll need to cauterise the clean flesh once I've cut away any corruption. Believe it or not, a healer treated this wound – and didn't even stitch it. He must have introduced the infection into the wound when he was playing with it. Sometimes I wonder just how the Roman Empire has survived for twelve centuries.'

Cadoc heated a special scalpel in the flame until it started to glow cherry red, and then, while Finn stood at the ready across from his master, Myrddion made a deep, clean incision the full length of the ragged gash. Just as neatly, he trimmed the edges of the wound as he went, removing flesh that was an unhealthy colour. Periodically, Finn soaked away blood and pus with clean cloths, although there were fewer obvious signs of infection than Myrddion would normally have expected.

Suddenly, his blade struck something hard within the part of the gash where the wound was deepest.

'Cadoc, I need you! Finn, clean out the blood! I can feel a strange object in here.'

While Cadoc sterilised a long probe with a curved scoop at the end, Myrddion cut around the foreign object. A sudden rush of pus obscured his vision.

'Turn the arm and let it drain directly onto scrap rag,' he ordered. As the pus began to stain the cloth, the absence of clean blood warned the healers that they still had much work to do. Wielding the probe carefully, Myrddion extracted a long sliver of wood that had been driven deep into the flesh until it lay against the bone.

'How did Cleoxenes suffer this injury?' Finn asked as Myrddion continued to cut away dying flesh, leaving an ugly hole that exposed part of the long bone of the lower arm. 'Was it a hunting accident?'

'Cadoc? Summon Pincus, but don't touch anything. Your hands must remain clean at all costs. And be polite to the man because we need his co-operation.'

Cadoc summoned the servant by shouting through the shutters until he roused another house slave. Pincus opened the shutters and closed his eyes momentarily when he saw the blood-soaked cloths that had been discarded on the floor.

'How may I assist you, master?'

Myrddion turned away from Cleoxenes's bloody arm and Pincus paled at the sight of the healer's bloodstained hands and leather apron.

'How did your master come by this wound, Pincus?'

'He told me he fell down a set of wooden stairs during a business transaction. The staircase must have been weakened in some way and a slice of timber tore his arm open.'

The healers exchanged knowing glances.

'Have you ever heard of a Jewish healer called Isaac? I'm

worried that my efforts will not be sufficient to save your master. This Isaac is said to be a healer of uncommon skill.'

'My old master used the Jew when he caught an unpleasant disease from a prostitute,' Pincus responded, making a little moue of disapproval. 'I don't know where Isaac might now be found, but I can consult the steward of the Tullius household. Tullius Triagula advised my old master to see the Jew to ease his symptoms.'

Myrddion sighed with relief. 'If you could oblige me in this matter, Master Cleoxenes would be very grateful, and would pay any fees in compensation to other persons involved in gaining access to Isaac.'

Pincus eased himself out of the sleeping room and Myrddion continued to remove flesh until he was satisfied that the wound was as clean as he could make it. Finally, he used his supply of spirits to give it one final wash.

'Right. We'll pack the wound with radish paste, bandage it and immobilise the arm,' he told the others. 'And then we wait. We'll need to clean up this apartment, and then pray that Pincus finds Master Isaac and that Master Isaac agrees to leave his bed to help a Christian who is also a Byzantine noble. Christians and Jews rarely live amicably together.'

Master and apprentices completed all that could be done and then watched Cleoxenes in shifts. The wooden floor was hard, but cushions eased the discomfort.

Myrddion was so exhausted that he felt he could have slept on a bed of hot coals. His injured shoulder still ached when he used it, especially when he was tired, and this had been a particularly long day.

Then, when the dead of the night approached, and men's souls most often relinquished their hold on life, Pincus returned with Isaac the Jew.

*

The shutters of the sleeping chamber were thrust open by a forceful arm, jerking Myrddion and Finn out of a deep sleep. Cadoc almost dropped the oil lamp in surprise, causing their shadows to dance on the wall in a crazy jig.

'Light!' a booming voice demanded. 'I need more light so I can see what these idiots have done.'

Pincus looked apologetically at Myrddion over the large man's shoulder before he scurried off into the dark corridor.

'Who are you?' a coarse voice snapped at Cadoc. 'I've got better things to do in the middle of the night than clean up your messes.'

'Now listen here, whoever you are,' Cadoc began, striding pugnaciously towards the stranger.

'Be calm, Cadoc. I believe we're in the presence of Healer Isaac, of whom I have heard so much good report. You don't need to defend me, so come close with the lamp. Our patient, Cleoxenes, is all that matters, not any misconceptions Healer Isaac might have. After all, he has come at my bidding in the middle of the night.'

Cadoc backed away from Isaac, but the line of his jaw was a clear warning that he wasn't prepared to accept any nonsense from this stranger, no matter how skilled he was.

'Sir, I am Myrddion Emrys of Segontium. I, too, am a healer. I was called this evening to treat an infection in the arm of Lord Cleoxenes because he was alarmed that he had become feverish and the wound was giving every indication of being poisoned. The envoy is required by the emperor to be part of a delegation to confront Attila in a few days, so he would not on any account permit me to remove his forearm. I promised to do whatever was necessary to ensure that he remains a part of the delegation. I have done everything that my knowledge and experience permits but fear it is not enough, so I instructed Lord Cleoxenes's steward to seek you out.'

'Brevity! That's a virtue in Rome, where gibble-gabble passes for conversation. So, let me see the patient,' Isaac responded gruffly. His voice rose to a bellow. 'That is, if anyone ever brings me enough light to see by!'

On cue, Pincus and four servants entered the room. Little more than children, the boys were knuckling their sleepy eyes and trying not to yawn, but the oil lamps in their hands immediately brightened the sleeping chamber.

Myrddion had expected Healer Isaac to be a small, ascetic man with deft fingers and a learned manner. On the contrary, the man who was now clearly visible by the light of the lamps was proof that appearances could be deceiving, and Myrddion grinned at his foolish assumptions. This man looked, and spoke, like a blacksmith.

The Jew shambled over to the patient and removed the loose dressings without touching the wound. As he stared at Myrddion's handiwork, the Celts stared in turn at a man who stood almost six feet in height. He was powerfully built, like a wrestler, especially across his wide shoulders, while his huge, square hands were strong and lightly dusted with black hair. His bushy black eyebrows almost met above a nose that was bulbous and flattened from several breaks along the bridge. He wore an equally lush beard and moustache, with streaks of yellowing grey extending from the corners of his wide lips. With relief, Myrddion saw that his flesh and clothing were scrupulously clean and the instruments that he ordered Finn to unpack from the bag he had brought with him glittered in the lamplight and were obviously well maintained.

The wound was now exposed to the light. Although the flesh was very swollen and red, Myrddion could see a slight improvement in the skin colour now that much of the poison had been drained away.

'You've cut deeply. Why?'

Isaac had yet to touch the arm, other than unwrapping it, but Myrddion was certain that the healer's narrow black eyes had evaluated every element of the younger man's surgery.

'When I lanced the tear, I removed any dying and ragged flesh and skin. As I sought the source of the infection, I found a large splinter of wood which I have kept for you to see. I was forced to drain the abscess and remove all the compromised flesh. Finn, show Master Isaac what was taken from Lord Cleoxenes's arm.'

Isaac nodded absently, and carefully examined the three-inch-long piece of tapering wood. 'How could a fragment this large be missed during the original treatment?'

Isaac's palpable scorn shrivelled Myrddion's resolve to remain calm, no matter how insulting the Jew might be. He felt his spine stiffen in response.

'I don't know. I didn't treat the original wound, which occurred some seven days ago. Cleoxenes used the services of a noted Roman healer to clean and dress the wound. I suppose I was the envoy's last resort when he realised it wasn't healing.'

'Where by all that's holy is Segontium?' Isaac demanded irrelevantly. The Jew obviously didn't know how to be polite – or didn't care. 'I've never heard of it.'

'Segontium is in Cymru, Master Isaac, in the isles of Britain. I have come to Rome seeking knowledge of our craft.'

'Well, you won't find too much of that in this pit of iniquity. What's this stuff in the wound?' He turned to face Cadoc. 'Remove it, please.' Cadoc complied resentfully.

'I use a paste of radish to fight infection when I'm treating injuries on the battlefield. As the bone is exposed in this instance, I decided not to attempt to close the wound, as I believe it will need to be regularly drained.'

Isaac grumpily cleared his throat. 'You're not a complete novice, Myrddion of wherever Cymru or Britain might be. You've worked as a battlefield surgeon?'

'Aye, in Cymru, and in other parts of Britain. I was also at the Battle of the Catalaunian Plain.'

'Hmpf! The casualties were rumoured to be enormous at that hellish place.' With a fearsomely intelligent stare, Isaac ran his eyes over Myrddion from head to toe, until the Celt was convinced that the Jew saw him clearly for the first time. Then he turned back to the patient. 'Ah, I can see what you've done now. It's very workmanlike ... a competent clean-up job.'

Myrddion realised that this was high praise indeed from the Jew, and thanked the older man.

'I need boiling water and a small bowl. Do you have a mortar and pestle?'

'Not here, master. Finn, please ask Pincus to boil more water and to comply with any other requests that Master Isaac might make. I always use boiled water and cleanse our instruments with fire, so Pincus is familiar with such demands.'

'You don't need to justify your methods to me, boy.' Isaac stared fixedly at the cleansed wound now that Cadoc had removed the radish poultice. 'This poultice would be effective if the wound was recent, but it lacks the power to fight such a nasty infection. I prefer a concoction made of seaweed and silver in injuries such as this. This patient was lucky that most of the infection was localized at the site of the foreign object.

The abscess, while large, hasn't compromised the bone. If it had, like it or not, Lord Cleoxenes would be minus the whole arm. But we'll see! I've been wrong many times over the years.'

Finn returned with a wet mortar and pestle, followed by Pincus carrying a basin of steaming water and a small pottery bowl. Myrddion thanked the steward and promised to inform his master of all Pincus's efforts on his behalf.

The Jew poured a little hot water into the small bowl, then stripped off his outer clothing and rolled up his sleeves above the elbow. From his bag he took a narrow brush with very stiff bristles, a container of salt and a small bottle, and proceeded to scrub his hands in the water basin, using a handful of salt crystals on his skin and the brush on his nails. Myrddion watched every move avidly. Then Isaac asked Finn to pour the clear liquid in the bottle over his hands as he held them over the water bowl. Finally, taking pains to touch nothing, he permitted his hands to dry naturally.

'Finn, in my pack you'll find two jars. One has dried seaweed in it. Grind that in the mortar, and then pour it into the small bowl of hot water. Avoid touching the seaweed with your hands.'

'Master, what was that liquid Finn poured over your hands?' Myrddion knew he was interrupting, but he wanted to learn the Jew's secrets.

'Distilled and fermented root vegetable. That humble tuber has excellent cleansing properties and can be used in a wide range of poultices and potions. Are you done, Finn? Yes, that's the consistency I want. Now, in a box in my bag, you'll find a wooden spoon. Wash it thoroughly without touching the bowl at its end, dry it with clean cloth, and then take out one spoonful of the powder from the other jar. Do not touch it! Stir it into the seaweed mixture until it forms a stiff paste.

Then bring the bowl to me and hold it. I don't wish to touch either the container or anything else. Do you understand?'

Myrddion was fascinated by every move the Jew made, and stood across the battlefield table so he could have an unimpeded view. He watched as Isaac spread the concoction into the hole in Cleoxenes's forearm, using the bowl of the spoon to pack the wound.

'Now, Finn! I want you to tie down the patient's arm. No matter how much discomfort he feels, the arm must be immobilised. Then cover the affected skin with a clean pad and tie it down, but loosely, mind. I want to view the injury every five hours in case I still need to remove the arm. I believe you should bind the patient to his bed in a comfortable position. By his deep sleep, I presume he's been sedated with poppy? Good. I'm afraid the use of a stupor-inducing potion must continue for the next six hours at least. Bodies heal better when they are pain-free and immobilised. When he does wake, induce him to drink some clean water, as much as he needs, but with a small amount of the poppy liquid in a second cup. He should pass urine, and he and his bedding must be thoroughly washed each time he soils himself. Can you obey my instructions, Myrddion Emrys of Segontium?'

'I can,' Myrddion replied grimly. 'And I will!'

'I'll return at dawn and we'll see what we will see,' the Jew murmured as he washed his hands thoroughly and repacked his supplies into his bag. 'You've done well, all of you. It's a pity the patient didn't consult you initially.'

The praise caused Myrddion to flush to the roots of his hair with pleasure. 'Thank you for your confidence in me, Master Isaac. We shall carry out your instructions carefully.'

Then Isaac the Jew laughed wryly and his thick-featured face was transformed until he seemed almost jolly. 'While you're at it, a few prayers wouldn't hurt either.' Then, as abruptly as he had entered, the master healer was gone. Suddenly, the room appeared larger, as the man's powerful personality deserted it. The silence was oppressive without that passionate, demanding baritone voice, while the shadows that lurked in the corners deepened, almost as if some evil influence had been driven away by his presence – and had now returned.

For now, all that could be done for the patient was to watch and wait, for the night would be very long.

MYRDDION'S CHART OF THE ROUTE FROM ROME TO MANTUA

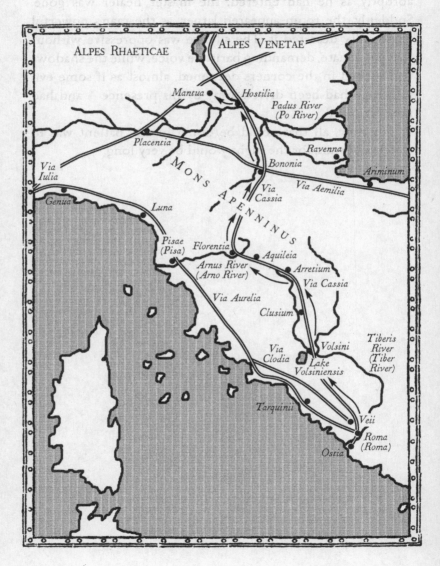

CHAPTER XIII

END GAME

With the shutters at the window pushed out to permit the early morning breeze to enter, Myrddion surveyed the dark city below.

Beauty, impossible layers of filth, grotesque contrasts and, over it all, a malaise that oozed out of the stones and gradually poisoned everyone who lived within its ancient streets. Rome! Harlot of the world! Myrddion recognised her nature, but was forced to admit that her charms were still seductive.

The half-light was kind to the city's ageing features. The first bloody streaks of sunrise touched the highest points of the Capitoline, rouging its outline with rosy highlights. Long gauze veils of midnight blue, rimmed with gold, blurred the ugly edges as night and dawn struggled for dominance. A light mist had risen from the Tiber and loaned the tenements the illusion of beauty by softening the raw wood, sagging doors and rusting iron.

Myrddion sighed reflectively and drew in a deep breath, and the illusion was broken. The air was heavy with the smells of distant garbage and rotting food, the foul stink of the river and a taint compounded of thousands of sweating bodies, excrement and sickly perfume. The healer wanted to gag, but Segontium's cleanly washed beaches were far away and the scent of wood smoke and burning leaves that drifted in from Mona belonged to a different time and place.

As on their first meeting, Isaac hit the shutters with the flat of his hand, sending them thudding back against the bedchamber walls. Finn and Cadoc stirred from their sleep on the floor, their cramped bodies stretching and flexing.

'A new day, praise be to the one true God,' Isaac boomed. 'How's our noble patient?'

He slung his healer's kit onto the nearest table and approached the bed with an infectious grin and a bracing eagerness that was, under the circumstances, almost indecent.

'Cleoxenes woke about an hour ago, and I encouraged him to . . . well, I bullied him actually . . . into drinking three goblets of cold water. I also gave him a small draught of poppy juice for pain relief. His kidneys voided involuntarily as soon as the poppy took effect, so his internal organs are still working effectively. He's been bed-washed, his linen has been changed and his forehead has been bathed in ice water throughout the night. Although he's been restless, the restraints have held, and his arm has remained immobile. His flesh is a little cooler to the touch, and that may be an encouraging sign.'

'Have you exposed the wound?'

Myrddion laughed wryly. 'No, master, I haven't disturbed your handiwork, although my anxiety and curiosity is driving me crazy. But I appreciate that the less the injury is touched, the faster it will heal.'

Isaac chuckled through his vigorous beard like a cheery, ageing wrestler. 'No, I'm not testing you, Myrddion Emrys of Segontium, but if I were you'd have passed the test. Has the patient spoken, or indicated his wishes in any way? Does he still plan to travel tomorrow?'

'As he drank the water, Cleoxenes asked me how bad the infection was. I told him that his injury could still cost him his life and we might yet be forced to amputate the arm. He was adamant, my lord. He insists that he will do his duty with Pope Leo's delegation and believes that the threat of Attila is far more deadly than any personal danger to himself. In my opinion, he won't change his mind.'

'A stubborn, arrogant Roman, huh?'

Myrddion's head snapped up and his black eyes flashed with a rage that was visible. 'Stubborn? Perhaps. Roman – by ancestry. But arrogant? Never!' He fought to bring his anger back under control. 'Cleoxenes is one of those rare and undervalued men whose personal code of honour marks him as an anachronism in a place as vicious as Rome. He is my friend and I, too, am therefore an anachronism, even if I'm a barbarian in your eyes. I'll do what he wants because that is the duty of a healer and a friend. Please don't play games with me, Isaac, for it's beneath your talent and your dignitas.'

Myrddion walked over to the battlefield table and looked down at the source of this crisis in confidence, a loosely bandaged arm. Cleoxenes was so much more than a patient. In this spacious room in an opulent, decadent city, he was that rare thing: an honest man. 'Let what happens, happen. Our gods will decide.'

'I stand corrected, Myrddion. Would you like to unwrap the arm yourself?'

'Aye!'

Myrddion washed his hands, copying Isaac's use of salt, nail-brush and spirits. Cadoc was asked courteously to bring a bowl of warm water and Pincus, who had remained quietly in a corner, immediately slipped away, unasked, to fetch Myrddion's requirements himself. Using forceps, Myrddion eased away the restraints and the loose bandaging to reveal a stained pad of light cotton over the long, open wound. The combined pus and blood that had soaked through the cloth indicated that the poisons were still oozing.

'I'm encouraged by the continued leaking of the infection, even if we have to soak the dressing off the treated area.'

'Yes,' Isaac said. 'I agree. The skin on his arm is a little cooler to the touch this morning, but we can't assume that his troubles are over. You know that God demands some kind of payment for turning His eyes away from one whom He has chosen to join Him,' he added, gently warning Myrddion that his friend's treatment was still likely to end in tears.

Servants returned with more clean linen, a container of boiled water and another of tepid water. Then, excusing themselves, they padded away.

Once the linen pad had been soaked away from the wound, the healers bent over the forearm to check its condition.

'More drainage?' Myrddion asked, taking a sterilised scalpel from Cadoc and raising one eyebrow at Isaac. 'And Finn can begin preparing the seaweed poultice, if you wish.'

'Aye. But you must cut very carefully. We only want to trim the compromised flesh.'

Myrddion began, relieved to see that the large outpouring of pus was greatly reduced. The shallowest end of the gash, in the soft tissue of the forearm closest to the wrist and the little finger, seemed healthy, although it gaped.

'The lower end of the wound can be stitched before an application of the seaweed,' Isaac suggested. 'I'll handle the needlework, being an old fart and trained in knotting.'

Myrddion snorted. He had difficulty knowing how to interpret Isaac's meaning when he was being flippant, so it was easier to remain silent when the healer made one of his more outrageous statements.

Isaac cleaned his hands and, using an unusual thread, began to stitch the skin of the lower half of the wound together. Unlike Myrddion, he created individual stitches set some distance apart. The lower half of the wound was then smeared with more of the healer's special salve.

'Why are the stitches so far apart?' Myrddion asked, having observed every movement of the Jew's large, deft hands. 'Won't the resultant scar be very ugly?'

'If the wound is only partially sealed, it will continue to drain. What's a scar compared with keeping your arm?'

The area where the abscess had formed was an ugly hole in the fleshy underside of the envoy's forearm, just below the elbow. Both healers agreed that the scarring would be considerable and the lost flesh would leave a hollow that would always mar the appearance of the arm. However, once Isaac finished the dressing, he stated his belief that the arm had probably been saved.

'You're certain?' Myrddion asked hesitantly, for the situation had been very grave only five hours earlier.

'No, I'm not certain. I'm a healer, not a prophet. But Cleoxenes has a fighting chance if he remains very quiet, doesn't move his arm and keeps it regularly dressed.'

'But he'll insist on leaving for the Padus river tomorrow. Surely he's endangering himself.' Myrddion saw the whole idea as foolish, even though he was sworn to assist Cleoxenes to fulfil his duty.

'He'll need regular nursing if he's to survive the journey,' Isaac warned, his bushy brows twitching with the energy that always seemed to fuel him. 'Are you prepared for that?'

'Aye,' Myrddion sighed. 'I'll go with Cleoxenes and prevent any stupidity on his part. I'll also take one of the women to watch over him if I need to sleep.'

'If you really intend to go, we'll let him wake naturally. But taking a woman on such a long journey isn't wise. This delegation is going into the heart of enemy territory and I, personally, wouldn't want the responsibility for a woman's life on my hands. You need to leave your apprentices behind to run your surgery – a reasonable decision – but you should take servants to share the nursing duties on the journey. The Lord knows there are servants enough in this house. Whatever you decide, that arm must remain immobile for the next twenty-four hours, with a new dressing every day from then on. Perhaps even two if you feel they are needed.'

'Your plan is sound.' Myrddion nodded. 'Thank you for your advice.'

'Can your apprentices watch over Cleoxenes for a while? They seem well trained.'

'They are.' Myrddion explained their abilities and backgrounds while Cadoc and Finn stood by, red-faced, as they heard themselves praised by their master.

'Then walk with me! We'll see if that steward can find us some ice water and something to eat. I left without breaking my fast and a man of my age needs to keep up his strength.' Isaac patted his ample girth and Myrddion clearly heard the Jew's stomach rumble.

As soon as food was demanded, Pincus became his usual deft self, and once Isaac was ensconced in the kitchens Myrddion was certain that no power on earth could convince the older healer to move. Fortunately, Pincus also realised that Roman manners were of no consequence to Isaac, who would happily sit and eat wherever he chose. Within moments, the kitchen staff magically conjured up a bowl of plump olives, two cold quails meant for Cleoxenes's meal the night before, a hefty wedge of goat cheese, flat bread, several fresh apples and a bowl of assorted nuts and seeds. Pincus offered them wine, but Isaac refused, his brows suddenly knitting like two demented caterpillars.

'Can we have ice?' he asked with the greedy anticipation of a child, causing Pincus to smile in a rather indulgent manner.

'Of course, master healer. Pincus will supply whatever you require.'

'Before you continue with your duties, Pincus, I need to organise transport for your master on the trip to Mantua,' Myrddion said. 'It's a task that requires your particular skills.'

Pincus nodded, so Myrddion explained that they must find the fastest possible, but least uncomfortable, means of transport. Pincus seemed unconcerned and explained that he had an acquaintance who could supply them with a good carriage and a litter, as well as a supply wagon to carry food, medical supplies and clothing. He assured the healers that everything needed for a trip from Rome to Mantua, likely to take several weeks, would be available by the next morning.

Myrddion gulped down a deep draught of ice water with a sigh of relief. The mechanics of the journey had been worrying him all through the night, and he thanked Pincus profusely. The servant appeared to be pleased and bowed before leaving the healers to their repast.

'I swear that you've got a smooth way about you, young man. That shifty slave was eating out of your hand by the time you'd finished flattering him. Tell me about yourself. Up until now we've not had time to scratch ourselves, let alone talk.'

As he spoke, Isaac did indeed begin to scratch himself, and

Myrddion tried hard not to smile. He was a little offended by Isaac's rude assessment of Pincus's character, but he was coming to appreciate that the Jew spoke intemperately as a matter of course. He gave Isaac a brief outline of his life and the path that had led him to Rome. The Jew asked some sharp, embarrassing questions about his parentage, which Myrddion tried to answer honestly, but his words seemed to choke in his throat when he described his mother's rape, his painful childhood and the death of his grandmother.

'Families!' Isaac said in disgust. The Jew's face was momentarily lugubrious, while his black eyes appeared suspiciously moist. 'It's amazing how we mess up our lives trying to live up to the expectations of others . . . or live down the sins of our fathers.'

'You speak from experience?'

'No . . . not entirely. Anyway, my past life is unimportant – as is yours. We're healers, and we live in the most diseased city in the world. We should be concerned with the fates of our patients rather than our own.'

Myrddion detected more than a trace of resentment in Isaac's voice, as well as anger that simmered just beneath the surface of the healer's expressive face. He also noticed that Isaac had deflected the conversation away from his own background.

'Why do you describe Rome as diseased? I know the city is in decline, that good food is highly priced and the river is polluted, but the population is the cleanest I've ever seen and most people have shelter and sufficient food for their needs. I've visited large cities that are far more filthy than Rome. Personal cleanliness is a natural part of daily life here.'

'That's true, my boy, but haven't you noticed the number

of patients who suffer strange maladies such as headaches, aching bones, walking difficulties, vomiting, too many bone fractures, madness? I can list dozens of strange, disconnected symptoms that make no sense to me. I have never seen the like in any other major city in the Empire.'

'Since you mention it, even in the short time I've been in Rome I've treated at least six patients with non-specific symptoms that I can't explain – but surely . . .'

Isaac slammed his fist down on a walnut with unnecessary force. The nutshell shattered and the plump kernel was pulverised.

'Shite, Myrddion, I've studied such patients for more than five years. I think of little else, for something is poisoning the citizens of Rome . . . reaching even beyond its borders. Something is killing the Empire . . . and I can't, for all my skill, discover what it is.'

Myrddion understood the frustrations of failure. One hand reached over the tabletop to grip Isaac's shoulder in sympathy. 'What symptoms have you noticed, master? Perhaps a new perspective might help. I'm an outsider, a newcomer. Perhaps I'll see something that you've missed.'

Isaac grinned at the accidental insult without taking offence. 'I've only established that the symptoms are infuriatingly vague. The mortality rate is huge and it strikes more patrician families than plebeians. But what does that tell us?'

'That the disease is somehow dependent on wealth? If that is so, it must be food-related.'

'But must it? I would hazard a guess that the slaves and servants in this house eat what their master does, only less of it. The same applies to all the patrician families I've studied. But the slaves never seem to have the symptoms. Or they have them so rarely that the number isn't worth considering.

Slaves of the patricians eat better than plebs in the suburas, so they should be sicker than the poor. But they're not.'

'It's a mystery,' Myrddion murmured. He cut a long slice of cheese and ate it reflectively. 'So the disease must stem from a specific food or drink that only Romans ingest. But I don't know where that conclusion leads us.'

'Agreed. It's easier to hold back the Tiber than to check each food item sufferers ingest and then try to cross-reference their diets for a commonality. I know. I've tried.'

'Permit me to dwell on the problem?' Myrddion asked hesitantly. 'I have been concerned about my patients since I first arrived in Rome, so the puzzle will be a profitable pastime for the long hours of travel that lie ahead of me. I'd be grateful if I could consult you when I return. I know I'm too old to be your apprentice, Isaac, but there is so much that I would like to learn from you. Perhaps I can assist you, in repayment, by offering a different perspective on the Roman disease.'

Isaac peered at his young companion from under his shaggy, expressive brows. 'Shite, boy, but I like you! You're a competent healer as well, which is a rarity in these days. You'll always be welcome at my rooms when you return. I don't envy you the days and weeks ahead of you, that's certain.'

'Nor do I. Somehow I've been manoeuvred into any number of difficult situations since I left Cymru. Do men ever control their own destinies?'

With a hoot of laughter, Isaac popped a handful of olives into his mouth and chewed vigorously before spitting out the pits. He slapped his leg and laughed again, even more loudly, once he'd swallowed. Myrddion began to feel offended.

'Don't stiffen up on me, lad, for I'm not precisely laughing at you. We're all such fools, trying to be free, yet choosing those paths that lead us into captivity.' He sobered a little. 'We're healers, lad, and so we can never be free. We must struggle to save others our whole lives long, at the cost of the freedom to marry, to choose our own place to live or to sleep through the night without interruption. We go where there is pain and suffering, and we do what must be done. Of course we don't control our own destinies. We are healers: we are the servants of fate.'

Myrddion stared along the narrow, rutted track that led to Mantua. Hostilia lay several miles behind them over the great Roman bridge that crossed the Padus river, servicing the Via Cassia that ran from Rome all the way through deep gorges in the Alpes Venetae to the lands ruled by Attila. The journey had been punishing on Cleoxenes and difficult for Myrddion, whose role was to ensure that the envoy could contribute to the delegation that would meet Attila, the Dread of the World, on the morrow.

The journey along the Via Cassia had impressed Myrddion more than he had expected, for these roads were not the more quickly constructed and rarely maintained Roman roads of Britain. The long dead engineers who had designed these networks had built them to last, as they had. On a foundation of carefully laid rock constructed over a gravel base, stone paving blocks were used as a finish to provide a durable and gentle surface for the passage of litters, wagons, carts and chariots. Every ten miles or so, fresh horses could be obtained, while inns dotted the countryside through which the great roads marched, as straight as a spear for the most part, so that weary travellers could find a bed on which to rest in comfort.

At the beginning of the journey, Cleoxenes had still been

very drowsy and vague because his abused body craved rest as it began the healing process. The envoy's manservants had placed pallets of wool, linen sheets and comfortable cushions in the travelling wagon so that Cleoxenes could lie in relative comfort under the covered roof. Two horses drew the cart, guided by a driver who sat in the open on a raised platform. One of the bodyguards served this purpose, although he grumbled throughout the whole two weeks of travel that this task wasn't part of his normal duties. A second wagon was piled high with supplies and a heavy carrying litter rested atop the leather cover. Before they left Rome, Myrddion realised that a litter would be necessary, especially in the Mons Apenninus, a mountain range that wasn't as high as the Alpes, but was difficult to negotiate by cart. The second bodyguard drove this vehicle.

Myrddion rode his horse, leading a spare mount. In addition, four other body servants accompanied the small cavalcade, taking turns on the wagons or riding the sturdy mules that made surprisingly good speed.

Concerned as he was for Cleoxenes's comfort, Myrddion was worried at first about the state of the roads. However, the heavy traffic out of Rome, consisting of litters, horsemen, farm wagons and carriages, not to mention several centuries of foot soldiers marching northward, slowed their progress to walking pace for long enough to reassure him that his patient would not be jolted too much on the well-maintained highway even when they picked up speed.

The ancient city of Veii, originally one of the great centres of the Etruscans, the first rulers of Italia, passed quickly. One sculpture in particular caught Myrddion's attention. Sited in a large square near the Forum, the figure appeared strange and inhuman, and seemed to stride on its plinth as if it was ready to explode out of its restraint of stone, leap to the ground and charge down the wide road. Strangely, the eyes were large and blinded, while the mouth smiled at its corners with a distant, peculiar knowledge that chilled the healer's blood. If Ceridwen were translated into stone, she would smile in just this way. Traces of brilliant paint could still be seen in creases in the marble, so Myrddion realised that the sculpture had once been coloured in red, black, white and ochre to ape natural colours when it sat in its temple. Wind, weather and more than a thousand years had bleached the sculpture white, like a spirit or a corpse.

'That's the Apollo,' one of the servants explained when he saw Myrddion's eyes riveted on the chilling, smiling face. Something about the gentle, all-seeing smile and the curls that clustered around the face before falling in long ringlets down the neck made the Celt shudder.

Later, the Via Cassia wound close to Lake Volsiniensis, a wide, glittering blue expanse encircled by rising hills that conspired to slow their passage. Then, as they passed the city of Volsinii, Myrddion noticed that many of the buildings were marred by empty, shutterless holes in their whitewashed walls which looked like so many blinded, black eyes. They screamed out that few occupants remained in what had once been a thriving community.

At Clusium, the party stayed in a rather smelly inn. Cleoxenes seemed much more alert, and after his dressings were changed Myrddion lingered with him to talk, in preference to joining the servants in the small, poorly ventilated space where all seven men were forced to lie on straw on the cold, unadorned floor.

'So! Will I keep my arm, Myrddion, worker of miracles?'

'So far, yes. The lower part of the wound is healing nicely. In fact, a scab is beginning to form. As for the place where the infection was at its worst, I won't need to drain it any further, which is a positive sign. Incidentally, you wouldn't be here without the salves of Isaac, so don't give me the credit for your cure.'

Cleoxenes sipped water, for Myrddion refused to permit him to drink wine at this stage of his recovery. Like most healers, he believed that wine overheated the blood. Myrddion had long adopted the 'better safe than sorry' axiom, so he had personally supervised the boiling and bottling of water during their passage along the Via Cassia, in spite of being the butt of many crude jokes for his precise instructions. He was unconcerned by the laughter, for he was practised at presenting a bland, uncomprehending face when he chose to do so.

'I'll turn into a fish if I keep drinking this stuff,' Cleoxenes joked. 'I won't complain, however. Frankly, two close encounters with death in a short period of time are two temptations of fate too many.'

'What was the first one?' Myrddion asked curiously.

'The fall where I was injured. I was called to meet a messenger from Constantinople at an inn on the Via Clodia. The building wasn't in particularly good order and some fool had failed to repair some of the rungs on the staircase. They were very loose. My foot went right through one, and as I pulled my leg out I leaned my full weight on the railing, which then gave way. The next thing I knew, I was falling. As I said, the building wasn't in good order, so I was lucky to save myself by hanging on to the rail as I fell, even though something slit my arm open as I slid downwards. I could just as easily have been killed.'

Myrddion wondered if Cleoxenes saw the flaw in his memory of the accident. 'What was the message?'

'The message?'

'The reason you were at the inn in the first place,' Myrddion prompted.

'I don't know. By the time my arm was cleaned up, the messenger had gone. I was rather annoyed, for I'd been waiting for instructions from Constantinople for days. But anyway, a scroll arrived by courier two nights later.'

Myrddion's face was thoughtful and troubled. Cleoxenes didn't understand the significance of the missing messenger, but Myrddion did.

After Clusium, they came to the ruins of Aquileia. Myrddion had seen the Hungvari techniques of terror at Tournai and Cambrai, but he wasn't prepared for the scope of the wanton destruction vented on this pretty walled town on the Arnus river. The roadway through the city had been cleared to permit the movement of Aetius's troops to the north, but otherwise it was left as Attila had last seen it from atop a nearby fortress.

All the timber structures of Aquileia had been burned to their foundations. The heat must have been ferocious, because the stone and marble had cracked and split in the maelstrom of the resultant firestorm. Here and there, a sculpture stood, headless, on its stone plinth, blackened and streaked by fire. Columns had collapsed in the heat, bringing down carved porticos and red brick roofs. In several places the heat had been so intense that the brick had melted and puddled. Within this hell of flame, nothing could have survived.

While Cleoxenes stared out through the opened hatch of the carriage with interest, Myrddion felt his stomach roil as he surveyed the aftermath of slaughter on such a scale. He tried to imagine Rome in a comparable plight, but the vastness of the resulting loss of life beggared even Myrddion's vivid imagination.

Ahead, the mountains were tall and rugged, inhabited on the lower slopes by hill people who eked out a precarious existence by raising sheep and goats, and tending vines and olive trees. The Roman engineers had cunningly used the natural landscape as their greatest ally, seeking out the sources of rivers and the tablelands between peaks to find a usable route for their road to cross a mountain range that looked almost impassable. And so Cleoxenes's wagons continued their slow, inexorable journey through Rome's greatest protection, the tall mountains that bisected Rome's most valued ally and traitor, the Via Cassia.

When they reached the last high point before the road gently sloped down to the plains, the vast valley of the Padus river lay before them like a blanket. Far beyond, the Alpes Venetae raised their snow-crowned heads in a great encircling bowl. Even in a fierce, steamy summer, the great plain was a patchwork of green and gold, full of verdant, bursting life created by a network of tributaries that fanned out from the Padus. If Italia had a vascular system, this was it, and, from a distance at least, the signs of decay and moral dissolution that affected the body were not evident in this part of the peninsula.

Myrddion was very tired but he felt his spirits revive as they approached the end of their arduous journey. Bononia lay at the entrance to the swelling landscape of natural beauty that the rivers had carved out of the primeval mountains that enclosed and protected these ancient lands.

'Praise to the Mother,' Myrddion whispered, when he saw

Bononia for the first time. 'For here she has birthed a place to nourish even the poorest of her children, where the earth is always replenished from the high mountains and the water is as clean and as sweet as the first springs that She brought forth out of Her sacred earth.'

The young Celt looked down on the ravaged city that marked where two roads crossed: the Via Cassia, running from north to south, and the Via Aemilia, running from east to west. From the Mare Adriaticum to the borders of Gaul, the people of Italia could move at will across many hundreds of miles with ease, because Rome had created the fastest and most efficient communications and transport system that the world had ever seen. In pride, arrogance and hubris, Rome had birthed a strong, stable society that had been impregnable for a thousand years and was only now beginning to crumble. Ironically, the great roads had proved as advantageous to her present enemies as to Rome herself, for Attila had used them to drive a great wedge into Italia, sending the feared Hun cavalry along Rome's arteries until her whole body was poisoned with his threat.

For the first time, Myrddion found himself imbued with the same desperate urgency that drove Cleoxenes and the rest of the delegation. Italia was an over-ripe bunch of grapes that Attila held in his mailed fist, and one by one he was smashing each bursting piece of fruit as his internal demons demanded. Rome couldn't defeat him, because her arteries were so clogged with the flow of Hungvari cavalry that the whole body of the Empire was choking.

Across the Renus river and over the Panaris tributary, vast Roman bridges eased the journey. Myrddion stared at these structures with their elegant, curving spans, and marvelled at the simplicity of the designs. Such feats of engineering made the healer's head spin. How could stone give the illusion of hovering over space as if marble and granite were as insubstantial as smoke?

'The stone is only a superficial decoration,' Cleoxenes explained from his carriage. 'Concrete is the secret to those great, arched spans – concrete bolstered and strengthened with rubble and iron. Roman engineers can build almost anything by pumping this mixture into wooden shells and then giving it time to harden in the open air. Stone is used to face the raw concrete to add beauty, but the real miracle is unseen – in the foundations and the structure of the framework.'

'It's hard for a Celtic barbarian to even imagine such building methods. In Britain, we can barely raise simple stone structures, and the Saxons only use wood. These ...' Myrddion's arms embraced the whole panorama of the bridge over the Renus river, 'these techniques are far beyond the skills of any of the peoples of the northwest.'

'And it could all disappear like wood smoke if the barbarians succeed,' Cleoxenes whispered.

The countryside unscrolled under the hooves of their horses with all its natural, panoramic lushness, but evidence of a vicious, one-sided war was everywhere for even untutored eyes to recognise. Farm cottages stood empty, and many of them were burned. The absence of fowl, cattle, sheep and other farm animals spoke eloquently of Hungvari pillage, but even human beings had disappeared, so that the landscape was completely empty.

By contrast, Hostilia was filled to bursting with refugees sheltering behind its inadequate walls or trudging south through the town in long, dispirited family groups, carrying all their worldly goods. The people of the Padus valley knew that Attila was primed to attack in the near future.

Finally, outside Mantua, Cleoxenes's cavalcade reached the camp of the delegates. Their arrival caused a stir, for Flavius Aetius had informed the other patricians that the Byzantine envoy was too ill to travel. Cleoxenes had barely enough time to settle into a snug pallet in the travelling tent brought for that purpose before his noble colleagues visited him.

Pope Leo wore the vestments of his office, liberally decorated with gilt and silver embroidery that featured fish, lambs and doves, all of which were sacred symbols of Christianity. His cloak was woven of dyed purple wool, for he was a prince of the church and, therefore, entitled to the royal purple. Myrddion had heard in Rome that this dye, called Tyrrhenum Purple, was extracted from small, toxic shellfish that poisoned the dye makers during its production. The first symptom was a form of madness, followed by blindness and a rapid deterioration in bodily functions. Death was inevitable. A cloak of Imperial Purple was grossly expensive in the human lives expended to produce it. Under his ostentatious, costly dress, Pope Leo was a narrow-faced, slender Roman, with blunt white fingers that were heavily decorated with rings of great value. His brown eyes were intense and clever, but his voice was soft and unassuming.

By comparison, Prefect Trigetius and Consul Avienus were archetypal Roman patricians. Trigetius was vigorous, middle-aged and arrogant, a trait clearly demonstrated by his treatment of Myrddion and the other servants who were snubbed as if they were invisible. A man of action, Trigetius was dressed in elaborate mail and armour, and carried a jewelled Roman sword and dagger. Even his manner towards Cleoxenes was curt and rude, as he voiced aloud his belief that a representative of the Eastern Empire had no place in such an important delegation.

'I am instructed to represent my emperor's interests,' Cleoxenes informed his fellow delegates. 'Before Italia or Gaul felt the lash of Attila's cavalry, my master's army met the Hun and suffered at the hands of his warriors. Flavius Ardabur Aspar met and was defeated by Attila, as you well know, your holiness. I believe your kinswoman, Leontia, has informed you of her husband's defeat in detail. For our burned churches, our murdered priests and nuns, and a population that has been butchered or left impoverished, Constantinople demands to be a part of this delegation. Further, we live in close proximity to the Hun homeland, so any agreements you make with Attila will have repercussions for us.'

'You aren't equipped to bargain with Attila,' Consul Avienus retorted. 'You're not a fighting man. And you're ill.'

Avienus was an older man who sported an elaborate wig of carrot-red hair, tortured into an exaggerated band of curls on his forehead. His purple-edged toga, a jewel of astonishing size that was used to secure his tunic and a quantity of rings and bracelets on both arms proclaimed his wealth, if not his good taste. He reeked of heavy, cloying perfume. Even Cleoxenes, who was accustomed to such epicures, wrinkled his nose at the overpowering scent.

'I am a diplomat, Consul Avienus, and am trained for just such negotiations. I am probably more experienced than you are.' Cleoxenes's face was flushed with annoyance, and Myrddion placed a cautionary hand on the envoy's shoulder.

'May I offer you wine, my lords? Or water, if you prefer? We were about to eat a simple repast, so my lord Cleoxenes would be honoured if you would dine with him.' Myrddion spoke soothingly, with just the right balance of courtesy and subordination.

'Who is this person, Cleoxenes? He appears to be even more barbaric than Attila with all that hair,' Trigetius drawled, ignoring Myrddion's invitation. 'His Latin is very good for an oaf from Gaul.'

Cleoxenes presented Myrddion to the three dignitaries, but Pope Leo was the only one who acknowledged the introduction.

'He cannot be trusted, whoever he is,' Avienus sneered. 'How do we know he's not in league with Attila?'

'This young man was the chief surgeon at the Battle of the Catalaunian Plain. He served our cause with great distinction, so you speak nonsense if you try to blacken his name simply because he wears his hair long, as is the custom in his lands.' Leo examined Myrddion closely. 'Your Latin is very pure, Myrddion Emrys, so I presume you have read the classics.'

'Some, my lord. But my study has been largely confined to tracts concerned with healing and herb lore. I also read Greek.'

The three delegates raised their eyebrows, for not one of these notables had so high an educational pedigree as this outlander from the Western Isles. Out of embarrassment, annoyance and, on Leo's part, an earnest desire to spare Cleoxenes's feelings, the conversation was dropped. Myrddion excused himself and left the tent to instruct the menservants to present the best cold meal available to their guests, including the sweet wines that the Romans craved. The healer in him was thankful to see that his patient continued to drink water.

Outside, on a makeshift bed under the carriage, he watched the shadows of the Romans through the tent flap as they gesticulated and argued in raised voices. Even while the servants were offering them cold delicacies, the consul and the prefect continued to browbeat the envoy as they tried to convince him to stay out of the negotiations with Attila. Quietly and with little inflection, Cleoxenes refused to accede to the Romans' wishes, and his clear, light voice remained adamant through the simple meal.

At last, Cleoxenes made his final declaration. Should the Eastern Empire not be represented in the delegation, Constantinople would refuse to recognise any agreements reached during the conference. Further, Cleoxenes assured the delegates that Attila's expressed position was that he wanted to make a binding agreement with all the parties involved. His ultimatum had teeth, for Rome depended on grain from the Eastern Empire and soldiers to bolster their armies.

Eventually, after eating and drinking Cleoxenes's bounty, the delegates bade the envoy good night. Dissatisfied with the outcome, they strode off in the direction of their luxurious tents.

Sleep eluded Myrddion, regardless of his exhaustion. Under his irritation, a surge of excitement kept his mind chasing ideas long after the fires were banked and the lamps extinguished. Tomorrow, he would see Attila with his own eyes and the fate of Rome would be decided by the diplomatic skills of four clever men and the mailed fist of another. And he, Myrddion Emrys from a small Celtic settlement in the north of nowhere, would be present at this historic meeting. Eventually, lulled by the snores of Cleoxenes's servants, Myrddion surrendered to the sweet anodyne of sleep.

Above him, the stars burned and wheeled in constellations named after the gods and goddesses of antiquity.

Cassiopeia, the archer and the long river of light from the girdle of Orion glowed above the camp while the gods laughed and moved their human chess pieces into new patterns for their own vast and unfathomable amusement. The darkness was warm and enveloping, and Myrddion caught the elusive scent of his grandmother's hair as he surrendered his consciousness to the valley of dreams.

CHAPTER XIV

ATTILA'S BANE

Gorgeous litters, liberally decorated with rare woods, gold, silver and ivory, and draped with gauzy curtains that were drawn to hide their occupants, bore the delegates to Attila's designated meeting place. Sturdy, half-naked body servants carried them while scribes, bodyguards, senior officers and advisers paced solemnly beside the litters. A small troop of soldiers assembled to provide protection for the delegation was able to report that the Dread of the World had come to the parley with a token force of five hundred men. All the participants, no matter how lowly, were dressed in their finest clothes and largest jewels. Although Myrddion had been unable to wash his whole body, he had scrubbed his hands, feet and face until he glowed with health and cleanliness. Dressed in his new clothes, which had been brushed clean of any dust, Myrddion did credit to Cleoxenes with his elegance of form and the gravitas of his manner.

Attila awaited the delegation at the entrance of a large leather tent that was painted in bright colours with depictions of his victories. Flanked by his guard, who were dressed in furs, polished armour and naked swords, he presented a barbaric but exotic magnificence.

The Dread of the World was a middle-aged man whose face was ugly by Roman standards yet radiated power and confidence. From his powerful, hooked nose and the dark, arched brows that led the eye upwards to the tall crown that rested on his head, the thickset king seemed to embody everything that Italia and its people considered uncivilised. His cheekbones were very high and slanted so that the dark eyes in their deep sockets were almost eclipsed by the breadth of forehead shining above them in the natural light. His greying hair curled and was cut long enough to protect the neck, but not so long that it could be a danger in battle.

By Roman standards, Attila was not very clean, and Myrddion saw dark crescents of ingrained dirt under his nails. However, to be fair, Vortigern had been none too scrupulous about bathing either, so the healer couldn't hold the Hun to Roman standards. Attila's body bore the physical signs of a lifetime spent in the saddle, for his legs were bowed and short while his arms were unusually long and heavily muscled. His robes and armour were gaudy but practical, and he rejected jewellery in favour of his heavy crown of purest gold, a clear statement that he was the only royal person present. With his chin lifted to stare slightly upward at the swaying litters, Attila was magnificent, deadly and terrifying.

Myrddion blinked abruptly as the litters were lowered to the ground and the body servants stepped back to assist their masters to rise to greet their host. Behind Attila, Myrddion swore he caught a glimpse of a dark shadow curling around the Hun's legs and trunk. Like smoke or mist, the shadow had no substance, and Myrddion knew that his eyes saw what was invisible to the rest of the delegation. Attila was dying, even though his body seemed hale and vigorous.

As he gave his arm in support to Cleoxenes, Myrddion

told the envoy what he had seen. Cleoxenes stared at the healer from under his narrow, expressive brows and nodded to indicate that he understood. The envoy's expression was inscrutible.

'Remain with me, Myrddion. I'll use my illness as an excuse to keep you beside me. I want you to tell me at once if any other images or ideas come to you, no matter how outlandish they might seem.'

'Of course, my lord. You understand that I can't interpret what I see, so I cannot guarantee that I am predicting future truths?'

'Yes, I understand. But you're my edge in this dangerous game, and I'll play you as my chief piece on the board. Forgive me for using you, my friend.'

Myrddion could only nod.

Flavius Aetius was already waiting opposite Attila. He had forsaken his guard, his weapons and his armour to don a simple Roman toga, tunic and sandals. The remnants of the general's great army of the Catalaunian Plain was in bivouac outside Aquileia, while roving bands of cavalry harassed the Hun from Hostilia to Bononia. Aetius was aware that his role was purely as an observer, but, as always, he carried himself as if he were the true power in the delegation. Even the narrow strip of purple on his toga, which, strictly speaking, he wasn't entitled to wear, demonstrated Aetius's wholehearted belief that he was emperor of the West in all but name.

For reasons known only to himself, the Hun king chose to ignore the presence of Flavius Aetius. Perhaps he thought that the general was the real threat? Perhaps his rage was still hot after his defeat on the Catalaunian Plain? Unfortunately, Myrddion knew that speculation was pointless. Offering a supporting arm to Cleoxenes, he assisted the envoy into Attila's tent, helped him to sit with a comfortable cushion under his arm, and then, his duty finished, stepped back to stand behind his patient as just another anonymous servant.

The meeting began without preamble or the offer of refreshments. Attila took the predictable stance of presuming that the Roman emissaries had come to beg for clemency and, as such, were the petitioners. Pope Leo remained standing and opened the negotiations by attempting to persuade Attila to return to Buda of his own accord. Leo explained that even if Attila defeated the Empire and burned Rome to the ground, he would never wed Valentinian's sister Honoria. At the first sign of danger to the Western Empire, Valentinian would pack her off to Constantinople where she would be held incommunicado for the rest of her life. She would never be permitted to imperil either throne by marriage to the Hungvari king.

'I don't need Valentinian's sister to defeat Rome,' Attila countered harshly. 'Or to take your holy city and rule it in my name.'

The room was stuffy with a press of nervous, sweating bodies and tense with unspoken motives and desires. Myrddion felt a sharp pain in his temple, where his mother had struck him with a rock in his youth. Attila's mouth moved but his words were elongated, so that the healer could scarcely understand the sense of his reply. And Flavius Aetius shot a glance over one shoulder and impaled Myrddion with his malicious monkey's eyes.

Myrddion knew, then, that Aetius was playing for a prize larger than any Attila contemplated. The general planned to rule the Seven Hills of Rome.

Moving forward and avoiding Aetius's basilisk stare,

Myrddion whispered in Cleoxenes's ear. 'Beware of Aetius. Everything that is said today is grist for his mill. He is gambling for a throne.'

'But he hasn't said anything,' Cleoxenes hissed.

'Pope Leo was the victor in the first verbal exchange. And Aetius is here only as an observer – it would draw attention if he were seen to engage Attila in debate . . . and win.'

Cleoxenes nodded and Myrddion straightened his arm on the pillow to justify his movement.

'But the difficult task for you would be to hold Rome permanently,' Pope Leo went on. 'Perhaps you could ask Alaric of the Visigoths for advice, if you could find his shade over the River Styx. For all his vast hordes, Alaric couldn't hold on to Rome when he took the holy city fifty years ago. The magnitude of the task eventually killed him.'

Pope Leo paused. Myrddion watched as a servant gave him a flask to drink from, and noted how Leo's fingers trembled. Attila saw the sign of weakness immediately.

'Eventually, our allies, including the barbarians of Gaul and Spain, will come to our rescue,' Trigetius interrupted in his aggressive manner. 'The Franks, the Visigoths and the Burgundians will not sit back while Rome languishes in your hands.'

Attila's head rose, exactly like the movement of a snake before it strikes. Aetius parted his feet and rocked on his heels. His narrow lips smiled, but at nothing in particular.

'But I can cripple the Empire forever if I hold Rome for even a month, least of all a year or more,' Attila countered with a chilly smile in the general's direction. 'For instance, I can remove the paterfamilies of the great patrician families, exactly like removing the heads of the hydra. I know how to destroy a civilisation, for I've done it before.'

'You wouldn't dare!' Avienus snarled unwisely, his face mottled with choler.

Attila was on the verge of making a snap decision, based solely on the unhelpful arrogance of the prefect and the consul, when Cleoxenes inserted himself smoothly into the conversation. Myrddion heaved a sigh of relief, for Leo still had a chance to be the hero of the hour.

'Of course, your majesty, any man with even a modicum of sense knows that you hold the whip hand at this moment.' Cleoxenes managed to keep his tone complimentary, with only a trace of ingratiation entering his voice. 'Your army is well trained, efficiently led and amply supplied. But my master in the Eastern Empire will not allow you to occupy the Capitoline for too long. You understand the politics of Constantinople as well as I do, and you know that we would find a hostile ruler in Rome totally unacceptable. My master wants to live in peace and friendship with the Hun Empire, but he has instructed me that such a peace and the promise of friendship must rely on mutual respect and equality of purpose. We ask that you show magnanimity to an empire that has benefited the world, even though we all know you have the power to destroy it, if you choose. We do not want your name to go down in history as a despoiler and a brute.'

Clever Cleoxenes, Myrddion thought. Attila is being forced to consider his place in history, now that he knows he is a ruler past his prime.

Attila pulled a sour face that indicated a certain element of agreement with Cleoxenes's words. The Hun stared around the tent at the faces of the delegates to gauge their reactions before shooting a look of active dislike and triumph in the direction of Flavius Aetius, who had taken no part in the proceedings thus far, except for several withering looks cast in the direction of Myrddion Emrys and a dour glance under his eyebrows at the interference of Cleoxenes.

Pope Leo smiled conspiratorially at Cleoxenes as if to thank the envoy for his diversion. Unfortunately, Attila saw the Pope's glance, and his face suddenly darkened with anger.

So easily are empires lost, Myrddion thought, for a glance out of place could give Attila an opportunity to deny the legitimacy of the delegation. Pray that Leo says nothing else to annoy him.

'What can you offer me to leave your churches unburned, priest? Aquileia made a very satisfying bonfire when I burned the temples, the churches, the palaces and the forums to the ground. Why shouldn't I sit on the Field of Mars and watch your holy places burn?'

Leo paled at the thought of Peter's city burning once again. He made the sign of the cross over his breast and tried to straighten his shoulders. Myrddion appreciated the weight that Pope Leo carried on his narrow frame. So many innocent children would die if he did not choose the perfect words to appease Attila, and convince this immensely powerful man to set aside his desire for total domination.

'I cannot stop you, for I'm a man of God. But consider, Lord Attila, ruler of the vast kingdom of the Hun, what became of Alaric after he burned God's holy city? He was warned to respect the houses of God, but he didn't listen. How long did he live after his desecration?'

A long, indrawn breath disturbed the stillness after Leo offered his veiled threat. Who reacted? Myrddion was unable to guess, but his own heart seemed to leap into his mouth.

Attila's dark eyebrows furrowed over his feral eyes, forcing the healer to consider just how dangerous the Hungvari were. Leo had been clever to appeal to Attila's superstitious nature, but the Dread of the World wasn't a child who could be frightened by tales of divine retribution.

'I believe that you can already feel it, my lord.' Cleoxenes added his mite in a conciliatory voice. 'I think that you can already sense the shadows snapping at your heels and the shades of the dead calling to you as they mass in the darkness when you close your eyes to sleep. What would you gain by bringing down all the prayers of the faithful against you across the whole Christian world? The weight of so much prayer can suck a mortal soul dry. Surely it would be better that such prayers be offered for your salvation, rather than your destruction? Especially if you permit God's city to remain free and unscathed.'

Attila's face suddenly became red and congested with ill-concealed fury, and his eyes darted from one face to another. 'This audience is over. Get you gone, scum of Rome. Get out of my sight – especially you, Flavius Aetius, traitor to your blood. Get out! You'll have my answer by morning.'

Regretfully, Pope Leo and the members of his delegation departed from the tent.

The delegates' camp was quiet and many rueful glances were exchanged between the patricians, their guards and their servants. Although noon had barely passed, the midday heat was beginning to fade, for autumn was coming and each day was shortening imperceptibly in the golden aftermath of summer. A scent of wood smoke sweetened the early afternoon and Myrddion felt a pang for a land of falling leaves, dim mists and the steady, thudding roll of long waves on the beaches.

'We failed,' Cleoxenes whispered. His hand shook as he tried to hold a mug of water.

'Not yet, my friend.' Myrddion smiled. 'We needn't despair until the Hungvari actually ride against Rome. Attila isn't a fool, although he has a superstitious nature that Pope Leo cleverly used in his argument. Attila didn't refuse the request of the delegation, which is encouraging. He didn't actually make any decision, except that he'd give his answer by dawn. Don't despair until you are certain of the Hun's answer.'

'I can guess what it will be. He'll choose to ride against us. He's in a pissing contest with Aetius, who's done precious little to save the valley of the Padus so far.'

'At least he hasn't any influence on Attila's decision. Or, at least, not that we're aware of. And you helped Leo significantly, my lord. You reminded Attila that he's facing not just the Western Empire, but Constantinople as well. He may have beaten your generals on the field, but Constantinople can amass a huge army if they are given time. Attila's forces are stretched thin. He can't face enemies on two fronts, no matter how brilliant a strategist he is.

'The moment Attila commits himself to crossing the Mons Apenninus, he loses the safe line of retreat that he enjoys in the valleys of the Padus and her tributaries,' Myrddion continued, becoming quite excited as he described Attila's predicament. 'How would he fare if the Visigoths used the Via Iulia, along the western coast from Gaul, to cut him off from a safe back door through the mountains? Just as easily, the troops of Constantinople could use the Via Aemilia to the east.'

'Myrddion, you are either an incurable optimist or a deluded mind reader, or both. And you seem to understand the road systems in Italia very well.'

'I mapped the western coast as far as Ostia, as you well

know. And I've taken an interest in the road systems in the east.'

Cleoxenes smiled.

'I'm not a mind reader, Cleoxenes. Nor, I hope, am I a fool. I could accept being an optimist. But don't despair until Attila decides to move – one way or the other.'

'By the by, Flavius Aetius could barely disguise his dislike for you,' Cleoxenes said quietly. 'You're more at risk from the general than you are from any number of Hun invaders.'

'It all goes back to Châlons and that damned prophecy I made. He's used it ever since as an excuse to hate me. Aetius is up to something.'

'I remember it well,' Cleoxenes murmured, sipping on his cup of tepid water. 'That day was the first time I ever saw you. I thought Aetius would choke when you told him that he was just another Roman caught up in the river of time. And you spoke about hubris, and how Aetius would succumb to it. Let me see . . . *you will seek to bolster your family power beyond common sense or personal safety* . . . Then you went on to speak of his death and how it marked the end of the Roman Empire. Something about Aetius putting the assassins' knives into their hands himself, and you rambled on about the Scythian Plains in his blood and the taint of envy. I think that was all.'

'Yes, Castor told me much the same, I remember. I wonder what I meant? About his family, I mean. I'm sure the key to the general's behaviour lies in his family dynamics. That's what he wants to keep secret, Cleoxenes, don't you see? But I don't know . . . I just get a headache when I try to work it all out. And he's not over fond of you either. The one time I really looked at him, he was glaring at you as if you were a chaos-demon.'

'That would fit, given the site of our meeting with Attila.

You probably aren't aware how Mantua got its name, are you? Mantus was one of the Etruscan gods from Hades, so the name came into being and stuck, even after the Romans defeated the old kings. Not a very propitious name, is it? I wonder if Aetius believes in Hades?'

Myrddion nodded absently, his mind now puzzling away at the problem of Cleoxenes's fall at the inn on the Via Clodia. 'Can I ask you about the day the staircase gave way under you?' he asked.

'I don't understand. What has my accident to do with Aetius and your prophecy?'

'Please indulge me, Cleoxenes. Who brought you the message to meet at the inn?' Cleoxenes raised one eyebrow interrogatively. 'I only ask because you were a witness to my ravings at Châlons,' Myrddion tried to explain. 'Merovech, Theodoric and several of the barbarian kings . . . they're all dead! Sangiban might be alive, but he's thousands of miles away. You're here! You're the only person of note who even remembers the words of that day – besides Aetius, of course.'

'There were soldiers present,' Cleoxenes protested.

'Yes, and servants too – but what do they count? I ask you again, who brought the message for you to meet the courier at the inn?'

'My apologies, Myrddion, but I received the message in writing. All I know is that the name of the courier was something like Willem.'

'That's a very odd name. I don't suppose you asked for a description from the innkeeper?'

Cleoxenes lifted the cushion that was supporting his bandaged arm and put it under his head. His deceptively lazy eyes were suddenly sharp.

'No, not then. I was a little busy at the time, bleeding all over the bottom of the staircase. But I asked the innkeeper later and he described a middle-aged, grey-haired man with dark eyes and a heavy build. He had an odd accent and wore his hair rather like yours, so I put the strange name down to peculiar writing. The man spoke Latin well enough, according to the innkeeper, who didn't seem to like him much.'

'And he wrote in Latin?'

Cleoxenes nodded.

'So we have an outlander named Willem who speaks and writes Latin, a rare skill among all citizens.' Myrddion's mind was racing. Could the messenger have been the same Gwylym who now works for Flavius Aetius? And why would he want to kill the envoy?

'What's amiss, Myrddion? You're as pale as a sheet.'

Myrddion explained his suspicions. He spoke hesitantly, because he couldn't see any profit to Flavius Aetius in Cleoxenes's murder. However, how many Celts were likely to be found in Rome – especially Celts who spoke Latin?

'The sound of Gwylym is near enough to that of Willem. And there's little chance the name would be remembered, especially if you were dead or incapacitated. The Gwylym I know is a mercenary, and he's obviously found a natural master in Flavius Aetius.'

'You might be correct, friend Myrddion. But if this Gwylym was involved, and he took the trouble to damage the stairs, I don't believe it was done out of a desire to see me dead – merely incapacitated. Perhaps Flavius Aetius didn't want me as part of the delegation for some reason that's not apparent to me.'

'But you did come to Mantua – and the general certainly wasn't pleased by your presence! He must be up to something that he doesn't want Constantinople to know about. Anyway,

I'm sick of thinking about it. All the same, I think I'll take a stroll around the bivouac before the evening meal to see what's happening.'

Cleoxenes looked grave. Myrddion planned to meddle in business that didn't concern him and the thought gave the envoy a twinge of anxiety. A part of his mind worried that Attila might act precipitately if Myrddion was caught spying on his campsite. But the envoy dismissed such fears as baseless and, worse still, disloyal. His friend had never acted rashly, nor would he willingly endanger the work of the delegation.

'Take care, Myrddion. These nobles will stop at nothing to achieve their ambitions, as you must have seen for yourself. Try not to be seen if you're going to stick your nose into Aetius's business. Your hair is too memorable, even among the Hungvari, and I won't be able to save you if you're caught spying.'

Myrddion spent several hours wandering through the delegates' campsite while he tried to memorise the layout of the tents of the various notables. Flavius Aetius had raised his campaign tent some distance from the more gaudy creations of Trigetius and Avienus, whose living quarters were colourful with bunting, so that they were indistinguishable from each other.

As he peeled a crisp apple with Captus's knife, the healer spied a distant figure that could have been the mysterious Gwylym or another of the barbarians that Aetius kept around his person. Humming under his breath, Myrddion established that a thin line of forest ran parallel to the track between the campsite and the river, and appeared to span the whole distance that separated the delegation from the Hun bivouac on the far side of a low hill. He was soon satisfied that he had found a direct route that gave him a clear view of Aetius's tent while still providing cover from the Hun encampment, so he sauntered back to the tent of Cleoxenes to disguise his dress and his appearance.

After changing into the rusty black clothes that had provided a certain degree of anonymity on the road, Myrddion began his small effort at espionage. With regret, he left his cherished knife in his pack, after deciding that it was too showy not to be noticed and could give him away.

As day turned into dusk and the evening breeze became cooler, Myrddion ambled through the camp and strolled into a stand of poplar and ash trees that grew beside the narrow stream that fed into the Padus river. He gave his name willingly whenever he was challenged by sentries, but failed to volunteer his relationship with Cleoxenes. His hair was bound around his head and covered with a crudely knitted cap, and he acted as if the sentries should know who he was. The guards forgot him as soon as he passed. Without his distinctive clothing and remarkable hair, Myrddion was just one more servant.

Once he had reached the trees, which had only just begun to shed their leaves in red and gold drifts, he slid behind a trunk and sought out a clear view of Aetius's campsite. The general's campaign tent was easy to spot, for it lacked the size and opulence of its fellows, being the workmanlike leather structure that Myrddion had last seen on the Catalaunian Plain. It was scarred, repaired in several places, and easily taken apart, a necessity in times of war. As well, several large barbarian guards stood at its entrance, carefully scanning the faces of the patricians and servants who moved around the camp by the light of flares.

Myrddion settled down under a cover of fallen leaves to wait for Aetius to act. The healer was at a loss to explain the reasons why he expected the general to leave the comfort of his tent, but instinct whispered to the Celt that Aetius was embroiled in some secret and hazardous plot. The general might attempt to regain the initiative in the parley with Attila by approaching the Hun directly, thus gaining any glory that could be dredged out of a private meeting.

Would Aetius use his Hun background to effect Attila's capitulation? Did the general want Attila to attack Rome so that Aetius could defeat him and become the saviour of the Western Empire? No, such ideas were nonsense. What did Cleoxenes know, yet not know?

Questions, questions . . . and no answers.

As the darkness deepened and the air became cooler, Myrddion spent the time considering Aetius's complex games. The healer had learned more of the general since he had served at Châlons, and now he knew that Aetius had been raised with the Hun and had a history with them. He had also discovered that the man was emperor in all but name, and the general would not have been human if he hadn't longed to enjoy the fruits of decades of warfare.

Myrddion's reverie was broken by a loud salute and a quiet voice speaking in response. Flavius Aetius was leaving his tent. Having instructed his guard to stay in place, the general strode off into the shadows.

As quietly as he could, Myrddion stood, allowing the leaves to fall from his lower body. Fearful of alerting Aetius as he followed in the general's wake, for ten minutes he kept to the tree line, observing but remaining unobserved.

Suddenly, out of the half-light, Myrddion heard a horse whicker as it pushed its way through the underbrush. Holding his breath, the young Celt pressed his body against a tree trunk while a Hun rider passed in front of him like drifting smoke. As soon as the guard was out of earshot, Myrddion swung up into the branches of the tree, rising as high as he dared so he could observe Aetius's movements from above.

He soon realised that Hun riders were patrolling a large circle round Attila's tent, while more sentries guarded the camp on foot. Aetius walked up to the nearest sentry and, judging by his pugnacious stance and fiercely gesticulating arms, demanded an audience with Attila. Eventually, the Hun entered the tent, and after a moment or two Aetius was ushered into the king's presence.

Hunched in the fork of his tree, Myrddion tried to ignore the cramps in his feet and the pain in his tailbone, which was wedged against a protuberant bole of wood. The light from the flares round the tent allowed him to see Aetius's shadow before he disappeared. The long shapes of the sentries danced on the hard ground, but Myrddion had no chance of hearing the brief conversation that took place. Within ten minutes, Aetius reappeared and strode away, while Attila bellowed for a guard.

Aetius's posture and his rapid, angry walk suggested that his impromptu meeting with Attila hadn't gone according to plan. If the Roman general had planned to use the Hun king for his own purposes, then he had failed. He had barely disappeared into the gloom before the mounted guard reappeared and trotted off into the darkness towards the Hun bivouac.

'What's Attila up to now?' Myrddion whispered to himself.

Within minutes, a handful of Hun officers came running, straightening their dishevelled clothing outside the tent before ducking in through the flap. The sound of raised voices floated to Myrddion on the night wind, but the distance was too far and the language too unfamiliar for clarity. Then, hastily, the Hun officers reappeared through the tent flaps and returned to their lines.

There was very little noise and very little movement that wasn't strictly necessary. Suddenly, Attila swept out of his tent and every gesture spoke mutely of rage and chagrin. He mounted a superb horse that had been brought into the light by a member of the guard, and as it bridled and flinched he used his quirt impatiently. Once the animal was forced into sullen obedience, a number of servants appeared and fell on the tent like a swarm of ants. The tent poles were removed and the leather panels collapsed and folded before being stowed in a cart and driven away before Myrddion could fully absorb what he had seen.

With the awesome speed that had brought the Hungvari huge success in battle, Attila and his guard were leaving and, surprisingly, they were heading in a northerly direction. For reasons that Myrddion had no way of discovering, Attila had broken camp in the teeth of heated opposition from his captains. If the Hun contingent was making for the north, and this sudden departure wasn't a ruse, then Attila was about to re-join his main force and abandon his attack on Italia and the Roman Empire.

Like well-trained and diligent servants, the Hun guard and attendants stripped, packed and loaded the whole bivouac. Within two hours, the entire horde had vanished like smoke into the forests surrounding Mantua.

Myrddion crouched in his tree and thought very hard as the disciplined Hun troops trotted quietly into the night. Behind them, only dust remained on the silent, black plain to indicate they had ever been there.

*

Attila had been angered by Aetius's unannounced appearance. His state, his crown and his jewellery put aside, the Hun king had been resting his ageing, arthritic bones on a camp bed. Years in the saddle in inclement weather, a hundred falls onto the hard earth in practice and in battle, had all served to produce bone and muscle damage that exacerbated Attila's fragile temper.

And now Flavius Aetius had interrupted his rest. Stifling a wince at the nagging pain in his knees, Attila climbed to his feet with a face that was thunderous with distrust and irritation.

Aetius began the conversation baldly as soon as the two men were alone. 'How much gold do you want to shore up the power of the Hungvari nation in the north and the west?' he asked.

Attila was silent.

'I can show you how to fight the Battle of the Catalaunian Plain again, and win – without the loss of a single man.'

'And what makes you think that I'd listen to anything a turncoat like you would suggest, Aetius, master of nothing and no one? You were one of us – you are one of us – but you have tied yourself to Roman curs. I cannot believe a word you say. However, you can spit out your proposal and I'll consider it, taking into account your capacity for changing sides.' Attila's face twisted as he strode across the tent and poured himself some wine. Unsurprisingly, he didn't offer anything to Aetius.

'I plan to rule in Rome and Ravenna, either through my son or by myself. As you have said, Rome is dying and its political system is rotten. I've served them for a lifetime, but I hate them even more than you do. I've bowed my head, I've bent my knee, I've plotted, manoeuvred and lied – and I will have my way or die in the attempt. And if you leave Italia be, and wait for the fruition of my plans, you shall have that stupid bitch Honoria and your kingdom will be secure forever. More important, as my ally I will cede to you the position of Overlord of the West. Gaul and the lands of the Visigoths will be yours without a single blow.'

Attila watched Aetius narrowly. 'You are giving very little away, at least initially, and I'm expected to give up everything, including the spoils of Rome, on a vague promise of possible future gains. You might die in the interim. So might I, for that matter, or you can fail in your ambitions through random chance. Why should I take such a risk?'

'You and I are alike, Attila. We both hate the patrimony of those Roman patricians who honour us to our faces, yet laugh at us behind our backs. They only show a modicum of courtesy because we fight and die in their place while giving them the wealth and leisure to pursue their pleasures. We have gambled all our lives or we'd not be here at Mantua, or in Hades, if you like. We both know what Hades really is, because we've both lived by the sword. What does Leo know? He prays and schemes to make his Church the real power in Rome. And Cleoxenes, an epicure who enjoys an effete life in Constantinople, has rarely lifted a sword in anger. They live in peace while we suffer the pangs of a life of struggle. My heart is sick from having to kneel before my masters. What of you?'

For the first time, Attila sipped his wine and examined Aetius dispassionately over the rim of his cup. His arched brows rose, but Attila recognised a fellow campaigner, regardless of the alliances that had been chosen in the past. In truth, Attila was tired of war. Perhaps a new strategy would spare his aching bones.

Attila laughed softly and maliciously, causing Aetius to experience a nasty little pang below his breastbone. Attila was dangerous, like all his brethren, even when he was tired and ageing. The general would be a fool to underestimate the Hungvari king. He waited as calmly as he could while Attila examined all sides of his proposal.

'Very well, I will do as you suggest, Aetius. But I have no intention of dying and leaving you as the undisputed master of the world. Cross me, or betray me, and you'll discover that I, too, can be a ruthless and secretive enemy. To date, I have never had recourse to the assassin or the spy, but I can change my methods, depending on how you treat me. In that event, the world will not be wide enough to save you from the Hun.'

'I'll not give my hand on the bargain,' Aetius replied, his heart singing with joy barely concealed. 'Amicable enemies like us need no empty gestures of friendship or loyalty. We'll deal with any breach of trust expeditiously. I will hold to my bargain, but I tell you now that this plan will be three years in the shaping.'

'I can easily wait for three years, Aetius. The question is – can Rome survive that long?'

Myrddion clambered down from the tree with a shriek of cramped muscles, resting only long enough to stamp feeling back into his numbed feet before returning to the Roman camp at speed. Thrusting his way into Cleoxenes's tent, the Celt breathlessly gasped out his news. The whole camp was soon roused and the information was confirmed – Attila had, indeed, departed into the darkness.

Outriders were dispatched to determine for certain the direction in which the Hun host was headed. The camp of the delegates heaved like an anthill stirred by a child with a long stick, especially when the scouts reported that the enemy was heading northwards out of Italia towards Buda. The Romans puzzled over Attila's intemperate departure and proposed many diverse reasons for the Hungvari retreat, but no one could fathom a reason why, at the moment of final victory, Attila should leave the diplomatic table without receiving a single concession from his opponents. Myrddion watched Aetius with cold, calculating eyes and wondered anew what such an elderly, unprepossessing man was planning for the Empire. What had sent him out in the darkness of night, in secret, to provoke Attila into intemperate action, when the general wasn't even born with Roman bloodlines?

So the delegation of Pope Leo was ultimately successful and the emissaries returned from Mantua to the acclamation of the citizens of Rome. Autumn had come, and those trees that were permitted to remain in the marble city were shedding their leaves like bloody tears, but the population ignored the first signs of the coming winter to enjoy a holiday of feasting, games and pleasure. The priests sacrificed on the Capitoline and the Palatine, and precious food was laid out for the household lares. The world was in a mood to celebrate and only Myrddion saw that blood would wash the holy city clean.

Myrddion returned to the embraces and back thumping of his apprentices and the widows, who wept, offered him food and proudly displayed the coin they had earned in his absence. Even Willa was excited and jumped up and down like a small puppy in her eagerness, although she remained mute even as she smiled and giggled.

Within weeks of the return of the delegation, Valentinian ordered a widespread campaign of posters, street speeches and promises of celebration. A proclamation was sent out through the city and its outskirts to advertise a week of free games that were to be paid for by the emperor, in honour of the peace that had been negotiated with Attila.

Even Cleoxenes was secretly amused at how quickly the delegation had claimed success for Attila's retreat, although Flavius Aetius was uncharacteristically silent, letting it be known that the marriage of his youngest daughter was demanding all his time. Myrddion grimaced when he was told by a patient of the amusements and free bread that would be distributed by the emperor in ardent thanks for the city's salvation.

'Will we attend, master?' Cadoc asked quietly when they had a moment to themselves.

'Should we, Cadoc? I've heard such unholy rumours about the games. The stories are so bizarre that I refuse to believe that a civilised people would tolerate such barbarism.'

'I've also heard the stories, master, but I was more interested in the free bread,' Cadoc half joked. 'Free is about the right price for anything in this stinking city – except for the baths.'

Cadoc had discovered the pleasures of bathing, so he attended every day, primarily as a treatment for his scar tissue. His visits earned a number of ribald comments from Finn, for the whole of Rome knew that prostitutes frequented the baths for the relief of interested customers. Fortunately, even Cadoc took his new passion for cleanliness as something of a joke, so he forgave Finn and the widows when their jesting became too pointed.

'Perhaps we should see what the fuss is about, master,' Finn suggested. 'I cannot credit that men fight for their lives while the crowds cheer them on. And they call us barbarians! Like you, I refuse to believe the stories I've heard – they're far too gruesome to be true.'

'We'll go tomorrow,' Myrddion decided. 'But don't blame me if your stomach isn't strong enough for Roman entertainment. We'll have to leave at dawn if you're to collect any free bread.'

Rhedyn was horrified that her menfolk wanted to attend the games. Like most Celtic women, she had a mind of her own and didn't hesitate to tell Cadoc that she thought he was corrupting her master for the sake of free food. However, like all women of her class, she had a healthy respect for the beneficial effects of a good meal, so Myrddion and his apprentices left the subura the next morning loaded down with enough cold delicacies to feed a large family.

The companions had no need to ask for directions to the games, because even in the hour before dawn a steady stream of slumdwellers – men, women and children – were wending their various ways to the great circular amphitheatre dedicated to a long-dead emperor. So many roads led to the circus that the crowd had swelled to fill the streets by the time the companions reached the huge entrance on the Via Nova. Myrddion couldn't believe that one building could seat this countless throng, no matter how large it was rumoured to be.

As the sun's rays touched the great gates around the circus, attendants threw open the entrances and allowed the citizens of Rome to flood in, scrambling to secure the best seats. Great baskets filled with bread of all kinds were distributed to the crowd, but the apprentices soon noticed that some men took more than their share, thrusting whole loaves into their tunics before returning for more. If the attendants noticed the ruse, the men were beaten with cudgels and forced to flee while still clutching their ill-gotten gains.

The arena was massive, a gigantic circle of white sand with a paved track round the circumference. Below ground level, lifts had been cunningly constructed with winches and pulleys that permitted wild beasts to be transported up to the floor of the arena and, thence, out onto the sand through an ingenious series of trapdoors and ramps. Men destined for the arena entered through large gates that led up from the nether regions, while large wooden gates were lowered behind them to prevent these unfortunates from deserting the area of combat.

The plebs poured into the amphitheatre and took up positions on the wide tiers of seating surrounding the arena. The hard stone benches could be softened with cushions, and some provident families had brought along a goodly supply for their comfort. Around the arena itself, and close enough to see the action clearly, patricians sat on special cushioned seats, while the emperor, his family and his special guests enjoyed a special viewing box that was fitted with every imaginable luxury.

For the next two hours, the circus filled with laughing, festive families, groups of young men eager for entertainment, the elderly with rugs, cushions and baskets of food, and girls in their finest clothing, giggling behind their face scarves and endeavouring to show the delicacy of their hands with much fluttering of their hennaed fingers. Even the healers began to feel excitement building in them, as the sun rose over the great open roof and the stone benches warmed pleasantly. Cadoc attacked Rhedyn's picnic basket with a ferocious appetite and Finn encouraged Myrddion to eat his share or he'd get nothing. In all, with Cadoc cheerfully munching on a folded envelope of bread filled with beef and vegetables, children running up and down the stairs, the noise of thousands of merrymakers and the warmth of the sun, Myrddion felt his reservations begin to drain away.

Brazen trumpets signified the beginning of the entertainment. A brilliantly cloaked and polished troop of the Praetorian Guard marched into the centre of the arena to protect an oiled, curled and beautiful courtier, who faced the crowd, bowed to the empty imperial box and then made a flourishing gesture to the waiting crowd. They responded with cheers, catcalls and wolf whistles. As the sound of the epicure's voice rose to the roof of the great structure, Myrddion marvelled at the understanding of acoustics that Roman engineers demonstrated through the amplification of this simple, reedy voice. For trivial entertainments such as this, a marvel had been built that trapped sound so that every word could be heard by every member of the audience as the drama unfolded below them.

'Citizens of Rome, proud descendants of Romulus and Remus, know you that Italia is now safe from the ravenous attacks of the barbarian, Attila. Emperor Valentinian gives thanks for the efforts of Pope Leo, Consul Avienus and Prefect Trigetius who acted as our emissaries to Attila. The emperor presents these games for the pleasure of his people as a gesture of gratitude for our salvation.'

To the sound of more trumpets, the courtier and his Praetorian escort left the arena, to be replaced by a group of muscular gladiators representing the four camps of Retiarii, Thraces, Secutores and Hoplomachi. Confused by the different names and accoutrements of the gladiators, Myrddion entered into conversation with a young, clean-shaven hairdresser from the district of Mons Ianiculus, who happily took the opportunity to share his knowledge as he described the different functions of the combatants.

'They don't all use swords, yet they're all called gladiators,' Myrddion argued. 'How can anyone follow what's happening when there're so many different categories of warrior?'

The hairdresser shrugged with a toss of his elegantly oiled and curled head. 'You have a beautiful head of hair, sir. I could sell it for several gold pieces for wig making if you should ever feel the need for coin. My name is Dido, and I live on the Street of Hanging Lanterns. You can find me on the Mons Ianiculus, where everyone knows me.'

Myrddion reddened but remained polite, resisting the impulse to twist his hair out of sight inside his cloak. 'Thank you for the offer, Citizen Dido, but I believe I'll keep my hair for the moment. I'll gladly consult you if I should change my mind.'

The gladiators began to spread out and take up their positions on the floor of the arena immediately below the audience.

The Retiarii fought naked except for a loincloth and a belt, and were armed with tridents, nets and four-bladed daggers, while a long armguard of leather and plated metal extended up their left arm and over onto their breast. This manica had a metal shoulder shield that offered flimsy protection for the neck and lower face. Myrddion was amazed at the deftness of these gladiators as they threw the nets with the left arm and snared the weapons of the Secutores, seeking to draw their opponents close to their wicked tridents or one of the four-bladed knives.

Equal in strength, the Secutores carried the rectangular shields of the legions and the gladius, or sword. Their helmets protected the whole head, including the face, so that only two small eyeholes permitted any vision. Greaves protected their legs and small manicas protected their arms. Disaster came speedily to any Retiarius who lost his net. The trident was a toy compared with the vicious power of the gladius, which was honed to razor sharpness by men who were dependent on that edge of iron for their next breath.

The crowd began to cheer for their favourites, but it took some time for the healers to untangle who was who. Burus wore a yellow feather on the crest of his helmet; Barca favoured red, while Colchis was from Asia Minor and wore a blue scarf tied to his gladius. One by one, Myrddion put names to the twenty matched pairs who were fighting in the arena. Colchis was one of the Thraces, who wore heavy leg wrappings to protect themselves from the waist down. His shield was perfectly rounded and decorated with a griffin dedicated to the goddess Nemesis. Waiting, poised and deadly, for an opening, the falx, a curved Thracian sword, was held in the right hand and to the rear as the combatants circled each other.

Against his better judgement, Myrddion felt a thrill of excitement as the superbly trained warriors fought each other in a ritual dance of death that was vile yet engrossing. Then, when Myrddion had almost succumbed to the seduction of the combat, a Retiarius was brought into danger by his net, yanked forward by a vicious grip on one end of the heavy, woven rope that his Secutore opponent had tangled in his shield. Caught off balance, the Retiarius was forced back with a sword at his throat. The swift manoeuvre was elegant and practised, and the healer would have admired it had a man's life not hung on the end of its smooth delivery.

The crowd screamed its approval or booed the loss of their champion. The successful Secutore looked around the arena, asking permission from the crowd to kill his prisoner – or spare his life. Myrddion watched aghast as some thumbs went up and others went down. Almost immediately, the crowd decided that a man's life should end. A slash of the sword, a backward step and a fountain of blood arced out from the Retiarius's neck, staining the sand around him with his life's blood. Dido whispered that, normally, gladiators delivered the fastest possible death blow, but the first blooding of the day demanded a good dowsing in gore. The crowd was eager, and they howled as the Retiarius bled to death and perished with their screams of enjoyment ringing in his ears.

Myrddion thought he was going to vomit, more at the reaction of the crowd than at the death of a single warrior. Children sucked their thumbs, played at cat's cradle or chewed on bread or honeyed buns while devouring the bloodletting below them with wide, curious eyes.

'What happens to children who grow up attending such displays?' Myrddion appealed to Dido for an explanation of the effects of seeing so much death. 'Are they more violent? More callous? I can't believe that nothing changes in them!'

'Shite, Colchis!' Dido yelled. 'What were you thinking?'

The hairdresser's champion had joined his dead companion on the sand, his torso streaked with blood and sweat. When Dido put his thumb down, relegating a man he had been cheering to a quick beheading, Myrddion turned his back on his neighbour in disgust.

The tempo of the battlefield speeded up as the gladiators wearied and sensed the boredom building in the crowd. Driven to increased risk-taking and flashy feats of arms, the gladiators began to fall and, almost uniformly, were sentenced to death by the crowd. Eventually, only the final twenty survivors of the tournament remained alive. Panting as they stood or kneeled on the sand, the men saluted the crowd with their raised weapons. Finally, Myrddion understood the reason for the opening salutation to the emperor, and his blood ran cold at the thought of such institutionalised murder.

'Cadoc?' Myrddion turned to his apprentice as servants scurried into the arena to sling bodies into a cart and spread fresh sand over the bloodstains. 'How can such a spectacle be entertaining? Don't the crowds see those men as real?'

'They seem to be enjoying themselves, master. They gamble on their favourites, scrawl their names on walls or send them love letters . . . or more.'

'How can you sentence someone to death if you know him – or even of him? I don't like this entertainment, Cadoc, I really don't.'

'It's no worse than battle, master,' Finn added, always ready to acknowledge both sides of the world. 'And we accept battlefield wounded without any qualms.'

'But can't you see that we don't take enjoyment from their injuries and death? Cadoc? Finn? There is a difference.'

'Aye, master, I suppose there is. I was driven almost to madness when I watched Katigern die, and yet this display doesn't affect me as much. Perhaps Rome is a . . .' Finn groped for words. 'Perhaps Rome is a moral stain that inhibits something in our souls?'

Myrddion lasted another two hours in the Amphitheatum Flavium.

He found himself watching mounted bowmen, called Sagittarii, as they fought bulls with iron spikes used to extend and sharpen their horns. Sometimes the bulls won. They watched convicted felons, the Noxii, struggle to the death, some blindfolded and armed with swords pitted against unarmed opponents who could see. Somehow, Myrddion's tangled and compromised sense of right and wrong was less offended by this punishment. That night, he would consider how far Finn's description of moral stains had infected him, that he should damn felons to an agonising and often extended death – as if the manner of their death were less important than that of other citizens.

Bestiarii fought a collection of exotic animals such as lions, spotted cats, long-horned buffalo and creatures stranger still, some with elongated necks. Myrddion's sympathies were with the beasts, which were so beautiful in their strange, vivid pelts. Whether armed with claws, teeth or horns, they invariably perished, although occasionally a bestiarius was wounded. Of greater interest to Myrddion were the Venatores, trained to create a spectacle by using a dangerous beast to perform amazing tricks. As neither man nor beast was hurt by this entertainment, Myrddion could bear to watch. He had watched several hundred men die while a band played jolly music and street sellers plied a brisk trade up and down the benches.

Eventually, he could stand the proceedings no longer. Although noon had not long passed, and the heat wasn't extreme, he surrendered his place on the bench and fled downwards towards the exits. He wanted to cover his ears so he was deaf to the noise of trumpets, lyres, horns and flutes played by capering musicians dressed in manic, highly coloured animal costumes.

Music and the brassy scent of blood followed him along the wide streets and back into the subura, where he stopped at a public bathhouse and scraped his flesh with a blunt strigil until it was red. Then, when the pain of his self-abuse shook him back to himself, he wept salty tears as he stood waist deep in water so that even the curious procurers who gathered at the baths refrained from accosting such a madman. When the cold water finally cleared his head, he began the long journey home. Hours had passed, and his apprentices looked up from a simple meal with eyes that were both sympathetic and guilty.

With a sense of profound shame, Myrddion suddenly realised that he was very hungry, so he devoured the stew that Bridie pressed on him. Then, without another word to anyone, he rolled himself into a blanket on his pallet and fell into a deep sleep.

CHAPTER XV

THE MORAL STAIN

Half a world away, a sacrifice of a different kind was being enacted, as ugly as the games in Rome, although smaller in scale. Instead of a sun-drenched circus, this place of blood was a cavern exposed by the waves at low tide, yet set deeply into a cliff protruding out into the wild ocean. To the north was the fortress of Tintagel, and to the south were the turbulent coves where the small fishing villages of the west clung precariously to the beetling cliffs.

The pebbles and crushed shells beneath the participants' feet were cold and wet, like the air in this dank, Styx-dark place buried deep in the heart of the hill. Fourteen cloaked figures had entered the cavern as darkness came, but only thirteen would leave when the rising tide began to lap the entrance to this natural temple.

The worshippers were swathed in dark cloaks that disguised their bodies and masked their respective sexes. Their faces were disguised by crude masks made of wood, plaster and coarse wool to mimic natural hair. The blank eye-holes of the disguises were edged with shell or polished stone, so that even in this preternatural gloom the glow of the single oil lamp caught their glitter, with its pretence of a baleful pair of eyes.

A gourd was shaken, and the dried seeds in its interior rattled eerily like tiny bones clicking together. The single light source, the grisly blank faces and the heavy shadows combined with this jarring sound to create a miasma of superstition and unseen, unclean gloom. The smell of rotting seaweed, tossed by the tide into the invisible corners of the womb-like space, was partially disguised by the heavy perfume of the oil being burned, a costly, oppressive muskiness that was female in suggestion, but too intrusive and powerful to be pleasant. A faint suggestion of dead fish permeated everything, as if this women's place was corrupted by unspeakable sins.

The cavern possessed only two items that suggested the hand of man. A single rock, smooth, black and roughly the length of a man, lay prone within the deepest part of the cavern beyond a shelf of stone that had been tumbled by the action of the sea. At some unimaginable time in the past, human hands had chipped this rock to trace curves and channels upon its obsidian surface. In shapes that were older than Celtic interlace, yet stronger and more vigorous than the carvings of more sophisticated artisans, the unknown artist had formed crude depictions of serpents, owls, strange birds with women's faces and a long worm with grotesque, over-sized wings. In the fitful lamplight the creatures seemed to move, although the carvings were raw and unpolished. The perfumed oil caused the brain to play tricks on the eyes, so that the shadows of the celebrants dancing on the walls mimicked the monsters carved into the stone.

One of the fourteen present was dragged to the stone by two large figures and stripped by indifferent, muscular hands. A naked girl was revealed in the yellow-green light, her hands bound together in front of her as she tried to conceal the triangular red fur that protected her genitals.

She was young and fair, no more than twelve, to judge by the mere buds of breasts that broke the clean lines of her boyish chest. Her hair was carrot red and tangled because her curls hadn't been brushed for some time, to judge by the cobwebs and dust trapped among her disordered locks. She had been stolen seven days earlier and had been locked in an underground room until the search for her body had been abandoned by her kin. Her captivity had been hard, as was evident by her gaunt, hollowed cheeks and the pinched look of hunger around her mouth.

Why waste precious food on a gift to the Goddess? Water kept her body alive, but the darkness, the persistent cold and the terror had crushed her spirit.

Twelve figures encircled the rock on which she was laid. She tried to rise, but one of her captors put a finger against the mouth of his mask in the age-old sign for silence. Then the same hand slapped her hard across her naked cheek, splitting her tender lips. The child curled on the unforgiving rock as she tried to make her gangling body as small as possible. Although blood filled her mouth, she was too terrified to make a single sound in protest.

Twelve of her captors began to chant softly, although the words were lost in the distant boom of the sea that reverberated through the tomb-like walls of the cavern. Presently, as the sound rose, the child heard the name of the Mother and she began to pray herself, muttering a childish invocation to Don, the protector of all children. A tall figure left the other twelve celebrants to approach the child and pushed a scrap of rag into her mouth to quieten her small defiance.

The chant grew louder in intensity, rising as the celebrants gradually surrendered to the mounting exultation of the ceremony. The growing gloom seemed more absolute, as if a dark force heaved the ancient body of the Goddess out from the substance of the cliff to bathe her feet in the salty waters as she drank the blood of an innocent. Perhaps her devotees would see her sacred flesh when she had accepted their gift? Perhaps she would deign to give them what they most earnestly desired in recompense for their faithful service, even though the practice of feeding the Goddess was forbidden. So here they had come, to her sacred place, where they could abase themselves before her naked breasts.

The chief worshipper approached the girl, who cowered away from him. He nodded and four more of the twelve worshippers left the circle and gripped her ankles and wrists, pinning her so she was exposed and helpless. Then the cowled figure brought his hand out of his robe and exposed a flint knife that had been knapped thousands of years earlier by a master craftsman. So fine was the construction of the weapon that the light seemed to pass through the stone blade.

With a flick of his other hand, the priest stripped off his robe and stood naked in the dim light. His body was spare, gaunt and hairy, while his sex was tumescent with the dizzying potency of the narcotic oil, the naked child and the web of power that they wove. The tall figure joined him and, once naked, revealed a woman's body. Her flesh was white-skinned, lush and seductive in the flowering of youth, and she bore a rudimentary cup carved from horn.

The chanting built in volume, louder and louder, until the walls were full of the sound. As the intensity of the ceremony swelled to fever pitch, the priest's arm rose until the invocation was cut off as if the Goddess had sliced out their tongues.

The stone blade descended and split the flesh that formed the child's breast. Because the flint blade was cumbersome and blunt-edged, the priest was forced to saw through the girl's flesh as she writhed under him, and he used all his body weight to drive the crude weapon through bone and muscle until it lacerated her racing heart. Even then her death was long, terrifying and bloody, but the ancient rite was merciless.

Once the blade was removed from the gross wound, the naked woman collected the dying pump of blood in her horn cup, and when it was full she raised it high and carried it to the furthest and darkest part of the cavern. There, in a natural niche, the second man-made artefact waited. A small female figure was crouched, grossly portrayed with swollen breasts, vastly pregnant belly and vestigial arms and legs, but the small sculpture had a malignancy far more powerful than its crude workmanship would suggest. After abasing herself before it, the woman poured the fresh blood over the figure so that the malevolent pottery object was soon stained glossy red. Excess blood ran from the niche to colour the rock walls where sanguine and brown marks showed that old gore had soaked into the porous stone. Then, with her fellow worshippers stripped naked around her, the woman returned to the corpse to smear her own body with arcane patterns using the blood that still oozed from the grisly wound.

Behind her avian mask, Morgan's dark eyes glowed with satisfaction.

*

To Myrddion Emrys of Segontium, Healer and
Physician.

Hail, friend. The last six months since we returned
from Mantua have been busy with much change, now
that I am living in Ravenna where Emperor Valentinian
has arrived for the summer months.

Ravenna lacks the beauty and age of Rome, while
the land around the city was once a swamp. I fear that
mosquitoes and insects must have been a severe trial
for the population in past centuries, before the marshes
were drained.

I trust that this missive finds you well and healthy.
For reasons that will become obvious, please destroy
this letter when you have read it. Normally, I would not
waste so much writing material when a courier could
learn my message quickly and deliver it personally.

I attended the bridal festivities of Flavius's youngest
daughter, Flavia, when she was wed to Thraustila, a Hun
nobleman. During the feasts, I saw your Gwylym and I
agree that he has a sullen, dangerous look about him.

While I was present, I heard a whisper from various
knowledgeable sources pertaining to our discussions at
Mantua. Aetius has brokered a marriage between his
son Gaudientius and Emperor Valentinian's daughter,
Placidia. By the time you hear this news, the marriage
will be in effect. Aetius has now placed himself, through
this marriage, within reach of the throne.

As well, be informed that a rumour is spreading that
Flavius Aetius stopped Attila, with very few troops,
from advancing into southern Italia. After all our
efforts, Aetius now stands so close to the throne that he

is, effectively, the ruler of the Western Empire in all but name.

Valentinian fears him and believes that Aetius plots against him. Worse still, the people are coming to believe that Pope Leo would have achieved nothing had Aetius not stopped Attila at the Padus river. He is the latest hero, if you can believe it. You should be aware, my friend, that Aetius aims high through the use of his family tree. Flavia's marriage cements the pro-Roman Hun camp, while the marriage of Gaudientius presents a claim to the emperor's crown through his blood ties with Aetius. All that stands in the general's way is Valentinian, who is very much alive. I fear for the future, my friend, so be safe and watch your back. I am recalled to Constantinople, and will be unable to protect you if Aetius bothers to move against you. Avoid Ravenna, if you can.

You'll be happy to learn that despite some stiffness and a really nasty scar at the elbow, my arm has almost healed. You cannot know how grateful I am to possess two arms that answer my bidding when I could so easily have had only one.

Be well, my friend, and call for me should you continue your journey to Constantinople.

In your absence, I will see if I can discover any man of the Flavius gens who is of an age to be your father. Perhaps Fortuna will aid you in your search.

Written in haste,
Claudius Cleoxenes, known as the Greek, and always your friend.

*

Autumn had come again to the City of the Seven Hills and Myrddion missed the softness of Britain, the brilliance of the wooded hills in their scarlet cloaks edged in gold and dim green and intermixed with swaths of yellow gorse. Soft skies streaked in pale grey and whitewashed blue were more beautiful in his memories than the hotter, denser skies of Rome.

In fact, he longed to be anywhere but where he was. He had come to loathe Rome and her class system, from her hard, geometric corners to the long, sweeping skirts of the outlying subura, soaked with grime and ordure almost to the knees of the city. He despised the toll that Rome demanded of his inner peace, and he had a strange, unnerving feeling that the city was contaminating his soul. Britain seemed a lifetime away and slipping further beyond his reach with every passing day.

Still, the subura had much to occupy him. The issues of life and death in the alleyways were as cruel and as immediate as ever. Each day merged seamlessly into the next, so that the young man was sure he sleepwalked through each day and each relationship, squandering himself in a pointless, squalid battle against the invincible armies of pestilence, violence and infanticide.

He had grown fond of his landlady, Mistress Pulchria, and had learned a little of her past, discovering in her insouciance and cheerful cynicism an optimism that no woman in her position should possess. Sold into prostitution when she was in her first, childish bloom at nine, she had wept when a rich old senator had deflowered her for an enormous price, but after those first bitter tears she had set about learning the fallibility of men, how to pander to their small vanities and feign the necessary passion in sex that soon made her a very desirable commodity in one of Rome's best brothels. Myrddion couldn't begin to imagine the depth of determination that the child Pulchria had possessed as she carved a reputation for sly, hot sex and a certain illusory fragility that appealed to wealthy men of all ages.

'You know what men are, master healer – well, you're one yourself. I flattered them by sitting on their laps and pretending to be a little girl. Then I told them how generous they were, so they queued to shower me with gold coins.' She giggled like a girl, and Myrddion could imagine the child she had once been, still trapped in her fleshy, tiny frame.

'I paid my purchase price, with interest, in fourteen years of hard labour on my back, master. But there are too many girls who can't give up the life. They get worn out and old, still hawking what's between their legs even after they've lost their teeth. Not me, dearie! Pulchria learned a thing or two from those fine gentlemen . . . and their ladies too. Now, don't colour up on me, for the world's not always black and white. I learned! So when I bought my freedom, I had enough left over for this insula – and here I am.'

Myrddion's relationship with Healer Isaac had been a stimulating bonus throughout the spring. The wily Jew had persuaded Myrddion to collaborate with him on the mystery disease, but so far none of their research had borne even the frailest hint of success. Myrddion enjoyed Isaac's company, his wealth of knowledge and a pungent sense of humour that tickled Myrddion's more serious nature. The Jew was a little casual about his craft at times, but the young Celt knew that Isaac possessed his own spirit of enquiry, so they managed to rub along together with little friction.

The last summer had been particularly vile. The heat had

been a series of brazen hammer blows that had assailed the city with thirst, furnace-hot nights and days when the stones of the city burned under hand and foot. Heat had shimmered over the streets, blurring geometric outlines so that the air was a gauzy curtain, thin enough to breathe but hot enough to burn the lungs. The stench from the subura, the latrines and the Tiber was overpowering and Myrddion imagined it as a virulent and rotting green that polluted everything it touched.

Disease had also come to Rome during the hotter months, born in the piles of refuse that rotted in the channels used to carry away rainwater, on the empty land and in the raw sewage that less scrupulous landlords dumped in the streets and in the river. Flies bred the illness and carried it from person to person on the hot air and in the polluted water.

At first, patients came to Myrddion complaining of a high temperature and headaches, followed by diarrhoea that was green in colour and uncontrollable. Myrddion consulted his scrolls and found a description of the gastric plague by ancient Thucydides, who described an outbreak in Athens during the war with Sparta. That disaster resulted in the death of one third of the Athenian population.

Myrddion was terrified of this plague, so, alarmed by the statistics collated by Thucydides, he pored over every scroll he had. Better Attila should have burned the city than it should die in its own vomit, fever and shit, so Myrddion sent word to Isaac, whose sector of the city was, as yet, unaffected by the disease. Myrddion knew that the Jew would come to his aid, for he was forever seeking out disease and trying to discover its root cause.

Isaac entered Myrddion's surgery in his customary fashion – noisily. Looking up from the series of tinctures he was preparing for patients who were too ill to leave their beds, the younger man breathed a sigh of relief that he'd no longer be floundering through the darkness of ignorance on his own.

'Here you are, Myrddion Emrys,' the Jew boomed out, frightening two small children who were waiting for Cadoc to treat a split head and a slash on the forearm respectively. 'A well-ordered room.' The Jew nodded appreciatively, but the children wailed shrilly at the sight of a huge bear of a man looming over them, all flashing teeth and curly hair.

'Hush, little ones. I won't let the nasties have you.' Isaac patted their heads with hands as large as terra cotta platters. Both children hiccuped and knuckled their wide eyes with dirty fists, overawed by the odd appearance of this huge newcomer.

'Noisy as ever, Isaac? Still, I'm very glad to see you. I hope you can spare the time to come with me to see some patients, as I'm at my wit's end to know how to treat Thucydides' disease.'

'That's the new name for the stomach disease? The plebs call it something else, but I won't sully the children's ears by repeating it in front of them.' Isaac laughed again, until the surgery seemed too small to hold that booming, titanic mirth. 'Are you ready, Myrddion? If so, I am totally at your disposal.'

The two men left the tenement and walked past several streets until they came to a dark laneway. As they picked their way through piles of rubbish, old clothes and the contents of countless slop buckets, Isaac clicked his tongue against his teeth and growled with disgust. When a rat as large as a small cat ran over his foot, he lashed out at it with a well-aimed kick, shuddering at the length of its naked, scaly tail.

'Don't you hate those damned things? They breed disease

and they feed on rubbish. When the Lord God created them He made a mistake, because they're true vermin – I would destroy every one of them if I could.'

'I can tell,' Myrddion responded drily. 'Here we are. This is the house of Arrius, the ironworker.'

'I've never understood how people can live next to such filth,' Isaac grumbled, attempting to clean something slimy off his sandal.

'They're poor, so they have no choice,' Myrddion retorted, a little sharply.

He knocked at the rickety door and it was pulled open by a worn woman whose black hair and excellent white teeth belied her ageing, faded appearance. The ruins of luminous beauty still lingered in her high cheekbones, almond eyes and dense white skin. She ushered them into two rooms that served the multiple purposes of bedrooms, kitchen and eating place. Five children clustered around her skirts, the youngest barely old enough to walk.

'A good day to you, Hadria. How is your man? Have your children become ill yet, or have you managed to keep them away from Arrius, as I asked you to do?'

'I've told them and told them to stay away from him, but it's very hard – them being so fond of their father,' Hadria replied in a whisper, twisting the hem of her peplum around her fingers.

Isaac surveyed the two mean rooms and recognised a valiant attempt at cleanliness, despite the filth of the alleyway. A twig broom obviously kept the uneven stone floor as clean as possible, and the low table had been scrubbed vigorously so that the wood was pale and smooth.

'Where's the patient?' he asked gruffly.

With instinctive courtesy, Myrddion quickly introduced

Isaac to Hadria, who coloured under the older healer's scrutiny. She ushered them both into the small room next door, which was little bigger than an alcove and was almost filled with a slim pallet stuffed with straw.

The man who lay on the bed was naked except for a loincloth. His body was slick with sweat and Hadria bent over him to coax him to drink a little water.

'Have you been boiling the water, Hadria?' Myrddion asked.

'Yes, master, although fuel is hard to come by. But I'll manage somehow.' She bit down hard on her lip, and Myrddion vowed silently to slip her several coins before he left.

Isaac examined Arrius's chest and slightly distended belly. 'See those small red spots? Thucydides was the first person to write down the symptoms of the stomach disease. I've seen it before.'

'What's the treatment?' Myrddion asked eagerly. 'I've never come across an illness like this before. Britain doesn't get hot enough for the disease to develop, even in summer.'

'Perhaps in Britain you have too few cities where filth can accumulate,' Isaac muttered as he knelt beside the prone man and felt his forehead. 'What colour are his stools, Hadria?'

She looked at him blankly.

'His shit, girl!' Isaac barked. 'What colour is it?'

Hadria blushed to the roots of her hair. 'It's green, master. I've used almost all the cloth we have to keep him clean.'

'Boil all the water! Boil his loincloths and force him to drink every hour. Better he should be sick than dry. If his temperature rises and he becomes too hot, then he'll die.'

Hadria hiccuped with distress and Myrddion felt a deep

pity for her. Isaac was being unduly harsh; he could be very sharp when the mood took him.

'What about feverwort, Isaac?' Myrddion asked, lifting a cloth bag out of his satchel. 'Will that help his treatment?'

'It wouldn't hurt, especially in boiled water. He can live for some time without food, but not without fluid.'

Hadria tugged at Isaac's sleeve. 'Will he die, master?'

Aware of Myrddion's reaction, Isaac answered gently and with more consideration than he had shown earlier. 'He's strong and not yet thirty. His labour as an ironworker has built good muscle, so he has an excellent chance. I'm more worried about your children.'

Hadria paled, rushed into the next room and clutched the children to her breast. Frightened by her panic, the youngest began to cry gustily.

'Myrddion, this disease runs wild in places where there is excrement, rats and flies. The subura is a breeding ground for this type of plague in the summer months, because it passes from human to human through contact with filth. If Hadria can keep her children clean and out in the fresh air, and not in that filthy alleyway, then perhaps she can prevent the spread of the illness.' Isaac shrugged. 'Otherwise, it's quite possible that a third of those who contract the illness will die because the citizens of this place cannot clean up their own filth.'

In the next room, Hadria wept fitfully. She understood the realities of life in the subura. Nothing would change, even if the streets were filled with rotting bodies. Slatterns would still empty night soil into the dark recesses of the alleyways, rats would still imperil the lives of infants, and flies would still swarm on the piles of rubbish and transfer their poisons into the eyes, ears and mouths of vulnerable humans.

Myrddion refused to accept that things would always stay the same. Thucydides had offered an excuse for the disease in Athens by saying that the city had been under siege for some time. Rome had no such excuse. The city had ample latrines and Myrddion refused to believe that there was no man or group of men able to force the denizens of the subura to clean up their living conditions.

'I have a possible solution, Isaac, but I'm not certain it will work. I need to explain the situation to some . . . er . . . citizens who might be able to help us with our hygiene problem, but it will probably take some time. Could you stay with Hadria and mix the henbane with boiled water? I hope I won't be long, if I manage to survive my negotiations.' Before anyone could try to dissuade him, he left the mean alleyway and picked his way to the local inn at the crossroads.

The tavernae, or public inns, were the unofficial meeting places of the many criminal gangs that offered protection to shop owners and street sellers. In their own brutal fashion, they controlled the insulae by ensuring that rents were paid and order in the streets was maintained. The emperor and his soldiers of the watch might have provided the overriding mechanism of law and order, but the street gangs, for a nominal payment, provided justice and peace, because it was a sensible way to do business.

Some months earlier, a thoroughly frightened Pulchria had aroused Myrddion in the middle of the night. She had been full of apologies, but an underlying terror had darkened her eyes and made her lips quiver with anxiety.

'There are two men at the door, Master Myrddion.' Her eyes darted from Myrddion to Cadoc and back again, and the young healer read the desperation in that anxious expression.

'They want you to attend a wounded man at the Inn of the One Armed Man. Please, master, speak to them. They'll not go away without you, and I will be the sufferer if you deny them.'

Unwillingly, and only for the sake of Pulchria's peace of mind, Myrddion had gathered up his satchel and clattered down the steps that ran down one side of the atrium. Although the night was still and sweetly perfumed from the orange tree that had grown as vigorously as a weed beside the pool in the courtyard, Myrddion was temporarily immune to its fragrance, being tired and out of sorts. After a very busy day in his surgery, he did not welcome imperious calls by strangers in the middle of the night – especially strangers who frightened his landlady.

The two men who were cooling their heels at the iron gate of the insula were heavy-set ruffians, a little above the usual Roman height and disfigured by scars and misshapen facial features. Myrddion decided that they were probably street toughs hired as bodyguards for their undoubted pugilistic skills. Myrddion noticed that the knuckles of the taller man were twisted, swollen and ridged with scar tissue, and wondered if this particular thug had started his career as a prizefighter.

'Are you the outland healer?' the taller thug demanded.

Myrddion nodded and tried to appear distant. He was offended by the man's disrespectful tone and the arrogance in his voice and eyes.

'You're wanted at the One Armed Man at once. You have an important patient who awaits your services. If you're worried about payment, we'll make it worth your while.'

'That isn't important. Who's my patient? I'm not stirring one foot until I know who I'm treating . . . and why.'

'Our master is a man with diverse business interests,' the shorter thug said smoothly. His voice was educated and honeyed, at odds with his rat-like eyes and scarred cheek, and his clothes were clean, elaborate and expensive. Only the knife he wore attached to a wide belt was worn and old.

'So his name is hardly a secret,' Myrddion countered.

'Osculus is his name, or the Kiss, as some of his friends call him. I know of no other name. An unhappy customer stabbed our master so he needs your assistance. Violence doesn't hold regular business hours.'

'Very well, I will come, as long as it is understood that I cannot be held responsible for the state of your master's health. I'll do everything I can, but I'm not a god.'

'Fair enough,' the taller tough replied and would have gripped Myrddion by the forearm, but the healer shook him off.

'All right,' the thug said softly. 'We'll escort you – if you don't like being touched. Agreed?'

'Agreed,' Myrddion responded with a set face. He stepped between the two men with as much aplomb as he could manage.

They moved through the predominantly empty streets with ease. The few drunkards or prostitutes who crossed their path cringed away and faded into the shadows, so that the three men walked within an invisible shield on the path of light cast by the flare that the shorter man carried. After passing a number of streets, they came to a crossroads with a large fountain in the centre where women collected clean water from the aqueduct. The Inn of the One Armed Man stood on one corner.

The inn was little more than a hole in the wall. Perhaps a dozen men could crowd into the small room if they stood shoulder to shoulder. A simple plank bar had been cleared of wine jugs, mugs and platters of chicken bones and was now an impromptu stretcher. The man who lay on it was slender and attractive in a coarse fashion, but was obviously racked with pain. Myrddion saw a knife jutting out of the hollow in his left shoulder.

'Osculus, I take it,' Myrddion said flatly. 'Is he conscious?'

The wounded man opened eyes that were an unusual shade of pale green, like drops of fine glass. Myrddion watched the head turn painfully, and the clear, flat gaze swept over him and measured him from head to toe. Self-consciously, the healer was aware that he had passed some unspoken test.

'I've heard of you, Myrddion Emrys of Segontium, and so far I've not asked for a share of your profits as my price for the safety of your business. Fortuna told me you'd be useful to me.'

'I'm flattered.' Myrddion replied drily.

'Can you treat this wound?' A reckless grin, of either pain or devilry, twisted Osculus's well-shaped mouth to expose yellowing teeth, at odds with his impeccable dress and clean hands.

Myrddion examined the shoulder carefully. The knife had been driven up to the hilt in the hollow between the shoulder bone and the start of the breastbone. Fortunately, the blade appeared to be short, although Myrddion worried that it might be barbed. Such a weapon could easily kill because flesh and muscle had to be radically torn to extract the barbs from the flesh. Even unbarbed, this blade was likely to cause major difficulties if it was close to the complex arteries associated with the shoulders and chest.

As if reading his mind, Osculus assured the healer

that the knife had a smooth blade. Myrddion carefully withdrew the knife, staunched the rush of blood and doused the wound with spirits while Osculus suffered his ministrations without complaint. The street criminal did become a little pale when Myrddion produced his needles and asked for an open flame, but the man was courageous and tolerated the five stitches needed to seal the wound without a sound. Once a poultice was in place to guard against infection, the wound was bandaged and the arm was immobilised.

Osculus tried to pay Myrddion with a gold coin, but the healer refused.

'No, I thank you – I prefer my money to be clean of suffering. However, I might need your assistance at some time in the future, so I may want to call in this debt.'

Osculus was insulted by the bargain, but he was forced to accept it to maintain his uncertain reputation for gentility; and from then on other associates of Osculus had occasionally made their way to the door of the healer's surgery, seeking treatment for knife wounds, broken bones, smashed teeth or head injuries, all of which Myrddion duly treated at no cost to the gangster.

Now the time had come for Osculus to repay his debt. With the beginnings of a plague in his subura, Myrddion came to the Inn of the One Armed Man once again, and found Osculus sitting in the small room like a king amid his brutal courtiers. Economically, the healer explained the situation while Osculus yawned delicately and sipped on his sweet wine.

'So? What has this plague to do with me? Do you expect me and my men to shovel shit? If so, you may go to Hades and rot.'

'No, Osculus, I know better than to ask men of your repute

to undertake such menial tasks. However, you are the only person who could marshal the able-bodied men of the subura and force them to clean up their own streets – which they should do anyway. You have the power to undertake this task, if you have the will. The plague will kill many of your men, and your customers, which is very bad for business.' He smiled thinly. Myrddion was learning diplomacy at the feet of violent men. 'It might even kill you – and yours.'

'Agreed, healer. Life is fraught with chance accidents and diseases. I could be dead tomorrow, so why should I do this thing?' Osculus feigned indifference. 'What's in it for me?'

'I remind you of your personal debt to me, Osculus. I told you I might call on you one day and I believe you to be a man of your word. I'm asking for something that is of far more importance than money: the lives of those who look to you for protection.'

Myrddion's voice was hard and demanding, for Osculus was his only hope to defeat the stomach disease. Osculus must be shamed into stirring himself to action.

Osculus shrugged. 'This request goes considerably further than anything I owe you.'

'Do you remember Ferreus? Would you like me to look into your eyes and tell you your future? If you deny your debt, that's precisely what I will do.'

Osculus blinked and his pale eyes burned with an internal fire. 'I'm not afraid of you, healer, but in view of our association I will help you ... this one time. After that, you'd be wise to stay out of my way.'

Myrddion instinctively thrust out his hand in the universal offer to seal a struck bargain. Osculus was nonplussed by the gesture at first, but quickly became amused by it.

'I'll say one thing for you, master healer – you've got balls.

It's been years since anyone dared to threaten me. Very well, you can stay in the subura for a little while longer.'

As Myrddion turned to go, Osculus called out to him with a mocking grin on his well-shaped lips. His eyes were as ancient as sin. 'Don't ask me for anything else, healer. I might not be amused next time.'

Somehow, with maximum coercion, Osculus persuaded the men of the subura to embark on a prolonged period of hygienic cleaning. Using wide-bladed wooden shovels, rakes and twig brooms, they filled cart after cart with accumulated filth and then removed it to prepared dumping grounds remote from the living areas. As they worked, Myrddion warned them to cover their noses and mouths with cloth and to wash their hands and feet thoroughly at regular intervals. At first the healer was met with stubborn resistance, but as the illness slowly declined over the ensuing weeks, rumours began to circulate in the alleyways that the young healer was a miracle worker and Osculus was a kindly patron who had always had their best interests at heart.

Myrddion smiled to see Osculus treated with the respect usually accorded to Emperor Valentinian, while Hadria was even moved to kiss the criminal boss's hands – to his confusion and pleasure.

Life returned to a semblance of normality and Arrius slowly recovered from the stomach disease at last, but he had begun to exhibit the first signs of the strange malady that so frustrated Healer Isaac. Myrddion pondered the puzzle for many weeks, but nothing in this set of symptoms made any sense. Hadria and her children showed no signs of the malaise, yet they ate and drank precisely the same food and drink as Arrius. Finally, Myrddion was left with only one other variable to consider – Arrius's workplace. Before his rational mind could persuade him to ignore his instincts, Myrddion organised a visit to the large ironworks where Arrius was one of the most proficient metalworkers.

The workshop of Claudio the Metal Manufacturer was large, run-down and reminiscent of a small slice of an inferno. Myrddion could imagine Vulcan, the Roman god of the forge, presiding over the workshop, his body running with sweat, his face red with fire burn and his teeth bared in a rictus of flame. After making enquiries, he found Arrius at his station at the far end of the foundry. The plebeian was wet with sweat, and had stripped off his tunic. Padded gloves protected his hands and forearms and more padding protected his legs from accidental splashes of molten metal.

In the lee of the huge brick ovens, Myrddion watched soot-streaked men stoking the firebox so that the heat built up to a white-hot intensity. Within the oven, crucibles of iron filled with a fast-liquefying metal had been placed on brick benches. Arrius demonstrated the sure touch of a master as he swung huge calipers to lift first one crucible and then another out of the oven and then, with infinite care, pour some of the molten metal into a large, pot-shaped mould. A deft twist of the calipers swirled the metal inside the mould so it covered the inside walls with an even coat before the excess was poured away. Then the pots and the cauldrons were set aside to cool.

Arrius was far from finished with the cauldrons. Myrddion watched him take up a cold one and use a coarse chisel to chip away the excess of metal at the lip, then clean the whole receptacle with an odd rasp so that it had a smooth finish. As he worked, Myrddion could see a cloud of grey dust in the air, and began to wonder.

'What are these vessels used for, Arrius?' he asked pleasantly.

'They're vessels to hold defrutum and sapa, master. Lead is perfect for these containers as it melts quickly and is quite soft. Defrutum is usually made in the leaden vessels, but the other iron cauldrons are used where a greater heat is needed to boil a distilled spirit called sapa. The heat can't be enough to melt the lead, though.'

Myrddion decided immediately that he would discover what defrutum and sapa were, as he'd never heard of either. Then, thanking Arrius for his lesson, he escaped the heat and stench of the foundry with his mind churning over a number of very unpleasant possibilities. For the rest of the day he tried to settle back into the numbing routine of his surgery, but his mind kept wandering until he realised he was offering poor treatment to his patients. Excusing himself, he plunged into the street and headed to Healer Isaac's rooms by the shortest possible route.

When Myrddion knocked, the Jew was bent over a scroll, trying to read notes that he had made some years before. He looked up, his caterpillar brows expressing surprise and his tousled hair standing on end where he had dragged his hands through his salt and pepper mop.

'Oh, Myrddion! I wasn't expecting you, was I? By the Most High, I sometimes delve so deeply into my notes that I forget if it's day or night.'

Myrddion had the grace to apologise for his abrupt arrival. He quickly explained that Arrius had begun to show symptoms of the Roman malaise, and then revealed his hunch that the foundry worker's livelihood might be at fault. As Isaac questioned him closely, Myrddion began to feel rather foolish. Surely lead couldn't be harmful, for it was in plentiful supply and was widely used in all aspects of Roman life. Water pipes, cooking utensils and even face powder were derived from this useful metal. In fact, Britain had supplied Rome with it for hundreds of years. A quick glance at Isaac's dumbstruck, slightly crazed expression confirmed Myrddion's fear that he had disturbed the Jew over a wild fancy.

'I'm sorry, Isaac. I fear that I may have raised your hopes over a nonsense.'

'Not so, Myrddion. Tell me, what are these lead containers used for? You must have asked.' All the hair on Isaac's head was now standing on end, including his beard and eyebrows.

'They hold some substances called defrutum and sapa. I have no idea what they are and I hoped that you'd know.'

'By the beard of my father! Defrutum, and the Roman passion for sweets? Could it be so simple? Yes, I suppose it is possible.'

Isaac settled back on his stool and calmed his trembling fingers. He reached for his wine jug, thought better of it and poured water into two cups instead.

'Defrutum is concentrated grape juice that is boiled to produce a sweet syrup used to flavour wine and food. Romans love it. If they concentrate it even further, they produce a sticky substance called sapa, which is even more potent. Heavens, Myrddion! It's used to make oenogarum that is put into almost all foods, just like salt. With honey, it's used to preserve fruit and even meat. Do you know what this means?'

'Frankly, I'll believe anything you say,' Myrddion replied slowly. 'The air was full of lead dust where Arrius cleaned the pots and the cauldrons at the foundry. As far as I can tell, that's the only substance he's in contact with that his wife and children aren't exposed to as well. But lead is used on all sorts of common objects. I must be wrong.'

'Leave it with me, Myrddion. I'll think your proposal through, but even if you're right we'll never convince anyone to believe us.'

Myrddion looked at him blankly. 'But if this defrutum is killing people, how can the authorities ignore it? It seems to me that toxins in the metal must contribute in some way to this illness.'

'Perhaps. But will your people in Britain welcome the closure of your lead mines? No. Will the makers of defrutum listen to us? Why should they? Think how much wealth is tied up in the production and use of the stuff. Do you truly believe that anyone will listen?'

Perhaps Myrddion's face expressed his horror. More likely, Isaac understood the young healer's idealism and was attempting to be cruel to be kind.

'No one will listen because women and children won't give up sweetmeats and everyone in Rome, except the slaves, drinks sweetened wine in preference to water. Perhaps in Gaul, Spain and Britain the wine is safe because it's allowed to ferment without defrutum, but what if it isn't? They'll call us madmen and fools, and avoid us as prophets of doom. No, Myrddion. If you're right, you'll have to keep your mouth shut if you want to retain any of your patients.'

'But to remain silent would be wrong,' Myrddion protested. 'You know more of our trade than I do, but the first rule of healing is to do no harm. We do harm if we remain silent.'

'Well, lad, what you do is ultimately up to you. I will examine the matter and the properties of lead in any event. My studies might take several years to prove anything, and even then I'd need to be very sure before I warned the authorities. If your conscience is so tender, then speak out, but I can't give any support to your hypothesis until I am convinced of the dangers.'

Myrddion felt everything he had believed in shudder and tremble under him, as if solid earth suffered a fit of ague. This Jew was dedicated to healing, but curiosity rather than alleviation of suffering seemed to be Isaac's motivation. His work was intellectualised, and was powered by a desire to know rather than to save. Behind the booming voice and the comical eyebrows, Isaac's dark expression suddenly seemed chilly and a little bored.

But worse yet was Myrddion's sudden understanding that intellectual curiosity also fired many of his own decisions – unthinking and casual nosiness that was sometimes dangerous to the health of the people around him. What inspired his journey to Rome if not personal curiosity? If he had set out for Constantinople from the moment they landed in Gesoriacum he would have avoided the wars of Attila. Today, Bridie would have two good legs, and even Cleoxenes would not bear a wicked scar on his arm. Had he not insisted on this whole, hare-brained journey, how many lives could he have saved by remaining in Segontium?

Curiosity and pride! Intellectual or otherwise, he was as bad as Isaac. The difference was only one of degree, so Myrddion could take no comfort from his relative ignorance of the repercussions of his actions. So he hadn't realised the probable outcome of many of his decisions. No excuse, he thought bitterly. Isaac is simply being honest when he cautions me to wait for my fears to be confirmed. None the less, Myrddion was disgusted with Isaac the Jew, whom he had considered a friend. All Isaac's learning and all his skills had been acquired to further his personal reputation for brilliance. His patients were a means to an end. With relief, Myrddion acquitted himself of using human suffering for his own enrichment in either coin or status.

As if pursued by something nameless and ugly, Myrddion backed away from his mentor and took to his heels. As he passed the grand marble buildings and the forums that were so pregnant with history and noble deeds, the disillusioned young man knew that Rome was one huge sepulchre and if he stayed within her rotting walls he'd be buried forever. Like Isaac, he'd relinquish his humanity for the world's acceptance and acclaim.

So Myrddion chose his fate and went his own way.

But how could he tell those people he loved and respected to avoid all food produced in Rome? Or was it already far too late?

CHAPTER XVI

RAVENNA AND THE GOLDEN CHAIN

The night was velvet dark and scented with perfume, moist earth, seaweed and salt. The city of Ravenna was perched on slightly higher ground just beyond the Mare Adriaticum with a huge man-made harbour at its ample flanks. Canals skirted her to provide for shipping, transport and defence, while sweet water crossed many hundreds of miles in a great aqueduct to make her defendable. Around the dark skirts of the city, the firm earth gave way to swamps that further scented the air with the rich aromas of rotting earth, dead water, fecund vegetation and flowering trees.

The city itself was adorned in finery. Marble and polished stone graced the public buildings, while the churches were rich in mosaics of glass, precious metals, pebbles and shell derived from the styles of Constantinople. In a wholly Asian intricacy, walls, floors and ceilings were decorated with fish, birds, animals and vegetation. But images of Christianity predominated over these rich, naturally inspired decorations, for Ravenna was devoted to the Jewish God and His Son, and the basilicas were famed for their beauty.

Two men walked along a marble colonnade and tasted the

perfumed night with delicate sensibility. Flavius Petronius Maximus and Valentinian's chamberlain, Heraclius, strolled slowly over the beautiful floors with the measured tread of men who are accustomed to the exercise of power. Any unwelcome observers would have laughed at the irony of these two unnatural companions walking together, for Flavius Petronius Maximus was a fabulously rich Roman senator and Heraclius was a slave. He was also a eunuch. Yet both men wielded considerable power within these gracious halls, power that extended well beyond the reach of Emperor Valentinian and his pallid, weak-kneed spite. Early winter in Ravenna was slightly cooler than in Rome, so Valentinian usually returned to the Holy City for the autumn and the winter. But the emperor hated Rome, having spent his youth in Ravenna before inheriting the throne of the West, and this year had decided to delay his departure. Ravenna welcomed his presence as Rome never could, for the Holy City was filled with vicious gossip and ambitious patricians who jostled for position at his court. Consequently, his courtiers must suffer the inconvenience of regular journeys across Italia if they wished to jostle close to the throne, allowing a festering resentment to gather around their timid emperor.

Ravenna enjoyed cool sea breezes to complement its temperate climate. The winds that blew in off the sea cleaned the wide streets and blew away dust, light rubbish and the marks of neglect that human beings often leave on their landscapes. Valentinian's mother, the sainted Galla Placidia, had ruled in all but name during his childhood and now, in death, her spirit looked down on the court from vivid mosaics that decorated any wall that Valentinian could find to dedicate to her, although no images of her face had been created in her honour. In life, Galla Placidia had ordered that her city should be kept scrupulously clean, and, like any good and provident housekeeper, she had arranged for flowering trees to be planted so that the air would remain sweet throughout the year. Ravenna was small by comparison with Rome, but love had endowed the city with grace, so that remnants of the empress's devotion still scented the early winds that came in winter from across the Mare Adriaticum.

Illuminated by the dark blue light, Petronius was quietly angry. The man whom Myrddion had met so long ago on the sea journey from Massilia to Ostia was almost wholly changed. Petronius had lost weight and his skin was now stretched tautly over his bones, suggesting athleticism rather than gauntness. Even more indicative, his eyes were haunted and all the smugness in his manner had been swept away by tragic circumstances.

Earlier that day, he had found himself embroiled in a distasteful argument with Flavius Gaudentius, who was even more pretentious than Valentinian, an emperor famous for his arrogance rather than his skills. Aetius's loathsome son had all his father's imperiousness, but lacked the ability and the intelligence that his father had demonstrated for generations. This Flavian didn't soil his pudgy white hands with work or the calluses of the sword, preferring conversation, gossip and devoting hours to dress and grooming. Aetius's son preened like any peacock within the royal court, consigning his noble wife to the role of a married mouse.

Gaudentius had stopped Petronius on his way to a private audience with Valentinian. Although months had passed since his family tragedy, Petronius was already on edge, having been forced to school his face so that the emperor remained oblivious of the senator's deep and undiminished animosity.

'Petronius, a moment! When does Valentinian plan to return to the Capitoline? I'll die of boredom if I'm forced to endure winter in this hellhole. My wife dislikes the weather and my father has urgent business levying the peasants to fill vacancies in the army. We can't languish here forever with nothing more entertaining than Valentinian's religion to keep us amused.'

The question was expressed with such languid disdain and condescension that Petronius had to bite his fleshy lower lip to avoid a rude, insulting retort.

'Master Gaudentius, I cannot presume to speak for the emperor. Nor is it my place to coerce or cajole my master to reschedule his visit to the Capitoline. We are all my lord Valentinian's servants, so we must await his pleasure.'

Gaudentius chose to be offended. His wide Hungvari face fell into a frown and his full red lips pursed with pique. 'You would do well to remember who my father is, Petronius Maximus, before you lecture me about my duty to the throne of the west. The day will come when you will be sorry that you were so curt with me.'

'Is that a threat, Master Gaudentius? I hardly think that the *magister militum praesentalis* would wish to put his needs above the desires of the emperor of the west.'

Had Gaudentius been a wiser man, he would have registered Petronius's lightly clenched fist and tensed shoulder muscles. Petronius might have been overly fond of good food, drink and pliant women, but he had been a soldier and he knew the imperatives of life and death on the battlefield. To be threatened and lectured by a spoiled and absurd young man who had forsaken the harsh life of his father was almost too much for the senator to tolerate.

Now, walking beside the lean and mild-faced Heraclius,

he relived a number of slights, insults and mortal blows that
he laid at the door of Aetius and his family. The secret revenge
of his heart was guarded, for equal to his hatred of the Flavians
was his loathing for Valentinian, who had turned him into a
pander and a cuckold.

Flavius Petronius Maximus had served the Western
Empire well, as a praetor, an urban prefect, consul and
praetorian prefect of Italia, all before his forty-third birthday.
Now in his late fifties, he was a man of extraordinary skill
who possessed talents that he disguised under the appearance
of a benign epicure.

And so, as he walked along Valentinian's colonnade, his gut
roiled with animosity towards Valentinian and, after him, the
loathed Flavius Aetius. Only the satisfaction of achieving his
revenge could wipe away a shame that was almost overpowering.
Petronius stopped abruptly, so Heraclius also paused, turned
and looked carefully into the senator's burning eyes. The
eunuch was always on his guard when he dealt with the senator,
for Petronius was clever enough to have retained his exalted
place within the maelstrom of power for many years. Petronius
was a man to fear under his gilded exterior.

Of course, Heraclius knew his secret humiliation. As the
Master of the Emperor's Bedchamber, Heraclius must have
organised the lavish dinner and prepared the fresh sheets of
seduction to entrap Petronius's wife, if not with his own hand,
then by his explicit orders. Petronius gripped his belt with one
hand, fingering the ornate buckle with its pattern of panthers.
Unconsciously, his manicured nails scoured the soft leather as
he imagined certain throats between his fingers. And one of
those throats belonged to Heraclius.

The eunuch saw those murderous fingers, but his eyes
remained untroubled. He had lived precariously for years as

he catered for the whims of crazed, ambitious men and women. He understood the effort of will that Petronius Maximus exercised to keep his face so bland and courteous, and was amused at how easily the senator betrayed his true feelings with those tell-tale fingers. Heraclius had learned to control every feature in his once-mobile face, so that now no twitching eyebrow or traitorous curl of the lip could betray the malice that coiled around his heart.

Heraclius was a eunuch, the *primicerius sacri cubiculi*, and a man in whom bitterness ran deep because of his castration and his ruined manhood. Having risen to the highest position that a slave could achieve, and being the man physically closest to Valentinian, he enjoyed extraordinary power over amateurs like Petronius Maximus who, for all his posturing and his vast wealth, was merely a useful tool. Unlike most eunuchs, with their womanish voices, overtly feminine mannerisms and excessive weight gain, Heraclius was thin, his voice was a melodious baritone and he seemed to possess an ageless youth. Time had stood still for Heraclius from the time his balls had been cut off shortly before his sixteenth birthday, an operation that usually resulted in death for a youth so fully grown. His survival had made him a very valuable commodity, for he was a man who had experienced the desires of the flesh, but could never relive the euphoria of masculine love.

Heraclius also burned for revenge, but the object of his hatred was Flavius Aetius, whom he thoroughly despised. Aetius might have been made a patrician, but by Heraclius's exacting standards the general was nothing but a jumped-up Scythian who exerted too much influence over his master. For his part, Aetius had devised a long list of insulting titles with which he tortured Heraclius whenever he was residing in Ravenna.

The eunuch wasn't thin-skinned, but he wasn't a natural homosexual, and he resented the barbs that Aetius lodged in his flesh so readily and so carelessly. Used to giving orders and having his way, Aetius had no respect either for Heraclius's position or for his manhood, an error that the eunuch nurtured in his heart during the long nights of servitude.

Petronius possessed the potential to sweep Aetius out of Heraclius's path so that his insults could be repaid in full. The senator had shown his loyalty to Valentinian by enduring the rape of his wife, so the emperor was inclined to treat Petronius like an intelligent lapdog. But Petronius was no man's tool, and Heraclius was biding his time until he knew that the moment was ripe.

And that moment had come. Petronius had been goaded once too often.

'I understand your mixed feelings concerning Aetius, my lord,' Heraclius confided softly. 'The general is a bully who has undue influence over my master, but he is also the hero of the Battle of the Catalaunian Plain. Who would the people believe to be the more able protector of Italia? I know he was central to your ... er ... problems with our noble emperor, in that Aetius provided the plan that Valentinian used to ... er ... gain his heart's desire at your expense. His only reason for that infamy was boredom and your great wealth, which he envies. Excuse me for speaking so bluntly, but candour should exist between men who are as devoted to the Empire as we are, and will make any sacrifice to remedy the threats to its safety. Aetius goes too far when he makes a jest of family and the sanctity of marriage.'

The tall, husky man beside him audibly ground his teeth at the reminder of his shame. His face darkened, causing the eunuch to smile inwardly at how easily this less-than-noble

Roman could be manipulated through his emotions.

'I do not wish to speak of my wife, Heraclius. Her name has been sullied quite sufficiently already. Remember your place!'

Heraclius resisted the impulse to bridle. Instead, he vowed inwardly that he would induce Valentinian to remove Petronius, once the Roman senator's influence was no longer needed.

'Of course, master. As long as you remember who is the real villain in your family tragedy. Flavius Aetius has set his sights on the throne, either by assassinating my master and taking his place, or by elevating his idle son. You are a threat to his strategy, for you have distinguished yourself during many years of service to the Empire. Aetius has made you a laughing stock to weaken your position, which indicates that his ambitions are so large that nothing will deter him from pursuing his chosen path. Regrettably, the barbarians of Gaul, Scythia and the north support him.'

'Aetius is what he has always been, a barbarian who courts the Hungvari and the Goths as his most ardent supporters,' Petronius retorted, his fleshy jaw stiffening with distaste. He neither trusted nor liked Heraclius, but if he desired to take revenge on Valentinian without being killed by the emperor's personal guard, then he must play a waiting game. He needed this vile, unnatural creature with his smooth, benign face and soothing voice.

Mentally, Petronius returned to his unpleasant meeting with Gaudentius earlier in the day. The senator's urbanity and temper had been tried to breaking point by Gaudentius's whining and threats, but he had somehow managed to maintain an air of patrician calm. Until Gaudentius took a parting shot.

'Give my . . . respects to your wife, sir. I have heard much of her beauty and her . . . chastity.'

Petronius's fists had clenched involuntarily at the slight. That the general should find his invidious situation amusing, and then share vulgar gossip with his odious son, filled the senator's belly with gall.

Petronius squirmed internally. If he had one dangerous weakness, then his love of gambling was his undoing, at least for a man of honour. The senator upbraided himself for agreeing to play dice with Valentinian, but he'd been in his cups and reckless with Bacchus's bravado.

When the time had come to pay his debt to the emperor, Valentinian had spurned gold as a means of payment. He asked for Petronius's family ring, a demand that the senator couldn't refuse, although it was an offence to the ancestors to hand a family heirloom to someone who was foreign to his gens.

How Valentinian had used that ring would shame the senator forever, while proving that Valentinian was a vicious rapist, in thought and in deed. That Aetius had sat at the gaming table, smiling and uttering pleasantries while he had hatched his cruel plan, made Petronius Maximus ill with hatred. Now, spurred by Gaudentius's jibes, he came to a decision.

'Aetius has spent a lifetime destroying everyone who stood in his path. What happened to Flavius Felix and his wife? Although Aetius owed Flavius Felix his loyalty as his supreme commander, he had them murdered! What happened to Bonifacius, who was also his commander? Dead, after a battle against Flavius Aetius! Where is Sebastianus? Exiled to Constantinople! Every great man who stood between Aetius and ultimate power has been thrust aside by the general. He does as he chooses, regardless of cost. He must be destroyed, or else we'll all be forced to bend our knees to him. I, for one, would rather perish before that day dawns.'

'Are we agreed that Aetius must be prised away from Valentinian?' Heraclius asked, smiling with mock servility. 'And that we will use whatever force is necessary?' The slave could tell that Petronius was like a frightened horse that must be gentled before he was ridden.

'Yes. I will speak to Valentinian in private. But he'll not believe me because of our past disagreements and the situation with my wife. Our master will only act against Aetius if he is sure. He will distrust me and think that I am motivated by anger and a desire for revenge. That's where you come in, Heraclius, because Valentinian trusts you. Your word will go far towards persuading him, because he will be unable to sleep comfortably if we both repeat the same tale. I'll provide the facts and explain the distrust that the patricians feel for the Scythian, but Valentinian will take more notice of you.'

Heraclius smiled tightly. 'I'm here to serve my master's interests, which I will do to the best of my ability, for Aetius's continued existence imperils my master's life.'

Petronius felt a momentary twinge of caution. He hadn't survived to the respectable age of fifty-eight without knowing deception when he saw it. Heraclius's smile was like that of a satisfied cat torturing a mouse.

I refuse to be devoured by this obsequious fucking eunuch, Petronius thought recklessly. He's just a means to an end. The senator's mind swam with imperial possibilities, but they could only be considered if Aetius was permanently removed. In perfect accord and enmity, Petronius and Heraclius recommenced their steady, measured stroll along Valentinian's colonnade. The velvet dark muffled their footsteps so that they became one with the night until they disappeared into the enveloping shadows.

In his tasteful villa, Petronius's beautiful wife, the chaste Gallica Lydia, reclined on her perfumed bed and wept as if her heart was breaking. Her pride in her patrician ancestry and her determination to be the perfect wife in the style of Galla Placidia had come crashing down from the moment Emperor Valentinian had made his first advances. Like Caesar's wife, she had deflected his overtures as gracefully as she could, but Valentinian refused to listen to her polite rejections.

The shame burned within her, more potent than her fear of the emperor. When Gallica Lydia had returned from Valentinian's palace, her husband was missing. Lydia was almost glad. Almost. She had been lured to the palace by her husband's ring, trusting the messenger who had explained that she was ordered to attend upon the empress, Licinia Eudoxia, but the whole ruse became obvious when she found herself in a distant bedroom in the palace. Valentinian had offered her a sumptuous meal, as if the gross immorality of his actions was normal and gallant. She couldn't bring herself to eat, lest she should vomit and further shame her noble ancestors.

The rape had not been the worst part of the whole business. Valentinian had taken her roughly as if she was a servant girl, but afterwards he had ordered her out of his room as if she was a woman of the streets. He had stated bluntly that he was tired and wished to sleep, so a woman would be in the way. The dismissal, uttered so casually, cut her pride to its roots and tore it loose from her soul.

Even worse, she felt betrayed by her husband, who must

have known the uses to which the family ring could be employed. The man who should have protected her was her ultimate betrayer. When Petronius returned and divined the situation, he swore his love and devotion and begged her to believe he hadn't been aware of Valentinian's plans for her seduction. But the eunuch had lowered his guilty eyes as she fled from Valentinian's sanctum, and she had seen the servant's lips curl with mirth. Then, three days later, a courier had delivered a message from Placidia, daughter of Valentinian and daughter-by-law of Flavius Aetius. The message was short, cloying and unkind, although only someone who was aware of Valentinian's perfidy would recognise the evil intent behind the message.

To Gallica Lydia,
Honoured wife of Flavius Petronius Maximus.

Hail. I have heard you are indisposed, so my husband wishes me to relay to you his earnest hope that you will soon be well once more.

Unkind words and innuendo have been spread through the court, but I beg you to believe that no one in our house will listen, knowing the whole truth. Flavius Aetius reminds you that names cannot hurt, but he is well aware, from experience, that reputations are lost through unwise indiscretions. On the occasion of your visit to my mother's house, he saw your disarray, but will not speak further on the subject in the hope that any scandal will wither on the vine.

I will close my ears to any unkind words that I should hear in the hope that you will remain a model of the Roman wife and a loyal subject of the Empire.

There is no need to respond to this message. I refuse to believe that you would choose to compromise my noble father but, perhaps, to silence the rumour-mongers, it would be advisable if we did not meet in future.

If you refrain from dwelling on cruel gossip, perhaps this whole affair will soon be forgotten. As the Christos tells us, it is only the sinless who have the right to throw stones.

I shall pray for you.

Written by Flavius Aetius, Magister Militum,
For Livia Placidia,
Daughter, wife and friend.

Poor Lydia! Every word chopped away her confidence. She was obliged to ask Petronius to read the scroll to her, for like many women of her class she did not know her letters very well. Having demanded an accurate reading, she had been further humiliated when he had stumbled over the words. His face was red and swollen as he tried to comfort her clumsily when she had begun to cry, but a part of her brain was angry that he didn't attempt to soften the ugly message through the device of harmless lies. Lydia knew she was being perverse, for she truly preferred to know the worst, but Petronius hadn't even remonstrated with her when she demanded that every word on that hateful scroll should be spoken aloud.

The gulf between Petronius and Lydia widened into sullen silences as she found herself effectively ostracised by the patricians of Ravenna. Fortunately, she was unaware that Gaudentius was informing anyone who chose to listen that his noble wife had publicly prayed for Lydia's compromised reputation, for such knowledge would have caused her to rage and weep uncontrollably. As it happened, even as Petronius tried to protect her from the worst of the gossip, Lydia was insulted when she became aware of the whispering and giggling of some of her servants. Her old nurse, after much persuasion, eventually told Lydia the brutal truth that further lies were being bandied about the fair city of Ravenna – tales implying that the wife of Petronius Maximus was a harlot at worst, and at best a credulous fool who had tried to cement her husband's standing with the emperor by trading her body for preferment.

Unkind whispers were not the worst of it, for Lydia could laugh off the suggestion that she hid a lascivious nature under a skin of feigned piety. When the gossip implied that she had been seduced because her husband had traded her body for a gambling debt, Lydia felt her heart begin to break. She had borne four living sons for Petronius. All were married advantageously and settled outside Italia, but her waist was still tiny, her feet and hands were delicate and her face was still unlined. The clean lines of her features and the perfection of her thick, white skin had defied time, and many men still watched Gallica Lydia with hot, lascivious intentions.

But Lydia had loved her older husband, although he was often foolish and hasty in his decisions, and responded with his emotions rather than with his reason. Even if he had been ignorant of the use to which Valentinian put his family ring, Petronius had not left the court when his wife became the subject of vulgar gossip. He had said nothing in answer to her critics, and continued to bow low to the emperor to maintain his position at court.

Her husband's apparent indifference to the destruction of her good name was the most painful cross she had to bear.

Petronius must not love her, so she had based her pride on the shifting quicksand of an unrequited devotion.

The misunderstandings that exist between husband and wife are commonplace in any marriage, but the tragedy for Gallica Lydia lay with her inability to broach her feelings with Petronius Maximus. Dumb as she was with misery, her husband knew that something was seriously amiss with his wife, but his natural reserve with women made any confessions of guilty feelings quite impossible to repeat to her. Just as he brought no hint of his many frustrations at the emperor's court home to Lydia, he did not expect to be confronted with her hurt feelings and shame. And so the silence festered between them.

Eventually, Lydia could cry no more and she rarely left her rooms, preferring solitude to the looks of pity or amusement in the eyes of her staff. She became pale and silent, a shadow of her previous self without the animation that had kept old age at bay. Hopelessness was her constant companion and silence became her lover.

For two months, Gallica Lydia withered. Desperate to avoid her dark, wounded and accusing eyes, Petronius began his campaign to poison the emperor's mind against Flavius Aetius. With a fixed and implacable determination, Petronius used subtlety rather than warnings, by innuendo and apology rather than by character assassination. In short, he praised Aetius constantly and spoke with respect and reverence of the general's strategic gifts, his capacity to survive all his commanders and his intelligence in marrying his children to useful allies. In particular, Petronius expressed admiration for Aetius's cleverness in binding the Romanised Hun nobility to his person through the marriage of his youngest daughter, Flavia.

'It would be easy, my darling,' he explained to Lydia as he shared a simple evening meal with her in her rooms, 'and it would be foolish to make disparaging remarks about the marriage of Valentinian's daughter to Aetius's son. The emperor would see any such warnings as spite. He knows how close Aetius stands to the throne, so I don't need to belabour the point. But, puss, when I remind the emperor that Aetius also has a son-in-law who is wealthy, and a Hun, then Valentinian will start to wonder.'

'Good!' Lydia murmured tiredly, and Petronius scanned her pallid face with real concern.

He was increasingly worried over the health of his frail but still lovely wife, which perhaps was the reason for quitting a game of chance early to return to his villa with its red-tiled roof and crisp white walls. As the afternoon shadows barred the forecourt with deep blue stripes, the bare poplars rattled their skeletal branches in the winter breeze coming in from the sea. A tang of salty air caught in the back of his nose and reminded him again of the sea journey to Ostia in company with Aetius's daughter and her chaperon, and once again he relived the feelings of impatience that he had experienced at the realisation that he was being used as an escort for a spoiled girl who lacked even the distinction of patrician birth. Petronius should have been fighting the Hun, but he had been reduced to performing the insulting duties of a tame watchdog, not to mention fulfilling the role of a spy. At the time, Aetius had been distracted by Attila's advance southward, but in spite of the urgency of the situation the general had also been obsessed with the whereabouts of a Celtic healer and his followers. The man, named in his heathen way after their sun god, Myrddion, had been interesting for any man of action, for the healer had confined himself to treating any sailors who were ill and watching the shorelines along the route of the voyage. Petronius had scorned to mention the Celt to Aetius, forswearing the role of eavesdropper.

Aetius had used him whenever they had met and, unpardonably, the general had used Petronius's sweet and gentle wife nearly as terribly as had Valentinian, the man who raped her. Aetius was a pestilence, an evil that must be eradicated if Petronius was ever to sleep easily.

So Petronius was quietly angry when he tossed off his toga with its narrow bands that indicated his pedigree. His steward rescued the fine wool from the tiled floor of the colonnade as Petronius strode towards the mistress's rooms to assure her that he would be home to dine with her. When he knocked at her door, he heard no answer. Even with his ear against the heavy timber, Petronius could hear nothing in the stultifying silence.

He opened the door carefully in case Lydia should be sleeping, and wasn't surprised to discover her curled like a weary child under the fine bleached-wool coverlet. Frightened in case he should disturb her, he almost tiptoed away, but something about her stillness and the quiet of the dim room made the hair rise on his arms.

'Lydia?' he called softly. The silence was eerie and he realised that her small dog lay curled around her feet. The little creature looked up at him with piteous eyes.

'Lydia? Wake up, Lydia,' he exclaimed, his voice rising as her stillness chilled his skin. When he gripped her thin shoulders to shake her to wakefulness, her flesh was icy.

Petronius let her corpse fall back upon the cushions on her bed. Her open hand, with the blue veins pathetically exposed at her wrist, filled his heart with pity, loss and a growing wave of hot, scarfing loneliness. Against his volition, a sob escaped from his tight throat so that the delicate, liver-spotted dog howled thinly in his own poignant misery. The small glass bottle that had held something very poisonous rolled off the sleeping couch and smashed to splinters on the tiled floor, releasing and giving voice to his misery. As man and dog howled in unendurable pain, the running servants could not tell which cry was human, so that they held their hands over their ears lest the gods forsake them.

In the heavy darkness, the senator wailed inconsolably behind the door he had locked to ensure that his wife could not be taken from him. The entreaties of his desperate steward were ignored by the suffering Petronius, whose cries swirled through the villa and set the teeth of all the servants who dwelled within it on edge.

As Flavius Petronius Maximus gave voice to his pain, far away in the City of the Seven Hills Myrddion Emrys started and dropped the bowl of hot stew that he had been holding, so that the searing liquid splashed his feet and burned his flesh. Six pairs of eyes swivelled to watch him, shocked and staring.

Both Finn and Cadoc had seen those open, sightless eyes before, but Willa screamed shrilly and Bridie moaned once in shock and fear.

Myrddion stood up like a man in a trance and walked towards the windows, opening the rickety wooden shutters to their full extent. With eyes that saw a different world from the shadows of the dark city, Myrddion moaned . . . then began to speak.

'Woe is come to you, City of the Romans, and you will burn before five years have passed. For fourteen days and fifteen agonising nights, the wild men will rip your fine old flesh apart before you crumble into ash.

'Woe to your children, dead in their beds, for there is nowhere else for your people to flee.

'Woe to your women who will be raped and enslaved, whether they be patrician, plebeian or slave. The barbarians will not care whether you suffer or die.

'Your roads will lead to scattered hills of corpses and your aqueducts will shatter and run dry. Cursed are these hills when the last vulture has fled, for no Roman will ever wear the crown of Empire again. As slaves you will know the travails of defeat, people of Rome, and suffer the pain that you have inflicted on so many other enslaved peoples for more than twelve hundred years.

'Carthage sings in its salt-sown ruins. Rome is dead! Greece rejoices in the memory of its greatness that you are on your knees. Gaul is free to tear itself into bloody rags, while Hispania shivers in the darkness, waiting for the warriors of the crescent to cross the Middle Sea and enslave its people anew.

'Look down from your heights, Holy City, and know that the glory is all fled . . . and will never return, although untold centuries wash over you, rebuilding and destroying, until the end of all things.

'Woe to you, Flavius Aetius! For you will die at your master's hands.

'Woe to you, Valentinian! You have cut off your own strong hand and now you await the assassin's knife. Beware the Field of Mars.

'Mourn, Petronius Maximus, emperor for three score days before the mob tears you limb from limb and, later, no man will care to speak your name.

'A river of blood has been shed in your name, whore city, but now you will drown in the tides that you have loosed.

'And woe to you, Myrddion Emrys, for you will lose what you valued, to hold that which you sought.'

Then Myrddion turned and would have spoken, but his eyes rolled upward in his head and he collapsed like the boneless straw men that are used to frighten away the crows that gorge on the wheat fields.

For one agonised moment, his own face loomed over him in his inner darkness and pointed to a bloody child. Then the infant lifted a long, steel sword and stabbed his heart.

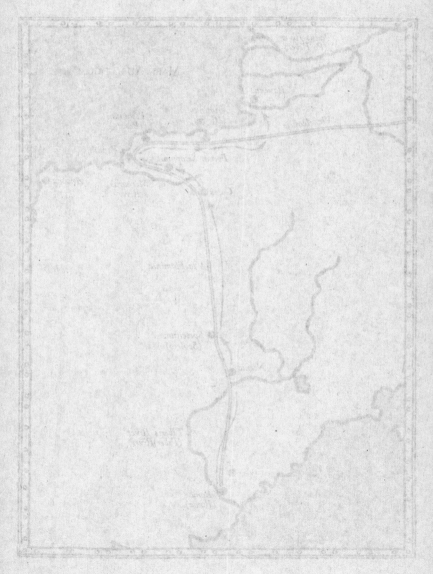

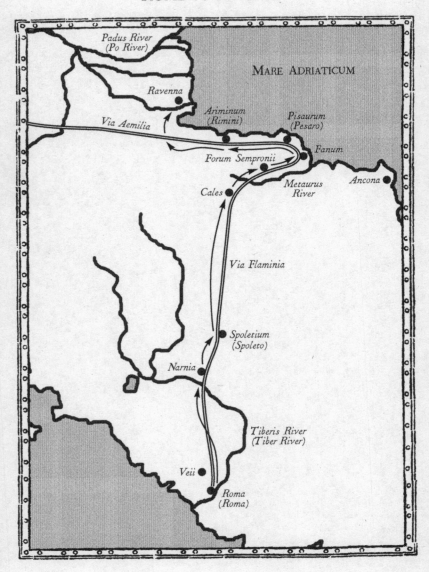

CHAPTER XVII

A ROSE-RED WOUND

'Every man slaughters his true desires by trying to hold them too closely,' Myrddion cried out as he woke to a grey morning. His head thudded with an insistent headache that threatened to cause it to explode. As he opened his eyes to dim, rain-drenched light, he imagined that his brain was leaking out of his ears, eyes and nose. He vomited weakly over the edge of his pallet.

'Master? Praise the gods, you live!' Finn called out. 'Cadoc, come quickly! The master is awake – he's sick, but awake.'

Over the agonised pounding in his ears, Myrddion recognised the rich, deep voice of Rhedyn, now high-pitched with distress. He closed his eyes to lessen the pain and experienced a corona of dancing, jerking, coloured starbursts behind his eyes. Trying to move his agonised head as little as possible, he vomited again into the bowl that the widow held to his mouth.

'What can we do to help you, master?' Finn pleaded, but his voice had a far-away sound.

'Are you a spirit, Finn?' Myrddion asked, his mind dazed in childlike confusion. He frowned as the weak light struck at

his senses, so he closed his eyes once more and the world
went away for a few minutes.

In response to an insistent hand shaking his shoulder,
Myrddion dragged his eyes open with an enormous effort of
will, and there were Finn and Rhedyn standing before him as
they tried to support his shaking shoulders.

'I'm ill,' Myrddion explained unnecessarily, as if to
backward children. Nothing made any sense, as if his flesh
and his spirit were dislocated and he couldn't reassemble the
shattered pieces.

'Drink, master,' Cadoc ordered, his face looming out of
the darkness at the edges of Myrddion's vision. 'Open your
mouth and don't force me to pinch your nose shut.'

'Would you poison me, my friend?' Myrddion whispered,
so Cadoc took the opportunity to force the bitter liquid
down his master's throat. Choking and protesting, he tried to
shrug his apprentice away, but his arms refused to respond
to the orders from his brain. He felt himself flailing at the air
like an invalid.

'I'll not poison you, master, trust me,' Cadoc pleaded as he
forced the cup against Myrddion's teeth until the healer
submitted and swallowed the last of the soporific draught
with a choking cough.

As a roaring, echoing darkness carried him away, Myrddion
felt the inner part of himself release its rigid hold on his mind
and body. Then, in a long, slow wave, he felt his senses slip
away. Mercifully, that cruel inner vision let him be.

Ravenna was shocked, titillated and thrilled by the suicide of
the noble Gallica Lydia. For the first time in many months,
the older, more distinguished citizens of the second City of
God spoke of her with affection and nostalgia for the old days

of the Republic. The gossip was pointed in its change of public opinion. Petronius's wife had been pure and noble, so she could not bear to live with the shame of her rape. Perversely, the old women nodded over their watered, warmed wines and agreed. Only a decent and self-respecting woman would kill herself out of shame, therefore Gallica Lydia must have been innocent.

Valentinian heard the whispers and the rumours that were circulating behind his back and experienced a frisson of anxiety, which was made more keen by the ritual hand-washing of Flavius Aetius, who now loudly proclaimed that his family had written to the beleaguered woman to offer her their sympathies, prayers and support. Valentinian watched the tide of positive public opinion turn against him and settle upon the ever-willing shoulders of Flavius Aetius.

After the inhumation of Gallica Lydia and the prescribed period of mourning, Petronius Maximus returned to Valentinian's court. He was a changed man, for the super-fluous flesh on his jaw, his shoulders and his belly had melted away, leaving him leaner and harder. Those courtiers who could meet his eyes discovered that Petronius viewed them all with a hollowed, tortured gaze that spoke eloquently of his loss. With Lydia's suffering always in the back of his mind, contempt flared in Petronius's face when noble citizens expressed their sympathy or pressed his hands encouragingly. Even Gaudentius refrained from making jokes or leering in the senator's direction, reading something stark and deadly in the set of Petronius's lips. Nervously, the young epicure lowered his eyes whenever the senator passed.

Heraclius was uncomfortable in the presence of the newly silent, introverted senator. Petronius was far too brooding to be predictable, and for the first time the eunuch wondered if he had been wise to embroil himself with a man who was so inexplicably volatile. Had Heraclius realised that Petronius actually loved his wife, he would not have approached the senator so blithely with his treasonous plot.

'Romans don't usually care for their wives overmuch,' he explained to his lover that first evening of Petronius's return to the court. 'Marriage is more about treaties, the size of the dowry and the purity of the bloodlines than affection. I'd swear that the senator was half mad with grief – dangerously so, in fact.'

'My dear, Romans don't think like rational men and women,' his partner responded casually. 'Who'd be foolish enough to kill themselves over a sexual misadventure? Those who serve the throne in menial matters know that shame can be survived, but death is final. Instead of being treated like a fool, Lady Lydia is now praised. It's ironic, my darling boy. Yet earlier, at a time when sympathy would have helped her, she was castigated by her own kind. And it all happened because she was raped. Better to serve barbarians than belong to Romans.'

Heraclius's hirsute lover kissed the eunuch's shoulder until the Greek grew impatient and pushed him away. The strapping young man pouted and stalked out of Heraclius's private bedchamber.

Can I control Petronius? Heraclius wondered. What will Valentinian do when he is forced by proximity to meet the senator? By the gods, I wish I had left well enough alone.

Meanwhile, Valentinian tossed in his luxurious bed. He had ordered his wife to leave him, preferring to sleep alone as was his custom. Part of his need for privacy was driven by fear – of assassination and of having to comply with the needs

of others – but it was also motivated by his burning desire
to be invisible in a world where nothing and no one was
ever solitary. From his earliest memories, Valentinian had
been conscious of having to share every aspect of his
privileged life with others. His adored mother had belonged
to the empire rather than to himself, and something of that
small boy still endured in his desire to be free of the bonds of
his position.

Poor Valentinian! Like the possessions of all weak men, his
Empire had come to resemble his own inner qualities. In the
wake of Attila's invasion, the Empire was weak and dependent
on the strength of ambitious and clever acolytes who were
more able than he was, causing him to become terrified of
the world that existed outside his luxurious apartments. But
now Valentinian had cause to fear the powerful family that
hovered on the very edge of his throne, especially its paterfamilias, Aetius, who was the direst emergent threat to
Valentinian's continued trouble-free existence.

'Can I trust my guard to rid me of Flavius Aetius? Would
the Praetorians obey me? Not a chance! Many of the guard
are barbarians and those ruffians love the old fox, damn his
eyes. So who can I trust to serve my needs?'

Valentinian's voice rasped harshly in the silent room, even
though he whispered in the darkness so that the guard
outside his door should not hear the words he shared with
the night. To speak his internal anxieties aloud gave strength
to his thoughts. One after another, he discarded possible
assassins who could be trusted with the task of murdering the
greatest general in the Western Empire.

Outside the locked door, Valentinian's personal guard
heard the muffled rumble of the emperor's voice as he spoke
to himself. They wondered if, at last, their master had

succumbed to the madness that affected so many members of the Roman patrician class.

Throughout the night, Valentinian tossed and turned in an agony of indecision. He admitted to himself that he was frightened of the *magister militum* who had wielded influence over the Empire for the whole of Valentinian's adult life. He couldn't imagine a world without Aetius in it. Even a glimpse of that compact, bandy-legged figure with its bald dome and fringe of iron-grey hair filled Valentinian with dread. His smile! Valentinian had a child's certainty that Aetius used those cruel, narrow lips to point out the emperor's craven inner self to anyone who would listen. The emperor squirmed with self-knowledge.

What could Aetius do? How would he begin his attack on the emperor? Valentinian was certain that the Scythian was aiming his sights at the throne of the Western Empire, not because Petronius Maximus had suggested it, but because of the bad blood that now lay between Aetius, Petronius and himself. Gods, the senator had gone so far as to voice his suspicions of Aetius openly, and to swear that the general would enjoy the spectacle of the emperor's death throes.

In his usual self-serving fashion, Valentinian was exaggerating. The first day Petronius Maximus had returned to court, ghost-ridden and guilty, Valentinian had made the mistake of speaking publicly of the senator's loss.

'My regrets, senator. Your wife was a beautiful and accomplished woman. I'm sure you must miss her.'

In hindsight, Valentinian admitted that he should never have grinned quite so widely or so obviously. Petronius Maximus had glared at him with grief-stricken, angry eyes, so the emperor knew in the pit of his stomach that he had made a careless tactical error.

'I swear that I will do nothing to imperil the throne of the west, my emperor,' Petronius had vowed. 'Not in word, nor in deed. My love for Rome has been tested a thousand times and my wife's . . . death is but another test of my loyalty. I prefer to put my trust in the Three Fates and the goddess Fortuna, whose wheels, shears and caprices rule us all.'

Valentinian was not a fool, merely lazy, spiteful and spoiled. He noted Aetius's sudden rigidity at the ambiguity of Petronius's little speech, so he was sure that the general had read messages into those words that Petronius refrained from voicing. As the long day trailed away in doubt and anxious indecision, Valentinian drank too much wine to spare himself from the horrors of his dreams. Eventually, supported by Heraclius and a member of his personal guard, he staggered drunkenly to his bed.

Once he was safely ensconced in his room, he latched the door from the inside and, with a dagger for company and consolation, plunged into a drink-sodden sleep. Heraclius listened to the iron and wood latch fall into position and walked away down the colonnade, smiling gently as he went about his duties.

In Rome, winter had come with a vengeance and the city shivered in her damp and mud-draggled skirts. Myrddion had taken more than a week to recover from his illness, terrifying his servants, who had been deathly afraid for his survival. Stray draughts and breezes were banned from his room by the use of the last of their heavy linen from Aurelianum, which was nailed over the window frame, an action that Myrddion thought wasteful once he returned to his senses.

'Never fear, master,' Bridie replied equably, as she sat and spun lamb's wool into long threads on her spindle. 'When we leave this cursed place, we can easily take the linen down and boil it, and then it will be as good as new.'

During Myrddion's frightening illness, Cadoc and Finn had decided that they should all leave Rome as soon as they could retrieve their wagons and horses. Pulchria was visibly upset at the news of their impending departure, and would bury her face in a piece of colourful gauze, burst into tears and totter away on her tiny feet every time she saw any of the small group of healers.

Once Myrddion was in his right mind, he insisted on seeing all his patients who suffered from the mysterious malady. In each case, the patient was made aware of Myrddion's theory concerning the poisonous nature of residual lead in wines and sweets. Unfortunately, most of the sufferers chose to believe that the healer, while gifted and kind, had become a little disturbed during his illness. Sadly, Myrddion was forced to accept that most Romans would not take precautions. Wine was drunk in preference to water and Romans adored their sweet, sticky treats. He sensed their incredulity in the whispered conversations that were conducted behind his back. Poison in the wine? Poison in sweetmeats? Ridiculous! Frightening! Impossible! Only Arrius, whose bodily strength was vital to his family, chose to listen. As a skilled metalworker and blacksmith, he had observed many other men become strangely ill and die when they worked with lead, and his innate intelligence eventually forced him to arrive at a decision. He managed to persuade Claudio, his master, to place him in a position within the foundry where he would work solely with iron.

So, when Myrddion closed down the surgery and paid Pulchria considerably more than she was owed for her trouble, their departure was graven in stone. The healer had done everything in his power to fulfil his oaths and meet his responsibilities, so when Cadoc or Finn asked after Isaac the Jew, Myrddion pursed his lips into a thin and bitter line and refrained from responding to their queries.

'From what you have told me, I prophesied the conquest and sacking of Rome . . . and soon. I'll warn Pulchria, for she should have the opportunity to sell her building in the subura and depart into the safety of the countryside – although I don't believe for one moment that she will. Then, within three days, I want to be on the road to Ravenna.'

'Ravenna, master?' Finn Truthteller protested. 'Aetius is in Valentinian's city, and we'll get short shrift from the general. It would be better if we found another port on the east coast to take passage to Constantinople, if you insist on continuing this journey.'

'All true, Finn, but Ravenna has the best port on the east coast. Rome has enriched our coffers, so all we need to do is take the Via Flaminia until it meets the Via Aemilia and turn to the north. A smaller road leads off the main coastal route to Ravenna, and we can take ship directly to Constantinople from there.'

Cadoc frowned. Myrddion's plan sounded reasonable, but who would have expected the greatest Roman general in the west to vent his spleen on a female servant, as he had done with Bridie? Such cruelty had left the small woman perm-anently crippled, and she still had nightmares that proved that the rape had harmed her gentle, happy soul. Could Flavius Aetius be depended upon to leave the travellers in peace?

No!

Since recovering from his illness, Myrddion was quieter

and more determined than usual. He had learned the depths of courage that dwelled in the hearts of ordinary people. Against all the odds, Pulchria had risen above her appalling childhood and youth, so that now she fought a gallant battle against the dirt and poverty in the heart of the subura where she lived. Even the ruthless egotism of Osculus and his thugs was capable of being circumvented when his community faced a threat from within.

On the other hand, Myrddion had learned that those men, and some women, who had an opportunity to improve the living conditions of society often failed because of personal pride, fear of failure or unbridled hubris. For instance, Isaac the Jew could watch patients suffer while he turned their pain into an abstraction. Isaac had been proved right in his assertion that the citizens would not give up their wines, their sweet flavours or their love of luxury – but the Jew had refused to even try to convince his patients of the dangers of the metal. How many lives would be lost while Isaac watched with cold curiosity, making notes for his studies? For a famed, charismatic healer, Isaac chose to forget the golden rule of Hippocrates whenever it suited him to do so.

But the arena had exposed the depths to which even decent people could sink when they became accustomed to death as some grotesque sport. Could the Romans be saved from themselves? Probably. Would any person in a position of power choose to do so? Unlikely, because banning the games would breed ridicule among the citizenry. Yes, Rome had taught the young healer some valuable lessons that he would carry for the rest of his life.

In the dark of night, Myrddion still hungered to meet his anonymous father, although the need was more abstract and less emotionally demanding than in the past. The healer had discovered a great deal during his journey to Rome, and little of it had come easily, but he was now so close to Constantinople that it called to him with a promise of learning and self-fulfilment that couldn't be resisted. Like Isaac the Jew, he was tantalised and taunted by the need to know, although the size of the Flavius gens mocked Myrddion's search with the likelihood of failure.

Still, Constantinople is the source of modern knowledge and we shall see far-off and important places, the healer thought as he attempted to justify his needs. Even the sea journey will take us to Greece, and the ancient land of Homer.

So Myrddion crushed any feelings of futility and forced his small, loyal flock of companions to embrace his quest. He smothered any residual feelings of guilt with the promise of enrichment at the completion of their long journey, for the wealth of Constantinople was fabled and every large city needs healers. So Myrddion succumbed to curiosity once again, while deluding himself with many practical reasons to complete their journey.

Two weeks later, the small party climbed into the loaded wagons and prepared to leave the subura. Pulchria had presented the ladies with small pots of rosemary, thyme and mint, knowing that these simple, commonplace herbs would be useful for preparing food during the journey. Finn and Cadoc were given bunches of radishes, lavender, rue and mandrake, and amidst floods of tears the tiny woman was kissed for her thoughtfulness and generosity.

But it was for the young healer that she kept her most precious gift. Myrddion unwrapped a small twist of cloth to find an ugly iron circlet that could be snapped together and secured around a child's narrow ankle. A short length of chain was still attached to the object, though the iron was pitted with rust.

Myrddion raised his wondering eyes to search Pulchria's wet face. He raised an eyebrow in an unspoken question.

'Yes, my boy, that is my slave shackle. When I was first sent to the brothel, I cried enough tears to cleanse all Rome. I'd often run away, so they chained me to my bed. Even when I had learned my lesson and realised that I had nowhere to go, I was still forced to wear it, and the chain was a constant reminder that I no longer owned my own body.'

Myrddion's thumbs caressed the metal as his compassion grew for her lost innocence.

'I outgrew it, of course, as well as any silly notions of having any control over my life. Even when they cut the chain off me, I still wore it in my heart, if you know what I mean. Perhaps I will begin to feel like a free woman now that I've given my manacle to you.'

'Why do you give me your slave chain, Pulchria? Surely you need it to remind you of how much you have achieved in your life?'

'You need it more than I do, dear boy. We all have our separate forms of slavery, Myrddion, and you are chained to your craft by your essential goodness. When you look at my old anklet, think of what stops you from being all the things that you can be ... and remember old Pulchria.'

They said their farewells to their landlady with kisses, laughter and tears, and as their carts moved along the crowded streets to the Via Flaminia the citizens of the subura who had been Myrddion's patients came out to pass on their best wishes. Some gave loaves of flat bread, while others gave bunches of flowers, mushrooms, strips of ribbon, or finely polished pebbles. Even the poorest of the poor tried to find some small gift, which most could ill afford, out of gratitude and friendship. One huge ex-wrestler even presented ten small golden coins imprinted with the head of Janus and his two faces as a gift from the street gangs of the subura.

Myrddion would have wept if he had believed that his tears and prayers would intercede with the Goddess to help these people. Rome might still be doomed, but he held this moment close to his heart to remind himself not to prejudge from superficial appearances.

Isaac the Jew chose not to offer any farewells, an omission for which Myrddion was grateful. He knew he had outlived his usefulness to the master healer.

The road to Ravenna was long, and the landscape teetered between barren dust bowls, dispirited farms clinging closely to the river bottomlands, and opulent villas that crowned the high, healthy vistas. Olive trees, goats, some grain farms and small vegetable plots were forced to bear produce, but Myrddion was nostalgic for a dim young land that still wore her green fields and her golden cloak of trees like a queen. Homesickness ate at them all as the alien landscape of Italia unrolled before them like a slightly soiled scroll.

Myrddion comforted himself with the knowledge that all things, both good and bad, eventually end. The rule of Rome would soon be finished, so anything was possible for those distant lands on the edges of the world that remained part of the crumbling Empire.

Still, the journey offered diversions. Once more, Myrddion saw the Apollo of Veii and pointed out the cruel triangular smile of the god to Finn and Cadoc. With round, amazed eyes, his apprentices and servants took in the beauties of Narnia and marvelled at a stone bridge that crossed a raging river at Interamna. The town of Spoletium stood in the mountains and the apprentices were dumbfounded by the engineering feats that made it possible for villages to clutch to the steep cliffs like eagles' nests. Aqueducts marched out of the mountains and turned towards Rome like enormous serpents with multiple stone legs.

'Italia is a place of wonder, even in decay,' Brangaine murmured with glowing eyes. Willa did not speak, but she nursed her caged bird to cushion it from the bumps in the road surface and gazed around in excitement.

The wonders of a majestic past were all around them – in beauty, awe and symmetry – so why did Myrddion feel as if he was walking through a sepulchre of old graves that had sent up their ancient bones to bleach in the sunlight like strange, whitening driftwood?

Long before Myrddion left Rome, Valentinian was suffering on the rack of his imagination. Petronius Maximus heard the whispers and saw the deep purple shadows under the emperor's eyes, so he wondered if Lydia's shade waited by the River Styx to see her murderers pass into the underworld with her. Then, with a snort that spoke volumes for his conflicted feelings, the senator rejected the idea. Gallica Lydia had converted to Christianity, although she hadn't listened to its tenets on suicide. Perhaps she hoped for justice in Heaven.

Valentinian couldn't sleep . . . and couldn't rest. Fear is a potent spur and it gored his mind, day and night, as if he faced a maddened bull. He was frightened of Flavius Petronius Maximus, but he was terrified of Flavius Aetius.

'I can't go on!' he muttered to himself, causing one of his guard to raise his eyebrows expressively at his fellow. 'I must do something! I must! What are you looking at, you barbarian cur? Keep your eyes downcast and your ears shut!' The two guards stiffened in unison and lowered their heads obediently. Fortunately, the much smaller Roman couldn't see their mutinous eyes.

Meanwhile, Aetius smiled and waited. He could feel the tidal currents of power gathering behind him, so he knew that the time was achingly close when it would propel him up and onto the throne to the acclaim of the crowd. He need only wait until Valentinian turned on Petronius Maximus, and when the senator was summarily executed, as he would be, then Aetius could regretfully remove the madman from power and install Valentinian's daughter on the throne under his regency. Girls were notoriously frail, especially in childbirth, so who knew what the future might bring?

Aetius nursed his amusement and bided his time, unaware that his hubris had stilled the small part of his brain that had always ensured his survival.

The mountains were high and harsh, but Myrddion was unsurprised by the great road that made the escarpments traversable. Cadoc kept their spirits high by inventing rude ditties about famous Romans, so that even Willa and Brangaine giggled cheerfully in the winter sunshine. The absence of rain made their journey pleasant, if cold, but for hardy souls who had been raised in Britain the bitter weather was simply bracing and invigorating.

So long...so far! The wagons snaked through the mountains with every turn of the wooden wheels jolting over loose stones that had fallen from the heights above. Myrddion wondered if their journey would ever end. And what would they find at the end of this endless Roman road?

*

Valentinian was outwardly calm when he ordered Flavius Aetius to attend him for a private audience on the finances of the Western Empire. The message suggested that the emperor also wished to discuss the difficult and tiresome presence of Petronius Maximus at the court of Ravenna.

Aetius read the small piece of scroll carefully and then destroyed it by thrusting one corner into a wall sconce and holding the scrap of fine leather by the opposite end as it slowly burned away. The words appeared to be inscribed in dried blood as the scroll withered and scorched.

The general smiled reflectively. The tide had turned and was roaring behind him.

Valentinian had chosen to meet Aetius in the same secluded apartments that had last been used for the rape of Gallica Lydia. As a thorough hedonist and egoist, Valentinian had forgotten the details of that night, if not its aftermath, but Aetius remembered the small tragedy keenly.

So now Valentinian must pay the Ferryman, Aetius thought, as he followed the vile catamite, Heraclius, down the long colonnade that led to Valentinian's lair. He had collected all the records of the army's expenditure during their recent campaigns, but he knew that the emperor's stated desire to examine them was merely a convenient excuse for a personal audience.

'Ah.' Valentinian sighed in welcome. 'Come in, general. Come in.' The emperor nodded to the guard. 'You may leave us. I'm sure I'll be safe with the *magister militum*, the hero of the Battle of the Catalaunian Plain.' The guardsmen bowed and closed the doors with a soft thud as they left the room.

'For privacy, Aetius,' the emperor murmured as he secured the latch behind the departing guards. 'I don't want anyone to overhear what we say during this visit.'

'How may I serve you, my lord?' Aetius bowed his head briefly – a little too briefly.

'Please, accept some wine. Falernian isn't what it was, but then again, what is?'

'Thank you, my lord, but only a clear head will permit me to serve you as I should.'

Valentinian smiled boyishly. Although his eyes were sunken from his poor sleeping habits, he seemed almost cheerful. 'I have asked you to attend on me because I am harbouring severe doubts concerning the mental health of Petronius Maximus. Since the unfortunate suicide of his wife ... well ... he's been strange.'

Valentinian paced around the room, seemingly at random, as if he was too concerned about the matter in hand to stand still. Aetius seated himself on a cushioned stool and waited politely, his face at rest. His self-possession irritated Valentinian, and frightened him as well.

'Do you believe our friend poses a threat to the Empire?' the emperor asked. 'Come, you may speak honestly and freely, general, for there are no spies in these rooms.'

Aetius cleared his throat while Valentinian continued his circuitous pacing. The sound of his leather sandals on the tessellated floor was oddly soothing. 'Well, master, Petronius is a very able man and a trained soldier. He has always been ruled by his intellect and his self-interest in the past, but the suicide of Gallica Lydia seems to have temporarily unhinged him.' Aetius shrugged expressively as Valentinian moved towards him with slow, even strides.

'Do you think he's dangerous?'

Valentinian moved away once more, turning his back on the general, just when the old man's razor-sharp instincts began to nudge his brain. Aetius forced himself to relax the involuntary tensing of his muscles.

'Yes, master. He is very able with the sword, and can attend your court at any time he wishes. He is nobly born from a line of emperors, so the mob would accept him in the event of your untimely death. I believe Petronius is capable of murder, especially after the tragic death of his wife. He has nothing else to lose that he values. Unfortunately, desperate men are dangerous men.'

Valentinian turned and began to move towards Aetius's left side with slow, deliberate strides. His eyes were thoughtful, almost abstracted. Stand still, you idiot, Aetius thought as Valentinian turned on his heel and started to pace away from the general, his hands gripped behind his back. The emperor paused a moment, turned and headed across the room.

'What should I do, Aetius? Advise me! I am loath to spend the rest of my nights fearing Petronius's blade.' As if putting his fear into action, Valentinian turned sharply and began to retrace his steps into the corner of the room.

This fool is on edge, Aetius thought, and had to quash the desire to laugh. He's jittery, and he's skittering around like a nervous colt. Come out and say what you want to say like a man!

Aetius feigned deep thought as the footsteps turned and moved back across the room. You have his attention now, the general thought as he slowly began to speak the words that would ensure Petronius's doom.

'You must execute . . .'

This time Valentinian did not turn away. He came up to Aetius's left shoulder and, as the general began to compose the words that would doom Petronius to the strangler's rope, drew a narrow eating knife out of the folds of his purple toga and plunged it deep into the general's exposed throat.

Aetius was shocked. His eyes bulged almost out of his head and his left hand rose to tear the blade from his flesh. With battle-hardened fingers, his mind numbed by complete incredulity, he plucked out the blade and sent it skittering over the floor, where it left a snail's trail of blood in its wake.

Valentinian scuttled behind a couch as Aetius struggled to his feet. By good luck rather than any skill on his part, Valentinian had severed the great vein in Aetius's throat. Now, released by the removal of the blade, a rich fountain of arterial blood spurted forth while Aetius watched with goggling, disbelieving eyes.

'What? Why have you done this thing?' the general whispered, as a red stain soaked down the left side of his pristine white robe. 'What have you to gain?' He began to fall, his eyes still open and fearsomely intelligent. 'You'll ... be ...'

Then Flavius Aetius, *magister militum* and the last of the great generals of the Western Roman Empire, died in an inglorious red pool of his own blood.

For a moment that seemed to drag out painfully, Valentinian could not believe how easily and fast the murder had been committed. Not a drop of blood marked his person, partly because he had left the knife in the wound and partly because he had run from the general the moment he had slammed the blade into Aetius's neck. Anticlimax made his knees suddenly weak, but he had no time to reflect on what had taken place. Although their conversation had been quiet and Aetius's death almost silent, the guards or a member of the staff could seek admittance at any moment.

Valentinian thought rapidly. No more gossip. Let Aetius appear to be a traitor because that's exactly what he was. He threatened me, and I killed him before he had an opportunity to assassinate me. But no more rumours.'

Shaking like a man with ague, Valentinian tried to still his trembling fingers. He hastily searched Aetius's body, but the general hadn't bothered to carry a weapon. He had never considered Valentinian to be a threat.

'Shite!' the emperor swore crudely. 'Fucking son of a whore!'

With a neat economy of movement that would have surprised all the courtiers who thought they knew him, Valentinian took an unadorned knife out of a clothes chest and placed it close to Aetius's hand. Then he cried out, loudly and in feigned terror, before sitting on the couch and waiting for the guards to batter down the door.

As the two burly guardsmen broke the latch and rushed into the room, the leader almost skidded in Aetius's blood. He cursed as his hand was soiled. Two pairs of eyes absorbed the scene and then fixed on the pale countenance of the emperor, who was huddling on an eating couch as far as possible from the flaccid body.

'Aetius tried to kill me!' he wailed. 'He missed, but my blow was true!'

His eyes took in Aetius's body. He had no difficulty in pretending to be panic-stricken, for reaction had set in and he was shivering as though on the brink of collapse. 'Clean up this mess!' he ordered, his voice rising to a petulant, frightened whine. He drew his toga tightly round his body and visibly tried to gather some rags of dignity. Unfortunately, he merely looked ridiculous . . . and guilty.

Heraclius came running and saw the object of his hatred stretched out within the stinking mess of fresh blood and voided bowels that spewed over the otherwise spotless floor.

'Master! Come away, master! Your guards will do what needs to be done. Come away, my lord, and I'll fetch you spiced wine.' Matching actions to words, the eunuch tugged at the emperor's lax arm.

Somehow, Heraclius arranged his face to show nothing but horror and concern, while one of the guardsmen kneeled in the general's blood and carefully closed the widely staring eyes. Oblivious of the blood that stained their hands and armour, the two guards then lifted the small form of Flavius Aetius as tenderly as they would a tired child, with gentleness and respect. Valentinian continued to explain Aetius's death in a disjointed, rambling series of disconnected complaints.

Neither man believed a word that Valentinian gabbled so repeatedly. If Aetius had drawn a knife, then Valentinian would be dead. Therefore, Valentinian had killed the general by stealth. Other than to exchange oblique, disbelieving glances, the guardsmen remained prudently mute. As they bore the body out into the colonnade, the guardsmen did not cast a glance at the Emperor of the West – or his eunuch.

So perished Flavius Aetius, and the Western Empire began to rot with him.

CHAPTER XVIII

A SPRING WITHOUT FLOWERS

Creaking and groaning with the strain, the healers' carts crossed the last mountain and Myrddion looked down at the sloping ground that shelved away into a verdant green valley, and, beyond that, the empty blue of the sea. The sun shone a little brighter and caught the reflected light from a number of rivers that cut through the arable land. In the far distance, although invisible, Myrddion knew that the Via Aemilia ran along the coast to Ariminum before it headed inland.

'Not too far now,' he encouraged his tired friends. 'I know the journey has been hard, but we'll soon be able to rest. See? The land here is fertile. The rivers carry silt down to the lowlands and enrich the farmers with black soil and clean water.'

'We need supplies,' Cadoc said bluntly. 'And the horses are very weary. Even though the grading of the road was brilliantly designed, those mountains took the strength out of them.'

'According to the tavern keeper at Spoletium, we can rest when we reach the coast,' Myrddion responded almost cheerfully. He knew how the journey had weighed on them all, so that the bright enthusiasm of their departure from

Rome had become lost in grinding weariness as they climbed the mountains over which the Via Flaminia snaked. Mounted couriers leading spare horses had thundered past them throughout their journey, and initially the healers had been curious. But familiarity soon bred the belief that this frequency of communication was normal, and their attention turned to their own concerns. They all needed to sleep on pallets, rather than on the cold earth, even though the first shoots of spring were breaking through the rock-hard, partially frozen earth.

'Well, let's get there before my bones become permanently crooked from sitting on this seat,' Cadoc complained. 'I swear I've got splinters in my arse the size of meat skewers.'

At least Cadoc could be depended upon to provide a moment's humour, even on the harshest of days.

The next morning, as they began the dangerous descent from the mountains, the healers' wagons blocked most of the road as Finn and Cadoc slowed their speed almost to a snail's pace. Tired and irritable, a courier galloped furiously up behind them, and after a brief shouting match with Cadoc over right of way, was forced to wait while the apprentices hauled the wagons aside to give him room to manoeuvre his mounts past the obstruction. Myrddion asked after the urgency of the messenger's errand. The soldier, for so his dusty armour indicated, looked down at the healer with a hard stare of scorn and frustration.

'I'm on the emperor's business,' he shouted, moving his sword aggressively in its scabbard with one hand. 'Hurry up and move these heaps of shit so I can go.'

'We are trying our best, sir, since we too are en route to the emperor's court at Ravenna. We would welcome any news of General Flavius Aetius or his daughter Flavia.'

Myrddion would later wonder why he mentioned Flavia's name, except that her face often came creeping into his mind when he was at the very edge of sleep. His conflicted feelings for the young woman were his secret shame.

'You're out of luck all round, man. Flavius Aetius is dead, killed by Valentinian's own hand, and all his kin are closely watched. I'd sever all ties with that family if I were you. Now let me pass.'

By this time, the wagons had lumbered to the side of the narrow roadway, leaving just enough room for the horseman to pass in relative safety. With a nod laced with wry irony, the soldier galloped off towards distant Ravenna.

On the whole, the healers were delighted by the news. The thought that the general was waiting at Ravenna had caused everyone, especially Bridie, to fear the future. But now...?

'Valentinian must have been crazed with fury,' Cadoc murmured. 'But whatever happened was a blessing for us. He's got rid of Aetius – permanently.'

'I hated Aetius, but as far as I can judge he was the only able general that Rome possessed, ample indication that the Empire is on the brink of collapse. The city will be at the mercy of the barbarians now that the only man who could have saved her has been executed. I think we should be profoundly grateful that we left Rome when we did.'

'Aye, master,' Finn agreed. 'I think we've had a lucky escape all around.'

Three days of hard travel brought them to the sea, which glinted grey under a drizzling sky. Showers rendered life unpleasant, but not unbearable, as the patient horses moved through the landscape incuriously, their brown flanks glossy with rain. A flat metallic sea stretched out towards the horizon, where a sky the colour of wood smoke met it in thick mists.

The land through which they were now travelling glowed with the lime-green flush of new growth. Fruit trees raised branches that were newly studded with shoots of bronze and pale jade, and the farmers had weeded, tended and ploughed the chocolate earth so that the furrows were furred with spear-points of green. The signs of new life gave the healers feelings of hope. Ravenna lay ahead and there was no longer an itch of fear lurking under Myrddion's encouraging words. Even Bridie was glowing with health and an internal incandescence that he assumed was generated by relief.

The small town of Fanum clung to the coast with a river on one side, the sea on the other, and a road to the north that would bring them to the Via Aemilia and, eventually, Ravenna. Fishing boats gave the seascape the sheen of industry, and even the old men and women who sat on the simple wharves and mended fishing nets and wicker crab pots were rosy-cheeked and picturesque. Exhausted and hungry, the healers sought out the first inn that looked moderately clean, took their valuables from the wagons and were ushered into a single, rather grimy room with dingy, whitewashed walls, drunken shutters that hung over a narrow window and palliasses of straw packed in coarse wool piled in one corner in readiness for sleepy guests. The faint smell of urine made Myrddion's nostrils twitch.

The innkeeper provided bowls of some kind of seafood stew that was rather tasty, although Myrddion had no idea what was actually in it besides some small grains of gritty sand. Out of caution, the entire group refused the wine, settling for water, milk or a rough, watery beer that catered for northern tastes. Although the meal was simple, it was filling, plentiful and comparatively healthy. At last, the healers began to relax.

Before the companions sought their beds, Finn asked Myrddion's permission to make an announcement. Hesitantly, and with Bridie in the protective curve of his left arm, the apprentice explained that he and Bridie were hand-fasted and that his new wife was almost positive that she was quickening with child. Myrddion gaped, for while he would have had to be blind to miss the obvious affection between the widow and Finn, the house in the subura in Rome and the enforced lack of privacy on their journey had hardly been conducive to passion.

'Well, Finn, it seems you've won a fair lady, one who's as good as she's beautiful.' Myrddion smiled to show his pleasure in their obvious happiness. 'I hope you know what you're taking on, Bridie, for he's a difficult man to train.'

Bridie blushed and smiled uncertainly, not sure if her master was jesting or serious.

'I know that Bridie could find a better man than I am – but she makes me happy, master, and I never thought I'd be happy again. I swear before you all that my girl will want for nothing as long as I have two strong arms to protect her and a strong back to work for her.'

Myrddion sobered as he stared at Finn Truthteller's earnest and embarrassed face. Out of the rubble of guilt, near madness and feelings of failure, Finn had not only carved a new trade for himself, but had also found the courage to fall in love. Myrddion felt a sharp pang of jealousy which he dismissed as soon as he recognised its taint. After Finn's dreadful experience on the Night of the Long Knives, when he had been left alive to bear witness to Hengist's revenge on

Catigern, the young man deserved a taste of happiness, even if Myrddion had never experienced the same depths of passion for himself.

The servant need not live as the master dictates, Myrddion chided himself internally, even as he clapped the newly-weds on the back and embraced the blushing wife. I'm being selfish and envious, for Finn is my friend – and not my slave.

Because the air was fresh and clean and their quarters were comfortable enough, Myrddion decided that they should rest for three days at Fanum in celebration of Finn's new status. The following evening, he proposed to host a modest feast to mark the good news. With his usual enthusiasm, Cadoc entered into the spirit of the occasion, persuading the dour innkeeper to prepare a special meal and to find a private bedchamber for the traditional wedding night.

The celebration even generated interest in Fanum, a town that was more used to rapid departures than to feasts. To the delight not only of the innkeeper, the healers were spending their coin in Fanum rather than Pisaurum or Ariminum, so the hotelier's wife bestirred herself to search out the finest ingredients available to her. Local musicians were hired and the townsfolk were invited en masse. Myrddion opened his chest, took out his gold, and spent his superfluous cash to give pleasure to his friends.

In provincial towns, especially after a hard winter, there are few opportunities for celebration. The people of the village around the inn arrived with small gifts, eager to enjoy a brief holiday from the rigours of everyday life. The flutes, lyres and drums played merry tunes, so that even the most sceptical guests found their feet tapping and their weathered faces cracking with smiles.

The food was largely the bounty of the sea, and was fresh and simply prepared. The luxury of soup made from tiny shellfish that grew on the rocks was a delight to travellers who had been starved of fresh meat for weeks. Apples kept in storage during the winter might be wrinkled with age but were still sweet and juicy. A large number of fish had been baked in a thick sauce made delicious with tiny shrimp and baby octopus that had been cooked whole. Although Myrddion had distrusted the food in Rome, he devoured this meal with gusto, even the octopus with their tiny, rubbery tentacles, satisfied that no sweeteners had been added, at his specific request, in its preparation.

He had unbent sufficiently to permit wine to be served, although the healers refused to drink it themselves, preferring the safety of beer. The amber, frothy drink quickly went to their heads and Cadoc led a crazed romp of dancers in a spirited British interpretation of village round dances. Joy gave the evening the sheen of magic that would live in their memories for many weary nights to come, while Fanum would remember the healers and their bounty in the harsh years of servitude under the occupation of the barbarians.

After much dancing, music and song, the newly wedded couple belatedly fled to the marriage bed, which was incongruously decorated with dried rose petals and some of Rhedyn's lavender.

'Don't ask, master!' Cadoc had warned when Myrddion had opened his mouth to enquire about the rose petals. 'What you don't know can't hurt you.'

Myrddion sighed, but then he grinned with boyish enthusiasm. 'Whatever makes them happy,' he responded, and clapped Cadoc's back. 'All we need to do now is find a wife for you.'

'There's no hope of that, master. Who'd love this ugly mug?'

'I'm quite certain there are many women who'd happily keep you. I'm aware of your many conquests in Rome, and by all accounts there are queues of women eager to mother you. Don't colour up, Cadoc. I'm simply speaking the truth as I see it, my friend. You can see how happy Finn is, so don't you long to experience such felicity?'

Cadoc's face fell into uncharacteristically sober lines. He threw one arm companiably over Myrddion's shoulders.

'Don't you, master? Hmm? Exactly! Like you, I'm becoming fond of the road and adventures. When I lost the full use of my arm and soldiering seemed beyond me forever, I thought I'd finish my days in some boring trade like farming. But I'm a healer now, and the world clamours for my skills. Bridie is used to the life, so she accepts travel as part of her love for Finn, but where will I find another girl who'll give up her family and any chance of a cosy, settled home?'

'Ah, then we'll be single men together, you and I,' Myrddion riposted, but his eyes were sad. Myrddion had seen the deep wells of affection that can enrich married life, so part of his nature hungered for a home and a family. Unfortunately, his experiences with his mother had taught him that love was not always unconditional, so he was cautious in all matters of the heart.

Alone on the strand, after the villagers and his own companions had retired to their beds, Myrddion sat on a crab pot and endured the advances of a small black and white dog with pricked ears and a wide, canine smile. He patted the little creature reflectively and it yipped with pleasure.

'Families are a problem, aren't they, little one?' he said, and the dog tilted its head towards him in answer. 'Marriage is a blessing where love dwells in the heart, as with Olwyn and Eddius. But when it is a matter of convenience and wealth, as with my mother Branwyn and her two husbands, then there's precious little happiness and a great deal of heartache.'

The face of his grandmother Olwyn seemed to materialise out of the sea mist. 'I loved you so much, Gran,' he whispered, realising he was a little drunk. 'You made me a man of some worth; you protected me and loved me. Your trust made me as whole as I'll ever be.'

Olwyn's lips smiled, and then faded to be replaced by his mother's scornful, hate-filled face. The old, unchanging expression of loathing seemed to radiate out of her to poison him, as it always did when they were together.

'I know why you hated me so much, Mother, and perhaps I would feel the same if I was raped and then forced to carry the result of that attack. I understand why you can't bear to even look at me, but I wish I could love you, and be loved by you.' The small dog licked his dangling hand, and the face of his mother vanished into the mist after his grandmother's, leaving Myrddion sick at heart.

'My loneliness is causing me to imagine things, pup, so forgive me.' He patted the small square head and was amused to see the dog's stump of tail wriggle with pleasure. 'I wish I could be as easily pleased as you are, but I suppose that's past praying for. Anyway, with luck, Finn and Bridie will be happy enough for all of us.'

With a twinge of regret, he turned his back on the sea, with its rime of phosphorescence from the slow, steady ripple of the tide, and made his way back to the inn and his solitary pallet.

*

The next morning, when the happy couple joined their friends in the sunshine outside the inn, it was to find that Myrddion had commandeered a table on which a pile of gifts from the villagers had been assembled. None of the objects on the table was valuable and few of them were new, but Finn's grin grew wider until his face was glossy with happiness, while Bridie burst into tears at this tangible proof of affection.

Fish hooks, a stew pot, a necklace of shells, dried apples, a potted lemon bush, loaves of unleavened bread, a conch shell and a strange little household god holding an iron trident stood on the table for the newly-weds to stroke and marvel at. Then the widows, Cadoc and Myrddion, who had scoured the town for suitable offerings, presented their own special bride gifts to the happy couple.

Somehow, Rhedyn and Brangaine had found a baby's dress made of fine thread that had been knitted, rather than woven. Ignorant of such women's work, Myrddion had no idea how the small, spider-webbed garment had been created, but he could recognise that it was soft from use and had a creamy appearance that spoke of great age. Tiny shells had been pierced and sewn round the hem so that they rang softly like little bells. The infant's robe was beautiful in its homely fashion, and alien in construction, so that it would become a fitting heirloom when the fledgling family eventually returned to the land of the Britons.

Bridie wept again and then hugged Rhedyn and Brangaine before clutching the lovely article to her breasts.

Cadoc had been mindful of practical matters and had found two silver spoons, although Myrddion chose not to ask where his apprentice had discovered such treasure, least of all saved the coin to pay for it. To own a single spoon was a sign of wealth, but to own two spoons was a wonder, so the newly wedded couple were incoherent with amazement.

Myrddion's gifts were thoughtful and strange, just as Cadoc and Finn would have expected. Myrddion had seen first-hand how his grandmother Olwyn had found little time for herself once the babes of her second marriage had been born, so he understood how women longed for personal adornment to make them feel pretty after the demands that childbirth made on their bodies. He had found a length of very fine linen that had been dyed a clear lemon shade that would enhance Bridie's lovely hair. A long row of abstract shell shapes had been woven into the fine cloth to create a border, thereby turning the cloth into a princely gift. Luck had been with the young healer, for such a piece of weaving could usually be found only in the centres of Rome, Constantinople or Ravenna, but a local trader had accepted the cloth from a fleeing kinsman of Flavius Aetius in exchange for a good horse. A wise man flees when an emperor kills the family paterfamilias. He had been relieved to exchange the cloth for two of Myrddion's store of Janus gold coins.

For Finn, Myrddion had purchased a bag that could be used to assemble his own healer's kit. The leather satchel was strong and serviceable, and was lashed together with strong thongs of the same material that had been dyed dark blue to create a self-pattern on the tanned leather.

'It's coloured with indigo,' Myrddion explained to Finn, who had gasped with surprise when the satchel was pressed into his hands. 'All that is needed now is for you to assemble a basic supply of salves, pain relievers, forceps, needles and lances and you can practise as a fully fledged healer.'

'This is too much, Master,' Finn protested.

'No, Finn, it's not enough. You and Cadoc have served me

well for so long that it's unfair on my part to consider you to be apprentices any more.'

Then, with a flourish, he produced a matching satchel for Cadoc, different only in that the thongs were coloured a rusty red to set it apart from the gift given to Finn.

'You have both served your apprenticeships, and I declare that you are now healers. You may choose to stay with me or to set up a practice of your own if you are tired of the road. I'll not blame either of you if you choose to stay here, or in Ravenna, or if you decide to return to Britain. As of now, you are free to do as you choose.'

'Master . . . how could I leave you?' Cadoc said emotionally. 'I owe you my trade, the use of my arm and my life. I am your man forever.'

'And I,' Finn agreed, standing back from Myrddion and saluting the younger man with one clenched fist over his heart in the Roman fashion. 'I would have died of shame and madness in Cymru if you hadn't taken me in and tried to stitch my damaged wits back together. We three are the healers of Segontium, and I'll not be parted from you. Forgive me, Bridie my love, but not even a thousand wives could force me to break my oath to my master.'

'Nor would a thousand wives want you to break your vows,' Bridie said proudly, drawing herself up to her full height like a perky little sparrow facing a cat that threatened her fledglings. 'We are your widows, master, and you've not asked anything of us but honest work in all the years we've served you. You've treated us as if we were ladies rather than camp followers. I'm a happy woman now because of you . . . and I don't deserve your gift. It's too valuable, my lord.'

Embarrassed and touched, Myrddion flushed along his high cheekbones. 'You are a lady, Bridie – as are Rhedyn and

Brangaine. You deserve more than I've given, because you've been loyal and true, which are qualities worth more than anything that can be purchased with coin.'

'I don't know about you, master, but all this sentimentality is getting to me,' Cadoc said with a wink, as he dried his face with his sleeve. 'Let's drink a glass of beer and then have something to eat from last night's leavings. I, for one, am starving!'

Even two months after the death of Aetius, Ravenna still seethed with fear, excitement and gossip. During those weary weeks before the New Year, the emperor had kept himself alone, preferring the company of Heraclius and his servants to that of the members of the court, whom he distrusted and feared. Every man and woman was a possible threat to his throne and his life.

Even the guards had been drawn into the after-effects of the execution of Aetius.

'I swear that the general was unarmed when he entered Valentinian's room. The knife in his hand was far too big to hide in his toga or in his boot. Besides, why would the emperor lock himself in a room with someone he hated and feared?' The soldier who spoke was Optilia, a captain in Valentinian's guard.

'Don't ask me!' a burly Goth snapped, his green eyes glowing in the lamplight of their quarters. 'The general wouldn't kill an unarmed man. Aetius was hard, but he wasn't a dog. I think . . .'

'Don't say it!' Aetius's son-in-law Thraustila had entered the guardroom and overheard Optilia's conversation with the Goth. To speak treason aloud in this climate of fear was crazy.

'We've already been soaked in the blood of our general

and I'd prefer not to be bathed in our own, so keep your mouths shut,' the Hungvari nobleman went on. 'There are plots and rumours everywhere I turn. Valentinian has cut off his own right hand to make his left hand stronger, but I think he's risking everything on a lie.'

'His lie, most like!' Optilia retorted.

'Maybe. Someone will eventually call Valentinian to account, but it won't be me.'

Optilia and Thraustila looked at each other, but neither man said anything further.

This conversation was repeated, in one form or another, all over Ravenna. Meanwhile, the empress Licinia Eudoxia kept to her apartments and avoided her husband. Her behaviour was so pointed that the dogs of gossip suggested she was afraid that the emperor could turn on her. In fact, the empress expected reprisals for her husband's murderous action, and she worried that her children could be killed in any struggle for the throne.

Valentinian did not fear his wife, but nor did he trust her to remain true to his interests. Because Valentinian lacked vision, he had expected his life to return to its normal luxurious and pleasure-loving pattern after Aetius was removed from the equation. All too late, Valentinian discovered that every action has its opposite reaction, and the entire court was watching him closely. His enemies had multiplied, so the dangers to his person had trebled.

'You must act, my lord,' Heraclius pressed him. 'Flavius Petronius Maximus remains your most potent enemy and he is waiting to take your throne as soon as he can have you removed.'

Valentinian rounded on the eunuch with reddened, angry eyes.

'I've had enough of your insinuations, Heraclius. If I execute Petronius, then the people will be sure that I've gone mad. The latest reports tell me that King Geiseric and his Vandals are massing near the border in the north. For the sake of all the gods, Heraclius, I must have some generals left alive. Are you going to defend the Empire? Or do you expect me to become a military leader so late in life? I need Petronius, else I'd remove him summarily.'

'You cannot trust either Petronius or your wife. They'd have you killed without a moment's hesitation.'

'Shut up! Shut up! Shut up!' Valentinian screamed, bustling Heraclius out of his rooms and locking the door behind him.

The eunuch might have been trying to bolster his reputation and the position of his protector, but he was very close to the truth.

In the New Year, Valentinian demanded that the court should move back to Rome, so while Myrddion and his companions were still in the mountains the court transferred back to the city of Romulus along the Via Salaria, leaving the empress, Placidia, Gaudentius and Flavia behind in Ravenna. Flavia's husband Thraustila and his friend Optilia accompanied the Praetorian Guard to protect the person of the emperor.

Valentinian distrusted everyone, but especially he feared the scions of Aetius, or those who had married into his family. By keeping Thraustila close to him, he was following the old adage of keeping your friends close, but your enemies closer. He judged, rightly, that Thraustila lacked the support or the patronage to attempt assassination in Rome, where his ancestry was hated. Rat-like, Valentinian argued with himself late at night when his fears of murder drove him to the edge of madness.

He's a Hun, and the people of Rome hate them and would tear them to pieces, Valentinian thought desperately. *It's in Thraustila's best interests to keep me alive.*

The emperor had never really understood the way ordinary people thought or felt. Thraustila's pride had been wounded, for his father-in-law had died ignominiously and no one had been punished for the murder. According to the beliefs of the young man's people, Aetius's shade was unavenged and could never rest peacefully in the grave.

Likewise, Optilia fumed inwardly that his master had died while he had been standing guard. He was certain that Aetius had been unarmed, so the general's death had been doubly shameful. By Optilia's exacting standards, Valentinian had forfeited the right to loyalty and Aetius's murder had now become an affront to the guard's manhood.

Had Valentinian considered the feelings of others, perhaps he might have decided that taking Optilia and Thraustila with him on the journey to Rome was a risky decision. But Valentinian saw the world through his eyes alone, and not with his mind and his heart, thus rendering him blind in a world of sighted enemies.

As soon as Valentinian departed, Licinia Eudoxia began to suffer from fearsome nightmares and terrifying suspicions. She believed that her husband had rejected her, while she feared Petronius Maximus more than she could express in words. Shortly after the suicide of his wife, the senator had spoken to Lady Flavia and expressed his dislike of Licinia Eudoxia, telling the red-haired beauty that he blamed the empress for complicity in the rape of his wife. Licinia Eudoxia would never trust Lady Flavia, who rushed to tell her of Petronius's enmity. But Licinia Eudoxia was not surprised that Petronius was seeking to find another scapegoat for the death of the lady Lydia. The empress was an easy target, especially if Valentinian died.

But even more than Petronius, the empress knew that she had cause to fear the heirs of Aetius. Flavia had been quick to swear her allegiance to the throne, but Eudoxia was nobody's fool. Flavia was Aetius's daughter and had inherited her father's cold-blooded intelligence.

'Aetius was loyal to you, your majesty, I swear! My father knew that he was too old to rule, so he would never have raised a hand against your husband. My brother is married to your daughter, so our families are tightly interwoven. A blow against one is a blow against all.'

Eudoxia was not deceived by Flavia's assurances. The girl might be married to a nobleman in Valentinian's guard, but she was still Aetius's daughter. Self-willed and careless, Flavia took every opportunity afforded by her husband's absence from Ravenna to surround herself with her own court of thoroughly disreputable persons, including handsome actors, freed gladiators, and gamblers, and was too fond of muscular young men to maintain a reputation for respectability. The empress's lips curled with barely concealed contempt.

Then, out of fear and doubt, Licinia Eudoxia made a dire and foolish error. She wrote a letter to Geiseric, trusting in the ambitions of the barbarian king.

'Should you be prepared to save me from the treasonous actions of those persons closest to the throne, then I will promise my daughter Eudocia to your son Huneric, in a marriage that will bind our houses together. I ask that you understand my womanly fears for my husband, Valentinian, who has been manipulated by unscrupulous men. Should he perish in Rome, I will know that he has been murdered, and I will need the support of your strong right arm to survive such treasons.'

Eudoxia paced her apartments after the letter was irrevocably sent, and she finally came to a decision. 'Call my daughters, Placidia and Eudocia, to join me at once, and then start packing their possessions for a journey,' she instructed her guard. 'You may tell them that I expect us to be on our way to Rome by noon tomorrow.'

And then, even though her daughters begged her to reconsider her decision, Eudoxia had her way and they were gone from Ravenna within twenty-four hours. Rome was a pit of sin and danger, but Licinia Eudoxia would be safer in a city that was so terrified of treason and violence that doors were always kept locked and barred. There she would be kept apprised of the entire political situation. In Ravenna, the empress was starved of information, and therefore vulnerable to attack from within the depleted court.

Gaudentius and Flavia attended the empress's court the evening before she left for Rome. Brother and sister had dressed in their best finery and Eudoxia noticed, with a pang of jealousy, that Flavia's gems rivalled her own.

How can that bitch have acquired a ruby the size of a pigeon's egg? the empress thought savagely, even while she framed aloud the graceful words that denied permission for the children of Aetius to accompany her. I swear she sleeps with wealthy trades-men and Asians. She's a trollop! As my father would have said, the fruit doesn't fall far from the tree. I'd have to be crazed to welcome these two serpents into my entourage. I'd never sleep in peace.

Her courtesy never wavered, but neither Gaudentius nor Flavia was deceived. Their brief period of influence was over. Although spring was coming, they felt a shiver through their veins.

To Flavia,   March
Beloved wife.

Hail! I hope this scroll finds you well. The messenger
who brings this greeting cannot read, so destroy the
scroll as soon as it is read. For safety's sake, perhaps you
should destroy the messenger as well, but I leave this
decision to you, sweet one. Be aware that Optilia and I
are now the emperor's guards. I have forgotten neither
your tears, nor the dishonour that was laid on your noble
sire's name after his death. Do not be afraid for me, for I
have entered into a pact with the noble senator, Flavius
Petronius Maximus, who has promised to reward us
with gold in exchange for our loyalty. I will say no more,
for I do not wish to imperil you.

I am in daily expectation of receiving a purse that
shows the senator's regard, so I shall dispatch this
reward in a strongbox with another messenger.

Look for word from the Campus Martius.

Trust to my honour, wife, and wait until I join you in
Ravenna.

Farewell, and know that I love you.

Thraustila,
Son of Thraustilius,
Lord of the Hungvari, and your husband.

*

As spring stirred flowers to life, the journey north to Ravenna
became a pleasure of unfolding vistas of beauty for the healers.
They marvelled at the difference between these gentle lands

and the sterile, depleted fields of the south. Wild flowers
grew in drifts under the burgeoning olive trees and the sea
breezes lifted the travellers' hair and cooled their faces as the
horses moved ever closer to Ravenna. Pisaurum passed in a
blur of fine new buildings, fishing fleets and fertile fields.
Ariminum was larger still, for it lay at the end of the Via
Aemilia that ran through the fertile valley of the Padus river
all the way to the Via Iulia and thence to Massilia and Gaul.
Both cities had become wealthy from trade, for they dispersed
the wealth of the eastern Padus to the south and to Rome.
Myrddion had already experienced the wide plains of the
north, but Cadoc and Finn could now see that Italia was more
than one great city and was far richer than they could have
imagined, given the nature of the subura of Rome.

'You can see with your own eyes, friends, that Italia isn't
dead, even if Rome is dying. These lands could still spawn
greatness, if Rome didn't persist in sucking all the wealth out
of it.'

'It's a pity, master,' Finn replied, although Myrddion could
tell that his friend was so preoccupied with his new happiness
that he wasn't really concerned with the fate of anything, or
anyone, other than those whom he loved.

As the party approached Ravenna, the landscape gradually
changed. The healers were in no particular hurry, for they
had learned that the court was back in Rome and the threat
of imminent danger had been removed, but when they
reached the swamplands they were soon forced to set a
brisker pace. Although the road ran above the lowlands and
the brackish water that lay in every hollow, mosquitoes,
wasps, crickets and gnats made their days and nights painful
until Myrddion ground up some herbs that he added to their
basic unguent mix. Once this cream was rubbed into their

skin, the women were no longer driven demented by the clouds of insects that had previously covered every inch of exposed flesh with itching, bleeding bites, but the discomfort was still sufficient for Myrddion to urge the horses forward at speed to escape their small tormentors.

Flavia and Gaudentius were lazing on eating couches watching several nubile young women doing something disconcertingly erotic with two large snakes and wild flowers. Unlike his sister, Gaudentius was amused by the women's gyrations and wasn't pleased when a stranger with long, greying plaits interrupted their entertainment with a message from Rome.

Flavia's heart sank to her bowels. Earlier, Thraustila's letter had terrified her because of the implications that were buried in the text, so she had ordered the messenger to be strangled immediately. But she still worried that the hapless man had shared the scroll with someone who could read. Now, as the new messenger looked at her sideways out of black eyes and opened his mouth to speak, she was certain that her husband had placed them all in peril out of some sense of misplaced loyalty. Thraustila had always been a sentimental idiot.

Gaudentius gave the messenger, who called himself Gwylym, a goblet of wine and bade him speak freely. After draining the cup to the lees and examining his host with a knowing grin, Gwylym began to recite the message from Thraustila.

'Aetius's murderer is dead, my lord, my lady, slain by your husband and Optilia at the Campus Martius. Your noble husband also slew the vile catamite, Heraclius, who plotted with the emperor to assassinate Aetius, so your father's shade has been fed with the blood of his murderers. Hail to Optilia and Thraustila, and to Flavius Petronius Maximus who protects them.'

Flavia wanted to vomit with fear. The rich food and sweet wine she had consumed caught at the back of her throat and her hands tore at the tassels on her couch until they ripped away from the rich pillow.

'Aye, praise to Optilia and Thraustila who struck these blows,' Gaudentius cried, and clapped his hands like a child. 'Tell us more – every detail.'

'I saw Valentinian's death with my own eyes, master, although I wasn't part of the assassination.'

'Every detail, Gwylym! The walls in this villa are safe, so you needn't fear discovery.'

'Rumour has it that Valentinian refused to give Petronius the full control of the army that Aetius enjoyed, so the senator was insulted.'

'A mistake, to be sure,' Flavia murmured.

'Aye, it was a mistake on the part of the emperor. On the sixteenth day of March, Valentinian decided that he needed to hone his skills with the bow, so he went to the Campus Martius with a full retinue of bodyguards. The emperor was so foolish as to turn his back on his guards to notch his arrow and, as he turned, Optilia struck him in the temple with his knife. When Valentinian looked back at his attackers, Optilia finished him off. At the same time, your noble husband slit the eunuch's throat. Heraclius squealed like a pig and tried to run, but the lifeblood only pumped out of him faster.'

'Didn't the rest of the guard try to save Valentinian?' Flavia asked, her knuckles clenched so tightly that the bone seemed to shine whitely through the skin.

'Why, my lady? We all knew that Valentinian murdered our general and that Heraclius put him up to it. We were glad when Optilia and Thraustila took his toga, his crown and his sword to give to Petronius Maximus, for we now have a new emperor, one who is also a warrior.'

'Gods, is Petronius Maximus the new emperor?' Flavia gasped.

'Aye, lady. Petronius has married Licinia Eudoxia and banned the marriage of her daughter Eudocia to the son of the Vandal king. The empress is very angry – but what can she do?'

'What indeed!' Flavia answered tersely.

'Your husband asked me to tell you that he now serves the new emperor, Flavius Petronius Maximus. Hail to Emperor Flavius Petronius Maximus.'

'Hail,' brother and sister murmured in unison.

'Your husband also sends this chest to you for safekeeping, Lady Flavia. He hopes to be with you soon, but Geiseric of the Vandals has entered Italia and must be repelled. The king of the Vandals is insulted that the marriage to Eudocia has been refused. Petronius has sent for the Visigoths to save the Holy City, but until they come, all loyal servants of the Empire must fight to save the throne and Rome.'

'Dear heavens,' Flavia muttered under her breath. Gaudentius nodded placidly.

As soon as Gwylym left the room with their thanks and a gold coin for his trouble, Flavia rounded on her brother. 'Are you insane, Gaudentius? Do you seriously expect that we will survive the murder of Valentinian? Petronius hates you – so you can lay any odds on the brevity of your survival when he returns to Ravenna. Have you forgotten his wife, Lydia?'

'Come now, Flavia. I'm still married to the daughter of the empress, and Petronius isn't immortal. What do I have to fear?'

With an exasperated expression on her pretty face, Flavia began to count off on her fingers the reasons why they should flee as soon as possible.

'First, I'm married to the murderer of an emperor, and he's your brother-in-law. Second, our father caused the death of the new emperor's wife. Third, the new emperor hates you for sneering at him, times beyond counting. Fourth . . . must I go on?' She paused, but her brother only shrugged. 'Obviously I must. Fourth, there mightn't be a Rome if the Vandals have their way, and even your marriage to Placidia won't save you from them.'

Gaudentius waved his hand in dismissal of her arguments, so Flavia tried a different tack. 'I know you think that Petronius is a fool, but I travelled with him to Ostia before my marriage and I can assure you that he is a man who cherishes a grudge. Why won't you listen, brother? Father would have understood, I know.' Flavia rang a small golden bell to summon her maid.

'Father is dead,' Gaudentius replied crudely. 'And a good thing too, if he ever learned what you really thought of your marriage vows. You might be my sister, but you'd make a street harlot appear almost virginal.'

Flavia slapped him with the full force of her arm and Gaudentius bit his tongue. He stifled an oath and would have struck her back if Flavia's steward hadn't interrupted them.

'Order my maids to pack, including that strongbox,' Flavia instructed the laconic, ageing Hun before turning back to face her brother. 'My plan is to catch the first available ship to Constantinople. You can take your chances with the Western Empire if you wish, but I'm heading to the east while I still have my head on my shoulders.' Flavia rose from her eating couch with all her natural, feline grace. 'If you plan to stop me, then good luck to you, my brother, for you'll need it. A street harlot knows how to protect herself.'

As she swept out of Gaudentius's perfumed presence, he threw one parting shot after his sister. 'May you have joy in Constantinople, Flavia, for they have no time for women who are less virtuous than God requires. And when you're forced to return, see if you can still find a man prepared to protect you in this city, for everyone here knows what a slut you are!'

Flavia's only response was a long peal of laughter, for she knew what was in the strongbox. It held a sizeable fortune in gold that was now hers – and her brother wouldn't know what a treasure she carried until she had slipped through his fingers.

Outside the villa, Gwylym waited in the shadows and grinned slyly to himself. Although he had been unable to break into the strongbox, he was certain he was right about the gold that lay within it. The weight had bowed down his spare horse on the long journey from Rome. He'd have stolen the whole thing and run for the nearest port, but Thraustila had taken the precaution of sending a troop of six trusted Hungvari officers with Gwylym to ensure his safety.

Gwylym had been shocked when Aetius had been murdered. Somehow, he had never expected the Roman general to be assailable like other, more fallible men, so his faith in the unshakeable power of all things Roman had been blunted. He was further from home than he could imagine, and surrounded by enemies who wouldn't hesitate to destroy him, so Aetius should pay for his straitened circumstances. Even dead, the *magister militum* could provide Gwylym with a little nest egg for the future through the agency of his upstart of a daughter.

All Gwylym had to do was wait.

*

Flavia drove her servants like a slavemaster, intent as she was on stripping the villa of everything that was portable and held some value. She even had recourse to a small whip which she used liberally on the back of any foolish maid who slowed the bruising pace she set as, hysterically, she jammed precious clothing into chests and secreted a pile of fabulous jewels in another strong box and buried it under a pile of linen clothing. Even small ivory, gold and silver figurines found their way into her chests as she looted the house for anything of worth that could be taken with her on her journey.

Grumbling, her brother had returned to his luxurious apartments while she was selecting the servants who would accompany her to Constantinople. Flavia had filled the entry hall with boxes and chests and was donning a travelling cloak when Gwylym used the knocker on her door to announce his presence. Having watched as a litter and a travelling carriage came to the door of her villa, the Celt had reasoned that Flavia was preparing to bolt for the harbour and a boat to Constantinople, so if he was to receive any benefit from the strongbox and its contents he must act quickly and with stealth. He had already ascertained that four strong bearers had arrived to accompany Thraustila's wife to the embarkation point, so it would be difficult to steal the strongbox by force alone.

Gwylym had served Aetius well, especially in the delicate task of engineering the accident that should have removed Cleoxenes from Pope Leo's delegation to Mantua. By chance, the nosy healer from Segontium had circumvented Gwylym's careful plans and frustrated Aetius's hopes of direct credit for Attila's retreat from Italia. During this time, Gwylym had provided the general's best intelligence and removed several other problems from his path, so in his own mind he was owed a parting gift for his services. Flavia, that spoiled and lustful creature whom not even her father had respected, would now provide a bounty, whether she desired to help him or not.

Flavia opened the heavy door in answer to his summons, and would have closed it immediately if he hadn't used his boot to prevent her.

'What do you want?' she snapped, surrounded by her chattels and frightened womenfolk.

'A moment of your time only,' Gwylym replied ingratiatingly. After all, honey traps more flies than vinegar, and he had no intention of using force until he had no other recourse. 'Preferably in private, madam, where I can give you a message from your father.'

Flavia was torn, just as Gwylym had intended she should be. As much as she loved anyone, Flavia had adored her father, and a message that was virtually from the grave was a compelling temptation. With an elegant wave of one hand, she indicated the ransacked scriptorium and followed the gnarled warrior into the disordered room, closing the door firmly behind her, but prudently refraining from securing the lock.

Flavia opened the conversation briskly. 'What do you want of me? A message from my father seems unlikely, since he's been dead for months.'

'He took great pride in your intelligence, my lady, and he deemed you to be more of a man than his son, if I may speak so boldly. He instructed me to call upon you if anything should happen to him. He also assured me that you would be . . . appreciative of my efforts on his behalf.'

Flavia frowned. What did this horrid little man expect of her? Was it money? If so, he was out of luck.

'He expected me to give you gold? My father wasn't prone to moments of generosity, so why should he have made an exception for you?'

'I hadn't planned to speak so bluntly, my lady, but your father entrusted me with any number of . . . delicate tasks, which perhaps were not so honourable as his reputation might suggest. Included among them was the delivery of the items from Thraustila that I left with you earlier. Surely you don't wish me to elaborate, Lady Flavia, for what I have done for your family is private and the details are best kept away from the prying eyes of the authorities, especially the supporters of Emperor Petronius Maximus. I haven't been paid by your father for my most recent services because his death occurred before I received my stipend.'

The oily threat in Gwylym's voice was absorbed by Flavia without comment. However, she smiled disarmingly and tossed her red bronze curls flirtatiously, leaving Gwylym to believe that she acknowledged his right to payment.

'I am certain we can come to an equable arrangement that will be satisfactory to us both, Gwylym . . . that is your name, isn't it? I will do much for any man who has given good service to my father, especially if he wishes to continue in my employ.'

'I'm sure the matter of your father's indebtedness can be resolved, Lady Flavia. It is my intention to return to my homeland in Armorica as soon as it can be arranged, and I understand that you plan to journey to Constantinople in the Eastern Empire. I'd not have the eastern emperor privy to your father's plans to assume the throne of Rome, for such knowledge would be dangerous for the daughter of a man I served with so much loyalty. In turn, I would appreciate your decision to assist an old soldier to return to his distant homeland. Once I am far away, there can be no chance of untoward gossip concerning your father's activities immediately prior to his untimely death.'

In a hard voice, Flavia summed up Gwylym's ambiguous threats. 'If I should pay you to return to your western home, then you'll make no trouble for me in the Eastern Empire, is that correct? Have I understood your unspoken demands correctly?'

Gwylym nodded. 'In a nutshell, my lady, that's it.'

His oily smile enraged Flavia, but she kept her expression calm. 'Very well, Gwylym.' She smiled softly. 'The strongbox is in the villa forecourt. Come with me.' With her usual grace, she led the way back to the entryway to the villa, where she paused before her steward, a tall and grizzled Hun.

'Fetch me my wrap so I can be protected from the chill,' she murmured softly.

Gwylym waited impatiently while the steward glanced down at the visitor with blank eyes before disappearing into the bowels of the house. Then Flavia passed through the double doors and into the forecourt. Her demeanour was icy, so Gwylym should have been warned, but the old Celt warrior had lived violently for five decades, and still trusted to his ruthlessness to save him from the consequences of his actions.

'Wait here!' Flavia ordered him imperiously, and strode towards the carriage, where three burly menservants waited.

'Take him,' she whispered quietly, and Gwylym immediately found himself surrounded. Unsurprised, he drew his sword with a wicked hiss and dropped into a fighting crouch. His face was bland and unconcerned because he still saw no difficulty in coping with unarmed men. After all, he had killed more capable men than these oafs while armed with lesser weapons than his fighting sword.

'You're making a mistake, Lady Flavia,' he hissed as he

backed away slowly, keeping his opponents in view. 'I expected you to try some form of treachery, so tell your bully boys to step away. I still insist on your coin for my silence, but I'm feeling far less friendly than I was when I first arrived here.'

'Kill him,' Flavia ordered crisply, and Gwylym raised his sword ready to cut through the unarmed bearers to make a dash for freedom. Then he noticed that her eyes were fixed on a point behind his left shoulder. Gwylym began to turn.

But Flavia was as quick-witted as her father.

Her steward had become alarmed as soon as he heard from the maids that the mistress was closeted with a barbarian. Then Flavia's request for a wrap she was already wearing had sent him into action. Fetching his hunting bow from the storeroom, he had positioned himself directly behind Gwylym's broad back with an arrow notched and ready for release. As a former Hun warrior, he was expert with the weapon and was oath-bound to protect Flavia from all harm. The bow string sang, and the black-fletched arrow struck Gwylym's back, burying half its length into his flesh. As the Celt fell forward on his face, his last vision was of Lady Flavia's sandals as she approached him across the cobbles. He heard her voice as if it came from far away, through a river of pain that radiated out from his left shoulder blade, and he swore crudely. 'Fucking slut! You'll pay!'

'Cut this creature's throat and continue loading the carriage. I must be at the docks within the hour.' Flavia's voice was bored, as if the Celt had been an annoying interruption to her urgent plans for the day's entertainment.

Then Gwylym had joined his master in the far-off, frozen place where that unquiet spirit had chosen to dwell.

*

Myrddion and his party avoided the city of Ravenna, choosing instead to travel directly to the port. The sooner they found a ship leaving for Constantinople, the faster they would be safe.

Ravenna's port was very large, capable of mooring two hundred and fifty naval fighting galleys at the height of the Empire's power. Now, the port hosted a steady stream of trade goods to and from Constantinople, Greece and Asia Minor.

Like all major ports, the town was a refuge for sailors who were seeking new berths or were running from the consequences of their crimes. A slew of disreputable men could be found at any of the dirty, primitive inns that lined the wharves and these villains could be hired to commit almost any wickedness. Unlike Massilia, which had been colourful and exotic, the port of Ravenna reeked of danger and dead fish.

Myrddion planned to pay for passage on the first available galley travelling to Constantinople. In a stinking, sod-floored inn on the edge of the harbour district, the three healers finally found a captain willing to take them aboard, but Myrddion was shocked at the price the man demanded.

'You can take it or leave it. You're not the only fellows eager to escape Italia, now that Valentinian is dead. I've several passengers who are fearful for their lives and desperate to leave Ravenna. If you don't take the berths, someone else will.'

'Very well, but I insist on two cabins if we are to pay this huge amount,' Myrddion snapped, his face showing his exasperation.

Cadoc realised that the captain was about to refuse Myrddion's peremptory demand, so the Celt donned his most obsequious manner.

'You're fortunate, sir, to be in the presence of Myrddion Emrys of Segontium. He is a healer of great renown. We travel to Constantinople to serve a noble patient, Lord Cleoxenes of the royal court, the senior envoy of the Eastern Empire and a favourite of the emperor himself. You need have no doubt that if you oblige Master Myrddion, then Lord Cleoxenes will be very grateful. I am quite certain that if you should have problems with the authorities at any time in the future, Lord Cleoxenes will prove to be a valuable mediator on your behalf.'

Even this blandishment would not have worked, for the captain was three parts drunk and inclined to be belligerent. Myrddion took his cue from Cadoc and promised to add a free bonus for the captain and his crew. 'Of course, we would agree to care for the health of yourself and your crew, at no charge, during the voyage.'

The captain stared at Myrddion craftily. 'The whole crew? Including the cook and the galley slaves?'

Myrddion sighed. The men who powered the oars on these galleys died like flies because of cramped quarters, poor food and bad hygiene. But beggars couldn't be choosers, and two cabins were necessary if any comfort were to be had on what could be a long and arduous voyage.

'Very well – all!' A quick handshake sealed the bargain, and the healers returned to the campsite.

Once again, Cadoc sold the horses and the wagons, and the fears of the population of Ravenna served to make him a good profit from the transactions. Whole families who lacked the price of a sea passage out of Italia were seeking to head northward as quickly as they could, so the healer's wagons were fought over and the funds that Cadoc obtained helped to redress the exorbitant cost of the voyage. Finally, with all their possessions stowed in their two cabins, the healers and their women prepared to embark.

With a clatter of iron-tipped sandals, four burly men carried a litter down to the quayside. They were followed by a large carriage piled high with boxes and trunks, all firmly tied down with rope. In response to barely polite requests from the cavalcade's servants, who were armed with long staves, the healers and the widows stood aside so a lady could disembark from her litter and climb the gangplank onto the ancient galley, which sported the imposing name of *Neptune's Trident*.

The watchers' first sight of the lady was a perfumed foot in a fine, high-laced sandal. Myrddion noticed that the soles of her feet had been rouged. The slim, tall form slid down from the litter and rested one hand on the arm of the nearest servant for balance. Her features were hidden behind a gauze veil of sea green that matched a peplum and robe of an exceptional fabric. The hand that rested briefly on her servant's bronzed arm was slender and beautiful, although slightly large for a woman. The nails were neatly maintained and stained a rosy shade of pink, and the palms were hennaed.

'Eeeeyaah!' Cadoc breathed. 'Now that is one perfect piece of woman flesh.'

The woman threw back her veil as she climbed the gangplank and Myrddion recognised the mass of red and auburn hair that cascaded down her back. His heart skipped a beat when he saw the broad shoulders set above the delicate breasts and the ridiculously tiny waist. Then, as his eyes pounded with the blood in his veins, the lady turned and revealed a proud, long-nosed face softened by the expert use of cosmetics.

'Yes, and the woman you see is Flavia, wife of Thraustila

and daughter of Flavius Aetius,' Myrddion whispered, as Flavia met his eyes and smiled slowly. 'May Fortuna save us.'

For an instant, the world reeled round Myrddion and he felt like a beardless boy in love with his first girl. Flavia had changed in the three years since they had first met, and now she was a miracle of beautiful artifice. Once again, Myrddion smelled the hot scent of sweet oranges, pine needles and warmed marble, and he was transported back to a garden in Châlons.

'In that case, Constantinople can't come soon enough!' Cadoc exclaimed under his breath as he herded the women up the gangplank. Boxes and trunks were unloaded from the carriage and prepared for storage on the galley. Myrddion followed and went straight to the men's cabin, where he prayed that Flavia would leave him in peace.

But the youth who still lived under his natural solemnity sang with excitement while, despite his most earnest wishes, his loins began to tighten. A sea voyage was just the place to learn to know Flavia better – and, perhaps, to remove her from his thoughts forever.

MYRDDION'S CHART OF THE VOYAGE FROM RAVENNA TO MARATHON

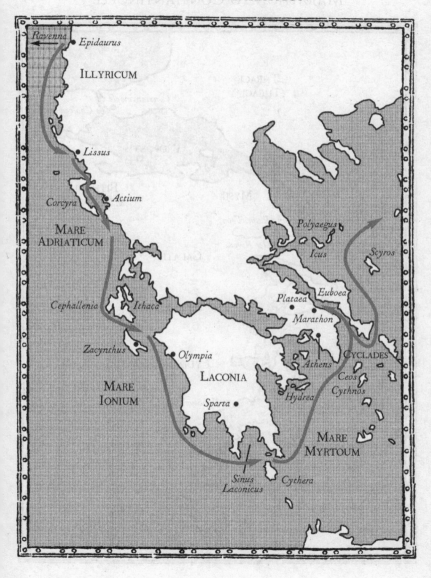

MYRDDION'S CHART OF THE VOYAGE FROM MARATHON TO CONSTANTINOPLE

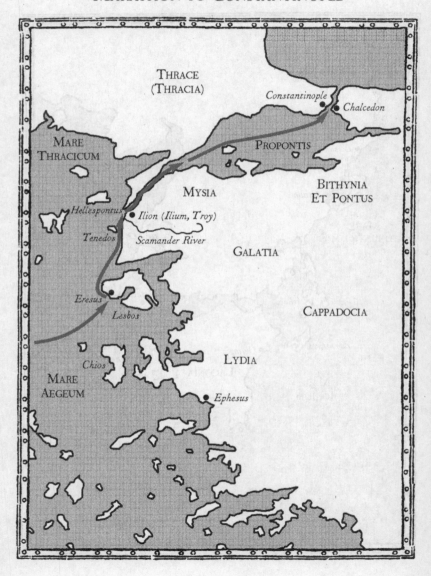

CHAPTER XIX

THE SIRENS SINGING

For the first week out of Ravenna, a fair wind sent the galley running briskly on the first leg of the journey that would take them to Epidaurus. Myrddion found himself drowning, not in the deep waters, but in his own tangled and confused emotions. The sea was very blue, shading to deep purple, colours that reminded the healer of Homer's description of the wine dark sea. Then he chastised himself, for Homer had spoken of the Mare Aegeum in the east rather than the Mare Adriaticum.

The ship ploughed across the wide, empty sea, heading for the coast of Illyricum and Epidaurus, where the galley would take on fresh water and supplies before heading south along the coast of ancient Greece. Catching any breath of wind in its great sail, *Neptune's Trident* pounded through the waves with all the grace of a duck, except when the oars were employed and the wide-bellied vessel fairly flew through the turbulent waters.

For the first few days of the journey, Myrddion was spared the distracting presence of Flavia, for the crossing was extremely rough and seasickness prostrated many of the passengers. As on the Litus Saxonicum, Cadoc suffered greatly and lay below decks, pale, wan and miserable.

Within her cabin, Flavia and her maid also suffered, but neither lady chose to expose the drawn face of illness to the small society of the galley. At any rate, the treatment for seasickness was always the same, so Myrddion ensured that all the sufferers sipped as much boiled water as they were able to keep down. Without food, a patient would weaken after several weeks: without water, a patient would die within days.

By the end of the first week, trembling and pale, the sufferers had improved sufficiently to enjoy the cleansing sea air, and as the galley was approaching Epidaurus they staggered above decks for a welcome change from the unvarying boredom of life in claustrophobic cabins. Myrddion discovered quickly that even seabirds on the wing became welcome diversions on days when only blue-green sea could be seen from one horizon to the other.

When Flavia eventually staggered out of her self-imposed sick bed, she was interestingly pale and seemed to have lost weight, so that she was almost as insubstantial as thistle-down. Myrddion was shocked by her pallor under the clever artifice of her cosmetics, and was touched by the bravado that drove her onto the decking, where she leaned against a mast out of view of the busy sailors who were bringing the galley about in preparation for a change of course to make landfall. Her careful coiffure was torn to long elflocks by the land breeze, but Myrddion decided that her beauty was enhanced by the tangle of russet curls around her face.

'Well, healer, we seem to meet under the most inauspicious circumstances,' she murmured softly, so that he was forced to lean forward to hear her. A heavy, musky perfume was trapped in her hair and in the delicate folds of her flesh, so that Myrddion felt her sexual pull, as potent as an aphrodisiac.

'Yes. We were landing at Ostia when last we met – and you were to be married.'

He ran his eyes over her tall, slender frame and realised that she had gained in beauty over the two years since their last meeting. She appeared to be more womanly and softer, as if circumstances had worn away her rough and abrasive edges.

'Ah, yes, my marriage to Thraustila. Father was forever scheming, so I became a chattel that could be used to cement an alliance with the Hun nobles. My father was clever, although he was remiss when he ignored your warnings about hubris. How does it feel to have been right all along?'

Flavia's mismatched eyes were mocking. He had forgotten the curious attraction of her one blue eye and the other that was a vivid green. Something glinted in the clear depths of those irises and Myrddion's instincts twitched a sudden warning.

'My prophecy was right, not I. I have no control over what I say at such times.'

'So meek, yet so lacking in vanity, Myrddion? My, how Father would rage if he was alive to see how the game finally played out. He reached too high, didn't he? Oh, well, Father was always his own man, and if hubris became his downfall, it had worked in his favour often enough in his past.'

'Aye, Lady Flavia, it worked in his favour his life long.'

'Let us speak of more pleasant subjects, for I'm wondering why you're going to Constantinople.'

Her full mouth had been stained a delicate rose pink so that her tongue appeared wholly erotic as it moistened her lips. Instinctively, Myrddion decided to avoid telling her of his quest to find his own father.

As the galley pulled into the wharf, a bronzed, half-naked sailor leapt onto the quay to tie off the rope that tethered it to the land. As he watched, Myrddion wished that affairs of the heart were so easily solved. Flavia was a sweet poison, a clever atrophy of the brain that sought out his reason and numbed it while she ensnared him with her extraordinary eyes. If only he could take her body casually and then have done with her.

'Did you know that my husband was one of the men who murdered Valentinian? I suppose he'll be dead soon as well. That's how I'll be remembered . . . as Thraustila's wife and Aetius's daughter. Is that all I am?'

Flavia spoke reflectively but even Myrddion's unsympathetic gaze discerned the bitterness below her words.

'How could anyone hope for more than to be remembered? Most of us will disappear in the great waters of time as if we had never been born.'

She laughed with all the arrogance of the old Flavia and her tossed head and aura of confidence stirred Myrddion's admiration. 'But not you, Myrddion-no-name. You will be remembered for something other than whom you marry or who sired you. In fact, I foretell . . . How does it feel to wonder what your future will bring?'

'I cannot match wits with you, Lady Flavia. I fear you are too clever for me – you always were.'

She laughed again, and the pleasant, contralto voice was laced with irony. 'Clever enough to accept Thraustila, a Hungvari simpleton, and to sit in Ravenna watching the Roman world split at the seams like an old tunic.' She nodded reflectively. 'Aye, I'm far too clever for you. Oh, to be young and green again, my Myrddion!' She turned her face away and the healer knew he had been dismissed from her brooding thoughts.

He walked away and returned to his cramped cabin. Nor did he re-emerge until after dusk fell and Flavia was safely below decks.

The ship left Epidaurus and took up a southerly heading to avoid the coastal strip where the land rose steeply into the jagged teeth of the mountains without the leavening of a strip of arable land at their feet. Straight from the shoreline, the mountains sheered upward, cut by the occasional river that ran in cataracts into the sea. Lissus passed, and the sapphire isle of Corcyra, followed by Actium and the jewelled islands of Cephallenia, Ithaca and Zacynthus that rose out of the Middle Sea like velvet green jewels on a cloth of deepest blue. The names sang in Myrddion's head with all the musicality and romance of the distant past. Homer could have seen these mountains and alluvial valleys before he lost his eyes. The fleets of Darius and Xerxes sailed among these dim islands as they sought weaknesses in the Greek defences. Wondrous names echoed in Myrddion's imagination, the sound of the marching feet of the hoplites as the phalanxes came to famed Thermopylae or glorious Plataea and created the history of the west, long before the people of Britain emerged out of caverns and raised the stones of the Giant's Dance at Stonehenge.

Here was history in every colourful, precarious village that clung to the forbidding coast. Here rang the echoes of conflicts fought in desperation and fierce loyalty over stretches of land too narrow and too mountainous to grow food and to bear new life. Here, history walked and still lived within human memory, although the men who had thought, fought and perished now existed only on scrolls or in the tales of peasants who still struggled as they tilled the soil in the ancient ways. Perhaps it was the dying glory of the land on their left, as it unrolled before their fascinated gaze, that stilled the small voice of reason in Myrddion's brain. Perhaps the fishermen who passed them in boats so flimsy that the Roman god Neptune could have struck them down with a single, violent wave reminded the young healer that life is fleeting and fragile, so experiences must be grasped and savoured before the sea drowned them all. Perhaps . . . perhaps . . . But Myrddion felt a sea change of recklessness rising in his blood like a hidden leviathan that was fighting its way towards the light.

One evening, as the galley drove towards the east with the great island of Cythera to the right and the broken teeth of Laconia to the left, Myrddion sat on a folded pile of canvas sails and stared out at the phosphorus-edged wavelets as they moved and slapped against the hull. The galley was quiet and the oars were at rest because wind filled the great sail, causing it to slap and rattle against its rigging. He was considering the wondrous and terrifying history of Sparta, the prime city-state of Laconia, with its dour warriors who had sacrificed their personal freedom to the machine of war. Although his thoughts were of bloody deeds of glory, peace enveloped him in a night that was lit by millions of stars. Had he known the lineaments of the constellations, he would have been able to trace the form of Andromeda, the Archer, or the Naiads as they wheeled in the sky for eternity. Their names filled his mind with resonances of wisdom and tragedies that were long gone, so that his heart was full of magic and sadness.

Suddenly, out of fragments of memory, a line of verse came to him. He recited it aloud in the original Greek in what he hoped was a reasonable approximation of the correct pronunciation.

'What did you say, Myrddion?' A female voice carried to

him on the sweet, salty air. Flavia stepped away from the shadow of the rigging, and he could see the outline of her body lit through her robes from a single lantern that hung on the mast behind her.

'Those whom the gods would destroy, they first make mad.'

Her laughter was wry, bitter, and yet as tinkling as the small brass bells that hung in the temples of the Mother, where they could catch the night winds and sing her name.

'Gloomy thoughts for a night of such magic! Can't you feel the ancient loves and dreams that lived here long before Rome came into being? So old, Myrddion! Our ancestors scrabbled like animals in the mud at a time when Athens spawned philosophers and Sparta made warfare into living song. How can you celebrate such beauty with so grim a warning?'

'Perhaps I'm trying to remind myself that all this . . .' he flung his arms wide to encompass the land, the sea and the wheeling, velvet-soft stars, 'this is all illusion! We struggle and scheme to win a small corner of the world and to gather up gold or jewels to protect us from the darkness that we fear, when all that truly endures through the ages are the shadows of our deeds and the generosity of our spirits.'

Flavia sighed and swayed towards him so that the lamp picked out the scarlet in her hair like threads of ruby and chalcedony. 'You think too much, healer. I believe I've told you so before. On a night such as this, how can you do aught but accept the power of your senses? Smell the scent off the land! Can't you imagine the olives ripening in the sun, the fish drying in racks and bunches of lavender perfuming the air? Can't you feel the wind as it caresses your naked flesh like a lover's touch? The gods give us eyes to see and ears to hear, but you persist in experiencing the world through the filter of your reason and your dusty scrolls. My father was the same. You miss the glories of being alive and being human, while you chase something abstract and impossible to define. Then, when you realise that knowledge is just another illusion, it's too late to taste the sweetness of living.'

'Why, Flavia, you surprise me,' Myrddion murmured without a trace of irony in his beautifully modulated voice. 'I never thought I'd hear philosophy coming from your lips.'

'Because I'm a woman – or because I'm Flavius Aetius's daughter? Am I any less capable of seeing the wonders of existence simply because I'm my father's daughter?' She made a small gesture of disgust. 'In Ravenna, they called me a harlot or an epicurean, because I want to experience all that life brings before I journey to the shadows. One life isn't enough to satisfy me, Myrddion. I'd live forever, if I could.' The healer could see her wilful, passionate mouth through the stray beams of moonlight. 'I want to devour life as if it was a ripe peach and feel its juices run down my face. Is that so wrong?'

Her appeal touched him, and involuntarily he stepped towards her. Wise to the passions of men, she took a half-step towards him and raised her hand to stroke his smooth, beardless face. Her pointed nails tracked deliciously over his cheek and his breath caught in his throat.

'Don't think, Myrddion. Be!'

And then Flavia was in his arms and her mouth was opening under his, as silky as the finest cloth and so smooth and warm that he couldn't resist her. Tongue and teeth captured his, teasing and biting as his heat rose and his work-strengthened fingers gripped her back, kneading her soft flesh and leaving bruises in their wake.

She pulled away from him and tilted her head so that she could see his blinded eyes, heavy with his body's longings. 'You have put aside your reason, healer. Will you regret what we do? Will you blame me for a night of beauty or love? If so, leave me now to the night and my feelings, for I am weary of recriminations.'

For a moment, Myrddion wondered at the courage and frankness of this woman who perceived herself to be outside the rules of society, not by choice, but because she was unable to adapt to the many hypocritical demands of her peers. He believed her. She really placed sensation above reason, a dangerous journey for even the strongest of men, for that path could lead to a life so dedicated to the senses that common sense and decency were lost.

'You'll receive no insults from me, Flavia, not if you act in accordance with kindness and compassion. I suppose you're a free soul . . . it must have been difficult to grow up under the rule of a man like Aetius, who was rigidly in control of every aspect of his life.'

Flavia shook her head with such finality that Myrddion sensed the heartbreak under her arrogance. His reason told him that Flavia was too damaged to change, but his body didn't care for arguments.

'No more talk, Myrddion. You use words like weapons. Just be, and let me be.' Then she moved back into his arms and their kiss was full of promise and hope. Flavia was demanding, with her mouth and with her hands, which stroked and insinuated themselves into his tunic and kneaded the muscles at his shoulders, back and buttocks. Only by an effort of will, and out of a need to remain Myrddion, did he pull away from her and bow over her hand, before kissing it gently.

'Goodnight, Lady Flavia. The night is lovely, but I must go before I make a fool of myself.' He almost ran to the stairs that led below decks, found the healers' cabin and leaned against the closed door. Cadoc stared at his master with wide, alarmed eyes.

'Don't fret, Cadoc. I've been enjoying the evening in company with Lady Flavia.'

Cadoc noted a long, shallow scratch on Myrddion's forearm, and leered knowingly. 'I can see what you've been enjoying, master. All that I'll say is that you should be careful with a woman like that. Ayeee! She'd suck a man's brains out through his mouth.'

'Don't say that, Cadoc, even in jest,' Myrddion cut in, but being young and vain enough to enjoy the admiration of other, older men, he allowed himself a small grin. He went to sleep on his scratchy pallet to dream of Flavia's thighs, her milky white breasts with their dusting of amber freckles and the rose pink crevices of her body that drew him towards her with a hot, musky scent that was all her own.

The galley drove on and was now heading north through the islands of the Mare Myrtoum. On the high ground to the left lay Sparta, out of sight but brooding over the south with all its reputation for discipline, unnatural courage and stirring deeds of heroism. Myrddion told Cadoc, Finn and the widows the story of Thermopylae and they marvelled at the stirring history of the three hundred Spartans who had held back a vast horde of invaders. As the galley continued across the sea, Myrddion dug into his store of legends and whiled away the hours of inactivity with tales of the ancients, what histories he knew and improbable tales of incredible courage.

Hydrea slid by and vanished into the distance. Cythnos and Ceos passed on their right, the northern tip of the famed

Cyclades where the souls of heroes were said to dwell. Then the galley pushed on to Marathon to take on a fresh supply of water before island-hopping across the Aegean Sea en route to the Propontis.

Although the days were a changing vista of many islands and dim, smoke-blue landscapes, the nights belonged to Flavia.

Though Myrddion might have hoped to resist her advances, in Cadoc's words, he had as much chance as a plump pigeon in a cage of peregrines. After an initial attempt at resistance, he submitted to his desires and took Flavia, rather inexpertly, in her narrow cabin among a pile of scented bedclothes. He had believed that to enjoy her body would free him from her thrall as had been his past experience, but Flavia was a fever in the blood, a disease in the mind and a poison in the heart. The more she kissed him, the more he wanted. When he had spent himself in her, the lust that should have sated him only served to whet his appetite more cruelly.

The nights were long and filled with wild sensations, but the days were governed by his craft. Sailors slipped often and he was kept busy with cuts, contusions and even the occasional illness. His assistants worked on their herbs, storing a fresh supply of completed unguents, fleshed out with new, strange ingredients purchased at the ports, fishing villages and islands where they picked up cargo or replenished their supplies of water.

As her waist began to thicken, Bridie sat among the women in the fresh air and sewed delicate baby clothes out of scraps of cloth. Each day fitted seamlessly into the next, like wool on a loom, and Myrddion prayed with a young man's ardour that the voyage would never end. He had his scrolls, now more interesting because he could see the lands that brought them forth, and he had his growing store of odd maps that recorded their journey. Even his ritual of plucking hair from his smooth skin, washing in salt water on the decks or combing and plaiting his midnight-blue mane assumed a kind of novelty.

So Myrddion began an odd double life, as strange as Flavia's mismatched eyes. The lovers spoke little, preferring to lose themselves in sensation. Besides, Myrddion feared to break the spell of Flavia, knowing in the deepest recesses of his heart that he would try to excise her from his life if he should learn the full measure of her manipulations and misdeeds. He was tortured by a persistent fear that something in him would bleed forever.

At Marathon, both Myrddion and Flavia left the galley, after a stern warning from the master that he must set sail quickly if the ship was to escape the tidal pull of Euboea, a huge land mass that ran parallel to the mainland. But the town of Marathon called to Myrddion with stories of Pheidippides who had run from the port to Athens to bring tidings of a great sea battle and, after imparting his news, had run back to Marathon without pause. Shortly after completing the return journey, he had died. The duty inherent in this tale of bravery and determination touched Myrddion's nature, so he longed to see the landscape on which such epics of the human spirit were based.

On the other hand, Flavia longed to purchase something pretty to adorn her throat, so Myrddion offered her his protection. Rouged and perfumed, the lady avoided the piles of refuse, old fish heads, fish scales and rubbish that fouled the wharf. Marathon itself lay slightly inland on the higher ground and was too far to visit, so Myrddion swallowed his disappointment and took pleasure in watching Flavia as she haggled with street sellers who tried to tempt her with trinkets of base metal. Eventually, she found a dark cavern of a shop-front that promised Greek jewellery within. Like a roe deer seeking sweet grass, she dived into its cool interior.

At first, Myrddion sat on his heels outside the unprepossessing premises but, out of sheer boredom, he eventually followed his lover into its dim recesses to remind her that they must hurry. He found Flavia poring over a strip of scarlet cloth on which lay bangles of heavy gold carved to resemble twining fish and a necklace that was a scaled serpent with a clasp shaped like a head swallowing its own tail. Its eyes were ruby chips and small, round emeralds decorated its spiny back.

'Buy the damned thing if you like it, Flavia, but hurry! The galley will sail without us if you don't make haste.'

'A moment, Myrddion. The captain wouldn't dare to sail without us. He has high hopes of a substantial sum at the end of the journey, if I'm satisfied with his services.'

Myrddion wandered around a whitewashed room that was far cleaner than its exterior suggested, except for spider's webs that lurked in corners out of reach. The dim shelves concealed all kinds of merchandise in a wild tangle that seemed without logic or order. Painted pots in blood red, black and white jostled with weavings of warriors and maidens that had been crudely coloured with vegetable dyes. In one dusty corner, a collection of pottery and carved wooden gods looked down with impassive, blind eyes, including a tall staff shaped like a sea serpent with a carved frill and fins encircling its scaly throat. The wood was unfamiliar and as smooth as silk.

'A fair piece of carving, master,' a voice croaked at him from out of the gloom.

Myrddion spun round and the staff fell to the packed sod floor with a dull clatter. The face that loomed out of the darkness was old and seamed with wrinkles, and the eyes were white and blind with cataracts. At first, Myrddion thought that the wizened creature was a man, but then it moved forward into a narrow strip of light from the doorway and revealed the dusty, bleached robes of a woman.

'How much is the stave, mother?' Myrddion asked, for in truth it attracted him strongly.

The old woman named a price that seemed fair, and although Myrddion knew he should haggle with her he was overly conscious of the swift passage of time. Searching through his satchel, he found the coin to pay what she asked and pressed them into her gnarled and twisted hands.

When their fingertips met, he felt an immediate jolt of precognition.

'Ah, master, I'll not need to read the portents for you. The Mother Serpent sits by your shoulder.' She paused, and her nostrils twitched as if she smelt the air. 'Beware of your woman, master. She may be rose-red, but like all pretty flowers her thorns are wicked and barbed. She will leave you weeping at the end of your journey.'

'You are a terrible old woman,' Flavia hissed from behind Myrddion's shoulder. 'How can you tell such lies?'

The old woman turned her milky irises towards the sound of Flavia's voice and smiled, revealing browned and broken teeth.

'Do I lie? You have learned to sell yourself to the highest bidder, but you still don't know your worth, Woman of Straw. You might deck yourself in gems and drape yourself in gold, but until in your heart you believe what you say, you will wander without a home or a man you can call your own.'

Flavia scoffed, but Myrddion could detect a faint tremor in her voice. When the old woman turned her wizened face back towards Myrddion, her features fell into a kinder expression. Chilled, Myrddion wondered if he was staring at the most terrible aspect of the Mother, the Crone of Winter.

'Remember, master, that you are like your father, but you don't have to be him. The gods decreed at your birth that you have free will, so you need not follow the ancient and wicked patterns of your bloodline. See what is real, not what your heart longs to see. Choose wisely, or you will never know your home again and a great destiny will be lost for all time.'

'Pay this charlatan so we can get out of this pesthole,' Flavia ordered rudely, turning away with the serpent necklace round her throat. The old woman was affronted and made a strange sign with her fingers behind Flavia's back.

'I will take no coin for what I have seen. You should beware that the serpent doesn't bite you when you least expect it, Woman of Straw. Beware of the eagle and the snake, woman, or you will die.'

With the old woman's words and the cackle of her laughter ringing in his ears, Myrddion fled from the mean little establishment and found he was gasping in the open air. Flavia was already disappearing down the narrow, cobbled street towards the wharf, her speed fuelled by temper, so Myrddion was forced to run to catch up with her.

'Now you know what it's like when someone tells your future. How does it feel, healer?'

For several days, Myrddion and Flavia avoided each other on the galley. The lady chose to eat in her cabin and Myrddion was kept busy caring for an outbreak of dysentery that had struck down the sailors and the galley slaves. The crowded conditions in the double banks of oars were unhygienic and filthy, so Myrddion ordered the whole space to be sluiced with seawater and scrubbed clean. The same treatment was given to the malodorous quarters deep in the belly of the ship where the slaves were shackled and the sailors slept in filthy straw. Gradually, under the twin cures of cleanliness and purgatives, Myrddion controlled the vicious spread of the stomach contagion, while he comforted himself with the knowledge that the disease wasn't more serious.

When he was finally able to assure the captain that the dysentery had passed, the galley had moved past Scyros, Icus and Polyaegus and was beating out into open waters as they headed towards the great island of Lesbos and landfall at Eresus. The captain was more able than most of his ilk and chose to cross open water, steering by the angle of the sun by day and by the points of the stars at night.

The sea was wide and very dark, like purple wine, and so still that at noontide Myrddion imagined he could see the reflection of clouds in its deep waters. The sun never seemed to dim in a sky that was so bright and so blue that the colour hurt Myrddion's eyes, while even the sunsets became glorious panoramas of gold, amber, scarlet and orange when the sea was set aflame. Myrddion felt a peace he had rarely known during his short life. For the first time in many months, he didn't regret the impulse that had driven him to leave Segontium for these strange climes.

Inevitably, Flavia and Myrddion renewed their passion, although his lady seemed to seek him out for comfort and affirmation of her worth rather than out of an overriding lust. He wondered occasionally if she even cared for sexual congress, considering their coupling merely as proof of her power and her attractiveness. She also chose to talk in the long, dark reaches of the night when the fires of the spirit burn dimly, as if she needed someone in the world who would understand the motivation that drove her to trade her body for feelings of adequacy.

When she revealed to Myrddion that her father and brother had awakened her into womanhood, the healer was appalled and sickened. That Flavia was only ten at the time added to the betrayal that the child had endured.

'It's a pity that Aetius is dead. He should have been made to suffer for what he did to you. From what you have told me, he died quickly and relatively painlessly. As for your brother Gaudentius, the Christian god has promised special punishment for such sins. I could almost wish myself to be Christian so I could pray for such justice.'

Flavia had wept and drawn comfort from Myrddion's sympathy, but she shared nothing else of a private nature with him. She remained a tightly rolled scroll, since enemies might find tools with which to torture her if she revealed too much.

Lesbos, the famous island celebrated for its ancient society of women, hove into view like a large hollowed triangle of green valleys and soft hills. So many places had swum through Myrddion's experiences that only the rudimentary maps that he continued to create could keep all the exotic places separate in his mind.

With fresh water and supplies of food on board after a brisk trading of Roman glass and pottery in exchange for amphorae of oil and wine, *Neptune's Trident* skirted Lesbos and headed for the Propontis, the inland sea that led to Constantinople. The names now had a glister of Asian strangeness – Lemnos, Hephaestia and the famed River Scamander where it flowed into the salt waters. There, on the heights, Myrddion could see a Roman temple gleaming whitely in the sunshine, and pointed it out to Cadoc and Finn.

'See how the temple glows in the sunlight as if it is lit from within. There, on the mount, is the famed city of Troy, which is also called Ilion by the local populace. It was there that Priam watched his son die in battle against Achilles, while his daughter, Cassandra, was thrown down from the walls because the Greeks feared her powers of prophecy. All for the sake of a beautiful woman called Helen!'

'Nothing ever changes, master,' Finn murmured, his eyes wide and glowing from the tales he had heard. 'For love, we tear down any obstacles in our path.'

Cadoc opened his mouth to joke, but Finn stepped sharply on his foot. Myrddion understood. His assistants feared that, like the Trojans, he was being led to ruin by a beautiful, flawed woman.

Perhaps I am, Myrddion thought, but he was so lost in the web of Flavia's complex personality that he no longer cared.

The Hellespontus was very narrow and the galley was now accompanied by a flotilla of ships of all kinds as they sailed through the channel towards the fabled city of Constantine. Once they had passed into the Propontis, they stayed within sight of land. The countryside was rich and adorned with groves of orange and lemon trees, huge swathes of olives on the higher ground and farms that clustered on the hills like neat, whitewashed boxes. Fishing boats strained under the weight of huge catches of fish and crustaceans, and everywhere the travellers looked they saw evidence of industry, wealth and rich trade heading for Constantinople from many far-flung nations.

Then, as dusk fell, lights filled the northern horizon ahead of them in a wide arc that almost dimmed the stars.

'What lies ahead?' a curious Myrddion asked the captain, as they lounged against the rail and enjoyed the evening air.

The man laughed through the bushy black beard that gave him a sinister air.

'I thought you knew, master healer. You will soon gaze on the Golden Horn. Ahead lies the jewel of the east – the lights of Constantinople. Tomorrow, we dock in the city.'

'Constantinople!' Myrddion breathed, and his heart sang in wonderment that the whole, interminable journey was finally coming to an end.

MYRDDION'S CHART OF CONSTANTINOPLE
AND ITS ENVIRONS

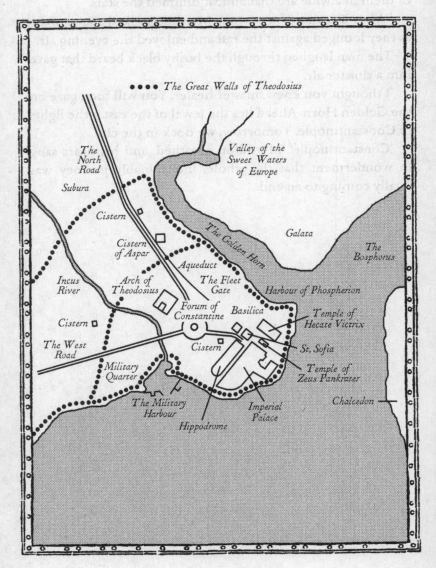

• • • • *The Great Walls of Theodosius*

The North Road

Subura

Cistern

Cistern of Aspar

Incus River

Arch of Theodosius

Cistern

The West Road

Military Quarter

The Military Harbour

Hippodrome

Forum of Constantine

Cistern

Aqueduct

The Fleet Gate

Valley of the Sweet Waters of Europe

The Golden Horn

Galata

The Bosphorus

Harbour of Phospherion

Basilica

Temple of Hecate Victrix

St. Sofia

Temple of Zeus Pankrater

Imperial Palace

Chalcedon

CHAPTER XX

THE GOLDEN HORN

The ship had sailed to the far end of the Propontis during the night, and a glistening summer sunrise rose over a city that spread across the narrow channel separating the Propontis from the huge inland sea called Pontus Euxinus. This narrow channel, wide and deep enough to permit the largest galleys to gain entrance to the vast inland sea, was called the Bosphorus.

'And that, young healer, is the Golden Horn,' the captain announced expansively.

Myrddion saw the huge flotilla of ships of all shapes, sizes and points of origin as they rounded the peninsula of land that protruded out into the Propontis. Here, Constantinople was built. A large natural harbour lay around the point of a sickle-shaped channel of water that divided the city from its sisters, Chalcedon and Galata, across the Propontis and the Horn.

The early light revealed wonders. A vast military harbour with special gates to protect its entry hove into view, filled with fighting vessels drawn up in orderly rows. As far as Myrddion could tell, a massive wall protected the promontory, although marble buildings were visible behind it. Still, an impregnable fortress of stone faced blankly towards the

Propontis, with the land rising in terraces above it. The galley rounded the point and the full wonders of Constantinople appeared before them. Light glowed softly on roseate marble and kissed the roofs of the city with a glimmer of gold. The rising sun gilded the rigging of ships and the black shapes of galleys were rimed with light. Myrddion's heart almost stopped with the beauty of the scene.

The captain of the galley was feeling in an expansive mood. He had reached his destination without major incident, his hold was filled to bursting with luxury goods from Italia and Greece, and he was already counting the sum he would receive from his noble passenger, Flavia, for making a safe landfall. Consequently, he was quite prepared to explain the importance of Constantinople to the worlds of the east and the west.

'You must understand, healer, the strategic value of this city. The Pontus Euxinus is huge and is ringed by great and alien nations such as Armenia, Dacia, Sarmatia, Cappadocia and the Parthian Empire. It lies along the direct route leading to the far-off silk and spice lands, so this city is the great trade centre where west merges with east. Without Constantinople, where would we find silk, fine cloth, exotic dyes, the strange scented woods from the distant lands of the east and perfumes that blind the senses?'

'I fully understand, master mariner. Constantinople is a conduit through which trade goods and culture pass in both directions,' Myrddion summarised. 'I can see that it is ideally situated for commercial and political power. What languages are spoken here?'

Myrddion was now a seasoned traveller and understood that communication was a vital tool for any stranger. In a city such as Constantinople, a man who could not be understood was virtually deaf and dumb.

'The aristocrats speak Latin, of course, as a sop to Constantinople's Roman origins, but to be understood in this city you will need to speak Greek. The Macedonians under Alexander were the first to see Constantinople's importance, so it's not surprising that while its inhabitants call it Imperium Romanorum, its neighbours refer to it as Imperium Graecorum, or the Empire of the Greeks. If you can speak Latin and Greek, you will have no difficulty, even in the roughest, most eastern quarters.'

'My Greek is learned from reading, so I don't know the correct pronunciations,' Myrddion murmured, his doubt rekindled by the captain's explanation. 'Will I be able to make my needs known to the citizens?'

'I don't see why not.' The captain was becoming impatient, bored and unwilling to gossip over trifles. 'You'll be understood if you can speak passable Greek, even if it sounds vile. The shopkeepers have to understand traders from the Indus or from beyond the columns at the end of the world and the Roof of Heaven. You'll get by.'

Briskly, the captain excused himself and strode away to oversee the complex details of docking the vessel.

Left alone, and without the distractions of other passengers, Myrddion watched the details of the vast city sharpen as the sun rose. Constantinople was beautiful, with fine marble structures built along the waterfront where Myrddion was accustomed to scenes of squalor in many western cities. The lure of fine views and cool breezes made the land closest to the sea the preferred sites for the palaces of the aristocracy and the wealthier citizens. Myrddion could see Roman and Greek columns of veined marble shining in the strengthening light, while the sandstone of ancient temples immediately attracted his attention. Low beams of sunlight were reflected from pools, fountains and decorative cascades, indicating that this was a city where water was plentiful and was used for beautification as well as the provision of drinking water.

Beyond the docks, in the commercial centres of the city, a swathe of plastered and rendered buildings marched backwards up slight hills. The land was mostly flat and Myrddion noted that trees, palms and gardens proliferated, even in the areas that housed the poorer citizens. A vast wall enclosed the central part of the city and Myrddion could tell that with water on three sides and a cyclopean wall of stone on the landward edge of the city environs, defence in time of war would make Constantinople almost impregnable.

The galley moved through the relatively still waters at speed, under the power of its two banks of oars. Myrddion never tired of watching the synchronised efficiency of the disciplined process of docking, so he noted every detail as *Neptune's Trident* sailed straight towards the dock on the left bank, threatening a disastrous collision in the process. At the very last second, the captain barked his orders, and the oars on the left side were feathered, raised and then drawn back into the vessel. At the same instant, the strokes of the right banks of oars were reversed with amazing smoothness. The galley stopped its forward motion, slowly slipped into reverse and then slid into the dock under its own momentum. Sailors leapt to the wharf and tied the vessel with huge ropes.

The long voyage from Ravenna to Constantinople was over. They had reached the Harbour of the Phospherion.

Myrddion and Flavia had said their farewells late the previous evening. Some belated sense of decorum prompted Flavia to insist that she should find refuge in the city of Constantine by herself. Myrddion, therefore, should wait until she sought him out.

'You'll forget me quickly enough, healer,' she had whispered against Myrddion's chest. A few tears slid down her cheek and Myrddion captured one on his finger and placed it on his lips.

'No, Flavia. I'll wait until you contact me, however long it takes.'

Flavia had lifted her chin and pushed him away with gentle hands. 'Don't depend on me, healer. My father would have been the first to tell you that I'm not to be trusted . . . and he was right. I'm not a woman made for hard times or troubles. I left my home, and when my husband returns, he will find his wife has flown the nest. I love you as much, or more, than I've ever loved anyone, but I don't believe I'm made to be loyal.'

Myrddion had reached for her in the darkness, his heart sad at the sound of defeat in her voice. 'No one needs to destroy your character, Flavia, because you do it all by yourself. Please, my dear, don't do this.'

Flavia hiccuped with distress. 'Don't say any more, Myrddion. Perhaps I'll see you in Constantinople and all will be well again.'

She had run from his arms then, her skirts swirling and her hair the only vital part of her that remained in his memory. She's searching for a better long-term prospect, Myrddion's rational self cautioned him. In truth, she'll only call for you again if she doesn't snare a wealthy, indulgent protector.

But the idealist in Myrddion, the sentimental part of him that Flavia touched, was convinced that their shared passion was more than just sensation and delight. He still had hope, for the day shone with promise.

*

As a temporary measure, Cadoc was sent to hire a wagon to transport their possessions to the best inn that could be found in the administrative centre of the city. Washed, brushed and wearing all his wealth on his body in a display of status, Myrddion assisted Finn and the women to take their possessions from their cabins to the dock. Then, with the women perched in relative comfort on their chests, Myrddion sought out a guide who could direct them to more permanent accommodation once he had located Cleoxenes. More than one dockworker stared at the tall, dark man with unbound hair bearing a serpent staff and wearing a barbarian sword at his waist.

On several occasions, Myrddion felt the eyes of his assistants rest on him with affection and anxiety. No one had commented on Flavia's absence. They simply watched him out of the corners of their eyes.

But there was no time for worries, fears for the future or doubts about a lover. Myrddion must work.

Using all his skills with Greek and with his judgement of human nature fully employed, Myrddion found, and rejected, a number of dark-complexioned men who were eager to serve him. Finally, he decided that a white-haired, muscular porter was suitable and the man was immediately taken on. The new servant, who went by the grandiose name of Praxiteles, was at least fifty years of age, but his cleanliness and the purity of his Greek suggested that he was a capable worker who had fallen on hard times.

Praxiteles was very brown of skin, which caused his white hair, curling beard and fierce moustache to contrast attractively with his complexion. His eyes were a startling bright blue with very clear whites, suggesting clean living and good health. His mouth was naturally red and he still possessed most of his teeth, which seemed cared for. Even Praxiteles's breath smelled sweet when Myrddion was close to him, and the healer noticed that his ragged tunic and leggings had been washed and bleached in the sun to a faded pale yellow and crisp white.

'You're hired, Praxiteles, for the duration of our visit to Constantinople. Do you have a family?'

'Aye, my lord. I have a grown son still living who is a baker. He gives me a pallet in his house because I have lacked the funds to own a home of my own since the death of my wife and daughters.'

The man held his head high, although Myrddion realised that such an admission must have wounded the porter's pride. Praxiteles was determined to explain his straitened circumstances, so Myrddion heard him out.

'I was a trader for most of my life, my lord, and never owed any man a single solidus in all my years of business. However, I fell on hard times when the vessel I owned was sunk off Ephesus and I was forced to repay the deposits that my clients had given me for the successful delivery of their cargoes. I cleared my debts, but I was left with nothing. Then an outbreak of fever killed my wife and two daughters, leaving me destitute and lonely.'

'I'm sorry to hear that, Praxiteles,' Myrddion murmured awkwardly. 'Sometimes the gods send harsh lessons to teach us how to live our lives.' What could anyone say to soften such dreadful blows of fate?

'Thank you, my lord, but the good God decides our destinies, and perhaps my wife is happier in heaven than enduring a life of grinding poverty. How can anyone know what God intends for us? Perhaps He intended me to serve you.'

'Perhaps,' Myrddion responded, and went on to discuss his

terms of employment with Praxiteles, who would be required to interpret for Cadoc and Finn, search out Cleoxenes and assist the women with all the heavy work.

Cadoc returned with a single wagon, so two trips would be needed to move their possessions to an inn. Praxiteles immediately proved his usefulness by suggesting an establishment within the city walls that was clean, refined and reasonably priced when its location was taken into account. He supervised their journey from the port to the inn and pointed out items of interest as they travelled along the route. Bridie, Brangaine, Rhedyn and Willa perched on top of the wagon with the trunks and boxes and stared wide-eyed at the busy bustle of the port. Finn remained behind at the dock to guard their remaining baggage.

'Look at how clean everything is here, master,' Brangaine marvelled. 'The open markets are well organised, and there's no rubbish in the streets.'

'Aye, and a good thing too,' Rhedyn agreed. 'It's so hot here that disease would soon breed in the garbage.'

Praxiteles looked puzzled at the strange language and asked what tongue they spoke.

'We come from the isles of Britain, far away beyond the Pillars of Hercules in the Middle Sea,' Myrddion explained. 'I am an Ordovice, and Brangaine comes from the Demetae tribe in a country called Cymru. Bridie is a Silure and Rhedyn is a Deceangli, like my grandmother. The child, Willa, is an orphan we treated after the sacking of Tournai by Attila's Huns. Our home country has many tribes, all with their own kings, but the land is ruled by a High King who has ultimate power over all the Britons.'

'So you aren't Christian then, master?' Praxiteles responded with a slight frown.

'No. We follow the old ways and worship many gods, but my whole allegiance is to the Mother. The Christ is worshipped in Britain by some, but most of us still worship the gods of our ancestors.'

Praxiteles stroked his magnificent moustache with one calloused forefinger. 'I see. You will find believers of all kinds in this city, although I follow the official religion of Christianity. No one is treated unfavourably because of their faith. The people of Constantinople are tolerant, although the emperor must follow the official religion. The state does not even permit Arian Christians to rule. Only the Christianity of Rome is considered legitimate for the emperor.'

'Such tolerance is rare,' Myrddion murmured, thinking of the artificial barriers that human beings erect between each other.

Praxiteles must have sensed that the conversation had strayed onto sensitive paths, for he changed the topic by pointing to the massive wall that encircled the central precincts of the city. 'See, master, there is the inner wall of Constantinople. In a few moments we will pass through the Northern Gate.'

Another, huge wall ran across the older sector of the city and extended from the Golden Horn over the peninsula and onward to the shores of the Propontis. This inner wall was nearly as large as the outer wall, several miles away, which Praxiteles explained was heavily fortified and guarded.

Praxiteles matched words with movement as he pointed to a long, winding structure with regular watchtowers that stood at least twenty to thirty feet in height. The walls were built of huge stones that had been positioned on a reinforced foundation and then mortared securely into position. The large stones decreased in size towards the top of the wall, and as they passed through a gate beautified with dressed stone the travellers realised that the whole structure was at least ten to twelve feet thick.

'This fortification is a wonder that rivals the buildings of Rome,' Myrddion whispered in Celt, and Praxiteles raised an enquiring eyebrow. 'My pardon, Praxiteles. I will practise my Greek on you, so you must tell me if I make errors in pronunciation.'

The journey through the wide, paved streets passed amicably as the young healer was instructed in the subtleties of the Greek language by his new servant. Praxiteles was an interesting man. Having been born in the country as the son of farmers, he had risen to prominence in the trading community through a wily, but honest, approach to business. When he had been reduced to penury he had begun again, thereby showing his courage and resilience. The more they talked, the more Myrddion warmed to him.

Open carpets of verdant grass were broken by groves of flowering and fragrant trees that were alien to British eyes, and all around them fountains splashed water melodically into deep ponds where large carp broke the surface and even turtles sunned themselves on ornamental rocks. Flowers bloomed everywhere in ordered profusion, while half-naked gardeners worked in the sunshine, shaded by large woven hats to ward off the bite of the sun.

Sunburned to a reddish hue and sweating in their dark, heavy clothing, the women fanned themselves vigorously as they attempted to assist the fitful breezes from the Golden Horn.

'The inn is past the inner wall and is a little inland, but the hostelry catches breezes from the water and is noted for the skill of its cooks,' Praxiteles assured them, and the women

thanked him in hesitant Latin. 'You can see Hagia Sophia and
the emperor's palace behind you from the top of the hill.
The basilica is a wonder.'

'What is Hagia Sophia?' Myrddion asked. The name was
exotic and beautiful, but the healer was unable to trace its
meaning.

'Hagia Sophia means the Great Church, and was named
when Constantine of blessed memory raised the first holy
place of that name on that spot. See?' Praxiteles turned on
the wagon seat and pointed behind them to the tip of the
promontory. A long, opulent palace hugged the walls on
the edge of the Propontis, and before it stood a Roman
basilica. As one, the Celts turned to stare back down the
North Road. 'This Hagia Sophia was built on the foundation
of Magna Ecclesia, which was burned to the ground in a riot
over fifty years ago. It's a lovely building, is it not?'

Myrddion stared at a roughly cruciform church with a
large marble portico which was decorated with a frieze of
twelve realistic lambs to represent the twelve apostles. The
white marble glistened in the sunlight and the short arms of
the church crossed at the nave, roughly in its centre. Although
the walls were of highly decorated and polished stone, the
roof was constructed of exotic woods. Fountains and trees
surrounded Hagia Sophia and a nearby structure called Hagia
Eirene, or Holy Peace, which Praxiteles explained was the
oldest Roman church in Constantinople.

'Very beautiful,' Myrddion began, only to be struck dumb
when his eye moved on to the large colonnaded palace
adjacent to the churches. The building backed onto the
water, and terraced gardens led down to the banks of
the Golden Horn.

'The palace,' Praxiteles explained unnecessarily. The

beauty of the large rambling structure screamed its importance.

For half an hour, the heavily laden cart drove down wide avenues until they reached a crossroads where an inn breasted the roadway and street markets attracted a steady stream of jostling customers. While Myrddion organised two rooms for his party, the women marvelled at exotic fruit and vegetables, pottery and eggs, while dressed goats, lambs, chickens and calves hung from hooks for the discerning buyer to pinch, prod and admire. Still another section of the market sold wine, a variety of cheeses, fish and crustaceans of all kinds, as well as brassware, carpets and lengths of cloth.

To the amazement of the women, another section of the market even sold live beasts. For the first time in their lives, they saw a camel.

Cadoc returned to the harbour with the wagon while Myrddion, the women and Praxiteles stowed their possessions in the two long rooms that Myrddion had procured. The healer was especially attracted by the large flat roof of the inn where guests could enjoy the long hot evenings in the open, fanned by the cool winds of the night. Praxiteles pointed out landmarks as they watched the traders organise their goods and thoroughly cleanse their flimsy market stalls. Even the animal dung was shovelled up and carried away to fertilise garden beds, so that customers never had to soil their skirts or foul their boots.

'Disturbing the peace or bespoiling public areas are punishable offences,' Praxiteles explained. 'This law ensures that the people will always keep their city clean.'

'Rome could use some of her sister city's rules,' Myrddion said acidly. Praxiteles looked puzzled by his tone, but the healer didn't explain.

They ate an early afternoon meal of goat stew, white cheese, dates and apples, washed down with a crisp white wine that lacked the cloying sweetness of the Roman vintages. Myrddion heaved a sigh of relief. One less problem to worry him. The wine was probably free of lead. Then, as was customary in the east, the population of the inn took a period of rest during the hottest part of the day.

Puzzled by the concept of an afternoon sleep, Myrddion decided that, as a custom, it probably had much to recommend it, especially as citizens were expected to work much longer into the evening than in other parts of the world. Some unpacking of baggage was necessary, but the search for Cleoxenes was an urgent matter and couldn't be postponed, so Myrddion apologised to Praxiteles and asked him to labour during what was the traditional rest break for most of the citizens of Constantinople.

'I must find an aristocrat called Cleoxenes who has served as an envoy to the Western Empire,' Myrddion explained to his new servant, while slipping several base coins to the porter to cover his expenses. 'See if you can find him after we have finished with the unpacking. I'm sorry to send you on such an onerous task in the middle of the day. I don't know where you should begin to search, but he is an important man, so someone in the bureaucracy must know him.' He paused. 'You're welcome to sleep at the inn if you wish, Praxiteles, and you may come and go as you choose while you are in my employ. My only requirements in this regard are that you should be available when I need you.'

Praxiteles bowed in agreement, his blue eyes expressing his gratitude.

'There's no need to bow all the time, Praxiteles. If I ever fell on hard times, I would hope that someone would help me, so there is no need for all this nonsense. I'm simply grateful to have found an honest man in a strange city, so if you serve me honestly you owe me nothing more.'

Praxiteles bowed once more and left. Myrddion raised his eyebrows questioningly at Cadoc, and his assistant grinned with his usual amusement at the follies of the world. 'He'll take a while to become accustomed to our ways, master, but he seems a good man. These eastern Greeks seem to bow and scrape endlessly. From what I've seen, you can't buy a loaf of bread in this city without bowing to the seller as you hand over the money. I swear they are the most polite people we've met – they'd probably be courteous to enemies who were murdering them.'

Without Myrddion's knowledge, Praxiteles had already told the innkeeper that his new guests were healers, albeit pagans. As a devout Christian, the innkeeper had initially been reluctant to rent rooms to a mixed group of men and women, so Praxiteles had explained the dynamics of the healer's extended family, emphasising the account of how Willa had come to live with them, because the innkeeper had been alarmed that a child should sleep with grown men. Once the innkeeper's mind had been set at rest, and he had acknowledged the generosity of Myrddion in providing refuge for such a motley collection of people, Praxiteles had left the inn with an inward smile of satisfaction. The innkeeper now accepted that Myrddion was a benefactor, so given his strict moral code Praxiteles was sure that his new master would remain respected and safe.

But no city is entirely free of crime, regardless of the firm hands that guide the reins of authority. In the darkest reaches of that night, Myrddion was woken by a hurried knocking at his door, followed by the entry of the innkeeper's wife, a plump matron who was encased in a huge nightgown that swathed her diminutive body in yards of pink-dyed fabric. Visibly upset and trembling within her voluminous gown, she carried a pottery oil lamp in her left hand and was fluttering the right in anxiety.

Half asleep, but fortunately still modestly clad, Cadoc and Myrddion tried to decipher the lady's garbled pleas.

'Come, sirs! Please come! Praxiteles has told us ... no, that's not important at this time ... but if you're a healer, and I've no reason to doubt Praxiteles, as he's a good Christian and a gentleman fallen on bad luck ... you'll be able to discover what's amiss with the trader. Well, if you can't, I'm blessed if I know who can. My man is a good innkeeper, honest as the day is long, but ... well, such injuries! ... You understand that a violent death in our house ... heavens, how could we explain to the law courts? Or his poor parents? You understand, I'm sure, why it's vital ... vital ... that we find aid for the poor young gentleman.'

She paused and took a deep, shuddering breath, but only because Myrddion had raised both hands in utter confusion. As the mistress of the house was speaking rapid-fire Greek much embellished with words in another language that Myrddion didn't know, her rambling request had fallen on deaf ears.

'Now, mistress. Slowly, please, because I can't understand you if you speak too fast. Is someone hurt?'

'That's what I'm saying, sir. I'm sorry if I speak in my mother's language, but she came from Armenia, you see, from Tripolis where I grew up. When I get excited I lapse into Armenian, although my husband says people don't understand me even when I speak good Greek.'

Myrddion turned to his assistant. 'Cadoc? My satchel,

please. You and Finn will probably be needed as well.' He shrugged on an old tunic and then nodded towards the woman. 'Show us to our patient, mistress, for time is wasting.'

As they followed her down a dark corridor to a large room far from the public parts of the inn, the lady continued to talk . . . and talk. Myrddion discovered that the innkeeper was called Emilio and had been born in Ephesus, while her own name was Phoebe and they had five grown sons and four married daughters, as well as a number of grandchildren and great-grandchildren. As he tried to filter the mass of information she was giving him, he also learned that the inn served the needs of travellers of distinction, that the streets in this district were generally very safe and that Mistress Phoebe had a natural aversion to grapes so she must beware of wine. Myrddion was still shaking his head in confusion when she pushed open a door and ushered him in to a scene of panic and confusion.

Even as he dragged his satchel down from his shoulder and demanded a supply of newly boiled water, Myrddion registered the fact that a middle-aged man, his face streaming with tears, was cradling a wounded youth. The landlord was standing helplessly on one side, looking pale and anxious.

With some difficulty, Myrddion managed to persuade the older man to let go of the injured youth so that he could begin his examination.

'Strip him, Cadoc. There's blood everywhere, and I can't see a thing.'

Without looking up from his task, Myrddion switched to Greek. 'What is the young man's name, Master Emilio? He's unconscious, but I must try to bring him back to his senses, so knowing his name will be useful.'

'He is called Yusuf el Razi and he is the son of a rich trader from Damascus. The older gentleman is his uncle, Ali el Kabir, who is a regular visitor to this establishment where he is an honoured guest.'

'Thank you, Master Emilio. Now, some clean cloths are needed. And that water, please – and hurry, for young Yusuf is losing too much blood.' He switched languages smoothly. 'Finn, find the preparation of radishes, my best needles, the usual poultice and the powdered root that enriches the blood. Oh, and the oil lamp we use to sterilise the blades. Quickly, Finn, there's blood everywhere.'

'He's been stabbed, master,' Cadoc said crisply, as Finn left the room at a run. 'See? He's taken a nasty pair of wounds, one to the big muscle across the upper arm and another in the hollow of the shoulder.'

'I can see them. Give me that piece of wool, please. Cut it, if necessary. Good. I'll try to stop the bleeding now.' He paused to collect his wits. 'Yusuf! Yusuf! Can you hear me? You're safe now. Can you open your eyes, Yusuf?'

The young man was very dark and his hair was as black as Myrddion's. His beard was still only half grown, while his skin had the smooth elasticity of youth and health. But his face had an unnatural pallor under his tan and the bluish tinge to his lips and nails suggested that he had lost too much blood to survive his wounds.

The room was mute testimony to this fact. Blood lay in a small pool close to the bed where he was lying and the cloth over the divan was saturated. The young man's uncle was also covered in gore and Myrddion felt a stab of regret that he might have been called too late. At least the pressure that he was exerting on the worst of the two wounds had slowed the flood to a trickle.

'We should give thanks to all the gods that the assailant missed the great vein in the throat and the one leading to the heart. If he had been struck in either of those two spots, he would have bled to death within a few moments of being wounded. Where was he attacked?'

'I don't know where the poor young man took his hurt, but it wasn't here,' Master Emilio answered, slowly and carefully.

'No. I saw the blood in the colonnade,' his uncle explained in heavily accented Greek, his hands twisting and turning with distress. 'I was about to discuss it with our good landlord when I saw that the trail led to Yusuf's room. Can you save him, healer? I cannot bear to tell his father that his only son is dead.'

'The boy isn't dead yet,' Myrddion said quickly. 'The first obstacle has been successfully overcome. But now we must discover whether the wounds are clean. His condition is grave, but he does have youth on his side. And we have stopped the bleeding.'

Suddenly, the room filled with a number of persons. A burly ostler carried in two pails of water, one steaming hot and the other lukewarm, while a young boy was burdened with folded cloths, a knife and several large basins. Finn arrived at the same time with a basket overflowing with Myrddion's requirements, and he and Cadoc began to spread the healer's equipment on a nearby table. Forceps, needles and scalpels were cleansed in the lamp flame and then washed in hot water.

'Cadoc, apply continued pressure to the shoulder wound while I wash my hands. Do we have seaweed, Finn?'

'Only dried, master. I brought some spirit, salt and your brush.'

'Mistress Phoebe, can you find me some fresh seaweed?'

'What kind, young man? Do you want broad . . .'

Myrddion cut her off before she could describe all the various types and told her that he would accept any that she could find.

By this time, he had scoured his hands with salt in a small basin, and was busy using the boar-bristle brush to clean his nails. Once satisfied with his ministrations, he took Cadoc's place over the patient.

When the pad of soaked wool was removed from the deep puncture in the shoulder, no blood flowed with the release of pressure. Myrddion grunted his satisfaction. Using forceps and clean rags, he cleaned the injury thoroughly before drizzling some of his precious spirit into the wound. Although unconscious, the young man still shrieked as the flesh bubbled and hissed from the raw alcohol.

'What are you doing?' Ali el Kabir cried. 'Are you trying to kill him?'

'I'm cleansing the wound. Please, don't touch him. He was attacked with a short, wide blade – thanks to Fortuna.' Myrddion had inserted a narrow probe into the wound to ascertain its depth and to determine whether any foreign object remained inside. 'Had the blade been longer a major organ or vein would have been cut, and he'd have had no chance. Nor are there any foreign objects in the breach. You can scrub up now and clean the other wound on his upper arm. It has bled cleanly for the most part, but any infection could kill him while he is in this weakened state.'

Cadoc obeyed smoothly, while Finn mixed up a poultice of crushed radish, garlic and the seaweed that Mistress Phoebe produced like a conjurer, with much puffing and panting from her exertions and haste. Thank the gods she's out of breath, Myrddion thought, otherwise, I'd not get a word in edgeways.

The seaweed was wide-leaved and was soon cut into ribbons that were plump with moisture. Myrddion later discovered that Mistress Phoebe had collected it from the household cooks, who used it as a vegetable in certain soups. The healer silently thanked the Goddess for her intervention and ordered Finn to pulverise as much as he needed for the poultice and then flatten out the leftover ribbons so that they could be used as a base on which to smear the finished poultice. When all had been carried out to his satisfaction, the whole concoction would be placed over the open wound in Yusuf's shoulder.

'You'll not stitch the puncture closed, master?' Cadoc asked in Celt, his hands busy as he cleansed the slash on Yusuf's arm.

'No. I'll want to drain the wound if an infection sets in. Any evil humours will weep out onto the dressings. I can stitch it together at a later date.'

Yusuf was still unconscious, so with Emilio's assistance Finn was able to wrap the young man's shoulder and chest in the ribbons of seaweed. Then, after washing his hands once more, Myrddion turned his attention to the arm wound, which he stitched together quickly and efficiently. Finn applied another poultice and the arm was quickly bound.

'He should be awake by now,' Cadoc said, his scarred face creased in a worried frown. 'We must have hurt him badly while we worked over him.'

'Aye. But let me examine his head to see if there are any other injuries.'

A clue revealed itself when Myrddion found a small bloodstain on Yusuf's headdress, suggesting that the youth could have suffered a blow of some kind. The healer's sensitive fingers soon found the knot of a nasty contusion at the base of his skull, and further examination revealed a small area of split skin in the centre of a lump.

'Check his eyes, Cadoc. Look for anything unusual about the pupils. Do you remember the sailor who fell on his head from the mast outside Colchis? If you recall, that man's pupils were different sizes? Something must have bled inside his head, because he died within hours of falling. I wish now that they had permitted us to explore the man's head wound after he died.'

Fortunately, Myrddion had spoken in Celt. Finn was certain that Yusuf's uncle would have been disturbed if he had understood the gist of the conversation.

'The pupils are the same size, master,' Cadoc reported after prising open the young man's eyelids.

'Good. If we ask Mistress Phoebe to make up a bed for us, one of us will stay with him until any danger passes. If he improves, we'll allow him to wake naturally.'

And so the night finished as Myrddion had decreed. It was fortunate that he couldn't hear Mistress Phoebe's comments on his skills, for his head would have been in danger of swelling. Phoebe praised him to everyone in the inn, speaking of his deftness, his cleanliness and the organisation of the three men who worked together as one.

'And so nice . . . and so handsome! I'm not ashamed to say that my heart flutters when I look at him. His hair, Mistress Dorcas! But he's no boy . . . and he gives orders like a general, even if it's done in a heathen tongue.'

Later in the morning, Myrddion broke his fast with a gigantic meal prepared by Mistress Phoebe's favourite cook, while the guests at the inn, the servants and various passers-by casually dropped into the public rooms to catch a glimpse of the foreign healer who had saved the life of young Yusuf el Razi. By the time Praxiteles arrived with welcome news, Myrddion and his assistants had treated a suppurating ulcer, drawn two teeth, provided a tonic for a child with colic, set a broken finger and removed a collection of warts. The healers' funds were growing already, as was their fame, while Ali el Kabir had sworn that he would assist them in any way he could.

Several officers of the city guard arrived at the same time, to report the result of their investigation into the attack on a prominent visitor. Fortunately, the innkeeper had insisted that the blood trail should not be washed away until the authorities had examined it, so they were able to trace the blood spoor back to a house where high caste prostitutes plied their trade for discerning customers. Yusuf had been attacked and robbed when he left the warm arms of one of the brothel's most expensive girls.

'Stupid boy,' Ali complained, but his voice was affectionate. 'The priests and rabbis would be most annoyed to discover that Yusuf had acted so unwisely.' Then he explained that Yusuf was the scion of a wealthy Syrian family who followed the Jewish faith rather than the pagan gods of the Amalekites. Finally, after giving Myrddion a purse of gold coins as an expression of his heartfelt gratitude, Ali went back to sit with Yusuf, and Myrddion was able to turn his attention to Praxiteles at last.

'I have found Lord Cleoxenes, master. He is at the royal court, and asks that you join him tomorrow evening for a private feast of celebration after he has introduced you to the emperor and the notables of Constantinople. If these arrangements are suitable, he will send a litter at dusk tomorrow to transport you to the palace. I am to return to Lord Cleoxenes's apartments as soon as possible and let him know your answer.'

Myrddion was elated. He thanked Praxiteles and asked him to pass on his acceptance to Cleoxenes, and then went back to treating the needy of the city. News that he would be visiting the palace on the morrow spread through the inn like wildfire, adding to his growing reputation.

The rest of that momentous day passed in a blur of patients, praise in a number of languages and regular monitoring of Yusuf, who remained in a deep, unnatural sleep. He went to his bed with a heavier purse and a sense that his journey to Constantinople had been ordained by the gods.

The next morning dawned with a glister of golden light that turned even utilitarian buildings into beautiful, romantic structures. Myrddion woke early and ran up the stairs to the flat roof so that he could watch the sunrise etch the many palm trees and other unfamiliar shrubs with pellucid light. His heart sang with joy and excitement when he contemplated the evening that lay ahead, and the only blot on his happiness was Yusuf's deep, unchanging sleep.

Later that morning Myrddion discovered that his fame had spread even further afield. Outside in the forecourt a line of patients was waiting, and Myrddion was kept busy for hours. Emilio and his wife were quietly ecstatic at the influx of citizens who crowded the inn, for they also spent coin on cordials, juices and food while they awaited the ministrations of the healer.

'To be called to an audience with the emperor and empress!' Emilio chortled, as he exhorted his cooks to prepare the tasty snacks ordered by those patrons who were eager to share in the reflected glory provided by the outland healers.

'What good news for this house! We must induce this young man to stay for as long as possible.'

'Don't be greedy, Emilio. Truly, the Lord God tells us to beware of vanity and the desire to enrich ourselves through the misfortune of others,' his wife warned him, her face creased with satisfied pleasure that belied her pious warnings. 'Besides, Master Yusuf is still gravely ill.'

Emilio's face fell immediately. 'You're right, my dear. It would be a tragedy if young Yusuf were to die. His death would become a blot on the reputation of our inn.'

'But sleep helps to heal the most terrible wounds, or so Master Myrddion assures me. He still has hopes for Yusuf's survival.'

Ignorant of the ambitions of his hosts, Myrddion worked through the morning and added significantly to his store of coins. Then, after devouring a plate of olives, cheese and cold sliced meats, he prepared to beautify himself for the audience at the palace.

But first things first, Myrddion told himself sternly, and hurried off to check on his patient. Yusuf had finally regained consciousness and seemed much improved, although he was trying to rise from his sick bed and hurting his damaged arm in consequence.

'If you keep moving that arm, Yusuf, you will cause your wounds to bleed and you've lost quite enough blood already. You could easily die if you fail to obey my instructions. I'll put a sling on your arm to immobilise it, and if you feel better tomorrow I'll stitch the shoulder wound and let you spend some time in the fresh air – as long as you remain in a chair. It's that or nothing!'

Reluctantly, after Myrddion had satisfied himself that infection had not set in, Yusuf agreed to behave. His uncle vowed that the boy would not be permitted to stir, so Myrddion left his patient in the Syrian's capable hands.

The afternoon passed quickly. Myrddion immersed himself in the baths, washing his hair thoroughly to remove the salt and smell of their voyage, and paid particular attention to his nails and hands. He relinquished several coppers for a very close shave to remove all traces of beard on his young man's cheeks, and also paid for a rather gritty paste of charcoal and something unpleasant that guaranteed sweetness of breath. As an afterthought, trusting to older, less dubious methods, he also used a twig to clean his gums and teeth.

When he returned to the comfortable familiarity of the inn, he found that Bridie, Brangaine and Rhedyn had excelled themselves by brushing his good cloak and his tunic, washing his underwear and cleaning his boots until they shone. His earring, his sword, his grandmother's necklace and his rings had all been cleaned and polished, although Myrddion put aside the priestess's necklace as inappropriate for an audience, even with an emperor.

Shortly before dusk, as if conjuring a rabbit from his sleeve, Cadoc brought out a small flat box of aromatic wood and presented it to Myrddion.

'From Ali el Kabir, master, to do you honour before the emperor and as thanks for saving young Yusuf's life – so far, at least.'

Myrddion opened the box and saw a cloak pin of extraordinary opulence. Circular in appearance, it was made of buttery yellow gold and had a diameter of some four inches, meaning that it was very heavy. Within the circlet were set two rows of cabochon gemstones, the outer ring of lapis lazuli and the inner of carved emeralds. The centre stone was a large piece of amber with a butterfly caught for eternity within its rich yellow depths.

'I can't accept this,' Myrddion gasped. 'This brooch is far too valuable. We've already been paid amply for our services.'

'Perhaps so, master, but you'll have to take your arguments up with Ali el Kabir, not me. One thing is certain – he will be offended if you attempt to refuse his gift. Moreover, there's no denying it will look very well at the shoulder of your cloak.'

Suiting the action to the words, Cadoc attached the spectacular pin to the sable cloak on Myrddion's left shoulder. The young healer was forced to admit that the garment looked far better with the addition of the jewel.

'If you wish, you can always return it to el Kabir tomorrow,' Cadoc suggested, ever practical. 'But for the moment, your litter has arrived and it's time that you were gone.'

Hustled out of the inn by his friends and with the farewells of fellow guests ringing in his ears, Myrddion found himself being hoisted up into an ornamental chair by four huge men whose skins were so black that they shone with the purple gloss of grapes. From their shaven heads to their sandaled feet, they were superb specimens of manhood. Their skins were oiled so they shone like polished agate and their white tunics seemed impossibly clean and starched by contrast. When they began to trot, bearing the gilded poles of the litter on their shoulders, Myrddion was amazed by their strength and co-ordination.

The journey was fast and smooth and a tribute to the skill of the bearers, but Myrddion was embarrassed to sit above their straining bodies. He could have drawn the curtains of the litter, but then he would have been unable to see the passing parade of men and women afoot, shopping, cleaning the streets, gardening or making their way to their own evening engagements.

As the litter approached the palace, Myrddion caught his first close view of Hagia Sophia and Hagia Eirene. He could see the long row of carved lambs, so lifelike that it seemed as if they might frolic out from the marble and crop the grass. A twisted column like his serpent staff rose up on its own plinth and he could tell that it was very ancient, hinting at religions that were far older than Christianity. Myrddion felt a thrill of something very like superstition.

Then, suddenly, they arrived.

Several wide steps led to a grandiose portico, supported by towering, fluted Corinthian columns. Guards in decorative armour, bearing a Roman eagle with spread wings embossed upon their breastplates, lined the stairs and the portico, providing a guard of honour for the guests who were arriving in litters. Unlike the foot soldiers of Rome, these men were tall and barbarian in appearance, and Myrddion remembered that Constantinople drew on a supply of healthy young men from the nearby nations of Samaria, Armenia, Thracia and Pontus. As Myrddion dismounted he thanked the bearers, who were quite puzzled by his reaction to the service they had provided. He found a number of copper coins and pressed them upon the four men, who accepted them with wide, white grins that made a sharp contrast with their wine-purple lips.

Then Cleoxenes was at his shoulder, clapping him on the back and embracing him with genuine affection. 'Myrddion, my fine young friend! I never thought to see you again, least of all in Constantinople. So, the last of your prophecies has come to fruition and here you are. I am so pleased to see you.'

Myrddion extricated himself from his friend's embrace

and stepped back so he could take in the envoy's splendour.

'Gods, Cleoxenes, I swear you must look finer than the emperor himself. Even the late unlamented Aetius would have been impressed had he seen you dressed as you are today.'

Cleoxenes was certainly magnificent. Head to toe, he was dressed in rich silks that had been dyed in vivid shades of blue. His cloak, which he carried over his arm, was dark as the midnight sky, while his tunic was a cobalt shade that gave his regalia a dazzlingly clean appearance. He wore soft dyed boots that laced up to the calf and his golden arm rings were decorated with cabochon turquoise and lapis lazuli stones. Round his neck he wore a heavy golden chain with a solid gold pendant embossed with a profile of Athena, the Greek goddess of wisdom. On the reverse was a depiction of an owl with tiny rubies for its eyes.

Under his friend's amused gaze, Cleoxenes blushed and then began to laugh. 'You think I'm dressed up like a Roman whore, don't you, my young friend? Don't deny it. But in Constantinople, this dress is considered conservative. Wait and see. You're positively funereal in your choice of clothing, so you'll cause quite a stir among the notables. Now I come to look at you, you're sporting more jewels than I am, and some of them are quite fine. That pin is damascene, isn't it?'

Myrddion nodded, confused by the unfamiliar term but trusting to Cleoxenes's greater knowledge. While they were talking they had climbed the stairs and passed between the huge, bronze-studded doors that were flung wide to allow entry for invited guests. Just inside, while Myrddion marvelled at the wonders of the tessellated floor, two guards relieved the waiting aristocrats of their weaponry in the way of all courts. Myrddion handed over his great-grandfather's sword without demur, although he demanded an assurance that the weapon would be returned.

The large anteroom inside the doors was gorgeously decorated with wall frescoes and mosaics of great naturalness and intricacy. Myrddion found himself gawping like a bucolic at the beautiful fabrics, the gemstones, the decorated tables and stools, and the sheer wealth of glass goblets and wine jugs of beaten gold that adorned the melee of courtiers and were treated with casual disregard. When a woman with an exaggeratedly curled headdress dropped a goblet of wine onto the floor and the precious glass shattered into glittering shards, Myrddion sucked in his breath with shock. A peasant family in Segontium could have lived for years on the value of that goblet. The woman looked accusingly at a servant who had come running to clean up the mess as if he was responsible for the wine stains on her elaborate robe.

Myrddion and Cleoxenes chatted idly, while a number of perfumed and gorgeous men of all ages joined them, ostensibly to renew their acquaintance with the envoy, but covertly studying Myrddion, who was fully aware of their curiosity. The gilded gentlemen were surprised at the purity of his Latin and were fascinated to hear his first-hand accounts of Flavius Aetius, Attila's meeting with Pope Leo and the situation in Rome. These aristocrats had rarely travelled to the west, for they preferred the more stable political conditions of Constantinople, but they were interested in the murder of Flavius Aetius and alarmed by the rapid decline of the social structure of Rome. Myrddion found his opinion sought by any number of influential gentlemen who marvelled at his youth, considering the vast distances the lad had covered to reach the Eastern Empire.

The healer suppressed his initial distrust of men who were

overly concerned with dress and ornamentation, once he realised that every courtier in the anteroom was competing to be the most elaborately garbed. His quick eyes discovered that smooth arms were bronzed and powerful under their golden bracelets, and clean-shaven faces were strong-jawed regardless of the occasional application of cosmetics. Myrddion was still very young, and he had yet to lose some of his provincial misconceptions about how men comported themselves. He was a little embarrassed that he had considered the courtiers to be foppish and decadent merely on the evidence of their dress.

He was also embarrassed by the many covert glances from noble ladies of all ages, who clustered together to talk behind hand-painted fans and to giggle at each other's comments on his face and figure. The aristocrats here are just as rude and vulgar as high-born people anywhere, he thought acidly. There's no real difference between nobility from different parts of the world, only the languages they speak and the affectations they adopt.

Then, with a fanfare and a sudden movement of the notables towards another set of brazen doors, the audience with the emperor began. Cleoxenes nudged Myrddion and the two men made their way to the back of the crowd. The doors leading to the emperor's apartment opened with a flourish to reveal a small dais at the far end of the room, on which Emperor Marcian sat in state beside his wife, Pulcheria, the sister of the deceased emperor Theodosius.

The emperor was a man in his middle sixties, and illnesses suffered when he was a tribune and, later, when he was taken prisoner by the Vandals, had left their mark on his long, large-nosed face. Rumour insisted that Flavius Ardabur Aspar, his *magister militum*, had engineered his rise to the throne after the death of Theodosius. Despite the emperor's negligible appearance, Myrddion felt a brief flicker of curiosity as he examined the lean, avian face with its muddy, greying complexion. Marcian was beardless, and wore what was left of his hair in long, curled locks that fell to his shoulders, aping youth, a look that was assisted by a series of suspicious curls that marched across his forehead beneath his domed crown.

Are men in Constantinople so vain as to wear wigs? Myrddion wondered. Probably. Especially if old age has wearied the flesh and the crown weighs heavily on an ageing arthritic neck.

Beside him, his wife was dressed in a robe that was so heavy with gold thread and seed pearls that she looked like a small idol. The enormous headdress, which added considerably to Empress Pulcheria's height, was obviously a wig, for her face below the tortured russet curls was far too raddled for hair of such an improbable colour. Unlike her husband, who appeared quite meek, Empress Pulcheria seemed comfortable as she called the courtiers into her presence with an imperious wave of her hand. Like her husband, whom she had chosen on the death of her brother six years earlier, she had an almost skeletal face in which forehead, cheekbones, nose and chin were extremely prominent and proud.

Another man stood in the shadows of the throne in such a position that Myrddion could barely see his features.

'Who's the aristocrat in grey?' he hissed in Cleoxenes's ear. 'He stands very close to the throne, so he must be a favourite of the emperor.'

Cleoxenes snorted under his breath, and Myrddion heard both respect and dislike in the sound. 'He's more than a favourite. He gave the throne to Marcian when our emperor was nothing but a minor commander, without background or ability. There stands the *magister militum* of the Eastern Empire, a man who has refused the throne of the east, supposedly because of his religion, but I believe because he likes to dominate weaker minds from behind. That, my young friend, is Flavius Ardabur Aspar, the most important man in Constantinople.'

'A king-maker,' Myrddion whispered.

On cue, Aspar stepped forward into the light of the sweet-scented torches and Myrddion could see him clearly. With a shock that seemed to travel downward to his toes, Myrddion recognised the ageing, handsome face that was lifted proudly to survey the crowd below him.

That face, with several decades added, was Myrddion's own.

CHAPTER XXI

IN A DARK MIRROR

Flavius Ardabur Aspar was still a beautiful man. His thick hair, which had been so black, was now white across the hairline at the front, but still retained some traces of sable at the back where he kept it militarily short.

Not for a moment did Myrddion doubt that the *magister militum* was his sire.

Aspar had yet to notice Myrddion, so the younger man enjoyed the luxury of examining his father in detail. The general was taller than most men, but Myrddion realised that he himself was an inch or two taller yet. Broad-shouldered, long of leg and ascetic in his clothing, Aspar was the most elegant man in the room ... and it was clear that he knew it, as he raised his clean-shaven chin to survey the faces that fawned on the emperor and his consort – and on himself.

'You can see the likeness, can't you, Myrddion?' Cleoxenes whispered in a voice so soft that the courtiers who clustered around them couldn't hear. 'I'm not mistaken, am I?'

'You knew, Cleoxenes! All this time. You knew!'

'I guessed. I'm sorry, Myrddion, but did you never wonder why I took such an interest in you from the time we first met? How could I not see Aspar in every line of your face and, especially, in your eyes? Although yours are kinder than his.'

'Hyacinth beauty, my mother said, and she was a very acute person, for all that she's been mad for twenty years. He is beautiful, but in a manly fashion. She called him Triton, you know, before he raped her – at twelve years of age.' Myrddion's face was set and bitter. Too many years of suffering and loss lay behind the young man's open face, which closed shut into rigid, uncompromising lines even as Cleoxenes watched.

'What was he doing in Segontium? In Britain, of all places – in the court of Vortigern, the High King of the Britons?'

Cleoxenes peered at Aspar over the crowd and then turned back to Myrddion and shook his head. 'You're two sides of a mirror, one young and one old. By my love of heaven, I don't know, Myrddion. All I know of Aspar is his role, in company with his father Ardabarius, in removing the Usurper, Johannes, and placing Galla Placidia and her son Valentinian on the throne of the west. Yes, Aspar is a king-maker, like his father. So he was certainly in Rome and Ravenna during those years. I believe he was only a stripling in his middle twenties at the time. I also remember that he then campaigned in Africa for some years. But he was home, and serving as a consul, during his middle thirties. Why he would have travelled to Britain is a mystery to me.'

'The timing of my birth would be consistent if Aspar is about fifty-six now, meaning that I was sired after Africa, and before he became a consul,' Myrddion murmured. 'Something, or someone, sent him to Britain and the visit must not have been to his credit.'

The crowd parted in front of them and the healer heard the emperor demand Cleoxenes's presence in a loud, querulous voice. Suddenly, Myrddion felt very vulnerable and exposed. Determined to face Aspar down, the young man also lifted his chin in defiance, unaware that more than one man in the room was experiencing a sudden spark of interest in the stranger.

'How may I serve you, highness?' Cleoxenes murmured in his mellifluous, easy voice.

'Who is the very tall stranger in black accompanying you? Come forward, young man. The light shines in my eyes, and I cannot see you properly.'

'I am proud to present Myrddion Emrys of Segontium in Britain. He is a healer of great renown who served under Flavius Aetius at the Battle of the Catalaunian Plain. Warriors perished in tens of thousands on that day, and many more passed through Myrddion's hands and still live because of this young man's skill. He was with me at Mantua when Attila turned aside from Italia, having saved my arm from amputation after an injury, and he served as a healer to the citizens of the city while in Rome. He is the great-grandson of a king and his grandmother was the chief priestess of his people. Myrddion Emrys offers you his obedience.'

Myrddion stepped forward and abased himself in the Celtic way towards Marcian and Pulcheria. His body formed a black cross upon the marble floor.

Cleoxenes had watched Aspar out of the corner of his eye while he addressed the emperor. Aspar had shown nothing when Segontium was mentioned, but Cleoxenes's trained eyes could see a certain rigidity in his stance ... and he wondered.

'So, Myrddion Emrys,' Marcian said in an avuncular voice. 'Arise, young man, so we can speak. Rarely do we meet men of your trade, although my dear Pulcheria swears by the skills of a son of Ishmael who cares for the empress's health. Usually, healers are Greeks, Jews or Persians, so we are very surprised to meet someone from the isles of Britain who has such a pedigree. Why would a nobleman become a healer?'

'I am landless, my lord, and the trade of war has been closed to me from birth. I was not willing to live on the charity of my aristocratic connections, so I took up the scalpel and have sworn myself to the oath of Hippocrates.'

Marcian smiled, but Cleoxenes could tell that the emperor had found a loose thread in Myrddion's narrative. Knowing the dogmatic nature of the emperor and his querulous curiosity, Cleoxenes was certain that Marcian would pull on that thread until he understood everything about the young man who stood before him.

More to the point, did Myrddion intend that Marcian should ask his questions?

'Highness, I could not become a warrior because I had no human father.' The crowd stirred and murmured, as if a wind soughed through the audience room. Myrddion stood tall in his sable robes, the centre of all eyes, as his voice, so suited to story-telling, drew them into his tale.

'My mother was twelve when I was conceived, a child who had been raised in a house of women, for her mother served the Goddess whose name must not be spoken. She swore she had been raped by a demon, but I was permitted to live because the serpents of the Goddess accepted me, as did the Lord of Light for whom I am named. I was called the Demon Seed, like King Merovech of the Salian Franks who perished on the Catalaunian Plain. I lived because I was feared.'

Marcian was taken aback. He was Christian and devout, but superstition existed side by side with his faith, and this young man openly proclaimed his demon status as he stood before the court of the emperor.

'Are you saying that you are allied with Satan, young man?

If so, my lands will be closed to you forever,' Marcian threatened, while Pulcheria made the sign of the cross over her breast.

'How could I be the son of a demon, my lord? Jesus would not damn a child, and your benevolent god would never curse an infant for the sins of the father. My mother was a child when she was raped on the beaches near her home. She invented the rest, fearing that she would be put to death because King Melvig ap Melwy, her grandfather, would be angry that her bride price was spoiled. She was a child, and she was deathly afraid and damaged. I was raised to be a decent and peaceful man, and I have dedicated my life to the saving of life – not the ending of it. No Demon Seed would be so magnanimous, if such a man existed. Such a man would want to cause discord and violence wherever he went.'

Sensing that Emperor Marcian was still unconvinced, Cleoxenes stepped forward again and exposed his right arm and the ugly scar that disfigured it. A deep hollow below the elbow showed where flesh and muscle had been removed.

'I would have died in Rome, Highness, had this young man not struggled to save my arm and my life. It was poisoned, and by the time I called for his assistance the infection had brought me close to death. A prudent healer would have removed the arm as quickly as possible, but I insisted that I must serve your interests in Mantua and forbade him to cut off the poisoned limb. He worked like a saint, rather than a demon, to scour out the taint in the flesh, to nurse me like a baby and then to travel with me all the way to Attila's camp so I could fulfil my duties to the Empire. He risked his own life, for Flavius Aetius had no love for him, but Myrddion refused to stay safely in Rome. He is not a demon, but is a gift from God to serve your interests. Rather the man who raped his mother is the demon, for such is a man who would cause pain to a little girl.'

So make what you want of that, Aspar Hawk-lover, Cleoxenes thought savagely as he watched Aspar bite his lip at the venom in the envoy's words.

'The poor child! So young to be ravaged by such an evil man,' Empress Pulcheria murmured. More than her husband ever could, she empathised with a noble, female child used as a pawn in aristocratic power struggles. 'Is she still alive, Myrddion Emrys?'

'Yes, your highness. My mother still lives, but she has been maddened since the time of my birth. She tried to kill me twice and she has tried to harm her younger children. She carves her own flesh out of guilt and shame, so she must be watched closely at all times.'

'Oh, my dear! How dreadful!' Pulcheria exclaimed. She dabbed at her eyes, although Myrddion was close enough to see that they were still dry. 'The sins of her despoiler were truly meted out to her. Did you suffer too?'

'Yes, your highness, but I was fortunate to be raised by my grandmother who protected me until Vortigern, the High King, attempted to sacrifice me to satisfy his own whims when I was but ten years old. My grandmother was killed while trying to save me from Vortigern's barbarians.'

The crowd of notables were riveted by the tale and strained forward towards the young man. Only Aspar appeared unmoved. He had stepped into a pool of shadow so that the light caught only his forehead, the straight line of his nose and the edges of those hatchet-sharp cheekbones.

'And what did your mother say of this demon?' he asked. 'Did she know who he was?'

'No, my lord. She always used the term, hyacinth beauty, to

describe her Triton who was washed onto the shoreline by a storm. She saved his life, sir, for all the good it did her. All I know is he purported to have killed his own mother and I still carry that woman's ring. I discovered that King Vortigern knew the man and he gave me small snippets of information before he burned to death in his fortress at Dinas Emrys. The High King told me that the man loved hunting with birds and that he was a natural killer – just like them. But I could never persuade Vortigern to give me his name.'

Aspar grunted, his eyes glowing in the dark hollows of his face.

'He must have been a cruel man,' Emperor Marcian said quietly, and Myrddion noticed how the older man's hands shook from nervousness or illness. 'You are permitted to stay in Constantinople, but mind you there must be no more talk of demons. Some of our priests take such chatter seriously.'

'I live to serve you, highness. Should you have need of my services as a healer, I would gladly place myself at your command.'

Marcian nodded. Myrddion had been quick to notice the lack of colour in the emperor's pallid face. 'You may call on me on the day after tomorrow, healer. Although, no doubt, my dear wife will prefer to have her Ishmaelite healer treat me.'

Marcian turned away and Myrddion's part of the audience was over.

As other notables pressed around the dais, Myrddion and Cleoxenes backed away, their heads bowed, until they could lose themselves in the crowd. Then, relieved of any need for courtesy, Myrddion spun on his heels and strode out of the great and glittering hall, his hands clenched tightly by his side.

'Where are you going, Myrddion? Stop. Or at least slow down. Your legs are too long for me to keep up with you,' Cleoxenes shouted as he hurried after his young protégé.

Myrddion ran down the steps of the portico and skidded to a halt on the empty roadway where the litters had disgorged their passengers. He turned to face his friend with a stormy face.

'I've travelled across the world to find him. I don't know what I expected, but I never imagined that he would be the *magister militum* and the most powerful man in the Empire of the East. My father has prospered while he left a storm of destruction and heartache behind him. There is no justice in the world, for the gods must surely be blind.'

'Myrddion, you can't really believe that evil goes completely unpunished. You know that most of us eventually pay for our sins in full measure, sooner or later. Look at Flavius Aetius!'

Myrddion stopped pacing and turned his sun ring round and round on his finger.

'Aetius lived long and well – and his death took but moments. For a person who caused havoc and despair to anyone who stood in his way, he paid a remarkably low price for his vices. It all seems so patently unfair.'

'Come, walk with me,' Cleoxenes urged, taking Myrddion by the elbow. 'My house is adjacent to the palace and a fine meal awaits us. We can talk further after we've eaten. There's an urgent matter I need to discuss with you anyway.'

Myrddion consented to walk with the envoy and the gentle pressure of his friend's hand on his arm calmed his churning feelings a little. The night was very clear, and although the city was full of light the stars were clearly visible, and seemed so close that Myrddion had only to reach upward with one hand to catch the starlight in the nets of his fingers.

The waters of the Golden Horn provided gentle background music now that the friends were walking down dark pathways far from the noise of the crowds. Aromatic plants scented the air with a heavy perfume that was both sweet and slightly rotten. Although the darkness under the trees should have been threatening, Myrddion felt at one with the breeze, the salt tang of the air and the soft soughing of palm fronds.

Then, suddenly, a villa appeared out of the darkness, brilliant with torchlight and lamps. As Cleoxenes and his guest strolled along the path, several servants left the building to usher them inside.

Myrddion examined Cleoxenes's villa with avid curiosity. The floors and columns were constructed from rose-veined marble, while the walls were painted with frescoes. The simplicity of the rooms, compared with the opulence of the palace, was tasteful and elegant. Myrddion noted that comfort was of paramount importance. The colonnade was wide, the rooms were spacious and well ventilated, and the atrium possessed a profusion of sweet-smelling flowering herbs, allowing the air to be scented with a combination of lavender and mint. In the triclinium, the eating couches were antique in design, with plump cushions and understated fabrics. Then, as they entered the scriptorium, Myrddion discovered a well-lit table used for writing or reading. The writing materials were presented in simple cedar boxes that perfumed the air with the scent of learning. One whole wall held cedar pigeonholes containing hundreds of scrolls, tightly bound within leather cases.

Cleoxenes ushered Myrddion out into the gardens, which trod a narrow line between functionality and aesthetics. On steep terraces leading down to the waters, orange and lemon trees glowed with globes of half-matured fruit, while garden beds were filled with cabbage roses and vegetables in equal measure. The night was sweet-scented and fecund with growth.

The promised meal, light and beautifully prepared by Cleoxenes's servants, proved to be pleasant. Cleoxenes had a preference for savoury foods rather than the cloying sweetness that dominated Roman cooking. Myrddion detected unusual condiments within the sauces, leading Cleoxenes to explain that traders occasionally brought spices from far-off countries to the south, most of which were especially appetising when used with meat and vegetables.

Myrddion was tentative at first with his food choices, but soon found that he enjoyed the spicy chicken and quail. He even drank a glass of white wine. It was very crisp and dry, and he too took comfort from the lack of sweetness.

Unlike the epicures of Rome, Cleoxenes did not provide a vomitorium, nor did he serve the enormous number of courses that required diners to void their stomachs in order to fit in more food. Myrddion had always considered that such gluttony was disgusting, and was glad that he was freed from the tiresome need to apologise for his lack of a Roman appetite. Now, pleasantly replete, the two men lounged over the remains of a fine meal and spoke desultorily.

Myrddion explained his suspicions about lead poisoning, especially with regard to wine. His words horrified his friend.

'I can't grasp the scope of the dangers you describe, my young friend. Every person who drinks sweetened wine, eats sweetmeats or prepares food with the powdered condiments of Rome is poisoning themselves. I've eaten their food myself. How terrible! And you swear that Isaac the Jew is aware of your knowledge and does nothing because some sections of

Roman society wouldn't believe him? If your diagnosis is true, may he be swallowed by his own Sheol.'

The healer shrugged. 'I could do nothing to persuade him to support my views on this matter. He holds his reputation to be higher than the lives of other, less fortunate people. You can have no notion how frustrating it is to be forced to stand quietly by while other men who are better placed choose to ignore a dreadful peril. I decided to sever all ties with Isaac once I realised that he didn't really care about his patients.'

'Many healers must be like Isaac. My understanding is that a healer isn't required to have any affection for his patients, just to treat them.' Cleoxenes played devil's advocate.

Myrddion's face flushed with passion and Cleoxenes reflected how different from Aspar this young man could be once his emotions were engaged.

'But we must not harm the sufferers of injury or illness in our care when we have the means to help them. Healers are obligated to do everything in their power to make patients well, not watch them while they die.'

'Oh, I'd far rather be treated by you, Myrddion, than by Isaac or his ilk, regardless of his skill.' Cleoxenes allowed the topic to lapse. Then he leaned forward, gripped Myrddion's arm and forced the young man to listen to him.

'You have a far larger problem than arguments about healer ethics. I can understand the temptation to strike Aspar where it hurts, but you don't know the man with whom you're dealing. In the last decade or so, he has used his religion as an excuse to defend his manipulative nature. He is a king-maker and has been the power behind the throne for over thirty years. He has dominated the emperors of the east for most of his life and wields power beyond our understanding.'

'I don't care how powerful he is. If I could, I would strike him publicly for his treatment of my mother,' Myrddion snapped. Obviously, the healer was still seething with resentment.

'For anyone with eyes to see, namely Aspar himself, you made your sentiments perfectly plain. Unfortunately, you are not in a position to negotiate with him, or threaten him with any semblance of impunity. I myself am always careful in my dealings with the *magister militum*.'

Myrddion stared at Cleoxenes. Rarely did the sophisticated aristocrat show any strong emotion, being usually almost preternaturally calm. 'I don't understand, Cleoxenes. What can he do to me?'

'Must I elaborate?' Cleoxenes frowned irritably. 'He can have you killed in secret. Why not? Who cares about one more missing outlander? Really, you are being quite naive.'

Myrddion's jaw dropped for a moment before he snapped it closed again. Of course, fathers also killed their sons in Britain. Vortigern, in particular, would have murdered all of his sons, if he could have. Like Cronos, who devoured his children, powerful Roman noblemen often went to great lengths to remove a younger rival. But until Cleoxenes had mentioned it, Myrddion had never considered that he was imperilling himself, or his friends, by his intemperate actions.

'What do you really want of Aspar, Myrddion?' Cleoxenes asked. 'Really?'

'To . . . to . . . be acknowledged, so that he admits that he caused harm to me and to mine.'

'And do you think he will?' Cleoxenes was inexorable.

Myrddion examined his hands and the sun ring that his busy fingers turned and turned. He sighed, and a world of self-knowledge was in that exhalation of breath. 'No. He won't do that. He'd be a fool to acknowledge me in any way. After seeing him, I have no doubt that he also has legitimate sons.'

The finality in the young man's voice comforted Cleoxenes. Perhaps the whole game of cat and mouse at the palace would pass unnoticed.

The two friends talked into the early hours of the morning, for although twenty years separated them in age both were contemplative in nature, and both were natural observers. Art, music and even the games in Rome and Constantinople were discussed, although the Eastern Empire rarely needed to descend to such barbaric methods to appease the population. Cleoxenes agreed that watching men fighting to the death for pleasure was reprehensible, but as a citizen of a society that sanctioned murder and war as entertainment he was inured to the idea, although he had vowed never to attend these entertainments himself. Myrddion sighed again. It was very difficult for anyone to resist the pressures of a world that had nurtured him, even for the best of men.

Cleoxenes and Myrddion parted company as good friends do – conscious that each had flaws, but able to accept the weaknesses as well as the strengths that existed in the other.

The next day, the three healers rose early for their impromptu surgery in the forecourt of the inn in the hope that they could keep the queue of patients to a minimum. Myrddion felt guilty that his absence in the afternoon had denied care to sufferers, but Cadoc pointed out that Constantinople had many other healers and he was simply a novelty. The citizens were coming to see the young men from beyond the fabled Pillars of Hercules rather than have their medical conditions diagnosed and evaluated.

'They're just curious, master. Boils, toothache, warts, cuts and bruises? None are fatal illnesses. They really only want to see you.'

'I don't like us being compared with market-place animals,' Myrddion complained.

'Well, we are,' Cadoc grumbled. 'But I must say that Constantinople seems a beautiful place to be on show, so I plan to enjoy the circus.'

Before their labours began, the three young men wandered through the market place and along the broad avenues. There was so much to see, to taste and to experience. The sun shone brightly with only a tiny sting in its heat, while the skies seemed wider, deeper and vaster than the dense, soft-grey skies of their homeland. From high points of land, they could see how the Propontis stretched away in dark blue waves, broken by small squares and triangles of coloured sail.

Finn bought a tiny manikin of bone, carved and dressed to represent a woman, as a gift for Bridie. The three healers were amazed at the skills represented in the market place, and Myrddion felt the coins in the pouch at his waist weigh heavily. Then, on a far stall, he saw a shimmer of glass and decided to take a closer look.

The stallholder specialised in glassware, so fewer people clustered around his expensive products. The array of gorgeous shapes, decorated and stamped to represent grapes or profiles of the emperor, glittered with a special brilliance in the morning sun. Although the stallholder frowned above his huge moustache, Myrddion stretched out his hand to stroke the surfaces. Then he saw the glass jars.

Compared with the other wares, these jars were plain, coarse things, clear in colour and rough in manufacture, and obviously moulded for domestic usage. They were approximately twelve inches high and six inches across the base, with a wide, open top and a rolled edge. Myrddion was fascinated. Already, he could picture his herbs, tinctures and specimens stored in those jars, so clear that the contents could be seen at a glance.

'Those jars . . . how much are they?'

The crafty eyes of the artisan scanned Myrddion's eager face before he set a figure so enormous that the healer gasped and turned away in feigned rejection. Quickly and smoothly, Cadoc took his place.

'Sir, your jars are very dusty, so it is obvious to me that you've had them for some time. My master admires them, but he can be soft in the head, because we both know that they are the simplest and cheapest glass that you make. Am I not right?'

The stallholder protested loudly and volubly with much waving of animated hands. His moustache managed to look aggrieved and insulted by turn as Praxiteles translated Cadoc's astute observations.

'What were they really for, hey? Were they a commission that went wrong? We lived in Rome for several years and I'm not as green as grass like my master. I'm curious and I've got no coin to spend, but my master usually takes my advice on matters of the purse.'

Cadoc grinned engagingly despite his scars and winked at the stallholder, who tried to look offended at first, then grinned in turn.

'You're right, young sir. A high-born lady ordered jars for her kitchens, although why she should bother surprised me at the time. She had more servants than fingers and toes. When the jars were finished, she decided that they were plain things and without merit, so she refused to take them. Stupid cow! Glass containers are too precious for household items. In truth, she probably changed her mind and simply left me to carry the loss.'

Even in Constantinople, common people nurtured a healthy disrespect for their masters, regardless of how low they bowed or how polite their words might sound. Praxiteles grinned knowingly and translated the glassmaker's statements carefully. Cadoc's reply was predictable.

'So you're stuck with them, right? All of them. Who's going to buy glass jars for storage? You'd be better off smashing them for reuse in your furnaces. Is that true?'

'No! No! No! My price was fair,' the stallholder protested.

'Yes! Yes! Yes! You tried to cheat my master,' Cadoc retorted. 'My master will now spend his gold coins on something useless such as carpets or golden jewellery, when my tasks for him would be far easier if he had purchased your jars. We might be from Britain – which I dare say you've never heard of – but my master is a healer of renown called Myrddion Emrys. Ask after him at the emperor's palace, if you don't believe me.'

'So? Is it better that I should break and grind these jars for reuse of the material, as you say? Or should I sell them to you for a silly price?'

The stallholder smiled, finally showing a flash of genuine feeling and not the glib, easy patter of the market place. Praxiteles sensed a weakening in his argument, as did Cadoc, and the two men had to hide triumphant grins.

'I could have used them,' Cadoc whispered to the man. 'You've no notion how many mushrooms, chopped basil, rosemary, rue, lavender, mandrake, henbane, et cetera, et cetera, I have to find in a moment among our pottery jars. And my master always wants it immediately, like all masters.

Glass jars would have been so very useful. Ah, well! You'll no doubt find another buyer, for all of them – one day.' Cadoc grinned wickedly as Praxiteles translated accurately, right down to the pregnant pause.

The stallholder was a pragmatist. Some coin is always better than no coin at all, so Myrddion found himself the owner of a score of glass jars for a tenth of the original asking price. What was more, the stallholder was perfectly prepared to transport the jars to the healer's inn, without a delivery charge, payment to be made in cash on delivery.

Below his elation, Myrddion was alarmed. 'I don't like to cheat a man out of his legitimate profits, Cadoc, no matter how much I long to possess those jars.'

'What is glass, master? It's mostly sand, right? And the world has more than enough of that, all for free. He would have made an enormous profit out of the aristocratic lady if she hadn't thought better of her whim. But, let's face it, master, who else was he going to sell them to, if not to us? He's happy. We're happy. And the world is good.'

With this homespun wisdom Myrddion was forced to agree, and his heart lifted with the thrill of his wonderful find.

And as the weeks passed profitably, the only blot on Myrddion's horizon was the lack of any word from Flavia. To all intents and purposes, she had vanished into Constantine's city as if she had never existed.

One day, after a strange lunch eaten piecemeal from market stalls, the three healers returned to the inn to find a messenger irritably cooling his heels. Myrddion insisted on washing off the dirt of their morning jaunt and checking on the condition of young Yusuf, who was almost healed, before he was prepared to listen to what the messenger had to say. When he came back, the messenger wiped his face clean of stormy exasperation and began to recount his memorised tidings.

'Greetings to Myrddion Emrys, healer, of Segontium, from his honour the *magister Militum* of all Constantinople and its lands, Flavius Ardabur Aspar. My lord begs that you will accept an invitation to wait upon him next week, to break bread with him and to learn something that is to your advantage.'

The messenger bowed deeply and waited patiently for an answer.

Do I go? Myrddion thought furiously. I would be walking into Aspar's territory and that, on the face of it, would be crazy. For my own safety, I'll need someone with me who can ostensibly be my witness and translator. But whom can I use? Anyone I choose will be placed in danger.

But not if they know nothing, Myrddion answered himself inwardly.

'Of course,' Myrddion whispered aloud. 'Of course! I will beg the *magister Militum*'s indulgence and take an interpreter in case my skills fail me.'

He turned back to the messenger. 'Wait here and I'll re-join you shortly.'

Once Ali el Kabir had been found and the situation had been explained to him, Myrddion returned to the *magister militum*'s messenger with a polite acceptance of Aspar's invitation. Ali el Kabir had not hesitated. If this outland healer needed his presence, then he would comply. His family owed the young man a debt that could never be repaid, for Myrddion had informed him that Yusuf would almost certainly live and have full use of his arm.

The intervening week passed uneventfully, with work,

visits to various places of interest and another audience at the palace. Cleoxenes had warned Myrddion that Marcian was probably motivated more by curiosity than by medical need, but the young healer was still looking forward to meeting the empress's healer, the Ishmaelite. Although several weeks had passed since the original invitation, Myrddion understood that kings live to different time patterns from ordinary men, so he wasn't offended by the long wait.

Unaware that he was being singularly honoured, Myrddion was escorted by armed guards to the emperor's private apartments, where Marcian awaited his arrival. The emperor was accompanied by a lean, swarthy man dressed in garb that seemed more suited to the southern lands of shifting sands and terrible heat than to Marcian's palace. His white, flowing robes and burnous were ideal for counteracting the extreme conditions of the desert. Myrddion grinned as he considered how differently the two healers were dressed.

'Myrddion Emrys, you have come,' the emperor exclaimed, rather unnecessarily, as he rested on the edge of his sumptuous bed. 'I suppose you want to poke and prod me, like Eleazar here?'

Marcian was dressed in a simple robe of indigo linen, so a physical examination would be relatively easy. Eleazar, who was an Amalekite, stood to one side of the emperor's bed and watched sardonically as Myrddion lifted Marcian's eyelids and peered into the emperor's rather yellowish eyes. He noted the grey tinge to the old man's complexion and, with an apology, placed his hand over the emperor's heart, frowning as he felt the heart stutter irregularly under his sensitive fingers.

After a few more questions and a measured observation of the emperor's laboured breathing, Myrddion hazarded a diagnosis.

'Your heart skips a beat occasionally and it is a little rapid, my lord. I am sure my respected colleague has told you as much.'

Eleazar nodded with a slight smile.

'I have observed that the heart can grow old faster than the rest of the body, and when this occurs the lungs weaken and sap the patient's strength. I would suggest, your highness, that you avoid too much wine, because it exacerbates the problem. Also, your eyes indicate that you have internal problems, so you would do well to avoid prolonged periods of heavy exercise. A little walking, however, is always good for the circulation. You must avoid rich foods, too much sweetener and very large meals. Finally, you must rest for several hours every afternoon, and sleep in a propped-up position with pillows behind your back.'

Marcian almost pouted at the thought of all the rich foods that were barred to him. 'Do you also want me to live like a priest, healer? Eleazar has already pronounced that I must rest and live an abstemious life.'

'Better to live like a priest than die before your time,' the Amalekite stated baldly, and Myrddion's innate honesty forced him to nod in agreement.

A little more time was spent as Eleazar and Myrddion decided on the most effective tonic to prescribe to their patient, after which Myrddion was presented with a gold coin bearing the emperor's profile by a rather sour Marcian. The audience was over.

The rest of the week passed slowly and tediously, although Myrddion fretted because there was still no news from Flavia. Heartsick, he was certain that he had been supplanted, and he tried hard not to imagine the red-haired witch in the arms of another man. Regardless of his efforts, jealousy seared him, and only the approaching meeting with his father, Flavius Ardabur Aspar, distracted the young healer's mind.

One surprising incident served to briefly lift Myrddion's flagging spirits. A patient came to the inn, a hawk-nosed trader from far to the south who was suffering from a persistent cough that disturbed his rest. As Myrddion prescribed a cleansing tonic for Finn to prepare for the merchant, he noticed a curious, leaf-shaped knife hanging from the patient's belt. Suddenly, Myrddion's fingers recalled the blade picked into the stone of the Giant's Dance, and his previous recognition of the Phoenician knife. His curiosity was piqued.

'Praxiteles, my friend, could you ask the gentleman if he would allow me to examine his knife?' he asked softly.

When the weapon was handed to him, hilt first, the young healer saw that the blade was identical to the ancient carving.

'Could you ask the trader if he would tell me the place that he calls home, and who his people are? Is he Phoenician?'

Praxiteles spoke quickly to the merchant in a strange tongue, and the trader responded just as rapidly as he resheathed his weapon.

'Yes, he is a Phoenician, master, and he hails from Tyre on the edge of the Middle Sea. His people are great sailors and traders who have travelled throughout the waters and beyond. Or so he boasts,' Praxiteles reported doubtfully.

As if Fortuna's wheel had once again begun to move in earnest, Myrddion sensed that fate was closing the circles of his life and proffering the answers that he had sought for many years. He sighed as he contemplated the future.

'Give him my thanks, and explain that his people once reached my land, which lies beyond the Pillars of Hercules. Express my gratitude, for he has solved a mystery that has eluded me for many years.'

CHAPTER XXII

THE SINS OF THE FATHER

Gorlois was riding to Sorviodunum from his summer palace at Isca Dumnoniorum when he chose to detour to the Giant's Dance. Time after time, he had seen the huge and ancient monument from a distance, for the route to Venta Belgarum passed close by the enigmatic circle of stones, cradled within the huge mounds that surrounded them. He had never examined the Dance closely before, deeming it to belong to the ancient, barbaric time before his people had travelled across the Litus Saxonicum from Armorica.

The last years had been difficult for Gorlois and his beautiful wife. Beside Ygerne's miscarriage, their younger daughter, Morgause, had married Lot, the powerful king of the Otadini tribe who ruled the fertile lands between the two fortified walls in the distant north. Ygerne had wept inconsolably at being parted from Morgause, although the vain and self-willed girl was often a trial. Almost immediately, Morgause had fallen pregnant and had borne a son, while the tyranny of distance had prevented the new grandparents from meeting their first grandson.

Added to this sadness was the strange behaviour of their eldest daughter, the beautiful Morgan. Although the young woman was close-mouthed and wilful, and preferred her own company, whispers had reached the king that his daughter was mixing with unsavoury characters. Gorlois had been enraged by these formless rumours of ancient, arcane rites, and had been forced to interrogate a village wise woman who had stated publicly that Gorlois's daughter was a filthy, murderous witch.

When the wise woman had defied him by remaining mute, Gorlois had ordered her to be imprisoned and starved until she became more compliant. What he learned gave the Dumnonii king no pleasure, for he discovered that his elder daughter had begun to dabble in the dark arts that promised unlimited power. To think that his beloved Morgan had come to such a pass almost made Gorlois sick with sorrow. While Ygerne had the solace of tears, Gorlois could only rage at Morgan, demanding answers that she stubbornly refused to give.

Finally, she had offered an explanation – of a kind. Red-faced and shocked, Gorlois had wondered where his flower-crowned little girl had fled in the years since her childhood.

'I was born female, Father. Do you understand what that means? No, how could you? I will never ride to war or wear a crown, because I was born a female. The best that I can hope for is what my sister possesses, a wealthy, noble husband and the chance to bear a clutch of mewling, squabbling sons. Well, Father, such a fate is not enough for me. I will not be fulfilled by putting a man's needs ahead of my own. I'm determined to win renown by myself and for myself.'

'Home and hearth is enough for your mother, and she is one of the best people you will ever know,' Gorlois snapped in reply, his mind whirling with his daughter's rejection of their whole way of life.

'I'm not as beautiful as my fabled mother, my lord, and I'm certainly not the fairest woman in Britain,' Morgan retorted. 'But I am clever and I have a man's will. So I shall use everything I have to win a name. Can you deny me my ambition?'

'Where did such arrogance and pride come from, girl?' Gorlois retorted, his honest face furrowed in confusion. 'Why must you be the best?'

'What is so wrong with desiring to be the best? Would you deny me the right to a fulfilled life? Answer me, Father, if you care so much for me.'

'Yes! If it means you must descend to murder to achieve such aspirations. How dare you mock the gods of our people by taking part in ritual sacrifice to the Old Ones? Don't you fear the retribution of the Tuatha de Danaan?'

Morgan giggled, as if she were discussing a new robe rather than the murder of peasants in ancient rites. Gorlois was well aware of the licentiousness of the rituals and his heart sank to think of his daughter involved in such filth.

'Anyway, I've learned all I need to know of the old ways, Father, so I can promise that I'll go no more to the Cavern of the Mother. The priests are only using their spells to frighten the peasants anyway, and it has degenerated into an excuse for debauchery. Instead, I've decided to look to the Druids for knowledge.'

Gorlois was both thankful and appalled. He was relieved that Morgan had cut her ties with the nasty little cadre at Tintagel that he planned to put to the sword as soon as possible. Yes, he wished to silence any further rumours, but their perversion of worship affronted Gorlois's blunt but honest sensibilities. However, his daughter's continued interest in magic still appalled him. The only mercy was that the Druids had been more circumspect in their forms of worship before the Romans had wiped them out.

'If you really felt the power in the ancient places like the Giant's Dance, then you would know why I search for answers,' Morgan explained defiantly, and Gorlois had been struck dumb by the passion and purpose in her dark, elegant face. So, on this visit to the court of Ambrosius, the High King, Gorlois had halted his troop near the Giant's Dance, and against his custom had advanced alone into the dreaming circle.

The day was bright, with a clear blue sky marred by just a few scudding clouds. Grasses waved their willowy seed-heads in light breezes and a rabbit leapt out of the grass at his destrier's hooves to run madly through the radiating stone circles. The scene was peaceful, and several black-faced sheep cropped the verdant grass beside the altar stone in the very centre of the Dance.

'There's nothing dangerous or powerful here,' Gorlois muttered defiantly, speaking aloud for reasons he didn't fully understand. 'These are just old stones, and they're not even well cut at that.' A shadow crossed the sun for a moment, darkening the day. Gorlois shook his head as he felt a moment of superstition chill his blood.

'Now you're imagining things,' he muttered, and strode inwards with a warrior's firm tread. As he reached the centre of the circle beside the altar stone, he leaned one hand against the largest upright and slapped the rough surface as he would a horse or a dog.

His fingers tingled immediately, as if the cold stone had energy running through it, or was very hot.

Gorlois replaced his hand so the palm was flat against the rock. The tingling returned, but it was so subtle that he wasn't sure if he was imagining it. A sense of dread bubbled up in his spirit and an icy coldness seemed to clutch at his heart, as if some hidden threat in his future peeped out momentarily and showed a naked, ugly face.

The Dumnonii king recoiled and stared at the pastoral scene around him. The sun burst out from behind the single cloud and flooded the landscape with light, while the sheep still cropped the grass, unconcerned, and a robin landed on the altar stone and looked directly at him without alarm.

'I'm being a fool,' Gorlois muttered, to break the strange mood that had captured him. 'But one thing I do know. The Giant's Dance is not for mortals to play with. Old things should be left in peace, in case they damage our minds. Morgan should take care.'

Then, his mood darkened and sombre, Gorlois rode away from the Dance to his next meeting with the Lord of the West, Ambrosius Imperator.

Watched pots never seem to boil, nor long days ever come to an end. Myrddion existed in an agony of apprehension, counting the hours until he could visit Flavius Ardabur Aspar's mansion and talk privately with the man he believed to be his father. Eventually, accompanied by Ali el Kabir, he sallied forth to learn the worst.

The *magister militum* lived in great state for one so ascetic in appearance. His palace was decorated with the wealth of a man who held the whole of the Middle Sea in the palm of his hand. Statues from Egypt that had been carved from green malachite and white alabaster rested in niches in his walls; scenes of hunting birds decorated his scriptorium; pots, basins and huge jars in attic red, black and white were in daily use and his gardens were small miracles of exotic trees and shrubs. As soon as Myrddion and Ali arrived, a very superior servant ushered them through the house to a superb garden house on the edge of the terraces overlooking the Golden Horn, where Aspar was busy with his hunting birds.

'Ah, there you are, Myrddion Emrys. And this gentleman is?' Aspar turned to Ali el Kabir, bowed low and waited for his son's introduction. 'I have heard of your trading house. You're a man of the desert, I hear, so you will be familiar with my aviary. My servant will show you my treasures.'

With a quick glance at Myrddion for confirmation, el Kabir consented to be led away.

'Come, Myrddion! These hunters are my special darlings. I'm sure that Vortigern told you how fond I am of hawks, eagles and peregrines.' He gazed at his son in grudging admiration. Myrddion had taken special pains to dress with care. 'I learned to love them from the desert peoples who worship their dogs, their horses and their hawks above all things. Are they not beautiful?'

Aspar's face was filled with love as he stood outside a cage in which three birds perched with their heads covered by finely embroidered hoods that hid their fierce faces. Long jesses of leather trailed from their legs. When they moved on their perches, bells rang with a sweet tinkling.

'Aye, I also love the hunting birds, but I'd never wish to own them,' Myrddion whispered in agreement. 'I've seen them hovering in the wind over the long grasses by the sea. Their grace during the kill can stop the heart.'

'Stop the heart?' Aspar murmured with a crooked grin. 'You have a poetic turn of phrase, boy. I hadn't expected that from you. Come and meet my beauties.'

With a negligent wave of one graceful hand, Aspar sent a

servant into the cage with small platters of meat which he placed within reach of each bird. Then, using the hand that had been encased in a padded leather glove and forearm guard, the servant removed their hoods.

Two of the birds, the two largest, moved to their meat without hesitation. The first was a huge desert eagle, banded and beautiful, with powerful, sand-coloured wings folded against its body. Its talons were huge, polished and glossy implements of death.

'That is Interfector, my killer.' Aspar entered the cage and, against all common sense, stroked the eagle's breast with his naked hand. The superb creature narrowed its eyes, perhaps with pleasure, and lowered its savage head.

The second bird was a peregrine falcon, a creature that had always represented kingship in Italia, Gaul and Britain. Again, it was a superb specimen whose feathers shone with health and strength.

'This lady is Regina Atrox, my cruel queen,' Aspar crooned. 'You kill on my command, don't you, my beauty?' The bird seemed to understand him and bobbed her noble head several times.

The third bird was the smallest, but its golden eyes were sinister and wild. It had chosen to ignore its meat and stared out at its master with blank eyes that seemed charged with endless malevolence, as if it still hungered for the wide, free skies.

'And this beauty is Nemesis, my merlin. He refuses to be trained and will never consent to love me – but I still have hope. He's beautiful, isn't he? His eyes see right through you.'

'He dreams of freedom. He will never submit to the glove, my lord, no matter what you do. Only death will break his spirit.'

Aspar looked at Myrddion with a sweetly smiling mouth and eyes as cold as the seventh ring of Tartarus, or Hell. 'Like you, Myrddion? Be careful, honoured guest, for men who do not bend can easily break in a strong wind. Perhaps you should be called Merlinus?'

'I am,' the young man said.

Myrddion smiled in turn and even Aspar saw something in those eyes, so like his own, that made his blood run cold for the briefest of moments. But Aspar had lived a long and fruitful life on the edge of a sword blade, so he feared nothing and nobody. And Aspar was very, very careful.

Myrddion looked around the quiet aviary and gardens. They were alone, except for the servant who cared for Aspar's birds.

'Don't mind Tofus. He's as deaf and as mute as the sandstone he's named for. I saw to that myself. You may speak freely,' Aspar murmured, his mouth and voice expressing his amusement.

'Why did you rape my mother? What pleasure could you have gained from such a congress? I've never understood.'

'You're blunt enough, Myrddion Merlinus, I'll say that in your favour. She was there, I could take her without fear of retribution – and she amused me at the time. Better I should have killed her, which, I'll admit, was my first intention. I recall that she pretended to enjoy my ... ministrations. I admired her for her effrontery at a time when she must have felt endangered, so I permitted her to keep breathing. The final decision was made for me by the gods.'

'I thought you were a good Arian Christian,' Myrddion countered ironically, while his mind processed what his father had told him. I'll not vomit, he thought as he spoke. I'll not give Aspar the satisfaction of a reaction.

'I'm a good anything-that-serves-my-purpose. I'm sure you understand me, Myrddion. That name! Lord of Light! By the Sacred Cross, it almost suits you.'

'What do you plan to do with me? Poison my wine? Cleoxenes has warned me that it's not in your best interests that I should live.'

Aspar threw his head back and laughed. For a moment his bronzed throat was exposed and both the merlin and the young man looked at his smooth neck hungrily. Myrddion shook his head imperceptibly.

'You're safe with me, I assure you, even though you've brought a desert kinglet with you as your bodyguard.' Aspar laughed again at Myrddion's confusion. 'Didn't you know who el Kabir was when you asked him for assistance? Oh, Myrddion! I'm really enjoying your company. You collect great ones so easily.'

The *magister militum*'s face lit up with amusement. 'As for Cleoxenes, he's always read my character correctly, but he's wrong in this case. I've nothing to lose and much entertainment to gain by keeping you alive. Somehow, I don't think your oaths would permit you the luxury of assassination, so I'm prepared to take my chances on you. You see, I know rather more about you than you know about me.'

Myrddion stared at Aspar, his eyes flat and disbelieving.

'Come along, my boy, and we'll ask el Kabir to re-join us.' Aspar almost giggled. 'We shall eat well and come to know each other better. I have several strong and clever sons, but none who amuse me as much as you. You look like me when I was a younger man. What was the name that your mother used to describe me?'

'Hyacinth beauty,' Myrddion murmured as they retraced their steps to the palace, where Ali el Kabir stood waiting with a servant. 'You drove her to madness, you know. She has tried to kill me, or any man who came near her, on many occasions. You spoiled her.'

'Ah, but she still lives,' Aspar replied, as Myrddion saw a woman in a blood red dress sway out of the shadows of the columns. 'I believe you know my amour, Mistress Flavia?'

Myrddion felt the earth sway as Flavia bared her head and moved towards the small group of men with her wonderful hair glowing in the setting sun.

'Flavia?' Myrddion whispered, his heart clearly exposed in his eyes.

Flavia faced him evenly, her mismatched eyes calmly surveying him. In his imaginings, those eyes were Flavia's nature, false and true by turns, and now she travelled the way of least resistance. She was accustomed to being owned by a man more forceful than herself until he failed her in some way and she moved on to the next. Like a destructive force of nature, she lacked the soul to understand what havoc she wrought.

'You are as you were made by your father, my lady. You are as you were made.' Then Myrddion bowed low so Flavia could not see that his heart was breaking.

Aspar moved carefully from Myrddion's side to stand a little before his woman. As usual, he was wryly amused. 'I have heard from my friend that you are married, Aspar, with sons and daughters who carry your gens.' Myrddion glanced at Flavia, standing behind Aspar's broad back, then returned his eyes to his father.

'Of course I have sons, and I also have a noble wife. I've had three, in fact. What of it? Women are to be loved while the bloom lies on their cheeks and the pomegranate rouge is on their moist red mouths. You will learn the value of the moment, if the Lord High God sees fit to permit you to age.'

'I'll not spend my seed on the earth as you have,' Myrddion retorted. 'Nor will I scatter it on women of all castes with no concern for their suffering. I swear by the Lord of Light for whom I am named that I'll never use women as . . . receptacles for my lust. Even if I must live alone . . . lifelong!'

'Don't be tedious, boy. You'd renounce women for the sake of a lost love? Please! I had hoped for better from you.' He chuckled. 'Now we shall dine. I've discovered I have an appetite and I believe I'll be interested in the experiences of your friend, Emir el Kabir. Come. Flavia, my dove, you shall lead the way.'

Impotent, and completely outclassed by the urbane and dangerous Aspar, Myrddion followed the couple into the palace. There, the triclinium awaited them with soft-footed servants who offered light, sweet music and unwatered wine for the enjoyment of Aspar's guests.

A little confused by the undercurrents within the room, el Kabir attempted to maintain a civilised conversation with his host, while Myrddion picked at the dishes that were offered to him by silent women servants. He had no appetite, so he spent his time mentally cursing himself as an idiot for retaining hopes of regaining Flavia's favour. He tried hard to discover some vein of anger in the ashes of his desire — anything but the cold, sick feelings of loss and self-disgust that turned the most delectable food into so much tasteless muck.

'I'm sorry,' Flavia mouthed across the low table between them, from where she ate beside her paramour, who was fully occupied with a conversation about horses with el Kabir.

Myrddion turned aside so that only his profile was visible to Flavia. She flushed along her cheekbones and applied herself to her wine cup. Myrddion could tell that she was angered by his deliberate slight.

With a stab of actual physical pain, Myrddion realised that Flavia had seen the features of the son in the father, so her quick intelligence had led her to Aspar like a homing pigeon to its perch. Too despairing even for jealousy, Myrddion turned his face away from her.

Aspar had paused in his conversation with el Kabir to apply himself to a stuffed squab garnished with honey. Expertly, he spitted the bird's breast with his eating knife and carved off a leg which he devoured with relish.

Flavia caught Myrddion's eye. Her chin lifted and Myrddion knew that she intended to cause trouble for him. Suddenly, he realised that he didn't care.

'Despite his meek demeanour, your young guest has several hidden gifts, my lord. Perhaps you should ask him how he first met me at Châlons. And then ask him why my father hated him so profoundly.'

'Be silent, Flavia,' Myrddion cut in roughly, his voice thick with emotion. He applied Captus's knife to the task of dismembering a quail.

'You really mustn't tease the poor boy,' Aspar replied carelessly.

'Ask him about his gifts, then, and how few times he's been proved wrong,' she persisted.

Aspar turned to face Myrddion with a polite expression of vague interest. One eyebrow rose as he continued to tear at the meat on the point of his knife with his remarkably well-shaped teeth.

'It's nothing, Aspar, merely an ailment I've suffered since infancy.'

'What ailment, Myrddion? God's teeth, I had no interest in

her words until you seemed so unwilling to share your little secret. I'm sure my dove will inform me if you don't tell me yourself.'

'He has visions,' Flavia snapped. Her face was momentarily ugly and old, as if her baser self stripped away her youth. 'My father hated him because he saw through to Aetius's heart and foretold the manner of his death.'

Aspar scoffed. 'Impossible! No man can see through the veil of time, least of all an itinerant healer with neither wealth nor status.'

'You're wrong,' Flavia protested. 'I was in the palace at the time and the servants who were there told me word for word. Myrddion predicted the deaths of my father, King Merovech of the Salian Franks and King Theodoric of the Visigoths. They all died, exactly as he predicted.'

'I don't believe in the Sight. It's a trick used by charlatans to frighten the gullible – and silly women.'

Myrddion remained silent.

Yusuf's uncle looked at him with a strange expression and his dark eyes glowed in the torchlight. His hawk's eyes and long, narrow face remained impassive and watchful, yet they were sharp with curiosity.

'I have always found that those people who persist in cherishing hopes that the future can be opened to them are those who are unable to face the present.' Aspar's voice was laced with amusement and contempt. 'For them, anything is better than today, Myrddion, and I believe that sentiment and hope are for fools.'

'I agree – my words are only for fools. I've come to learn that only the highest of aspirations are of lasting value.'

Aspar stopped smiling. 'What does that mean?'

'Some men appear to be born to serve, while others are

born to take. You are one kind, while I am the other.'

Myrddion rubbed his forehead where a sharp, tense knot of pain had formed. He feared another terrible episode like the one that had made him so ill in Rome, so he dreaded this foolish game of cat and mouse. It exposed his emotions and exacerbated his pain, a vicious circle of tension and agony.

Flavia stared at the healer, hoping that this sudden change in behaviour would spark the onset of another fit. She had never seen one before, so she could not know the implications.

'Don't wish to know what the future will bring, Flavia, for you do not truly wish to hear your fate. No one does. The last time the fit came over me, I foretold the demise of Rome – and its imminent onset.'

'I don't care about Rome,' Flavia sniped.

'What, then, are a few hundred thousand people?' the healer retorted sardonically. Pulchria's face appeared before him. Somehow, the Roman landlady and former whore seemed so much more decent than this aristocratic young woman who lazed on her eating couch before him.

The room shuddered before his glowing eyes. 'What's wrong, Myrddion?' El Kabir's voice seemed to come from far away, and the young man struggled to hold himself back from the brink of unconsciousness. Even so, his voice began to build in his head, as if he were an onlooker and some demon really did inhabit his inner self.

No, he thought blankly. No. No. No. Never again! Please, Mother Ceridwen, save me from this curse. Don't let me betray myself in front of this terrible man.

But, as on so many occasions in the past, the wave within his skull could not be stopped, no matter how he tried. But this time he would be forced to listen to what his stranger's voice had to say.

'Woman, you will grow old before your time. That is all you need to know! Be silent!'

Myrddion's voice was so guttural that all the humour was wiped from Aspar's face.

'Prince of the desert, friend. Your descendants will own this city and all its wealth will, one day, come to your people. But many centuries will pass before the Christian god is cast out of Hagia Sofia, and the Children of the Prophet who is to come will answer the call to prayer in the great echoing vaults. Under the magical Dome of the Lord, the sons of Ishmael will triumph.'

'I don't understand, master healer,' el Kabir murmured. 'Why should we desire to cast out Christianity?'

'In centuries to come, my people and your people will be at war for ownership of the city of Jerusalem. Woe will come . . . and sadness . . . and the dreadful darkness.'

Without realising that he had moved, Myrddion rose and faced his father. From a great distance, he considered the death of any hope that he would find answers from this man, or a trace of the affection that his secret heart had yearned to see in Aspar's eyes.

Then he relinquished everything but pain and loss. 'You, Aspar, will live for many years. You will remain in power and will feast on the terror that you inflict on others. At your end, you will face the assassin's knife and you will be remembered for what you were not, rather than what you were. You never ruled and you never sat upon the eastern throne, but nor did your children. You were, ultimately, terrified at the thought of serving, for only great men can throw themselves away for the needs of the people. You do not have the soul to serve.'

'If you've said the worst you can of me, why should I fear your prophecy? If you speak the truth, then I will live long, die old and quickly, and be remembered. I thank you, Myrddion. I will permit you to be the one who serves, if you should so wish.'

'Be silent! You have given me my name, Merlinus, for the bird you'll never possess. When you are only scraps of information in scrolls that no scholar will ever read, every child in empires far larger than this one will know my name. And they will rejoice in their knowledge of the feats that have been achieved by me and mine. So it is without regret that I renounce you, and every root and branch of your family. I renounce your blood as trivial, an accident that the gods have sent me to repudiate. I have learned everything of you that I need to know . . . and what I have learned is not worth the knowing.'

Myrddion reached into his leather pouch and his blind fingers found the amber ring. Without further thought, and in the thrall of his words, the young man plucked it forth and threw it at his father's face.

'And, if you should doubt me, remember my words when Rome burns, and the Roman Church owns its heart and soul.'

Then, with Ali el Kabir at his back, Myrddion turned on his heel and strode out of Aspar's great palace. They passed the statues that smiled on eternity with carved faces, and hurried out into the perfumed night with the sound of Flavia's keening wails shivering the air in their wake. As the night embraced him, Myrddion didn't realise that he was weeping for his lost youth.

The inn was silent when Myrddion arrived at its door, while Ali el Kabir attempted to keep pace with the Briton's long legs.

'I shall come to see Yusuf in the morning, friend,' Myrddion said softly as they said their farewells. 'Don't be alarmed by my fits. I have been afflicted with them for many years. But you and your nephew will live well in the lands of your people. I wish you fortune with your horses and your hawks. I will smile often when I think of my friend in the warm south when the rain squalls fall chill on my face in Cymru.'

Ali el Kabir embraced the young healer and patted the sides of his beardless face.

'I cannot hope to understand what you said in Aspar's palace, or why you said it, but Aspar will now hate you for your words. I saw his face as you left and I knew that you had insulted the core of his vanity. We had planned to leave for Antiochia and Sidon tomorrow, but Yusuf will not be able to travel for many days yet. I will place my ship, the *Sea Shepherd*, at your disposal and I will give you a scroll for the captain to acquaint him with my wishes. Just send the vessel back to us in one piece! But go, young man – as quickly as possible. Aspar will lick his pride clean for a night or two, but then he will demand redress from you.'

Myrddion said everything that could be put into words of thanks and embraced el Kabir with gratitude. 'I hope our people never hate each other as I have foretold, for I could never see you as an enemy, my friend.'

'If it is the will of God, we will meet in Paradise, and, perhaps, we will weep for the greed and ambition that will rend this world apart in future times, my friend. There is nothing we can do but try to follow righteous paths.'

'Your sons are fortunate to have such a father,' Myrddion whispered, embracing him, and then he ran to rouse his friends.

'It's a good thing that Rhedyn and Brangaine refused to unpack,' Cadoc decided wryly when he heard the news that they would be fleeing Constantinople in the dawn. 'It's a pretty city, but it can never be home.'

'No, Constantinople can never be home,' Myrddion replied with a sob. No matter how he tried, Cadoc couldn't find the words to comfort his master as the young man wept.

Finn, Cadoc and Myrddion leaned on the rails of el Kabir's strange ship with its huge triangular sails as it beat its way out into the Propontis. Below decks, the women slept after a night of frantic activity, while Praxiteles fussed over the disposition of his master's possessions. Without asking questions, they had carried all their worldly goods to the forecourt of the inn, thanked Emilio and his still chattering wife, and started to load the wagons that Ali el Kabir conjured out of nowhere with a flourish of smiles.

Myrddion had sought out Praxiteles, who had been sleeping in the servants' alcove, and tried to pay him for his services, but the Greek staunchly refused to accept any coin. Eventually, his face very sad, Praxiteles insisted on accompanying them on their travels and all Myrddion's protestations couldn't change his mind.

Now, as sunrise gilded the Golden Horn and turned the city into a floating mirage of silver gilt, Myrddion hoped he would never see the Eastern Empire again. Aspar dwelled here, and after the Fall of Rome a wall of tall barbarians would stand between him and Myrddion. This son would never repeat the sins of the father, even if he must travel on his journey through life as solitary and as trapped as Aspar's merlin.

'Are we truly going home, master?' Finn asked hesitantly. 'Will my son grow up on his own soil?'

'Your child could well be a daughter, Truthteller,' Cadoc

joked. 'For all your potions and lotions, you still cannot determine the sex of an unborn child.'

'I don't care what sex the babe is, as long as it's healthy and strong,' Finn retorted with stern seriousness as the morning sun gilded his face with a rime of light.

'You'll be a good father, Finn,' Myrddion acknowledged with a sad face. 'Your child may be born on the journey home, but he'll be a Celt, and that's everything.'

Cadoc kicked Finn on the shin with his booted foot – hard. Myrddion heard Truthteller wince, but he was too deeply immersed in regret over Flavia, his father and the whole, ill-advised adventure that had absorbed six years of his youth to pay any attention.

'It will be good to leave these huge skies, for I've missed the rains that fall at home,' he whispered, almost to himself. 'In Cymru, everything seems softer and gentler, and I think I'll try to see Branwyn when I return. Perhaps, after all we have experienced, I can even try to heal her.'

Behind his back, Cadoc and Finn exchanged meaningful glances.

'You're not to blame, master, for whatever is making you so sad. It's not that damned Flavia woman, is it?' Cadoc asked angrily. Any blow to Myrddion was a major wound to Cadoc – and he'd never liked the flame-haired bitch. 'Sooner or later, a good woman will come into your life and love you. She'll be one of us rather than a Roman noblewoman who knows nothing of honour and decency. You'll see, master! Everything will come right once we get home.'

No it won't, Myrddion thought sadly. I'll not marry because it hurts too damned much. Better to be alone. I'd not willingly pass on my father's curse of casual cruelty.

But he couldn't put a voice to those thoughts. He had

pretended to be strong since he was very young, almost before he could remember, and now his pretence had become a second skin that hid his losses from the pity of others.

The city faded into the morning and the dhow, for so the black-bearded captain called it, fled before the wind into the Propontis as it took the healers on the first stage of the long journey back to Britain – and home.

'I'd like to be called Myrddion Merlinus from this point onwards,' Myrddion told Cadoc in the early morning, after the hours of silence that had weighed heavily on his heart. 'Of all the wonders I saw in Constantinople, the one thing that I truly admired was Aspar's merlin. It remained free, despite its captivity, and it convinced me that every man must learn his true nature.'

'Of course, master,' Cadoc replied quietly. 'You may choose any name you wish. But first you must eat, because I have no doubt that you need sustenance. Great events follow you closely, so we'll need to keep up your strength.'

Myrddion chuckled softly. His heart might be breaking for a faithless lover and his father might have humiliated him beyond bearing, but Cadoc would continue to baby him, regardless of his age.

'Why do you, Finn, and the women bother with me? I've dragged you into wars, to places so vile that I cannot bear to remember them, and then onwards into more pain and danger. Why do you travel with me?'

For a brief second, Cadoc looked thunderstruck and his mouth fell open in surprise. When he closed it, Myrddion heard the little snap as his teeth met. Then he repeated a response that Myrddion had heard before, in an earlier time of pain and death, and the young man's heart began the healing process.

'Ye gods, master! Surely you know by now? These things are done in the name of the love that we, at least, have long held for you. And ever will.'

Then Cadoc marched away towards the cabin below decks and Myrddion found that, suddenly, he was very hungry.

AUTHOR'S NOTES

I have always loved to write, but this novel was both the realisation of a dream and the hardest task I've ever attempted. Months of research, a very long journey over lands and seas, and hours of sweat and a bucket of tears went into the making of it.

The whole endeavour began when I started to wonder about the lost years of Merlin's life. What I'm referring to are the years between his attempted sacrifice by Vortigern and his role as Uther Pendragon's adviser. I looked at both Myrddion figures, namely the Merlin Sylvestris, or the Wild Man, and the Magician. I rejected the Merlin Sylvestris version, described in the Vita Merlini, as unlikely. I just couldn't visualise my Merlin as a man driven mad by loss. Such a man wouldn't be capable of guiding the destiny of such strong-willed kings as Uther Pendragon and his son, Arthur.

Once that decision was made, I was presented with a huge problem. Where was Merlin during his middle years, or at least a decade or so of that time? What would a clever, alienated and partially skilled healer be likely to do during this period? The Arthurian legends say nothing of these years, so I had no guiding lights to illuminate my path.

Eventually, after I had finished Book One of this trilogy, I puzzled over what I would do if I were in Merlin's shoes – and my answer came quickly. The ultimate, long-term goal would be to find his father, but in the short term he would be hungry for knowledge and would want to improve his medical skills.

So, where would he go? The answer to that question came quickly too. He would go to the world of the Middle Sea, literally the Mediterranean, as the source of all learning, but that empire was fragmentary and devouring itself. I knew virtually nothing about the finer details of that decay, so it was back to the drawing board for M. K. Hume. How fascinating it was to find that King Merovech, who gave his name to the Merovingian kings of France, was also reputed to be a supposed Demon Seed. This research result was surprising, to put it mildly. To trace the extraordinarily brutal and manipulative life of Flavius Aetius was historically fascinating. As I hunted for Flavius Petronius Maximus, Heraclius, Valentinian III and Flavius Ardabur Aspar, what struck me most was that the historical data was more violent and more bizarre than anything I could ever have invented.

And all of these men lived and died in the same period of time. The history of Europe was truly hanging in the balance. Attila the Hun and his murderous horde had the potential to change the face of Europe, so I wasn't really surprised when I discovered that the Battle of the Catalaunian Plain is numbered among the fifteen most influential battles of all time. That Flavius Aetius won this battle, in one day, was a victory for muscle and desperation over the force of numbers in Attila's massive army.

Then, after studying the ancient landscape of Rome

and the politics that rendered it almost moribund, I tracked down lead poisoning and the terrible toll in human lives that the Roman sweet tooth took. Would a young man like Merlin have made the connection between a distilled grape sweetener and this debilitating illness with its wildly differing symptoms? Possibly, or perhaps not. The Romans never made that leap, but then again, they never gave up their love of blood-soaked games either, even as Christians.

I travelled to Istanbul/Constantinople to see the Golden Horn and Hagia Sofia III. While I didn't see Hagia Sofia II, which existed in Merlin's time, I did see the basilica beside it that dated from a far earlier era. The land and the seas are unchanged and I embraced it, loved it and felt the past seep out of the walls and into my hands.

I make no apology for inserting Merlin into these fading days of glory. The Roman Empire saw strangers come and go by the many thousand. He could quite easily have been one of them. I had the opportunity to give him his modern name of Merlinus, or Merlin, and I bade farewell to the Middle Sea with regret.

I tampered with the truth as little as possible because there was really little need. I may have given Aspar an extra son and a rather fiendish, unspoken past, but historically we know little of him or the exact number of children he fathered. What is certain is that he could have become emperor on several occasions, simply by changing his branch of Christianity. Instead, he placed lesser men on the throne and remained a powerful, enigmatic figure that no one will ever be able to unravel. I invented his passion for hunting birds.

Incidentally, Flavius Aetius did indeed have a daughter who was married off to Thraustila, the Hungvari nobleman. The story of Valentinian's murder is also historically accurate.

My Flavia could easily have been given such a name, being the female form of the gens, but history doesn't record the daughter's name or her ultimate fate. My interpretation is thus as valid as any other and I confess I've been more generous with her than was likely to have been the case, given her father's character and the way girls were raised in the days of the late Roman Empire. I hope the historical Flavia escaped Italia and built a new life with Thraustila's gold, but I rather doubt it.

One last detail needs explanation. The prophet Muhammad had yet to be born so Islam, as we know it, did not exist in AD 456. The people of what would become the Crescent were followers of the Christian faith, the Hebrew faith or paganism, based on the beliefs of the Amalekites. This fact made me wonder why extremists from all three dominant religions in the Middle East are so intractably at war. What are we fighting over, as Myrddion would have said? So Ali el Kabir is an invention, but thousands like him traded with Constantinople and were believers in the Jewish faith. Still others were Christian, so members of that faith too moved freely within the world of the Middle East. Their love of horses, hounds and hunting birds were strong habits of the sons of the desert.

Just recently, a friend with a Celtic heritage talked to me about the physical differences that are so prevalent in my novels. I tried to explain that, in the bitter north, natural selection decided physical characteristics. Because of my own northern heritage, I am fair-skinned, blue-eyed and very long of leg for my height, which is short when compared with others in my family tree. My mother was six feet tall and my uncle was six feet seven inches. Only the tall survived as children of the snow. Conversely, kinder climes permitted shorter folk to live. So are legends made!

My friend also discussed the term Celt, and I admit that this word is a more modern description of the tribesmen who inhabited Britain between the eras of the Picts and the later invasions of the northerners. They called themselves by their tribal names but they were cohesive racial groups and, when attacked from outside, they put aside their tribal differences and united. Calling themselves the People, which most racial groups choose, wasn't an option for me, so I use the name Celts, given to these tribesmen by later scholars and commentators.

So that's it! I hope you enjoyed the journey we have travelled.

I was excited by it all because I fervently believe that when we cease to learn, then we are dead. And I hope my Merlin learned a great deal that would give him strength in the trials that were to follow in his adventures with Arthur, King of the Britons.

The Legion

Simon Scarrow

When the actions of a rebel gladiator in Egypt threaten the stability of the Roman Empire, Prefect Cato and Centurion Macro know he must be stopped. The locals are holding the Romans responsible for the attacks Ajax and his crew have been making along the Egyptian coast and, with the southern frontier under raid by the Nubians, Egypt is dangerously volatile.

Tasked by Egypt's governor with tracking and defeating the renegade, Cato and Macro are soon hot on Ajax's trail. Joining with the Twenty-Second Legion, they are determined to destroy the enemy. But will the strength of a psychotically fatalist gladiator and his new-found Nubian allies, hell-bent on destruction, defeat the Roman warriors?

Praise for Simon Scarrow's novels of the Roman Empire:

'Rollicking good fun' *Mail on Sunday*

'A rip-roaring page-turner' *Historical Novels Review*

978 0 7553 5376 7

headline

M. K. HUME

Prophecy:
Clash of Kings

Boy, healer, prophet – the epic tale of Merlin begins.

In the town of Segontium, a wild storm washes a fugitive ashore. He brutally rapes the granddaughter of the king of the Deceangli tribe, leaving her to bear his son, Myrddion Merlinus. Spurned as a demon seed, the boy is raised by his grandmother and is apprenticed to a healer who hones his remarkable gift.

Meanwhile, the High King of the Celts, Vortigern, is rebuilding the ancient fortress at Dinas Emrys. According to a prophecy, he must use the blood of a demon seed to make the towers stand firm. Myrddion's life is in jeopardy. But the boy has a prophecy of his own and a richer destiny to fulfil. Soon Vortigern shall be known as the harbinger of chaos, and Myrddion must use his gifts for good in a kingdom besieged by evil.

So begins the healer's journey to greatness . . .

978 0 7553 7144 0

headline
review

M. K. HUME

King Arthur: Dragon's Child

THE EPIC TALE OF THE MAN DESTINED TO
BECOME ARTHUR HIGH KING OF THE BRITONS.

The Dark Ages: a time of chaos and bloodshed. The
Roman legions have long deserted the Isles and the
despotic Uther Pendragon, High King of Celtic
Britain, is nearing death, his kingdom torn apart by
the jostling for his throne.

Of unknown parentage, Artorex is growing up in the
household of Lord Ector. One day, three strangers
arrive and arrange for Artorex to be taught the martial
skills of the warrior; blade and shield, horse and fire,
pain and bravery.

When they return, years later, Artorex is not only
trained in the arts of battle, he is also a married man.
The country is in desperate straits, its great cities
falling to the menace of the Saxon hordes. Artorex
becomes a war chieftain, and wins the battles that
earn him the trust of his Celtic warriors and prove that
he alone can unite the tribes. But, if he is to fulfil his
destiny and become the High King of the Britons,
Artorex must find Uther's crown and sword.

The future of Britain is at stake.

978 0 7553 4867 1

headline
review

M. K. HUME

King Arthur:
Warrior of the West

THE EPIC TALE OF ARTHUR
KING OF THE BRITONS

Twelve long, blood-soaked years have passed since
Artor was crowned High King. Against all odds, he
has united Celtic Britain and banished the Saxon
scourge. The legend of Camlann has begun.

But even as Artor's kingdom is at its zenith, even as he
has succeeded in conquering all external threats to his
rule, his kingdom is being undermined from within.
For Artor has chosen Wenhaver as his queen and
second wife. Wenhaver will always love what she
cannot have and have what she cannot love, and her
bitterness threatens to bring down all those around
her.

Not only has Artor been betrayed by the one person
he should be able to trust, he has also learned of
appalling perversion at the heart of his kingdom. He
must make a terrible choice. Could all that Artor has
fought for be lost?

Will Britain be torn apart?

978 0 7553 4870 1

headline
review

Now you can buy any of these other
bestselling titles from your bookshop or
direct from the publisher.

FREE P&P AND UK DELIVERY
(Overseas and Ireland £3.50 per book)

Prophecy: Clash of Kings	M. K. Hume	£7.99
King Arthur: Dragon's Child	M. K. Hume	£7.99
King Arthur: Warrior of the West	M. K. Hume	£7.99
King Arthur: The Bloody Cup	M. K. Hume	£7.99
The Legion	Simon Scarrow	£7.99
Empire of the Moghul: Raiders from the North	Alex Rutherford	£6.99
Island of Bones	Imogen Robertson	£7.99
The Gods of Atlantis	David Gibbins	£6.99
Sacred Treason	James Forrester	£6.99

TO ORDER SIMPLY CALL THIS NUMBER

01235 400 414

or visit our website: www.headline.co.uk

Prices and availability subject to change without notice